Rebuilding HOME

Gift of
Whispering Pines

Book THREE

KIMBERLY DIEDE

Gift of Whispering Pines Book Three

Rebuilding Home

This is a work of fiction. Names, characters, organizations, places, events, and incidents are either products of the author's imagination or are used fictitiously and any resemblance to actual persons, living or dead, business establishments, events or locales is entirely coincidental.

Cover by Carpe Librum Book Design – www.carpelibrumbookdesign.com.

ISBN: 978-1-961305-16-8

ISBN: 978-0-9992996-5-4 (pbk)

ISBN: 978-1-961305-09-0 (lg print pbk)

ISBN: 978-0-9992996-4-7 (ebook)

INTRODUCTION TO
WHISPERING PINES

Welcome to Whispering Pines—a quaint resort deep in the heart of Minnesota's lake country—where an unforgettable family will come together to learn how to heal and thrive, despite the inevitable wounds that life delivers. Join siblings Renee, Jess, Ethan, and Val as they struggle to make the most of the legacy entrusted to them by their dear Aunt Celia. If you enjoy a family saga filled with unanticipated twists, second chances, and the many gifts life offers, you'll love your visit to Whispering Pines!

Whispering Pines (Book 1)
Tangled Beginnings (Book 2)
Rebuilding Home (Book 3)
Capturing Wishes (Book 4)
Choosing Again (Book 5)
Celia's Gifts (Book 6)
Celia's Legacy (Book 7)

For release dates, news, and more, sign up to receive Kimberly Diede's newsletter on her website at www.kimberlydiedeauthor.com and follow her on Facebook and BookBub.

To Joshua,

*As you work on rebuilding
your own home*

*"If you want to change the world,
Go home and love your family."*

-Mother Theresa

Chapter One
Gift of Dirty Laundry

"Daaad! Where's my uniform? Tonight's our last game!"

Ethan Richter plunked his fresh cup of coffee down with a sigh, his enthusiasm for his first morning sip evaporating as a bit of the hot liquid sloshed onto the countertop.

Does this single dad stuff ever get any easier?

Even though he wasn't *technically* a single parent, it often felt that way. Ethan would be the first to admit going it alone sucked some days. Unfortunately, laundry didn't wash itself.

He strode down the narrow hallway to the boys' room. They shared one of the two bedrooms in the small apartment. Ethan knew they were fed up with the tight quarters.

Despite the light cast by the overhead bulb in the middle of their ceiling and the racket Drew was making, Dylan lay still, sprawled out on his twin bed, lanky legs hanging over the end with an arm covering his eyes against the harsh glare. His lack of movement signaled to Ethan the boy had overslept . . . again. Ethan sympathized with the kid, though—he suspected Dylan's growth spurt was at least partially to blame for how hard his youngest slept lately.

Drew, their middle child, was on his knees, rummaging through a tangle of clothes and sporting gear covering the carpeted floor. Based on the scent wafting up to meet him, Ethan feared the majority of the scattered clothes were dirty. He felt a pang of regret, remembering a similar mess in his own room when he was a kid. He probably still owed his mom an apology.

"Dylan, get up," Ethan said, tossing a discarded pillow at the boy's sleeping form. You've got ten minutes."

Groans met his directive.

He bent down to fish a blue sports jersey out of the mess piled next to the dresser. He gave the wrinkled garment a vigorous shake and a suspicious sniff. "Looks like you got lucky, Drew. It's not too bad. I'll toss it in the dryer with a dryer sheet and it'll be as good as new . . . or at least good *enough*." He chuckled.

Drew didn't seem to like his joke. "Dad, I can't wear a dirty uniform to what will probably be our last game of the season!"

"Well, I guess you should have thought of that instead of ignoring me last night when I told you to throw your uniform in the washing machine."

"But—"

"I don't want to hear it, Drew. Besides, no one'll notice if you're smelly in that sea of sweaty dudes."

Drew rolled his eyes in disgust. "*Mom* always made sure our uniforms were clean for game day," he said, standing to hold his black uniform pants up and inspect them.

At least they aren't white. Besides, they look better than the jersey, Ethan thought with a sigh. He was too tired to let Drew's dig get to him. It wasn't the kids' fault Stacey had bailed on all of them. And besides, his son was right: she *would have* made sure the uniform was clean. She'd made keeping up with household chores look like a breeze (minus her constant complaining). Now he had to listen to his kids complain instead of their absent mother—and worse, all while he tried to pick up the slack in the cleaning duties.

"Come on, we gotta get going," Ethan said, snatching the bottoms out of Drew's outstretched hands. He gently swatted Dylan's bare foot on his way out the door. "Dylan, get up. I'm not going to tell you again."

Moans from both boys followed him into the hallway.

He checked his watch; if he could get them out the door in fifteen minutes, the boys wouldn't be late for school. He tossed Drew's uniform into the dryer, groaning when he stood back up, his right hand automatically clasping his lower back. The damp fall weather always aggravated it. He hoped his boys would manage to escape the lifelong impact of pesky football injuries better than he had. His glory days on the field, now long past, had left their mark, making him wonder if all that had been worth it.

He looked around him, at his domestic life. Yes . . . they absolutely were worth it—he wouldn't give up his glory days for anything. Working hard on the field taught him how to work hard in life. It was worth a few aches and pains.

He'd been a bit of a legend on the football field back in his own high school days. They'd won the state championship his senior year—a rare feat not yet repeated. It was fun to feel like a winner back then. He understood why his boys both felt compelled to play the game, but on mornings like this, when his own body ached more than he suspected it did for most men two years shy of fifty, he half wished they'd give it up. But he knew better than to suggest it. Football was their *thing*, whether playing it or watching it. If either boy decided to quit, it would be their decision, not his.

Ethan had gone on to play two years of college football, but a torn Achilles' heel ended his semi-illustrious career far too prematurely. At the time he was absolutely devastated, but now Ethan was thankful his body hadn't endured another two-plus years of potential damage.

Slamming cupboard doors and bickering in the small kitchen behind him pulled him back to the present. His own schedule was jam-packed, and he needed to get the boys to school before he could start on it.

Come on, old man, he told himself. *Move it.*

"Richter, we've got a problem."

"Dammit, Rex, why is *that* the first thing you say to me almost every morning?" Ethan asked his foreman when the man met him at his pickup within two minutes of his arrival at the jobsite.

"Oh, you know, I live to make your life hell," the older man joked.

Ethan drew in a deep breath and got out of his truck, bracing himself for today's dilemma. Despite ribbing Rex, he knew from experience that his right-hand man seldom exaggerated. If Rex said there was a problem, it was going to be another long day.

"All right," he said, "what's the issue?"

"That shipment of tile we were waiting on arrived."

"And . . . ?"

Rex grimaced. "At least half of them are cracked, boss."

"Shit." Ethan dropped his head back in frustration, gazing up at the leaden sky. The forecast called for rain or sleet by midmorning. Not many days in November were conducive to working outside in Minnesota. Given the forecast, he'd asked Rex to schedule the subs to install the new cabinets and tile backsplash inside today. If they couldn't start the tile installation, they weren't going to hit their deadline.

Ethan cringed at the thought of having to deliver that news to Mrs. Holshan, the homeowner. The woman was difficult to please on a good day, and she'd be positively fuming if he screwed up her social calendar by not having her kitchen remodel complete in time for her upcoming holiday parties. And she wouldn't keep her displeasure to herself, that was for sure.

Ethan needed to avoid alienating the woman if at all possible. He knew his best option was to find replacement tile, and quickly, but he hesitated. Phil Ivers would have been his first choice to call, but the man was laid up with gout . . . which meant he was going to need to reach out to Brooke.

Brooke maintained a decent stock of tile over at her shop, and if she didn't have similar tile to what he needed already on hand, she could probably still find him some yet today. But because he hadn't hired her to do the install in the first place, it would make for an uncomfortable conversation.

The fact he hadn't called her back after their one and only date two weeks earlier wasn't going to help either.

You're a jerk for not calling, he told himself. And this was his karma.

He and Brooke had known each other professionally for a few years; she was one of the best tile installers in town, and he'd even hired her to work on the remodel of his own house. They'd gotten to know each other better over the past six months since his remodel started, and when she showed an interest in a Halloween party he was going to, he'd invited her along before he even realized how it would appear. She took his invite to mean he was asking her out on a date. The words were barely out of his mouth before he regretted them. Not because he didn't like Brooke, but because he didn't really want to date anyone—despite his well-intentioned sisters pressuring him to get back into the dating scene following his divorce.

Granted, Stacey, his ex-wife, was already on her third "boyfriend" since they'd split. Ethan hadn't been out on an actual date, other than with Stacey, in twenty-four years. He'd had plenty of opportunity to date during high school and college, but once he'd married Stacey, he'd given up his old habits and became a one-woman man. When things started to fall apart in their marriage, she'd accused him of many things—including cheating, but there she was wrong. He'd remained faithful through the years, despite some of those years being incredibly tough and lonely.

He'd grown up in what he considered to be the typical family structure—both Mom and Dad present and accounted for, raising him and his sisters together—and he'd expected to raise his own children in the same way.

Learning Stacey had other plans had come as a complete shock.

Since he wasn't a man to rescind an invitation, he'd followed through on his date with Brooke. He'd even enjoyed himself, once he'd had a couple of beers in him and reminded himself Brooke was fun and not the enemy.

The party was held at Whispering Pines, the lake resort they'd spent time at as a family since he'd been a kid. His sister Renee had owned it for almost two years now, and since Halloween was one of her favorite holidays, she'd started a bit of a tradition by holding an annual party in the resort lodge.

This year's party had consisted of family, along with a few close friends. If his folks or sisters had been surprised to see him show up with someone other than his kids, they'd hidden it well. They'd all enjoyed plenty of good food, a dance contest amongst the kids, and lots of storytelling and reminiscing. Brooke especially enjoyed his look of horror at the story his sister Jess shared, about the year he'd stolen some of her Halloween candy and then proceeded to eat so much of it that he'd thrown up in the station wagon before they even got home from trick-or-treating.

But aside from that one hiccup, they'd had fun. His own kids hadn't made the party; the boys had spent the weekend with their mother, and their daughter, Elizabeth, was away at college, too busy with her final year and two part-time jobs to get home very often. Since he wasn't sure how the kids would feel about him dating, he hadn't told them he took Brooke to the party. The kids were also the main reason he hadn't asked her out again. They'd been through so much, he didn't want his dating to be one more thing for them to get used to right now.

Brooke had seemed to enjoy herself at the party. It helped that she already knew Seth, the man his sister Jess was dating. Brooke spent much of the evening catching up with Seth, so Ethan hadn't felt like he had to keep her entertained the whole time.

She'd even invited Ethan up when he dropped her off. He'd begged off—he wasn't ready to go *there* yet—making some excuse about an early morning, driving off into the snowy night, and leaving her standing on her front step, probably wondering if she'd scared him off. He could have handled *that* part of the evening better.

He'd since ignored the two messages she'd left him and hadn't called her back.

"What do you want to do about the tiles?" Rex asked, pulling Ethan back to their dilemma.

"I'm gonna have to call Brooke." Ethan planted his booted feet wide and met Rex's eye with a steady gaze, as if daring his friend to make a smartass comment. Rex knew he'd taken Brooke to the Halloween party but, surprisingly, hadn't asked how the date went.

Rex grinned, as if reading his mind. "Did you earn a discount the other night when you took her out, then, or did you manage to piss her off so she's unlikely to take your call?"

And there it is. That's what he got for sharing anything more than work with a subordinate.

But that wasn't fair. He didn't really consider Rex to be a subordinate. There wasn't a single other person on his crew he'd have even considered telling, but things were different with Rex. They'd worked together for a long time, and Rex had saved his ass more than once while Ethan learned to juggle things at home and at work after Stacey walked out. He'd kept multiple crews running when Ethan was tied up with the kids, juggling even more than he usually did to help keep Ethan's construction business running smoothly. Rex even put new tires on Lizzy's car, not liking how worn they looked when she stopped by to say hello before school started back up in the fall, although Ethan drew the line at letting him *pay* for the tires too.

Ethan sighed. Rex wouldn't buy anything but the truth. "I might have screwed it up," was all he offered, turning his back on the man and heading into the house.

The sky was starting to spit icy streams of moisture and the clock was ticking. He had to make the call.

Brooke didn't pick up when he called, so he left a message asking her to call him back. He tried to keep his tone professional but friendly, hoping she'd forgive him for how he'd treated her. If she ignored his message, as he had hers, he couldn't blame her, but he would be in a bind.

Apparently she was a bigger man than him—his phone vibrated barely an hour later, displaying her name. Ethan stepped away from the kitchen, currently crowded with cabinet installers, to take the call.

"Hey, Brooke, thanks for getting back to me," he said, cringing when he thought his tone might have sounded a tad too friendly. The woman wasn't an idiot; nor was she likely to let him off that easily.

"Ethan. You said you were looking for some tile and it was urgent. What do you need?"

Keeping it professional, Ethan realized, noting her cool tone. He respected her for that—it made him like her even more than he already did—but he really hoped he hadn't damaged their friendship. His life was just too full right now to have to cater to one more person. But he could be professional and hope for the best.

He went on to explain his situation, referencing the order sheet he pulled out of his back pocket so he could give her the exact name and SKU of the damaged tile.

"I don't have that line on hand," she replied, "but I know someone who might. When do you need it?"

"Yesterday," Ethan joked. But when this didn't elicit a response, he tried again, saying, "As soon as possible. We're working on a tight deadline, and there'll be hell to pay with Mrs. Holshan if we don't hit it."

"Every job is on a tight deadline in our business, Ethan," Brooke said.

Ethan picked up on the irritation in her voice, but he refrained from defending himself.

"Listen," she continued, "I'm tied up right now. Let me see what I can find. If I can't get my hands on the exact same tile, I can bring you over some samples that should be close. What time works for you?"

"Whatever you can make work is fine."

"I'll be there at four."

Ethan sighed in relief. "Thanks, Brooke, you're a lifesaver."

"You're welcome. Oh . . . and Ethan?"

"Yes?"

"This is going to cost you."

Chapter Two

Gift of Competition

The alarm on Ethan's phone went off later that day.

Now what? he thought.

He glared at the screen, irritated by the interruption. He'd been deep in conversation with the guy overseeing the cabinet installation, because they'd just discovered the very last base was three inches too wide. He was surprised to see it was already 3:15 p.m.

Pick up Dylan at school.

Dammit. He'd forgotten . . . again. If not for reminders offered by modern technology, his kids might have disowned him by now.

"Hold on," he muttered to the frustrated contractor. Stepping into the other room, Ethan hollered for Rex.

"What?" the man yelled down from somewhere higher up.

"Can you come down here?" Ethan yelled back.

After bringing Rex up to speed, he hustled out to his blue Chevy pickup and made the now-familiar route toward Dylan's school. It had been easier when Dylan had football practice at the end of his school day, but his season had already wrapped up—eighth graders didn't play as long as varsity. Ethan knew Dylan would be mad when he found out they had to come back to the jobsite instead of going home; home, or the apartment they currently called home, was in the opposite direction and Ethan didn't have an extra forty minutes to spare. Even without the detour, Brooke would be on-site by the time they got back.

Brooke, Ethan thought, cringing. He still didn't want Dylan to know he'd taken her out on a date. Hopefully she wouldn't say anything in front of his son. He suspected *she* wouldn't, but Rex might not keep his trap shut.

"Dad, it's Friday night, I just want to go home for a while before Drew's game. And I'm starving!" Dylan complained when he hopped into the truck and Ethan explained why he didn't turn toward their apartment as he drove out of the school parking lot.

"Technically it's still Friday afternoon," Ethan replied to his son's whining. "I only ate one of my sandwiches I packed for lunch this morning—help yourself to the other one. We'll wrap up in plenty of time to get to your brother's game."

Dylan only grunted in response, staring out the passenger window, arms crossed over his chest in a sign of teenage disgust.

"Hey, have you heard from your mom?" Ethan asked, glancing over at Dylan. "Is she coming to the game tonight?"

Dylan's noncommittal shrug indicated either he didn't know or didn't care. Stacey hadn't been making any points with the boys lately. Ethan suspected Lizzy felt the same. According to his daughter, Stacey was inseparable from her latest fling.

Sighing, Ethan turned up the radio so he wouldn't have to make small talk with his pouting son. When they pulled into the long, winding drive leading up to the impressive façade of the house they were working on, his son sat up straighter, eyeing the residence with interest.

"Wow, who lives here? It's almost as big as our whole *building.*"

Now it was Ethan's turn to grunt, fully aware Dylan and Drew were less than thrilled with their current living conditions. Ethan reminded himself it was only temporary.

"The Holshans. We're doing a massive remodel on the lower level and the upstairs master bath. The kitchen was the biggest part of the project, and that's almost done. We need to be out by the middle of next week, but we hit a snag today. I need to take care of it before we can start our weekend."

Ethan shifted into Park behind his foreman's truck.

"Go find Rex. See if he needs some help. The sooner we get things wrapped up here today, the sooner we can get out of here."

His order was met with yet another sigh, but Ethan knew Dylan liked hanging out with Rex. The older man could order Dylan around and his son took it without back talk. He hoped the two of them would keep busy while he talked to Brooke.

She was pulling in behind them now. Ethan caught himself glancing toward his son to make sure the boy entered the house before he walked back to Brooke's truck.

This is ridiculous. Why do I feel like I cheated?

He didn't yet think of himself as a free man, but of course he was—and that meant he was free to see whomever he wanted.

Brooke jumped down out of her dark maroon, extended-cab pickup. Somehow the masculine truck complemented her personality, but she didn't look anything like the other workers on-site. Her long, silky ponytail poked through the back of her Carhartt ballcap. She wore jeans and a button-down flannel under a practical, quilted vest. The jeans were standard attire in their business, but Ethan couldn't help but wonder how she managed to find ones that accentuated her curves so nicely.

He gave his head a little shake, reminding himself to keep it professional. But as Brooke approached, freeing her ponytail out of the back of her vest, he caught a light whiff of her familiar smell. It sent his mind back to the inside of his own truck, the night he'd brought her home after the Halloween party. Even though he'd declined her invitation to come inside when he dropped her off, they'd managed some heavy necking before he drove away. Despite the many jobs he'd worked with her in recent years, he'd never seen her inky black hair down and loose before that night.

He rubbed the back of his neck—a nervous habit—and grinned sheepishly as she stopped to stand in front of him, hands on hips. Memories of their make-out session amplified his guilt over not calling her back.

"Well, look at you, all fit and healthy," Brooke said, looking him over. "Given the dead silence over the past couple weeks, I thought surely you were flat on your back in the hospital. That or you're just an ass."

He held his hands out in a sign of surrender, nodding. "I'm an ass. I'm sorry. I have no excuse other than lack of practice. You know I don't date much."

She snorted. "Much?"

"All right, I don't date. Satisfied? Taking you out was a whim and it was dumb. I regret it."

The look she gave him left no doubt what she thought of his fumbled apology.

Oh my God, this is a disaster, he thought, frustrated with his complete lack of finesse. What the hell was the matter with him? He'd had his pick of the ladies when he was younger, back in the day. Was it possible to get *this* rusty?

Brooke was glaring at him, looking like she was trying to decide between smacking him or walking away.

"Look, I'm sorry, Brooke. Can I just start over? I don't know what's the matter with me. I had fun on our date. You're great. I'm just not ready for anything serious. I don't have time to do half the things I probably should be doing with the boys these days as it is. You understand, don't you?"

"What I understand is you read *way* more into our date than you should have. What makes you think I'm looking for anything serious? Especially with you? It's not like you're a big catch, Ethan. You may still look good, despite your age, but you come with lots of baggage," Brooke said, motioning toward the front of the house. Ethan glanced over his shoulder and saw both Rex and Dylan carrying out toolboxes, heading toward the foreman's truck, and he was surprised to notice his youngest was nearly as tall as Rex. Brooke had never met his kids, but she might have watched Dylan climb out of his truck when they first arrived.

He looked back at Brooke and for a split second he thought he saw steam coming out of her ears. *Was she that mad?* No—it was her breath. The air was getting colder. Her eyes sparkled a bit in the fading light. He thought he saw a hint of hurt in them.

Time to man up. *Tell her she's right, old man.*

"You're right. Brooke, I'm sorry. I apologize for not calling you after our date. It was a fun evening and I enjoyed your company. But now I'd like it if we could continue to work together and be friends, like we used to. I'd hate to lose that."

She eyed him closely, considering.

A car door slammed and footsteps approached.

"All right," she said, holding out her hand to Ethan. "Truce."

He laughed, taking her peace offering with a firm shake and releasing it as his son and foreman approached.

"Hey, Brooke," Rex greeted the younger woman.

Ethan introduced Dylan.

"Did you bring us some tile?" Rex asked.

Brooke grinned at Rex. "Matter of fact, I did. Jensen had a shipment of similar stuff that a client of his out in Forest Hills didn't end up liking. Said it was too textured." She walked to the back of her truck as she talked, the two men and Dylan following her. She dropped the tailgate and pulled one of the heavy boxes out far enough so she could reach into it. She grabbed the top tile out of the box and handed it to Ethan.

"That gonna work?" she asked.

Ethan examined it, turning it over and sizing it up. Years of practice allowed him to be a pretty good estimator. "Looks promising. Let's take it inside and compare it to the sample I've got in there."

Brooke nodded and started to pick up the heavy box.

"Don't," Ethan said, stopping her. "We've got a strong young back here today. Dylan, bring that box inside with us."

"But *I've* got a strong young back," Brooke protested.

"And I've got an *older* strong back," Ethan replied. "Doesn't mean we have to do all the heavy lifting. Dylan can earn his keep, too."

Ethan turned to check Dylan's reaction, expecting complaints.

Dylan surprised him by coming around to stand next to Brooke, lifting up the first box, pulling out a second one as well, and hoisting them both into his arms. He grinned at her without saying a word and headed toward the house, Brooke close behind, eyebrows raised in amusement.

Rex laughed at the surprised look on Ethan's face.

"Nothin' like a pretty woman to get a young buck showing off," Rex said, playfully slugging Ethan on the shoulder as he walked past him.

Ethan shook his head, laughing despite himself. Apparently he wasn't the only Richter to notice Brooke's pretty face.

He followed the rest of them into the house and back to the kitchen. Brooke was already comparing a piece of the tile she'd brought to the sample propped up against the wall next to the massive, recently installed Sub-Zero refrigerator.

"What do you think?" Ethan asked her. She was one of the best and he trusted her eye.

"I think it'll work fine. I bet the homeowner won't even see a difference," she said, holding them side by side for Ethan and Rex to see. "Agree?"

Rex took them from her and walked over to the weak sunlight filtering through a west-facing window. "Yep, you're right, Brooke," Rex said, handing them back to her. "They'll work just fine." Once his hands were again empty, he motioned around the room. "Now, let's lock up and get out of here. It's Friday night and everyone else is already headed home. What time's the game?"

Ethan glanced at his watch. "Starts at seven. We've got an hour and a half. You're right—we better get going if we're going to grab a bite before it starts."

Brooke watched their exchange with interest. "It's a Friday night in November. Are you talking football?"

"We sure are, pretty lady," Rex replied with a wink.

Ethan watched Brooke, expecting to see her bristle at his foreman's comment. But she only grinned. Ethan should have known. Rex had a way about him that earned him a pass in most people's eyes.

Dylan chimed in. "It's our last regular-season game tonight. We've gotta win to move on, and it won't be easy. My brother is the backup quarterback."

"Sounds like you're proud of him," Brooke said.

Dylan blushed. He shrugged. "Drew's all right. Got a good arm. Like Dad here. Did you know Dad was a star quarterback way back . . . like, a hundred years ago? He was team captain the last time our school won the state title. Probably not much chance that's gonna happen this year. Our defense is weak."

Now Brooke turned her attention back to Ethan—something she'd seemed to avoid since they'd come into the house. She fiddled, nodding slowly. "Star quarterback, huh? Why doesn't that surprise me? Bet you thought you were God's gift to the cheerleaders back then, too. Not much has changed."

Rex let out a bellow of laughter, turning away to avoid Ethan's glare.

Ethan worried Brooke's comment might tip his son off, but Dylan, in typical thirteen-year-old style, ignored the part of the conversation related to his father. "Do you like football?" he asked Brooke.

"I love football! I have four brothers and they all played. If we wanted to hang out with them as kids, my sister and I needed to learn the game too. She never could get into it, but it's been a favorite of mine since I was young. I never get to games anymore, which is too bad. I have nephews and a niece who play, but they don't live around here. Closest I get to it is watching the Vikings play on TV on Sundays."

Dylan, a huge Minnesota Vikings fan himself, grinned wide. Ethan recognized that look and braced himself for the inevitable.

"Hey, why don't you come with us tonight? If you like football so much, we could really use more fans in the stands. To hear Dad talk, home football games used to pack the bleachers, but not anymore."

Brooke met Dylan's invitation with a look of surprise, quickly replaced with a slow grin. She looked between father and son, chuckling at Ethan's discreet shake of his head. "Why, thank you, Dylan. It's been a long time since I spent a Friday night under the lights at a high school football game. You sure you wouldn't mind?"

Now Dylan puffed out his chest, clearly intent on making a good impression with his father's pretty co-worker. "It'd be great! We always get a burger on the way. Want to just ride with us?"

Brooke laughed at the boy's enthusiastic reply. "Sounds like fun! Sure, I'll join you. Besides, your dad *owes me.* But why don't I meet you at the game? I need to run home, let my dog out, and get some warmer clothes. I'll see you both at the game. Seven, right?"

Dylan's animated head-bob did little to reassure Ethan.

How did we go from me keeping my date with Brooke a secret . . . to having her tag along to Drew's game tonight?

He'd convinced himself he was done with her, and dating in general for the foreseeable future. But now Dylan had to step in and unknowingly screw that up.

Brooke seemed to have a talent for securing invitations. He'd do well to remember that.

The sky cleared before the game started, but the air had a definite bite to it as Ethan and Dylan climbed the bleacher stairs. The smell of popcorn permeated the cold, and an enthusiastic pep band's rendition of an iconic song from the '80s added a sense of nostalgia to the evening.

Four of Ethan's best years of his life took place right here, back when he had nothing more to worry about than whether or not he'd live up to his coach's expectations and if his current crush would say yes when he asked her to the homecoming dance. He needn't have worried. They always said yes. Things used to come easily for him.

At least, that's how he remembered it. The passage of time had likely muted the disappointments and highlighted the wins. He grew up before kids faced all of today's pressure to specialize. Even though he'd been the star of the team back then, he knew he probably wouldn't have measured up to some of the boys playing out on the field tonight. Natural talent used to be enough. Now talent was ruthlessly shaped and molded from an early age. While this might result in higher skill levels, Ethan couldn't imagine it was as much fun.

Would the kids playing tonight look back on their high school years with fondness? He'd have liked that for his own kids, but he wasn't sure how to help them achieve it.

Hell, I can't even manage to send Drew to his biggest game of the year in a clean uniform.

His son scanned the bleachers. There were a fair number of fans, but the seats were far from full. "Oh man, Dad. I don't see Brooke yet. I hope she didn't change her mind," he said, a frown on his face.

With any luck, she won't show, Ethan thought.

Aloud he said, "Game doesn't start for twenty minutes yet. Let's find a place."

They got situated, saving a few extra spots. Ethan's mom had texted him an hour ago to say they'd decided to come, too, since the weather cleared. Lavonne and George tried to get to most of their grandkids' sporting events, but Lavonne's knee had been bugging her and it was tough to climb the bleachers.

Together, father and son watched the teams warm up out on the field. His middle child looked smallish out amongst his team. Dylan's earlier comment was spot on: Drew had a great arm. He was fast, too. He just hadn't bulked up, or shot up, like many of his teammates. Even Dylan was now taller than Drew, despite their three year age gap. Ethan was starting to get the impression Drew didn't love playing the game as much as his dad and younger brother anymore. He hadn't said as much, but Ethan wasn't seeing the spark he used to when Drew talked about his teammates or the excitement of a close game.

"There she is!" Dylan cried out, jumping to his feet and waving enthusiastically.

Ethan peered around him and found Brooke in the line of fans streaming in now that the game was about to start. Her bright red jacket and white knit stocking cap made her hard to miss. She waved back at Dylan, heading their way.

Before Ethan could again curse his bad luck, things got more complicated. Another familiar face caught his eye as it topped the stairs and turned to face the crowd.

"Um, Dylan, your mom's here, too."

Dylan plopped down next to Ethan, clearly deflated. "What's *she* doing here?"

Despite his bitterness toward his ex, Ethan was careful to avoid showing his true feelings for Stacey in front of their kids. "Hey now, don't be like that. Of course she'd want to come, Dylan. This will probably be Drew's last game of the season."

"Way to think positive, Dad," Dylan said, slumping down farther. "The game hasn't even started yet and you're already sure they're gonna lose. Hopefully she won't sit by us."

Ethan knew the "she" he'd referred to was Stacey and not Brooke. It hurt his heart to think the kids might also be getting bitter toward her. She'd screwed up, *a lot*, but she was still the only mother they'd ever have.

Brooke continued to make her way toward them, squeezing past other fans farther down their row. A few had to stand to let her pass, the big blanket she carried making it harder to slip by. As the cold permeated his aching back, Ethan had to admit a blanket was a good idea. The newer metal benches weren't quite as comfortable as the old wooden bleachers had been. Or maybe it was just his slightly older bones complaining.

Ethan stood as Brooke reached them and Dylan slid down, clearly indicating she should sit between him and his father.

"Hi, guys! Man, it's cold out here. Didn't you bring anything to sit on? Here, stand up, Dylan, this thing is big enough for all of us."

Dylan got out of the way and Brooke smoothed the blanket out so all three of them could sit on it. As they got settled, Ethan glanced back toward the walkway along the front of the bleachers and caught Stacey's eye—years of habit had left some type of honing ability in Ethan's mind. She gave him a finger wave and turned to talk to a woman he didn't recognize who was walking behind her. He watched Stacey point to an area slightly above where they were sitting, and the two of them started up in their direction.

Ethan held his breath, hoping they wouldn't sit too close. Juggling conversation between Brooke and Dylan was going to be enough of a distraction from the game for him.

What ever happened to a simple game night out at the field?

He glanced over at Dylan and caught him watching his mother out of the corner of his eye, pretending not to see her when she gave him a more generous wave than the one she'd given Ethan. The women continued up the stairs, past their row, and Ethan let out a sigh of relief. Brooke and Dylan were holding an animated conversation, pointing toward the home team now lined up along the edge of the field in their impressive royal-blue uniforms.

A flag quartet approached the field from the north end zone and a signal from the band had the crowd rising to their feet. Hats came off and hands came up to cover hearts in a show of respect as the national and state flags were paraded onto the field. Ethan recognized the strong young voice singing out the first few bars of the National Anthem. He scanned the sidelines for her, the daughter of family friends, but couldn't locate her in the crowd.

Aside from a soft ringing of an errant cell phone and the laugh of a young child somewhere in the crowd, the fans and athletes were silent as she finished her impressive rendition of the song that had kicked off nearly every Friday night game on this football field for the past forty years. The honor guard took their measured steps toward the edge of the field, and applause erupted when they reached it—a signal for the festivities to begin.

"That girl is good," Brooke said, leaning toward Ethan as she spoke, trying to be heard over the racket.

Ethan nodded, smiling back. "Her name's Holly. I actually went to high school with her dad. We played football and baseball together. She's been singing at these games for a couple of years now. Drew has had a serious crush on her for years, but as far as I know he still hasn't asked her out yet. They're the same age. He's never even told me he likes her, but I can tell."

As they all sat back down again. Brooke fussed with her stocking hat, still holding his gaze, looking as if she had something to say.

"What?"

"It's probably my turn to apologize," she said, breaking their eye contact. "I know you didn't want me to come along tonight. But I really *do* love football, and when your son invited me along, I couldn't resist. I might have seen it as a chance to tick you off a little, too, like you did to me when you didn't call after our date. I had fun that night . . . and I thought you did, too. But I think I get it now."

Ethan was having a hard time following her.

"Get what?"

Brooke leaned in closer so no one but Ethan could hear her. "You know, the whole 'it's complicated' thing. I knew you had kids, and an ex, but until I met Dylan it wasn't really a big deal. Now that I've seen what a great kid he is, I understand. You don't want them hurt."

Ethan looked into her eyes for a beat before glancing away. He couldn't help but wonder whether or not Stacey, the *ex* Brooke had referenced, was watching their exchange now, sitting somewhere behind them. Would she wonder who this attractive young woman was, tucked between him and their son? Was it juvenile for him to hope it bothered her?

"Tell you what," he said. "Now that we've both admitted we're far from perfect, let's forget it. It's no big deal. Let's have fun and enjoy the game."

She smiled. "I'd like that."

They cheered as the announcer named the starters and the teams took the field. Ethan found Drew in his jersey, number twenty-eight, standing amongst the players along the sideline, yelling encouragement to their teammates.

The first quarter was a battle, with one interception against the home team allowing the opposition to score. A fumble a few minutes later resulted in a touchdown and a tie game. Drew got in for a few plays and helped his team advance down the field. At the blare of a buzzer signaling the end of the first quarter, people again stood at the end of their row. Lavonne and George, Ethan's folks, made their way toward them, followed by Rex.

"Hey, guys," Rex said, "look who I found out in the parking lot!"

Brooke and Dylan slid closer to Ethan to make room for everyone, and there was a round of greetings. Lavonne looked from Brooke to Ethan questioningly, but he ignored it.

"Hi, Lavonne," Brooke greeted Ethan's mother. "Good to see you again. You look different without your Halloween costume, but I suppose the flowers in your hair and whole hippie-vibe thing wouldn't really fit in at a cold November football game, huh?"

Lavonne smiled in response. "Nice to see you again, Brooke. And hey there, Dylan, how's your brother doing?"

"Hi, Grandma. Hi, Grandpa," Dylan said, leaning over to wave at his grandparents. "You're late—Drew's been out a couple times now. Rex, why didn't you tell us you were coming?"

"Last-minute decision. I figured you could use a few more fans in the stands tonight," Rex said, looking around at the crowd. He paused at one point, his eyes snagging on something, and then turned back to face the game. Without glancing in Ethan's direction, he added, "I thought things might get interesting. Looks like I was right."

"It's a good game," Ethan replied, ignoring the innuendo in Rex's comment. "Drew made a few good plays, Mom, but he hasn't been in all that much. Maybe more in the second half. Our starting QB hurt his hand in practice, so I'm not sure he can last the whole game."

The six of them continued to enjoy the game and add colorful commentary when warranted. The home team held their own, and the first half ended with the game still tied.

Ethan's pocket vibrated deep inside his jacket. He pulled his glove off, fished out his phone, and glanced behind him when he saw who was texting him. He nodded in Stacey's direction and dropped the phone back in his pocket.

"Dylan, why don't you go up and visit with your mom, now that it's halftime?" Ethan suggested to his son.

Even though he'd said it quietly, Brooke heard him. "Wait. Your ex is here, too?"

"Why wouldn't she be? Her son's on the team," Ethan said, a bit too defensively.

To this Dylan snorted. "She must not have had anything better to do. Do I have to go up there, Dad? I was going to go find the guys."

"Yes, you have to. Then you can go find your buddies. Now go."

Lavonne stood as her grandson dawdled. "It's colder than I thought it would be tonight. Dylan, listen to your father. Go see your mom. Give him a little time with his date."

Dylan looked at his grandmother as if she'd grown horns. "*Date?* Brooke isn't here on a date with Dad! *I* invited her."

"Oh, well, I just thought since—"

"Mom, why don't I run down and get you a cup of hot chocolate," Ethan interrupted, cutting her off before she could finish. "Dylan, just do as I say. You can come back down and sit with us when the game starts, unless you want to sit with your friends."

Heaving a dramatic sigh, Dylan turned to search out his mother in the crowd and then started in her direction. "Save my spot. I'll be back."

By the time the game hit the two-minute warning, everyone was on their feet. Few had expected the score of the game to be this close. Drew had been playing the quarterback spot throughout the final quarter, just as Ethan had predicted. They were on the twenty-yard line and it was third down. If they got a touchdown, their team would advance. If they didn't, they'd lose by three, their season over.

Ethan watched the snap, not daring to breathe. His son backed up, scanned for a receiver, and pulled back. One man was open in the end zone and Drew threw a hard pass his way. Before Ethan could even see if the pass was caught, he watched a kid twice Drew's size launch himself at his son, catching him around the knees. Ethan didn't think Drew even saw the guy coming. He went down hard, and Ethan was up on his feet on the bench in front of them, straining to catch a glimpse of his son in the mass of bodies.

The school athletic trainer ran onto the field, followed closely by two student trainers.

The other players backed out of the way and a hush fell over the crowd.

Ethan could see the head coach signal the boys back to the sidelines, out of the way. Now he could see Drew on the ground, prone and not moving.

"Oh . . . that doesn't look good," George groaned.

"Honey, you need to get down there," Lavonne ordered her son, shoving him toward the end of their row.

Ethan again looked behind him, searching for Stacey. She was already halfway down the bleachers. "Stay here," he directed over his shoulder at the rest of their party.

Together Ethan and Stacey hurried down the bleachers, but they hovered at the edge of the field, trying at first to be inconspicuous. If Drew wasn't badly hurt, he'd be humiliated if they made a fuss.

"God, I hope he's all right," Stacey said, sparing a fleeting glance at Ethan but keeping most of her focus on their son's prone form out on the field.

Ethan could only nod, fear curdling the burger he'd wolfed down with Dylan on the way to the game.

This is taking too damn long. Why isn't he moving?

Three boys on the team stepped in front of Stacey and Ethan, unintentionally blocking their view. Before Ethan could move, he felt a wave of relief wash over him at the sound of the crowd bursting into applause. Drew's teammates high-fived each other. It could only mean one thing.

"Oh, thank God," Stacey said. "I *hate* football. I *told* you I didn't like Drew playing anymore. He's small now compared to most of the other guys out there."

Ethan grimaced, leaving her on the sidelines to go check on their son.

Leave it to my wife—ex-wife—to twist this to be about her.

The trainer had just helped Drew up onto the portable table they used to treat injuries on the sidelines when Ethan reached them. Drew's eyes were shut against the pain, so he didn't see his dad's approach.

"What have we got, Sam?" Ethan asked the trainer. Sam had been around forever—since Ethan had sat on a similar table after getting banged up on the field himself, more than thirty years earlier.

Drew's eyes popped open with a groan.

"Dad, what the hell are you doing down here? I'm fine," he said, although he didn't sound fine to Ethan. Drew seldom swore, at least in front of his dad—a sure sign he was hurting.

"Hey there, Richter," Sam said, acknowledging Ethan. "He should be fine. I've gotta follow concussion protocol, make sure, but my gut tells me he just got roughed up."

Drew strained to look at the scoreboard. "How close was it?"

"I have no idea," Ethan replied honestly. "I was watching you, and when you went down, I couldn't have cared less about the pass."

Drew rolled his eyes at Ethan.

"Jesus, Dad, you're starting to sound like Mom."

"Speaking of your mother, she's worried sick about you."

I might be giving her the benefit of the doubt, Ethan thought, but managed not to mention that out loud.

"She showed? That's surprising," Drew replied, leaning back onto his elbows for a second before he shot back up. "Wait—don't let her come out here!"

Ethan glanced back at where they'd been standing. Stacey was walking back toward the fence, away from the field. "She's not."

"Seriously, Dad, you need to get out of here," Drew insisted. "Sam's got it."

Ethan looked to Sam for confirmation. The old trainer nodded.

"He'll be fine. I'll send a sheet home with him," Sam said, then walked a few steps with Ethan as he retreated from the sideline. The old man lowered his voice. "Make sure you read it so you know what to watch for and what he needs to avoid doing for a bit. And keep a close eye on him."

Ethan knew his son's request was reasonable. He fought his natural urge to stay and continued walking back toward Stacey, who'd stopped at the fence. He knew Drew was in good hands with Sam.

"He'll be all right," he said when he'd caught up with her. "Sam's checking him over. I'll call you if anything changes."

Stacey nodded but didn't look his way. She was chewing on her thumbnail—something she'd always done when she was nervous to tell him what was on her mind.

"You can go back and sit down, Stacey. Drew is going to be fine." Ethan glanced at the scorecard. "Looks like they're not going to be able to pull this one off. Are you still planning to take the boys to Minneapolis with you for that thing next weekend?"

"Yeah . . . about that, Ethan," she began.

Here we go again, he thought, recognizing her tone. It was the same one she took whenever she was going to back out on plans she'd made with the kids.

"Yes?"

"I've got some *big* news. I wanted you to hear it from me before the kids find out."

Ethan couldn't remember at what point Stacey had acquired a flair for the dramatic. And when it had started to bug him so badly. Eventually, he came to realize it was a cover for her insecurities. She'd always had a jealous streak. He'd thought that would fade with time, but it didn't. Then, once they'd had kids, she'd gone on and on about how she slaved away as a mother, getting little help from him. He thought she was exaggerating.

Now that *he* was doing much of those domestic things alone, while still trying to keep his business afloat, he realized she might have had a right to complain once in a while.

He waited impatiently, anxious to get back up to Dylan and everyone else and tell them how Drew was doing.

Stacey took a breath. "I'm getting married."

He couldn't help it: he drew a shocked gasp at her announcement.

Well, I didn't see that one coming.

Chapter Three
Gift of Moving On

"DREW, DID YOU KNOW Dad had a date a couple weeks ago and didn't tell us?"

"Yeah, right," Drew replied, more intent on his phone than what his brother was saying. "Dad doesn't date."

"That's what I thought, too, but Grandma told me he brought Brooke to Aunt Renee's Halloween party."

"Who's Brooke?"

Ethan pulled the skillet of scrambled eggs off the burner and took it over to the table to fill the boys' plates. Most mornings, their breakfast was a bowl of cereal or piece of toast, but it was Saturday and they weren't rushing off anywhere.

Since he'd tossed and turned all night, he hoped a big plate of eggs and plenty of black coffee would help him wake up. Stacey's bombshell the night before was still bothering him. The fact that her news cost him a good night's sleep bothered him even more. After everything she'd put them through, he shouldn't still care. But he did.

Maybe his concern over his kids' reactions when they would eventually hear the news was what kept him up the night before. Or maybe it was the footsteps coming from the apartment above them, accompanied by the wail of a newborn. Either way, it had been a long night.

Drew crossed his left arm over his chest and stretched it with his right, grimacing as he did so.

"Stiff?"

Drew glanced at his dad. "A little."

Ethan tried to change the subject before Dylan's tidbit about his date registered with Drew. "Do you guys have anything planned today? If not, I could really use some help over at the house."

"Just a minute. Who's Brooke?"

So much for keeping Drew in the dark.

"Just somebody I know from work."

"And you took her to the party out at Whispering Pines? Why?"

Ethan dumped the rest of the eggs on his own plate and took the pan over to the sink, dropping it in the basin with a clatter. He grabbed his steaming cup from the coffeemaker and sat down at the small kitchen table with the boys.

"Look, guys, it wasn't a big deal. That's why I didn't say anything. She's a friend. You guys were with your mom and Elizabeth was at school. When I mentioned the party to her, she said she thought it sounded like fun, so I asked her if she wanted to come along. It wasn't really a date."

Ethan took a bite of his breakfast. The boys had already wolfed down half of their eggs.

"Grandma said it was, and it sounds like a date to me," Dylan shot back, frowning at his dad. He'd grilled Ethan about it on their drive home from the game the night before.

"What's she look like?" Drew asked.

Dylan grinned. "Hot. Hot and a *lot* younger than Dad."

"Dylan, seriously? She's not *that* much younger than me," Ethan objected between forkfuls of scrambled eggs.

Dylan put his elbows on the table and leaned toward his father, looking him in the eye. "How old is she, then?" he challenged.

Ethan put his fork down and sat back in his chair, holding Dylan's gaze, not appreciating either his son's tone or the direction of the conversation. The fact Brooke was fifteen years younger than him *did* bother him a bit.

"Old enough to go on a date with me."

Drew dropped his fork onto the table, scattering little bits of cold egg. "You admit it was a date then," he said, grinning triumphantly. He turned to Dylan. "Describe her."

Ethan had had enough. He stood up and started clearing the table, his appetite gone. "I'm warning you guys, knock it off. This is exactly why I didn't tell you I took her out for one lousy date."

Dylan drained the last of his orange juice and pushed away from the table. "I find it hard to believe any date with Brooke would be lousy." He went on to describe Brooke to Drew.

Ethan tried not to listen, but he had to admit, Dylan got it right. The woman was attractive. But what Brooke looked like wasn't really the point. He needed to find out if it would bother them if he *did* eventually start dating more often.

He set the plates down on the counter and turned back to the two. "I'm sorry I didn't mention taking Brooke to the Halloween party. Dylan, can you sit back down, please?"

The smile slipped off Dylan's face.

"Look, forget about Brooke for a minute," he said, once again taking a seat in the third chair at their minuscule table. "Your mom and I have been divorced now for over a year, separated for a year before that. I really haven't given any thought to dating up until now because, honestly, I didn't have time."

I also was feeling pretty burned by your mother, he thought, but he didn't want to say that out loud.

"Would it bother you two if I *did* start to go out once in a while?"

Drew and Dylan looked at each other and then back at their father. Dylan shrugged. Drew, being the older of the two, often took the lead in conversations like this.

"It's about time you started to do some fun stuff, Dad. Mom sure didn't wait. You've been great, picking up all the slack around here, but we're fine."

Ethan knew Stacey's leaving had come as a shock to the kids, too. Even though she'd been unhappy, often complaining to Ethan both directly and in front of all of them, no one had expected her to walk out like she did. Then, when it wasn't long before she was openly dating, they'd been incredibly hurt, feeling easily replaced. She never used to miss any of their events, but suddenly she was often too busy to make games or teacher conferences. Ethan hated that she'd hurt them and didn't ever want to do anything to make them doubt *his* commitment to them as their father.

Ethan nodded at Drew and then looked to Dylan for confirmation. He got it in the form of another shrug.

"All right then. If I go out on any more dates, I won't try to hide it from you. But I'm not interested in another serious relationship right now. Got it?"

"Yes, sir," they replied in unison, standing and heading for the hallway and their room.

"Wait up, guys. Since we're having a heart-to-heart, I might as well bring you up to speed on something else."

"I don't know, Dad, I've had enough of this relationship talk to last me a while," Dylan said, hesitating at the hallway. He was clearly ready to get on with his morning.

"I know, bud, but this is important. Come sit back down."

They stayed standing by the hallway, so he continued anyway. "Your mom told me something last night, and I'm not sure how you'll feel about it. She asked me to talk to you both about it."

He thought back to the phone call he'd made to Stacey after they'd gotten home from the game. He still couldn't believe she expected *him* to tell them she was getting married again and had tried to talk her out of the ridiculous notion. Wasn't that *her* news to tell?

He'd considered refusing her, keeping his mouth shut and letting her tell them herself when they were in Minneapolis the next weekend. But he also didn't like the idea of the boys being blindsided with news like that. He'd learned the hard way that surprises could hurt like hell.

Drew walked slowly back to the table with a bit of a limp.

"You hurting?" Ethan asked.

"I'm fine. What did Mom want you to tell us that she couldn't wait to tell us next weekend when we go on that stupid trip with her?"

Ethan, tired of finding himself in the middle of the strained relationship between Stacey and the kids, sighed. "She's decided to get married again."

Drew visibly stiffened, but his face didn't give away any emotion. "Is that it?"

Ethan felt his heart break a little more. This was another blow to what used to be, at least in his opinion, his near-perfect little family.

How can I isolate the kids from all this crap she keeps putting us through?

"That's all I know at this point."

Dylan took a cue from Drew and held any emotion he might be feeling deep inside. Ethan couldn't tell how either of them were taking the news.

"Come on, guys, talk to me. What's going through your heads right now?"

"Honestly, Dad, this isn't a huge shock," Drew said. "She's already living with the guy. She's moving on. We already knew that. She moved to Minneapolis, doesn't care if you have to raise us pretty much by yourself, and once in a while she manages to fit us into her schedule."

This discussion wasn't making Ethan feel any better.

Dylan must have read the anguish on his face. His youngest came back to the table, hugged him with one arm, and gave him a forced grin. "Drew's right, Dad. Mom is making a new life for herself in Minneapolis. And even though we have to go visit her once in a while, this is home. It doesn't matter if it's in this crappy old apartment or over at the new house. As long as we can hang with you, life is good. If you add a saucy new girlfriend into the mix, we're good with that, too."

Now Dylan's grin didn't look forced. Drew nodded his agreement and Ethan watched his sons walk back to their bedroom and shut their door.

He couldn't help but wonder what they'd say to each other, out of his earshot.

Telling the boys about their mother's impending nuptials had been tough, but the phone call to Lizzy would be worse. He hated to even tell her. The relationship between his daughter and her mother was already strained. But now that he'd told the boys, he had to call her. He suspected Lizzy wasn't planning to see Stacey, Drew, or Dylan when they were in Minneapolis the next weekend, even though they wouldn't be far from her school.

"Hey, Dad."

"Hi, girl. What are you up to?"

"Hold on a sec."

Ethan could hear rustling on the other end of the phone.

"Sorry about that, just leaving a coffee shop. I've got two tests this week and they're going to be tough. I've been here since seven this morning."

"Did you do anything fun last night?" he asked. She'd always been a private person. She never shared many details about college life with him, but he was curious. He knew she used to tell Stacey more, and his wife would often keep him updated, but Ethan didn't think Lizzy was telling her mother anything these days.

"Yeah, we went to the hockey game. Then over to a house party afterward. Now I'm regretting staying out so late. It's hard to concentrate with a headache. What did you guys do? Oh, wait, I forgot about Drew's game. How'd they do?"

Ethan almost started to lecture her on how she needed to be careful at house parties but stopped himself. That would be the quickest way to shut her down. Besides, she was twenty-two years old and in her fourth year of college. She knew more than he did about what went on at those parties.

"Let's just say the season is now officially over for Drew."

"Darn. They lost, huh?"

"They did. Drew got banged up, too, but he's just stiff and sore today."

Ethan sank onto their tattered couch and muted the college football game playing on the television so he could give his daughter his full attention.

"Who went?"

"To the game? Mom and Dad came, even though your grandmother's knee has been bugging her. You should give her a call. She'd appreciate it. Let's see, who else? Rex came. Dylan, of course, and"—he almost didn't mention her but it just came out—"a friend."

Lizzy didn't seem to catch on to the part about his friend. "Was Mom there?"

"She was. I talked to her after Drew got hurt. She was there with a friend, too."

Ethan heard a car door slam through the phone. Lizzy must have gotten into her car.

"Do you mean her *boyfriend*?" Sarcasm dripped from her voice.

"No, it was a woman, but I didn't recognize her."

Dylan wandered into the room. He pointed to the television. "Turn it up."

Bossy kid, Ethan thought, shaking his head and pointing to the phone against his ear.

"Oh . . . sorry. Go in the other room."

Ethan sighed. "Just a sec, Liz," he said, then covered the phone with his other hand. "Dylan, don't be rude. I'm on the phone with your sister."

"Hey, sis!" Dylan yelled, loud enough for Lizzy to hear him. "Did you tell her about your date? Or Mom's wedding?"

Ethan glared at his son. He could hear Lizzy talking on the other end.

"Hey . . . Dad. What did Dylan just say?"

"Hold on," Ethan said into the phone. He lowered it against his chest so he could address his youngest again as the boy watched the silent TV. "Dylan, go fold your laundry and make your bed. I'm leaving for the house in ten minutes and you just earned yourself a few hours helping me out over there."

Dylan started to protest but apparently decided he'd pushed his luck enough. He stood and headed to the laundry, tucked away in the large closet off the kitchen.

"Sorry, Elizabeth. I did call you to catch up, but I thought I better update you on a few things, too."

"Sounds that way, if I heard Dylan correctly."

Ethan sighed again. *No point in stalling.* He went on to tell Lizzy about the bombshell Stacey had dropped the night before.

Lizzy didn't say anything for a minute.

"Lizzy, you still there?"

"Yeah, I'm here, Dad. I can't really say I'm that surprised. You know Mom. She's not good on her own. And this guy is rich, so . . ."

"I'm sure she isn't marrying him for his money. Your mom's not like that," Ethan said, surprised by the implication. He hadn't even considered why Stacey might be in such a hurry to get married. Ethan had only met the guy once, and it was a brief encounter. He had thought the man seemed quite a bit older than Stacey.

Kind of like you and Brooke, he thought, surprised as that thought popped into his head.

But as far as Stacey went, he didn't *think* she'd marry for money. Then again, she'd surprised him too often over the past couple years for him to be sure.

"Whatever," Lizzy said. "I've given up trying to figure that woman out. Listen, Dad, I gotta run. Anything else?"

Ethan heard an engine turn over in the background and Lizzy murmuring something to someone.

"Well, I was going to ask you one other thing, if you have another minute."

"I guess," she replied.

"Who are you talking to? Are you in your car?"

"Dad, come on. What is it? I gotta go," Lizzy said, clearly impatient.

"Never mind. It can wait. When are you coming home? Will we see you before Thanksgiving?"

"No way. I'll be lucky if I can make it home *for* Thanksgiving. My schedule is crazy."

Ethan suppressed another sigh. He felt like his daughter was turning into a stranger. He'd wanted to ask her how she felt about him dating, but that conversation would have to wait for another day. She was clearly distracted and in a hurry.

"Maybe we'll road trip to see you instead, then," he suggested.

"Well . . . *maybe* that would work." Lizzy didn't seem too thrilled with the idea. "Call first, though, if you do. Gotta run. Oh, say hi to Rex for me, will you? I miss that guy. Love you! Bye, Dad."

Ethan stared at his now silent phone. His daughter missed Rex?

What about me?

By the following Friday, Ethan was ready to do something that didn't involve either work or his boys. With their school football done, they would be around more, but that wasn't the problem. The problem was, once the news about their mother sunk in, they were mad about her getting married again, and since Ethan was the one around, not to mention the one who'd broken the news to them, he was on the receiving end of their frustration. They still weren't willing to talk about it, but they weren't acting like themselves.

Ethan called Brooke. He used the excuse of thanking her for helping him out with his tile debacle, but their conversation soon turned into a rehash, first of Drew's football game and then the Vikings' disappointing loss on Monday night. By the end of the phone call, they'd decided to try another date. Nothing serious. Dinner and a movie. Seemed casual enough.

Ethan walked down to the parking lot with the boys when Stacey picked them up after school on Friday. They tossed their duffle bags in the trunk.

"What are you going to do this weekend, then?" Stacey asked Ethan through her rolled-down window as she waited for the boys to get situated. "Got any plans? Or are you working . . . like usual."

She'd been pleasant enough up until that point, but Ethan felt the dig. "You say that like all I do is work."

"Isn't it, though?"

He let that comment go, deciding not to take the bait. "Yeah, I guess I do work a lot. I have a lot of responsibilities. And I'm trying to get the house done so we can move out of this cracker box. But not tonight. I have plans, too. Dinner and a movie. Have you seen that new one with the '80s band? I heard it was good."

Stacey looked confused. "No, not yet. Who are you going to the movie with? I didn't think Rex liked movies."

Ethan pushed away from the side of her car with a smile. "He doesn't. I have a date. You three have fun. I gotta go or I'll be late."

It was all he could do not to give her a wink as he turned away from her stunned expression. The boys could fill her in. Hopefully they'd remember to tell their mother his date was *hot*. Stacey shouldn't object to the age spread. She was doing the same thing.

Chapter Four

Gift of Averted Disasters

Stacey was right about one thing. He *did* work a lot.

First thing Saturday morning, Ethan headed over to Celia's house.

Celia, his aunt, had died two years earlier. She'd been a successful business woman, but she never married or had any kids of her own, so when she died, she generously split her worldly possessions among her extended family members.

Celia's gift to Ethan was property—rental properties, plus her own home. He was still trying to figure out how to make the best use of them. Most of his weekend time was spent working with the different properties. Celia had long-term renters in most of the units, so other than a few maintenance issues from time to time, he was satisfied to be making a small amount of money off each rental. Celia, always looking out for the underdog, used to keep her rents on the low end, but she always made sure they more than covered the mortgage, tax, and insurance payments, with a little to spare, each month. She'd been generous *and* astute. And her low rental rates and fair nature meant very little tenant turnover.

The property that was taking up most of Ethan's time lately was her house: a grand old Victorian, solid but tired. He was renovating it and planned to move his family in as soon as it was finished. When he and Stacey split, neither wanted to stay in their old house. He'd hoped to have the renovations done before their previous home sold, but Stacey knew of a potential buyer and it sold immediately. Now he and the boys were making the best of apartment life until Celia's house was ready.

Today he needed to finish painting the upstairs bedrooms so all the new trim could be installed. He'd just opened the paint when he heard someone come in downstairs.

"Anybody home?" a male voice echoed up the impressive staircase and through the double doors into the master.

"Up here!"

Heavy footsteps made their way up the stairs and down the hallway to where Ethan was on his knees, stirring an industrial-size vat of paint.

"You know you can't wear those boots in the house once the new floors go in," Ethan said, not bothering to look up.

"No shit," Rex replied, looking around the room. "Got an extra one of those?"

Ethan looked down at the roller next to his knee. "Sure, but what are you doing here? I thought you were driving over to your brother's for the weekend."

"I was, but something came up. Thought I'd see if I could give you a hand."

"Can't say no to an extra set of hands. The boys are with Stacey this weekend, and I need to make some progress if we want to be in here by Christmas."

Ethan turned back to the paint. He appreciated the help but felt bad for his friend. He was convinced Rex's brother was a loser, always calling Rex when he needed help with something but often canceling on him if they were scheduled to just hang out. But Ethan didn't want to make Rex feel worse by pointing out he had a jerk for a brother.

They settled into a routine, years of working together making the exchange of directions in order to accomplish such a mundane task as painting a room unnecessary. Ethan was preoccupied about how the boys' weekend was going with their mother and her new fiancé. Rex was quieter than usual, too. The two men soon moved on to the second bedroom.

"Oh, before I forget—I was supposed to tell you hello from Lizzy," Ethan said, glancing over his shoulder at Rex, who was currently crouched down, cutting in near the floor.

"How is Lizzy? She sure doesn't come around much anymore. I miss that kid."

Not as much as I *do,* Ethan thought. A phone call now and then just wasn't enough.

"I think she's all right. She's keeping busy with school. This is her last year, you know," Ethan replied, thinking back to the day they'd first dropped her off at her new dorm room as a freshman. U of M was a huge complex in downtown Minneapolis, and when Lizzy started there three and a half years ago it was like it had consumed her. Ethan couldn't be sure if it was the school or the implosion of her parents' marriage that kept her away. He suspected it was a combination of the two.

"Will she be home for Thanksgiving?" Rex asked.

"She *better* come home for Thanksgiving. But probably not before that."

Rex nodded. "Seems like once they leave the nest, you don't see much of them after that. At least that's what I've seen with my nieces and nephews. But that could be because they're tired of life with my brothers, too."

Ethan grinned. Turned out Rex didn't need to be told his brothers weren't perfect.

Ethan paused before loading his roller up with more paint. "She's barely seen this place since we started renovations. She has an eye for design, too. I'd hoped to get her input, but no such luck."

Rex laughed as he slathered paint up on the south wall in a large *X* pattern, filling in gaps as he went. "Remember when she was on a jobsite with us years ago and she convinced that crazy woman she should go with a sage green on the walls instead of the obnoxious purple the woman picked out? She couldn't have been more than, what, eight? You had zero luck convincing the woman, but for some reason Lizzy, an eight-year-old girl, was able to convince her. After that, it was hard to keep her away. I half expected her to want to join you in this business, you know, after college and all."

This surprised Ethan. While he knew Lizzy enjoyed coming to work with him back when she was younger, he'd never considered the possibility she might want to do more with the business as an adult. He admitted as much to Rex.

"Jesus, Ethan, are you blind?" Rex asked. "I'm a crusty old widower with no kids of my own and even *I* could see how much working with you meant to Lizzy."

"Since when is fifty-eight old and crusty?"

Rex waved off his comment. "Don't try to change the subject. Have you ever talked to Lizzy about it?"

Ethan shrugged. Rex's rant had him thinking. All he said in reply was, "Guess I should ask her about it."

Rex shook his head but said nothing more on the subject. By the time they were finished with a third bedroom, it was noon.

"Let's go grab a burger and a beer," Rex suggested.

"A burger *and* a beer?"

"Hey, as they say, it's five o'clock somewhere."

Ethan rolled his shoulders to flex his sore muscles. He could come back tomorrow and finish the walls. "You talked me into it. Where to?"

"You're going to make me ask, aren't you?" Rex said, a sly grin on his face, before he took a bite out of his burger.

"Ask what?"

Rex swallowed before answering. "Come on, Ethan, how was your second—wait, no—*third* date with our little friend?"

Ethan took a pull on his beer, eyeing Rex across the table as the din of football and car racing provided background noise to their conversation. The walls of the sports bar were lined with televisions, all tuned in to different sporting events.

"How'd you come up with a third?"

"The party, the game, and a movie. Three."

"Technically the game wasn't a date. But it went fine. Fun, I guess. By the way, I wouldn't let Brooke hear you call her 'our little friend.' She wouldn't appreciate it. And when Brooke doesn't like something, she'll let you know."

Rex laughed. "That she will. That woman knows her own mind. What's it like to be around a woman like that for a change?"

Ethan frowned at him. "What's *that* supposed to mean?"

"Look, you know as well as I do that Stacey was always a pushover. A people-pleaser. She didn't have much of a backbone."

Although Ethan hadn't really thought of Stacey as a pushover, Rex made a valid point. Stacey followed the crowd. He remembered how she always seemed desperate for the approval of her small group of lady friends. It used to drive him nuts. He wondered what they thought of Stacey walking away from her family and shacking up with an older, *wealthy* man. For all he knew, they'd encouraged it.

Ethan snorted into his beer. "I think she might have found her backbone now. But I don't want to talk about Stacey. Oh, other than to let you know she informed me at Drew's football game that she's getting married again." Rex's eyebrows raised, but Ethan kept going. "And I don't want to talk about Brooke. Stacey is old news and Brooke is a work buddy I've gone out with a couple times. No biggie."

Rex was obviously enjoying this. "Back up a minute. Did you say old Stacey was getting *hitched* again? Boy, that was fast. What's the rush? She get herself knocked up?"

This brought a laugh out of Ethan. "Even if that were medically possible for *her* these days, I doubt *he* could accomplish that feat. The man has to be deep into his sixties."

"Then it must be money."

"You sound like my daughter," Ethan said, dropping his napkin onto his now empty plate. "That was her theory, too."

Rex shook his head, clearly trying to come to grips with Stacey's news. There'd been a time, years ago, when they'd all been friends. They'd even come to this bar together.

He caught the waitress as she passed by and ordered a second beer. Ethan declined.

"Did you do the walk of shame this morning, then? Since the boys aren't around, that is."

Ethan downed the last of his beer.

"Of course there was no *walk of shame*. Christ, man, it's not like we're in a 'relationship,' " Ethan said, making air quotes with his fingers around that word—*relationship*.

Rex shrugged. "In this day and age, you don't have to be in a relationship to be having sex. From the stories I've heard, that didn't used to be one of your requirements either, back in your college days."

The waitress stopped to drop off Rex's beer and laid their bill on the table. Ethan scooped it up.

"You didn't even know me back in those days. And those stories have become exaggerated through the years."

"Doesn't matter. People talk. You had a reputation for being quite the ladies' man."

Ethan was about to deny it but couldn't muster the energy. Besides, there was enough truth to Rex's words that Ethan knew his buddy had found a decent source for his information.

"Why don't we talk about something else," Ethan suggested, tired of the ribbing. "Talked to anybody who's gone hunting?"

The two of them talked for another fifteen minutes and then Ethan headed back to Celia's.

Wonder how long I'll think of it as Celia's and not mine?

He wandered through the empty house, checking progress. As he did so, his mind traveled back to time spent here as a kid. Until he started the reno work, everything had still looked relatively the same as it had for the past forty years. Now, the big parts of the reno were done, and they were down to just the cosmetics.

He wasn't sure what he should do with all of Celia's personal belongings. His dad had him box up her things and put them upstairs, in the large attic. Now it was a mess up there. At some point, something would need to be done with all of it, but he didn't feel like it was his place to take the lead on that.

He was just opening the door to the attic when his cell rang. It was Lizzy.

"Dad?"

The tone of her voice set off alarm bells. She sounded like she either had a very bad cold or she was crying.

"Hey, kid, what's wrong? You sound sick."

"Dad . . . I'm sorry, but . . . I . . . I—"

Ethan shut the attic door and walked back toward the stairs.

"Elizabeth. What's wrong?" he repeated, more forcefully this time. His guts twisted with nerves.

"Umm . . . I'm really sorry. I had a car accident."

Ethan headed down the stairs, starting to think he might be taking a road trip.

"Are you hurt?"

"No, but my car is bad," Lizzy said, breaking into tears.

It *must* be bad. Lizzy seldom cried.

"Do you need me to drive over? Your mom's in Minneapolis this weekend. She could get to you quicker than I can."

Lizzy sniffed loudly. "No! Do not call Mom. No way! I don't need any of her shit right now."

Ethan took a deep breath, trying to figure out how best to handle his upset daughter so he didn't make things worse.

"Daddy, I'm okay, but I don't know about the other guy. It looked bad. Real bad."

"Did you hit another car, honey?" Ethan asked, trying to stay calm and not get frustrated with how difficult it was to pull the story out of Lizzy.

"No, he was riding. I mean he was driving a motorcycle."

"In November? In Minnesota? What . . . is the guy crazy?"

Ethan hustled through the house, making sure the back door was locked before going out the front. He'd already decided. He had to get to Lizzy. His daughter needed him.

"What the hell was somebody doing riding a motorcycle in Minneapolis in November?" he repeated.

Lizzy was crying again. Ethan heard a shuffle and then a male voice came over the line.

"Mr. Richter, this is Officer Benton with the Falcon Heights Police Department. Your daughter is awfully distraught. I think she needs someone to come help her, calm her down."

"I'm on my way."

He called Rex from the pickup, since he'd agreed to go over there for pizza later. He explained about Lizzy's call and that he was driving to the campus right away.

"Why don't I come with you?" Rex suggested, concern in his voice. Ethan suddenly remembered Rex's story about eight-year-old Lizzy, remembered that Rex cared about her too. "I'm not doing much and maybe I can help you out with the car. You know, drive it back here or something if it isn't too dinged up."

Ethan considered this. Rex was right—he might need an extra set of hands.

"If you're sure?"

"Are you kidding? This is Lizzy we're talking about here. I'm sure. Besides, you never learned your way around a vehicle."

On any other day, Rex's criticism would have ticked Ethan off. Just because Rex learned to rebuild vehicles from the chassis out as a kid, he thought anyone else who couldn't do the same was worthless around cars. Ethan didn't know as much as Rex, but he could change a spark plug or fix a starter. But today that didn't matter. Today he needed to get to his girl.

"I'll swing by and pick you up on the way out of town."

By the time they got to Lizzy's apartment an hour and a half later, she'd calmed down some. She was still waiting on news from the hospital about the guy driving the motorcycle. The police had just left after questioning her for over an hour.

Someone was with her, a guy Ethan hadn't met.

"Dad, this is Hunter. Hunter, my dad. And our family friend, Rex."

"Hello, Mr. Richter, nice to meet you," the young man said, shaking Ethan's hand. He greeted Rex as well.

"They had to tow my car to the shop," Lizzy said, her voice still quivering ever so slightly. "Want to go look at it now?"

Ethan shook his head. "In a bit. First, why don't you tell us what happened. Are you sure you didn't get hurt at all?"

"I didn't. We didn't. Hunter was in the car with me. I was just driving along . . . pulling out of a gas station, actually . . . and, all of a sudden, BAM! Something hit the door behind me, on the driver's side. At first, I couldn't see what hit us. But then . . . oh God, Dad, it was awful. I opened my door and saw the motorcycle. Really just the underside of it, because it was laying over with the wheels facing me. They were still spinning. I couldn't see the driver . . ."

Lizzy's voice got louder as she fought to contain her emotions. She started pacing her small living room. Ethan had never seen her like this.

"Then . . . I saw a foot. We were afraid he was *dead*, Dad. He wasn't moving. Someone in the station must have heard the crash, because the cops came almost right away. An ambulance came, too."

Rex, standing near Lizzy, put a comforting arm around her shoulders. Ethan glanced at his friend, not surprised to see his face drained of color. Rex lived with the pain of a tragic accident that had claimed his own wife years earlier. He'd never stopped blaming himself, even though no one else blamed him. A deer jumped out in front of them and Rex swerved to avoid it. The roads were slick. Rex barely tapped the brakes but the car still spun out of control and rolled into the ditch. For whatever reason, Gail's seatbelt failed and she was thrown out. She never had a chance. Rex hadn't had a day of peace since. Hearing Lizzy's version of her own accident had to bring it all back for him.

"Was the driver wearing a helmet?" Rex asked. He'd never want Lizzy to see his own pain. Besides, Rex was a Harley driver, too, adamant about always wearing a helmet. He'd lost more than one friend over the years who hadn't opted to wear one.

Hunter chimed in. "He was, and he was in full leathers too. Probably helped that it was cold out."

"I'm still confused as to why someone would be riding a motorcycle this time of year," Ethan said, shaking his head.

"Probably doing some work on it would be my guess," Rex said. "We haven't had much for snow or ice yet. Might have been moving it somewhere for winter storage, even. Do you have any idea how bad his injuries are?"

Lizzy shrugged. "He was sitting up and talking by the time they went to load him into the ambulance. He had some blood on his face and he was holding his arm. I hope he's going to be all right."

Despite already having hugged his daughter the minute he arrived, Ethan couldn't resist another. He'd been so damned scared after talking to her the first time.

Lizzy hugged him back for a minute but then wiggled out of his embrace. "Dad, really, I'm okay. I want to show you my car. See if you think I can drive it. I'm glad you brought Rex. He'll know."

Ethan threw up his hands. "Again with busting on me about not knowing my way around a car. I already had to listen to Rex give me a hard time about that." He saw a smile begin to creep onto his daughter's face, and he sighed. "All right, let's run over there. You can show us where it's at."

Lizzy and Hunter grabbed their coats and followed the men out to Ethan's truck. It was starting to snow and dusk was falling. As they climbed in, Ethan turned to Lizzy in the backseat. He was surprised to see Hunter was holding her hand. "Tell me you at least called your mother like I told you to."

"Uh . . . I tried. Honestly, I did. But she didn't pick up. I didn't want to leave a message 'cause she'd freak."

Ethan sighed. Stacey was surely going to blame him for not telling her right away.

Ten minutes later, they drove up next to Lizzy's 2011 Honda Civic, parked outside an auto repair shop.

Rex whistled as he rounded the back corner of the small black car and surveyed the damage to the rear quarter panel. "They don't make 'em like they used to, do they?"

Ethan cringed as he took a look for himself. The motorcycle had certainly done a number on his daughter's car.

"Thank God no one was sitting in the back," he said, turning to the kids. "You two sure you feel okay?"

"Dad, for the millionth time, we're fine," Lizzy said. She stayed back, eyeing the damage from a safe distance.

Ethan knew from her wide eyes and rapid blinking that she wasn't as "fine" as she wanted him to believe, but he wouldn't embarrass her by pushing the issue in front of Hunter.

"I can't drive it like this, can I?"

"Afraid not," Rex said, dropping to his knees to check for damage to the underside of the car. The setting winter sun offered little light, so he used the flashlight on his phone.

Lizzy stepped away to take a phone call. The three men checked the car over more closely. The shop itself was already closed, given it was late on a Saturday afternoon.

"What do you think, Rex, is it salvageable?"

Rex straightened, removed his hat, and pushed his graying hair back from his forehead, a thoughtful expression on his face. Ethan knew the news would be bad. It was always bad when Rex took off his hat.

"Need to get it up on a lift to be sure, but there's fluid leaking out onto the ground and the rear axel looks like it might have been tweaked. Do you have full coverage on it?"

Ethan nodded. "Yeah. I can't even imagine what this is going to do to my rates, though. Two young drivers on my policy is expensive. Add in a significant accident and my bill is going to be even uglier."

"We can't do any more tonight," Rex said. "It's late, and I'm starving. Are we going to drive all the way back home tonight?"

Ethan didn't get a chance to answer him before Lizzy wandered back.

"That was the police. The good news is the guy who ran into us was released from the hospital. They couldn't tell me anything more than that, I guess, due to privacy laws. But he must not be in too bad of shape if they already sent him home, right? The bad news is they still need to do more investigating before they decide who was at fault."

Lizzy walked around her banged-up Honda, despair evident on her face.

"I don't know what I'm going to do, Dad. How am I going to get to work and class until it's fixed?" She looked at him hesitantly. "Are you sure I can't just drive it like this for now?"

"Come on, let's go get something to eat," Rex said, walking purposefully back to Ethan's truck. "We'll figure something out."

Chapter Five
Gift of a Home-Cooked Meal

A week after Lizzy's accident, Ethan and his crew were putting the finishing touches on the Holshan house, only a few days past their initial deadline. Rex had spent most of the morning over at another project but stopped to see Ethan to get the final choice on finishes nailed down.

"Any updates on Lizzy's accident?" Rex asked. "I hope you made the right call, trying to fix her car instead of letting insurance total it out."

"It's not like I had much of a choice. The money they were offering wasn't going to be enough to replace it with a car as nice as the one she had before the accident."

Rex gave a grim smile. "Welcome to the world of negotiating with insurance companies."

Ethan nodded. "The shop is still waiting on parts. Thanks again for letting Elizabeth borrow your spare car. Now she's going to like you even *more* than she likes me—and it was already bad to start with."

Rex chuckled. "Yeah, it's great to be the *favorite* family friend to your kids."

Ethan flipped the light off in the kitchen, now that he'd had a chance to assure himself the room looked just as he'd hoped. The homeowners were due back any minute. Rex followed him out into the foyer. Despite Rex's tough-guy act, he knew the man had a huge soft spot in his heart for Lizzy, Drew, and Dylan. Rex and his wife hadn't been able to have kids. Rex got to be like a fun-loving uncle, while Ethan was the parent tasked with disciplining, harping, and all the other difficult challenges of raising kids.

"Are they pressing any charges in the accident?"

"It isn't sounding like it. Even though Lizzy pulled out in front of the biker, there was a car parked illegally and it blocked her view. It blocked the motorcycle guy's view, too. I asked why we couldn't make the guy who parked the car in a bad spot pay for damages, but that argument didn't get any traction."

"Is your insurance company only on the hook for her car, then? What about the motorcycle or the guy's trip in the ambulance and his short stint at the hospital? That had to have been expensive."

"We'll let the two insurance companies battle it out and see how things sit when the dust settles," Ethan said with a shrug.

"You do realize this was a pretty decent outcome, don't you?" Rex asked as he helped Ethan carry tools out to their enclosed trailer. "No one was badly hurt. If that guy on the motorcycle had been killed, Lizzy would have been scarred for life, maybe even face manslaughter charges. That's not something you get over . . . ever."

"I know, buddy," Ethan replied. "I know."

Later, after finishing up at the Holshans', he headed over to the fourplex where Rex was overseeing a small crew. The property was one Celia had left to him. Three of the four units were occupied; however, the tenant in the fourth unit had died recently, leaving it empty. Little had been done to the unit—to any of the units—in a long time. Ethan decided it was time to start giving the units a facelift. He'd begin in the vacant unit and then decide when to tackle the others.

He parked along the curb. The driveway was already full of vehicles. The four-unit building was designed with two distinct halves mirroring each other, each half with an upper and a lower unit.

Ethan was frustrated to see the outer door on the north half standing wide open. Someone working in the lower apartment must have neglected to close the door. A cold wind whipped dead leaves around, some of which were now swirling inside on the landing and making a mess. Whoever'd been too lazy to shut the damn door was going to clean it up. As Ethan entered the building and pulled the door shut behind him, a voice greeted him from above.

"Hello there, Mr. Richter. I am *certainly* happy to see you. I was going to call you today," a tiny, white-haired woman said from the top of the stairs, the door to her upper unit standing open behind her. The expression on her face didn't look happy. In fact, she sounded as irritated as Ethan felt.

"Hello, Mrs. Jarvis," Ethan said, bracing himself for the inevitable complaints.

"What in heaven's name are they doing down there?" she asked, pointing downstairs. "Poor Theo is barely cold in the grave and now there is all kinds of racket coming from his unit. Never heard so much noise in my entire life."

I do not *need this today,* Ethan thought, his irritation level ratcheting up another notch. Mrs. Jarvis was a decent tenant, always paying her rent on time (she was set up on automatic payments), and she kept a close eye on the property. Ethan knew she had him on speed dial, but he tolerated her constant complaints because her nosiness served a purpose. If there was any trouble in or around the building, the old gal let him know.

"Penelope, don't you remember? We talked about this. I explained that I needed to do some updating, now that this lower unit is empty. You'll thank me for it once it's done because, eventually, I plan to update all the units, including yours. I suspect you'd appreciate some new carpet, wouldn't you?"

"Hmph," the old woman snorted, shaking her head at Ethan. "You'll probably wait until they carry me out of here feet first, too, *then* you'll fix it up all nice and fancy."

And with that parting shot, she grabbed hold of her walker and turned her back on Ethan, the door slamming behind her. He could feel the tension knotting itself in the back of his neck, sure to become a nasty headache before the day was done.

The scream of a table saw sounded from below. He better go see what kind of progress they were making before a second tenant made a complaint.

He walked into chaos. Rex and another guy were wrestling a dark, pressed-wood cabinet down off the wall. It was tight quarters and, based on the cuss words he was hearing, they weren't any happier than he was today. He would've stepped in to help, but there wasn't room for him in the tiny kitchen.

"Why is it so cold in here?" Ethan asked when a blast of freezing air hit him. He strode back into the rear bedroom and almost shouted. "Who broke the goddamn window?"

The day was getting better and better.

He headed back to the kitchen area.

"Doesn't matter who broke it," Rex said between grunts as he eased his end of the short bank of cabinets onto the ground. "It was an accident. I knew you were stopping by, so I didn't bother to call you. As soon as we get these beasts out of here, I'll grab a piece of plywood out of my truck to cover up the hole until we can get new glass installed."

"And who left the outside door open? A bunch of crap blew in and it needs to be cleaned up."

"Aren't *you* just a ray of sunshine?" Rex inquired over his shoulder as he pulled out his tape measure and measured first the width of the doorjamb and then the size of the bank of cabinets.

A man wiped his hands off against his stained blue jeans and brushed past Ethan, heading for the stairs. "Sorry about that, boss, I'll go sweep it out."

"Don't be so careless next time, Skip," Ethan instructed, some of the irritation cooling in his tone when the construction worker took responsibility. Ethan knew he needed to keep things civil on the jobsite and not contribute to bickering. Skip was a decent worker.

Ethan turned back to the others. "Lenny, get over here and help Rex cut these old cabinets in two so we can get them out of here. I need to measure that broken window."

As he walked back toward the bedroom, he snatched a file folder off the kitchen counter. The folder contained rental and repair information on the unit. Ethan was also storing his notes related to the remodel in the file. He jotted down the size of the window pane he needed to order.

When he returned to the kitchen, Rex was trying to get Lenny to turn the bank of cabinets so they'd fit out the door. The kid didn't appear to know his left from his right. Ethan tucked the file folder into the back of his jeans and stepped in to help. Between the three of them, they got the disassembled cabinets out to the dump bin.

A cell phone went off and Lenny hurried back into the building, ahead of Ethan and Rex. As the two of them reentered the fourplex, Rex muttered, "Damn kid thinks I can't hear that phone of his ringing. I've already had to tell him to put it away three times today."

"Are you about done making a racket down there?"

The voice from above stopped Ethan in his tracks, and Rex nearly ran into him from behind. With a sigh, Ethan looked up to once again address Penelope, snapping the overhead light on as he did. "We'll be wrapping up in about a half hour, Mrs. Jarvis. I know you don't like us here past five."

The older woman nodded. "And we have a whist game this evening . . . have friends coming over. Wherever would my friend park when she arrives if all you boys' trucks are still out there?"

"I understand. We'll be out of your hair soon," Ethan assured her.

He expected her to leave it at that, but now she seemed to be staring at Rex.

"Ah . . . hello?" Rex said. He'd noticed her staring as well.

Penelope didn't immediately reply. She kept staring.

"Penelope, do you need something else?" Ethan asked impatiently.

"I just can't get over it," she finally said.

Ethan looked between Penelope and Rex, unclear as to what the woman was talking about. "Get over what, Penelope?"

"How much you look like Theo."

"Theo?" Rex asked.

"Yes, you know—Theo . . . the man who used to rent that apartment you're tearing apart, now that he's dead. My heavens, but you look like him. You aren't his son, are you?"

Rex pointed at himself, frowning in confusion. "Me?"

"Yes, you. But of course you couldn't be his son. That's silly. Theo only had a daughter. Don't mind me," Penelope said, patting her walker with a slightly shaky hand. "I'm just a silly old woman. For a second there, I thought I was seeing a ghost. You boys go finish up now. I have guests coming."

Ethan and Rex watched as the woman disappeared back into her apartment, slamming the door behind her.

The clatter of something behind them made both men jump.

Ethan clutched at his chest, laughing when he saw a broom lying on the floor. Skip must have propped it in the corner after he cleaned up the foyer, and the slamming door caused enough of a shake to knock it over.

"What, did you think it was a *ghost*?" Rex teased, picking up the fallen broom and heading back down the stairs with it. "You know, I swear this broom looks just like the last broom that was here—you know, before it died."

Ethan followed, chuckling, close on his heels, pulling the folder out of the back of his jeans. He rummaged through the sheets and then let out a low whistle when he found what he was looking for.

Rex was already using the broom to clean up the mess they'd made, cutting apart the cabinet. "What?"

"You gotta see this, man."

Dropping the broom, Rex came over and looked down at the photo Ethan had pulled out of the folder.

"You *could* pass for this guy's son," Ethan said, shaking his head.

Rex grunted as he turned away. "Well, since my old man was a no-good drunk and died a good *forty years* ago, that's not exactly possible."

Ethan was surprised by Rex's reaction. It seemed he'd touched a nerve. He gave the photo one last glance then snapped the folder shut, dropping it back onto the counter. There was work to be done if they were going to get out before Penelope's whist game started.

They covered the broken window with plywood, finished cleaning up the debris from the day, and headed out before they caused a parking shortage outside.

Ethan drove home in silence, trying to let go of his bad mood. Drew was supposed to have their dinner on the table by 6:30, and Ethan didn't want to be late. They were trying something new, each of them taking two nights a week to be responsible for making supper. Neither boy knew how to make anything other than mac and cheese (which, if he were honest with himself, Ethan would admit sounded great), but it was time they learned. With football over, there was no reason they couldn't help out more around the apartment.

Drew was making sloppy joes for supper, and Ethan was cautiously optimistic the sandwiches would be edible. Stacey had written down a handful of simple recipes for things they liked before she left. It was one of her more charitable moments.

The smell of something delicious met Ethan at the top of the stairs of their third-floor apartment. Knowing that delectable scent couldn't be coming from *his* kitchen, he reminded himself he wouldn't complain about Drew's cooking, no matter what.

He unlocked their door, which led straight into the small combination kitchen and eating area. He was met with noise, a mess, and the source of the mouthwatering scent he'd noticed a minute ago.

He stopped cold, wondering for a second if he was in the wrong apartment. But there were both his sons, along with a surprise visitor, draining noodles over the sink and stirring sauce on the stovetop.

"What's this?" Ethan asked.

"Oh hey, Dad," Dylan said as he stood over a steaming pot.

"Dad!" Drew was pulling plates out of the cupboard. "Surprise!"

"Hi, Ethan."

Brooke shot him a smile over her shoulder as she shook a colander of hot noodles over the sink.

"Brooke? What are *you* doing here?"

Brooke was the last person he'd expected to see in his kitchen tonight.

Drew smirked at his father as he set the table. "We didn't have any buns."

Like that explains it? Ethan thought, still not following. Drew hadn't even met Brooke before—but of course Dylan had when they went to the football game.

"Rex gave me a call about a job," Brooke said, setting the colander down in the sink and wiping her hands on a dishtowel.

Ethan had come to learn over the past two weeks that Brooke sported two different types of outfits. Her work attire consisted of jeans, T-shirts, and flannel tops. She also had her "date night" outfits, which were much more stylish and feminine, sexy even. Since he'd found her in his kitchen with his two very impressionable teenage sons, he was relieved to see she wore jeans and a flannel.

Ethan looked at her expectantly. He hadn't yet shrugged off his dark mood from earlier in the day and wasn't pleased to have his loosely planned evening of a beer and a sloppy joe in front of the television ruined. Entertaining the woman he was *kind of* seeing wasn't on the agenda.

"Rex mentioned you were in a nasty mood today and suggested I should see if I could cheer you up. He thought maybe my world-famous spaghetti might do it, so he gave me Dylan's number. Said none of you can cook worth a damn. Dylan was more than happy to invite me over instead of suffering his brother's cooking tonight." She turned to Ethan's eldest son. "No offense, Drew."

"None taken," Drew replied, grinning as he glanced between this woman Dylan couldn't seem to stop talking about, and his father, currently not looking too pleased.

"I was supposed to babysit for my niece tonight," Brooke went on, "but she got the flu, so I found myself with a free evening and a package of thawed hamburger in my fridge. And here I am."

And tomorrow Rex'll give me crap about a fourth *date.*

Ethan shrugged out of his jacket and went to hang it in the large closet to his left. He groaned at the pile of dirty clothes next to the washer. The machine lid was open, the washer empty. *Add laundry to tonight's list of unwanted interruptions.* And a lecture to his boys once their guest went home for the evening.

As he searched for a hanger in the mass of jackets and sweatshirts suspended on the short rod, he couldn't help but overhear Drew and Dylan talking with Brooke. The three of them laughed at something. He paused and listened.

They hadn't had enough laughter in their lives lately. He needed to snap out of his mood and let everyone enjoy the evening. He was going to kill Rex the next day for putting his nose in where it didn't belong, of course . . . but for now, he'd try to make the most of it.

He closed the closet door behind him, not wanting Brooke to witness his inability to keep up with the laundry.

They sat down to their first decent home-cooked meal in weeks. Ethan had two or three dishes he could make without issue, but they were all sick of his standbys.

"Wow, I didn't think we'd get a home-cooked meal before Thanksgiving when Grandma cooks for us again," Dylan said, trying but failing to keep a straight face.

Drew busted out laughing.

"Keep it up, boys, and you'll eat mac and cheese every night between now and then," Ethan warned as he filled his plate and took his first bite.

"Is this Prego?" he asked Brooke through a mouthful of pasta. He knew it was the wrong thing to say when she narrowed her eyes at him and picked up her own fork. In his defense, there had been three jars of Prego in his cupboard.

"Seriously? Even *you* could make spaghetti by dumping a jar of bottled sauce into a pound of hamburger. No, Ethan, it's not Prego. It's my grandmother's recipe. She was by far the best cook in our family, and my sister and I grew up in her kitchen, learning as many of her tricks as we could."

Ethan felt a twinge of guilt at his unintended insult. She was just trying to be nice, and he didn't like the hurt he'd caused in her huge brown eyes. Clearly he was rusty at this, despite all of Rex's talk of him being some kind of "ladies' man." He wiped his mouth with the paper towel Drew had tossed onto each plate when he set the table.

"I'm sorry. This is great. Your grandmother taught you well," Ethan said, hoping to take the sting out of his words.

"This *is* good," Dylan chimed in. "It reminds me of Aunt Val's spaghetti. Unlike Dad, she's a great cook, too."

Brooke asked what the boys were doing now that football was over. Dylan talked about his new practice schedule for basketball. Drew surprised them all with news of a job he'd just taken.

"I didn't even know you'd started looking for a job already," Ethan said. "Guess this means you've definitely decided against basketball this year?"

"Yeah. Last year kind of sucked. Dylan got the height in this family. I know I can play a decent game as guard, even though I'm short, but we've got plenty of good guards on the team. I'll spend as much time on the bench as the court during games. Besides, I need to beef up my college fund."

"I like the way you think," Ethan said, although he felt a twinge of disappointment Drew wouldn't be playing in the varsity games this winter. Dylan's games would be fun, but those were always challenging to get to since they were in the middle of the afternoon.

Drew stood up and took his empty plate over to the sink. He'd managed to polish off two helpings before Ethan finished one.

"I am playing intramurals, though, and we start tonight. I gotta run."

"Not so fast, bud. You already managed to get out of preparing this meal. You need to clean it up."

Drew groaned but had learned not to waste time arguing. He got the leftovers put away and washed up the pans while the rest of them finished eating.

"Good enough?" he asked Ethan, clearly anxious to get going.

Ethan could see Drew had done what he could without being rude. He nodded. "Go. But be home by ten. It's a school night."

After Drew was gone, they finished cleaning up the kitchen and Ethan invited Brooke to watch the football game on TV with them.

Despite his earlier reservations, Ethan enjoyed the evening. There was a friendly banter between Dylan and Brooke since they were fans of opposing teams.

"What are you doing for Thanksgiving, Brooke?" Dylan asked.

"Going over to my sister's on Thursday. I'm on pie duty. We have some other friends coming, too," she said, pushing up out of the deep sofa and collecting empty cans. It was halftime. "Thanks, guys. It's getting late and I have an early job in the morning. I better get going. What are your plans for Thanksgiving?"

"Lizzy should get in Wednesday night, and we'll go over to my folks' on Thursday. There'll be lots of food, games, and competition. Then I'm not sure what we're doing on Friday and Saturday. My sister mentioned maybe spending the day out at Whispering Pines on Saturday."

"Why don't you come with us to Whispering Pines?" Dylan suggested to Brooke. "Aunt Renee said we could bring friends." He grinned. "She didn't specify I could only bring *kid* friends, though."

"Oh, I don't want to impose," Brooke said, glancing at Ethan. "It sounds like a family weekend."

Ethan hadn't been sure whether he'd even go out to the Pines. He needed to get their house done. But he had to admit it might be fun to have Brooke join them out at the resort instead. He already knew Drew and Dylan liked her, but Lizzy hadn't met her yet. It might be a good way to have the two of them spend time together in a larger group setting. Brooke had already met most of the rest of his immediate family.

Rex's voice entered his head: *That'd be date number five . . .*

"You should come along," Ethan said. "I'm not sure what we'll do, but we always have fun out there. Or do you have other plans?"

Brooke shook her head. "Not really. I'll probably babysit my niece for a while on Friday so my sister can go do some shopping. That Black Friday circus is *not* for me. But the weekend is open. If you think it'll be all right to tag along, it sounds like fun."

"Awesome!" Dylan chimed in. "I just hope my big sis isn't too hard on you. She's been on a bit of a rampage lately."

"You guys don't have to spend any of the weekend with your mom?" Brooke asked.

Ethan tried to formulate a quick response, in case her question made his son feel awkward, but Dylan jumped in before he could utter a word.

"Nope, we did our duty last weekend when we went to Minneapolis with her. She's on some ski trip in Colorado with her new squeeze." Dylan rolled his eyes. "They're probably planning their wedding or some crap like that."

Brooke blinked. "Wedding?"

"Oh yeah, didn't Dad tell you? Mom's getting married again."

Brooke looked questioningly at Ethan.

Ethan smiled uncomfortably. "It's not like I go around advertising that, Dylan."

"You should have heard Lizzy go off about it. She is *not* digging this whole split-family thing. You'll want to be extra nice to her on Saturday, Brooke. That or bring your boxing gloves." Dylan pretended to size her up. "I think you could take her."

Chapter Six

GIFT OF HERITAGE

THURSDAY PLAYED OUT MUCH like every other Thanksgiving Ethan could remember. It was a relief to have all three kids with him and not have to share them with Stacey for a change.

They feasted on the same holiday meal they'd all grown up enjoying. Variety was fine most days of the year, but heaven help whoever tried to screw around with tradition at the Richter house. They'd eaten their big meal at one o'clock. The mess was cleaned up, at least until they got out all the leftovers later for round two.

The kids were clustered around the dining room table, playing a wicked game of Spoons. The adults were gathered in the front living room, catching up on each other's busy lives.

"How is the house coming along?" Ethan asked his sister Renee and her husband Matt. The newlyweds were building a new home out at Whispering Pines.

"The weather cooperated these past couple of weeks," Matt said, "so the shell is up, but that's about it. If they can get the windows and doors in, then we can start on some of the inside work. If not, we're on hold until spring."

"I hope that happens. The longer it's still in these early stages, the more time I'm going to waste tweaking the plans and changing my mind," Renee said with a laugh.

Matt smiled. "The truth is, we're lucky with how things have been going. I had my doubts about getting anything accomplished before winter, given our late start."

Ethan knew his brother-in-law had experience in construction, despite a career in law enforcement. Matt had told them he took a year or two off when the pressures of police work got to be too much, signing on with a crew that specialized in rehabilitating old mansions on the East Coast, back before he'd met Renee.

"I had my doubts, too," Ethan agreed. "When you first started talking about building out at the resort this past summer, I figured it wouldn't happen until next spring. Now maybe we'll both be moved into our new homes come springtime. I'd hoped we could get in to our house by Christmas, but now I'd put the odds of that at less than fifty-fifty. It doesn't help that I started remodeling one of the units over at the fourplex. One of the tenants died and I figured I better get moving on that, too."

Jess, one of Ethan's other two sisters, had been listening. "I am so glad you two are the ones doing the moving and not me this time."

Ethan grinned back at her. He was relieved Jess had seemed to finally get settled and find some happiness. She'd moved into the other half of Renee's duplex out at Whispering Pines the previous summer when she'd started the process of divorcing her cheating husband. Since then she had adopted a new baby daughter and was seeing Seth, a decent guy who appeared to treat her well. Despite being happy for Jess, however, he couldn't help but give her a hard time.

"You do know you owe us, right, sis? What with moving and all?"

Jess screwed her face up at her oldest sibling. "Yes, dear brother, I fully intend to make myself useful when the time comes."

"Good, see that you do," he teased. He was enjoying spending the day with his family. No one seemed inclined to rush off—except for his youngest sister. "It's too bad Val had to take Jake home. I hope his belly ache was because he ate too much turkey and it's not the stomach flu."

"Oh my God, the flu is the last thing I need," Lavonne piped in. She had her leg propped up in the recliner. Hours of cooking had taken a toll. "It's the last thing *any* of us need."

"Mom, why didn't you let the kids do the dishes after dinner?" Jess asked. "They're old enough."

"Most days I'd be all for that, dear, but *not* with my crystal and Celia's china. They can clean up after we use paper plates for leftovers tonight."

"Actually, *I'll* clean up if we're using paper plates!" Renee said with a laugh.

Conversation continued around the room. An occasional scream could be heard from the dining room, along with the scrape of chairs on the hardwood floors.

"If you kids break anything in there," George yelled from his recliner, "you will have your grandmother to answer to!"

"Why do I always have to be the bad guy?" Lavonne asked. "You are such a pushover."

"Speaking of bad guys . . . any updates on Will?" Ethan asked Jess. Will was Jess's ex, currently doing time for prescription fraud and embezzlement. "Did they ever figure out where all the money went that he and that woman stole?"

Jess sat forward on the sofa and rolled her shoulders, as if trying to shrug off the distasteful topic of her ex. Seth rubbed her back, and she sent him a grateful glance before answering Ethan.

"Most of it went to fund their insatiable appetites for the finer things in life. There were a couple of timeshares, one in the mountains of Colorado and another one on St. Thomas," Jess reported in her signature, matter-of-fact tone. "Turns out some of those medical conferences he claimed to be going on were really nothing more than a getaway with his mistress, too."

"He really is a bastard, isn't he?" Ethan said with a sad shake of his head, sorry he'd brought up Will. He hoped he hadn't ruined the holiday for Jess. Seeing Seth sitting next to her now reminded him of how Will had seldom come to family functions in the last years of their marriage. As a surgeon, he'd claimed to be working, but no one really believed that anymore. Ethan could only hope Seth would treat her better. So far, their relationship looked promising, even to an overprotective older brother.

"That he is, Ethan, that he is," Jess agreed, but then her face brightened. "The good news is my adoption of little Harper is final now and I no longer have any reason to interact with him. I haven't been back to that jail in months, nor do I intend to ever go back. I do feel bad for the kids. It's humiliating to have a father in prison. I wouldn't be surprised if they just tell people who don't know the whole story that he's dead."

Renee, having lost her first husband and the father of her children to a terminal illness many years earlier, said nothing but shifted in closer to Matt's side as she listened to the exchange between her siblings. Jess must have noticed the pained look on her face the minute the words were out of her mouth.

"Oh, Renee, I'm so sorry . . . that was a terrible thing for me to say. I can't imagine how Julie and Robbie feel, having to tell people their dad really did die."

Renee waved off her sister's apology. "Jess, aren't you always the one telling us not to worry about putting our foot in our mouth when talking about the tangle your life has been the past year or so? Same goes here. Jim died a long time ago. Of course, it still hurts, and probably always will, but we've all found ways to move on." She reached over and squeezed her new husband's leg.

Matt patted Renee's hand. "What about Tiffany? Harper's mom? Do you hear from her?"

"Only through our lawyers," Jess replied. "She told me she needed to distance herself from all of us, including Harper. It was too difficult for her, I guess, and she's trying to build a new life. I'm just so thankful she finally realized she wasn't the type of woman who could ever give Harper a stable home."

Jess stopped talking and tilted her head slightly, listening. "And speak of the devil. Sounds like Harper is up from her nap," she said, pushing up out of the couch where she'd been tucked in next to Seth.

"Want me to go get her?" Seth asked, catching Jess's hand.

Seth's willingness to help Jess with Harper, and his efforts to build relationships with her two older kids, Nathan and Lauren, earned him points in Ethan's book. He knew Will's mistreatment of Jess through the years had turned his sister a bit cynical, but based on the expression on her face when she talked with Seth now, she was opening up again.

"Thanks, but I've got her," she said, squeezing Seth's hand before dropping it as she headed for the stairs.

"Anything new with you, Seth?" Ethan asked, always interested to hear what he was working on. Ethan, as a contractor, knew all too well the amount of quality architectural elements that were destroyed every year. He liked the idea that Seth had made it his mission, and his business, to save as many treasures out of old buildings as possible.

"Next week I'm heading over to Brainerd. There's a big old lodge out on Gull Lake that they're tearing down in the spring to build a new condominium complex. I'm going to take a look, see what there might be that's salvageable."

Renee shook her head. "I hate to hear about another old place on a lake getting torn down. Makes me think how lucky we were that Celia took care of Whispering Pines like she did."

"I know," Seth agreed. "I hate it, too. This is just a chance to take a look and see what there is. If I like what I see, I'll bid on it. I can usually find something."

"Is there a decent market for the old things you pull out, then?" George asked.

"Usually. Just like anything else, styles change. I need to keep my finger on the pulse of what buyers are looking for, too. I'm willing to pull most anything still in good condition out of buildings so they aren't destroyed, but how I repurpose them or position them for resale changes."

Renee said, "I should introduce you to my friend, Tabby. She's an interior designer back in Minneapolis. She was a big help to me when I first got Whispering Pines, and the project even inspired her to help clients with their lake homes."

Seth looked genuinely excited. "Thanks, Renee, that'd be great. So much of this business is based on networks and who you know. I can always use more contacts."

The stairs creaked as Jess came back down, little Harper in her arms. The ten-month-old still looked groggy. She rested her head on Jess's shoulder, white, baby-fine hair sticking out in all directions, her cheeks rosy red.

Lavonne held out her arms to the child as Jess again entered the room. "I know that look," she cooed to Harper, settling the child on her lap when Jess handed her over. "She's cutting teeth. George, go get me a cold washcloth from the kitchen, will you? Grandma will make you feel better, honey."

Never having to be told twice to do something for one of his grandchildren, George hopped up to do as he was asked. When he returned with the cool rag, Lavonne asked him, "Hey, did you tell the kids what you want some help with on Saturday?" She showed Harper how to chew on it to help relieve her teething pain.

George settled back into the recliner. "No, I hadn't had a chance yet. Renee, you still thinking about having people out to Whispering Pines on Saturday?"

"Sure, Dad, but I'm not sure what all we'll do. With the college kids home, I thought everyone might want to spend more than just today together, but there's more room to spread out there. Maybe we can do some early holiday baking and freeze stuff. Or, if that snow comes in that they've been talking about tomorrow, maybe the kids could go sledding. Is everybody coming?"

Her question was met with affirmative nods from around the room.

"Good. It'll be fun! Did you have something else in mind, Dad?"

"My service club wants to find some ways to help local seniors over the holidays. I was trying to think of a project I might be able to do. And I think I have an idea. Remember that tie blanket Julie made me for Christmas last year? What if we made a bunch of those for the residents over at one of the nursing homes? Maybe smaller blankets, for their laps if they're in wheelchairs."

"And were you thinking maybe we'd make it a group project? Make a bunch of them on Saturday?" Matt asked.

"Yep. That's exactly what I was thinking about. What does everyone think?"

"Are they hard to make?" Jess asked.

Renee shook her head. "No, not at all. There's no sewing involved. Just some measuring out of the fleece, cutting tabs all around the edges, and tying them together. Any of the kids could help—well, except for Harper, of course."

"Then I say let's do it," Jess said. "Everybody can contribute, and it's for a great cause."

Ethan called Brooke on his way home from his parents'. He was alone in his car, as his kids were all in Drew's vehicle behind him.

"How was your Thanksgiving?" Ethan asked when she picked up.

"It was a madhouse. Lots of food, lots of drama, plenty of noise. Got home a couple of hours ago. I'm actually working on my website now. A nice, quiet task."

Ethan navigated the tricky sharp turn entering their neighborhood, a thin coating of new ice making the road slick. *I hope Drew is careful.* Having teenage drivers was definitely contributing to his gray hair.

"If it's quiet you're craving," he said, "you might want to reconsider spending the day with us on Saturday. My whole family will be around, and that always comes with plenty of noise and confusion."

Brooke assured him she was looking forward to spending time with all of them. She was sure a quiet day on Friday babysitting her niece would leave her fully recharged and ready to face the masses again. "What's on the agenda?"

"Probably some time outside, maybe some baking, and a project my dad came up with—making tie blankets for local seniors for the holidays."

"Hey, I knew I liked George. Those hippy costumes your folks wore to the Halloween party exuded good karma."

"The idea of baking holiday cookies and doing craft projects doesn't sound like a bust of a Saturday to you, then?"

"No, not at all," Brooke assured him, but then she paused. "Unless you don't want me around all of your family again. I get it if you don't want them to assume we're in . . . like . . . a *relationship* or anything."

Ethan considered this. *Did* he worry about that? Probably. If he was being honest with himself, he still wasn't sure how he felt about Brooke. He liked her as a friend, but sometimes she just seemed so different . . . so *young*, maybe. But he did want Lizzy to meet her. He was curious to find out what his daughter might think of her. That might help him decide whether or not to let this thing, whatever it was, continue with Brooke. He was still keeping her at arm's length, but he suspected Brooke wouldn't tolerate that for long. She might want more than he was willing, or able, to give.

"They're usually pretty good about not jumping to conclusions. We'll pick you up at nine o'clock, if that works for you."

"I'd like that."

Chapter Seven
GIFT OF TEAMWORK

"UM, JESS . . . Ethan mentioned he might bring Brooke along today," Renee said, glancing at her sister as they hauled groceries from their vehicles into the lodge. She said it like a question, as if she were worried Jess might bite her head off at the news.

"Oh great," Jess said. It was more of a groan than a statement.

"Did you ask Seth about her?"

Jess balanced two paper grocery bags on her hip as she wrestled with the front door. "Not really," she admitted. She hated to admit to anyone, especially Seth, that she was jealous of Brooke. He'd been friendly with Brooke since they'd run into each other at Celia's old house when Brooke was helping Ethan with the remodel and Seth was helping Jess search old records in the attic. It was evident they'd known each other for some time, and a few comments Seth had made led her to believe they'd dated in the past, though she was too afraid to ask him outright. Even her own hesitancy to discuss her feelings about Brooke with Seth irritated her. She didn't usually have a problem speaking her own mind, but she *really* liked Seth, and she didn't want to screw it up.

Renee said, "And what, oh practical sister of mine, have you always told me about this kind of thing? About assuming things?" She pushed past Jess through the open door and back toward the lodge kitchen, leaving Jess to again struggle with the door behind them.

"I know, I know. But it's always easier to give advice than to take it—even if it's your own," Jess said, making her way through the early morning gloom in the entryway. The welcoming scent of coffee filled the kitchen as they entered and dropped their heavy bags down on the massive island.

"Morning, Val," Renee greeted their youngest sibling. "I didn't know you were here already. Where's your car?"

"Hey, guys," Val replied from the floor, where she sat in front of a large cupboard full of pots and pans. An assortment of cookie sheets surrounded her. "The older boys had to help get the tree lot set up this morning before the first shift starts at nine, so Luke dropped me off then took them in that direction. He's going to take Jake for doughnuts to kill some time until they're done. Then they'll all be back out here to help."

Renee took butter and cream out of one of the grocery bags and put them away in the fridge. "Jake must be feeling better, then? Was it the flu on Thursday?"

Val snorted. "No. He only threw up the one time. I finally got him to admit Dave dared him to eat all the black olives on the kids' table. And of course, Jake can't ever back down from a dare issued by his oldest brother."

Renee and Jess both laughed. Jake, the youngest grandchild before Harper entered the picture, held a special place in all their hearts. His big personality was entertaining, although Jess suspected Val and Luke would have their hands full raising him. Jake was a lot like Val—which wasn't surprising, since both were the youngest of four.

"No sign of Mom and Dad yet?" Renee asked.

"Not yet. I'm sure they'll be here any minute. Hey, Jess, is Seth coming?"

Jess started unloading the rest of the groceries. Based on all these baking supplies, they had a full day in the kitchen ahead of them. "Yep. He'll be out soon. He needed to call his daughter's mother to make arrangements for Christmas. Kaylee is flying out here on Christmas Eve."

Renee paused. "Does *that* bother you?"

Jess laughed. "You mean Seth talking to *Dawn*? Not at all. What Seth had with her is ancient history, and from what he says, other than the daughter they produced together, what they had wasn't much. Mostly friendship with a one-night stand thrown in to complicate life. Besides, she's married now and expecting another child."

"Tell me again," Renee said, "why you're jealous of *Brooke*, then?"

A cupboard door slammed and Val got to her feet, cookie sheets in hand. She dropped them onto one of the two stovetops, making a racket. "Did you say 'jealous'? *Jess*?"

Jess shrugged, searching the expressions on her two sisters' faces. "Tell me I'm being dumb and I have nothing to worry about and I'll try to let it go. Seth is coming out today, and I don't want to ruin any of the fun with a bad attitude."

Val made a funny face and turned away, busying herself with getting coffee cups out of an upper cabinet. She had to stand on her tiptoes to reach them.

Jess stared at her sister's back, groceries temporarily forgotten. "What the hell is *that* supposed to mean, Val? Come on, you're never one to keep your opinions to yourself. Do you think I have something to worry about where Brooke is concerned?"

"Jeez, Jess, settle down," Renee intervened. "You are *awfully* touchy."

"You'd be touchy, too, if you'd lived for years, questioning whether or not your husband was cheating on you. And since it turned out he *was*—and now he's in *prison* and I'm raising his illegitimate *daughter*—you might say I'm a bit gun-shy these days."

Renee rounded the large island, arms outstretched. Jess allowed herself to be hugged, but not for long. She didn't want her family's pity over her failed marriage. She was trying to move on. Outbursts like this weren't helping her.

"Never mind," she continued. "You two couldn't possibly know if I have anything to worry about. Seth hasn't given me any reason to doubt him, and I don't want to screw up our relationship by being petty. Besides, I've been telling Ethan for months that he needs to start having fun again, maybe go out on a date once in a while. I'm not about to tell him I don't like him dating Brooke. Who knows, maybe she's great and we just need time to get to know her."

"Tell me again," Lizzy asked her father as they all climbed into his truck, "who this Brooke chick is and why she's coming out to Whispering Pines with us today? You work together?"

"Look, Elizabeth, it's no big deal. We've just gone out a few times and I wanted you to have a chance to meet her," Ethan said, trying to keep his tone light. He did not want Lizzy to get upset about this—especially since they were already late picking Brooke up.

"Yeah," Dylan chimed in from the backseat. "Dad's got a hot new girlfriend."

Lizzy spun in her seat to look back at her brothers, then wheeled back to her father. "Are you frigging *kidding* me? Why am I just hearing about this now? You have a *girlfriend*? How can you spring that on me like this?"

Dylan wiggled his eyebrows at her, clearly enjoying her outburst. Drew merely shrugged at her, saying nothing.

"Honey," Ethan said, his tone still light, "it honestly is nothing serious. I'd actually planned to mention it to you a while ago, the same day I told you your mom is getting married again, but you were already upset about that, so I was just going to wait to tell you."

"Dad, that was over a week ago."

"I know, and I apologize. Now, please, rein in the drama a bit by the time she gets in the car and do your best to be nice to her. Who knows? Maybe you'll even like her."

He spared a glance at his daughter's face. Based on her stony expression as she stared out her window, no longer looking at him, he realized he could have put his directive into better terms. Women never seemed to like being told they were being overly dramatic.

He was spared from any further discussion when Brooke's townhouse came into view. He pulled into her driveway. "Liz, jump in back with your brothers. I'll be right back."

Other than a massive eye roll, she didn't comment as she grabbed for the door handle. She might be dramatic, but she still listened to him—at least occasionally.

He rang the doorbell and waited. Nothing. He glanced at his watch: 9:30 a.m. Maybe she'd given up on them.

But then he heard footsteps and the door swung inward. Brooke greeted him with a tentative smile. "I thought maybe you'd forgotten about me," she said, a slight pout to her lips.

Ethan tried to keep that same light tone he'd employed with Lizzy. He didn't need *two* crabby females on his hands. He'd enjoyed not having to walk on eggshells around anyone since his wife had moved out; if he was keeping a tally of pros and cons to this whole dating gig thing, he'd already have a couple cons racked up.

"Sorry . . . it isn't always easy to get out the door with three teenagers who think eight a.m. is an ungodly hour to be getting up on a Saturday."

Brooke glanced over his shoulder at the vehicle idling in her driveway. She took a deep breath and smiled. "You're forgiven. Let me just grab my bag and I'll be out."

The door shut in his face and he turned to walk back to his pickup.

I didn't know I needed forgiveness.

The drive out to Whispering Pines seemed to take longer than usual. Most of the conversation in the truck was between Dylan and Brooke. Drew added a few comments, and Ethan replied when spoken to, but Lizzy said nothing after the initial introduction between the two women. She kept her head down the whole time, listening to something on her phone and occasionally staring out the window. It was a good thing they had a busy day ahead of them. Maybe bringing Brooke along was a mistake, despite Dylan's obvious enjoyment.

They pulled into the lodge parking lot just as two other vehicles pulled in. One was Matt, in his patrol car, and the other was Seth's large white four-by-four.

Seth parked next to them and got out, nodding to Ethan. "Hey, guys. How's it going?"

A second door slammed and Nathan, Jess's son, got out of the passenger side of Seth's truck. Lizzy's face split into a grin.

"Hey, cuz!" she yelled over to him, grabbing her purse and heading in his direction. "I can't *believe* you weren't at Grandma and Grandpa's on Thanksgiving."

Ethan watched Lizzy make her way toward Nathan, relieved at the excitement on his daughter's face. Those two had always been tight, being the two oldest cousins, but they seldom saw each other now that both were so busy with the tail ends of their college years in different towns. Maybe Nathan would keep Lizzy occupied for the day and they'd get through it without any issues.

Matt yelled his name. "Can you give me a hand?"

"Looks like someone loaded you up with fleece for the blankets Dad wants to make," Ethan said, pulling out two stacks of fabric out of the back of Matt's patrol car to take inside.

"Thanks. Renee and Jess apparently had coupons and hit the Black Friday sales at the local fabric stores. I'm just the hauler."

Ethan glanced over to see if everyone else had made their way inside. The kids were gone. Seth was talking to Brooke. He'd forgotten they knew each other.

"We're heading in, guys," he told them. They waved and Seth said they'd follow in a minute.

There was lots of activity inside the lodge. Music blared from someone's phone. The scent of fresh-baked cookies had Ethan's stomach growling, reminding him he hadn't eaten yet today. Kids were working in the corner on tables, surrounded by bottles of paint and glue. Lavonne seemed to be directing things over there.

Following directions from George, they stacked the fabric in one of the sleeping rooms and headed out to grab the rest. During certain weekends of the year,

Renee and Jess ran women's retreats out of the lodge, so it had all been recently remodeled. Ethan had done much of the heavy lifting in revamping the layout of the lodge. An added benefit of the remodel was that now the whole family could spend more time out at the resort year-round, versus just during the summer months.

Another gift from Celia, he thought with a smile.

"Are you off today?" Ethan asked Matt on their way out the door. His new brother-in-law was in civilian clothes, but that didn't always mean he wasn't on duty.

Matt nodded. "Until later. I need to go in about five so one of my deputies can run home to celebrate a late Thanksgiving with his family."

"It was nice you had Thursday off," Ethan said as they finished with the boxes. He liked Matt, not just for his sister, but as a friend, and having him as an addition for Thanksgiving had been an unexpected treat.

Matt nodded again, locking his patrol car as they headed back inside. "Things have been relatively quiet. Hopefully it stays that way."

"You do know you probably shouldn't have said that, right?" Ethan joked. "That's the surest way to shake things up."

Matt laughed. "Let's hope you're wrong." But he knocked the wooden doorway as they passed.

The quiet lasted until early afternoon.

Those that enjoyed working in the kitchen helped Val with an assortment of goodies. They were careful to only make things that would freeze well. Brooke proved to be useful in the kitchen. When he peeked in on them, George loudly announced that he was impressed with their progress. Which of course meant he'd be more than happy to sample any of their creations.

The kids working on blankets measured, cut, and tied off fringes for nearly four hours, breaking only for lunch. Between the two nursing homes and one assisted living facility they'd talked to, they'd learned lap blankets were much appreciated by the residents as the weather turned colder. They were making as many as they could in the course of the day.

When they started to get bored with the process, George pushed his grandkids to keep going. Having donated things to similar facilities in the past, he knew the kids would get a kick out of personally delivering the blankets the following day.

Lavonne had decided last-minute to bring a bunch of craft supplies, to a messy result. Young Jake apparently thought it was more fun to spread glue on his hands and let it dry than it was to paint wooden ornaments. If he would have managed to keep the glue only on his hands, it wouldn't have been a big deal; the problem came when Jake grew impatient and accidently spread glue all over the place.

"I remember when your mother and aunts did the exact same thing with glue as kids," Lavonne said, grinning at her youngest grandson despite the mess.

George laughed. His wife wouldn't have been nearly that tolerant with her own kids back in the day. The years had mellowed her.

"How are things going with Harper, honey?" George asked Jess when she sat beside him to take a break.

He worried about all she juggled these days. Raising a baby, after she'd already managed to raise two kids and get them off to college, was an unexpected burden. Especially when that baby was born of an affair your husband had with another woman. Now that Jess's ex was out of the picture, spending years in prison for a long list of mistakes, Jess had stepped up and taken the child into her own home. She insisted Harper was a blessing and not a burden, but George worried nonetheless.

"Some days are easier than others, Dad, but I'm blessed to have her. I'm so relieved the adoption was finalized." Jess pulled out her phone. "Speaking of Harper, Lauren ran her back to the duplex for her nap, but they'll be back when she wakes up. Lauren hasn't been far from her little sister's side, ever since she got back from school for Thanksgiving break. It gives me a bit of free time, and they get quality time together. A win-win."

"I admire you, honey," George said, giving Jess's shoulder a squeeze. "It's been a hell of a year for you."

Jess nodded her agreement. "That it has, Dad, that it has. But I think we've weathered the worst of it. And I'm glad I found Seth. He helps a lot."

Just at that moment, Seth laughed at something either Matt or Ethan said. The men were clearly enjoying each other's company.

Jess seemed to think the same thing. "Will was never relaxed like that with Ethan," she said.

George shook his head. "You're right, honey. He always kept to himself."

Jess shook her head with him. "Turns out he wasn't really 'keeping to himself.'"

George grinned. "I like that you can joke about it now, hon. That means you're starting to move past it all. Good for you. Would you mind grabbing me a cup of coffee and one of those cookies? They smell awfully good."

"I'd be happy to, Dad, but then I better get back to work. Val mixed up an insane number of different batches of cookies. There's still lots of baking to get done."

A phone rang and George watched Matt take a call. His son-in-law stepped away and stuck a finger in his ear, obviously trying to hear the other person on the phone.

George gave a shrill whistle. "Hey, everybody, pipe down!"

Matt nodded his gratitude to George as he pulled a pen and small notebook out of a pocket in his sweatshirt. He jotted something down, stowed his phone in his pocket, and approached George and Jess.

"I've gotta run. We received a call about a big fire over at Forty-second and Eighth."

"In town?" George asked. "That's outside your jurisdiction, isn't it?"

"Yeah, but they think one building is fully involved and a couple others are threatened. They're requesting backup for traffic control. Sounds like there might have been some injuries. Can you tell Renee for me? I need to go."

At George's nod, Matt turned to go, but Jess stopped him with a hand on his arm.

"Do you have the full address?"

Matt shot her a curious look but pulled his notebook back out and read it back to her.

"Oh, no . . . Dad, that sounds awfully close to the address of Ethan's fourplex. You know, the one where he just started remodeling one of the units?"

"Damn," George muttered under his breath, "you're right. Ethan, come over here!"

His son dropped one of the small blankets he'd been folding back onto the tabletop. "I recognize that tone in your voice, Dad, and it never bodes well. What's up?"

"Come here," George repeated, waiting until Ethan was close so he didn't have to talk too loud. "Matt just got a call, kiddo. What's the address over at your fourplex you're working on?"

"Eight-two-five," he said, frowning, "Forty-second Avenue South. Why?"

Matt swore under his breath as he double-checked the address against his notes.

"What was the call about, Matt?" Ethan asked, his voice low and worried.

"A fire. A bad one. And that's the same address they gave me."

Ethan immediately started fishing for his keys. "Shit . . . I have to get over there! I've got tenants, and none of them are in very good shape. Pretty old. Jess, can you tell the kids where I went? Oh, and Brooke, too? I'll be back when I can."

"I'd just have you ride with me," Matt said, "but I have to run by the station and pick up one of my deputies."

George didn't want Ethan to go by himself. He clambered up from his seat. "I'm coming with. I don't want you going alone."

George turned to say something to Jess, but she held up her hand. "I know, I'll tell Mom, too. And everybody else. Now go. And call us when you know something."

Chapter Eight
Gift of Rescue

They could see the smoke and hear the faint wail of sirens before they even reached the city limits.

Ethan's father looked at him. "Ethan, you need to slow it down, son. You can't help anyone if you get in a wreck before you get there."

Ethan eased up slightly. Now that they'd reached a more populated area, his dad was right. *But what if someone's hurt?* It was all he could think about.

"Maybe they got the address wrong," his dad said, reading his mind. "Maybe it's not your place that's on fire."

Could I get that lucky?

Ethan tried to put all his dread and worry to the side and just drive.

A city police car was parked to block a main street and prevent any traffic from getting closer to the source of the thick smoke, now spewing above the treetops from this angle. Ethan rolled down his window as an officer approached.

"I'm sorry, sir, but I'm going to have to ask you to turn around. We're dealing with a situation here and need to keep everyone a safe distance back."

George coughed as the stench of smoke stole through the open window.

A loud crack shook the air.

"Look, buddy, I need to get in there," Ethan pleaded with the officer. "I'm afraid it might be my building on fire. I'm the owner."

"But you're not sure?" the officer asked, eyeing Ethan closely.

"My brother-in-law is the sheriff one county over and he received a call about the need for backup at a large fire. The address he was given matches my building."

The officer started to ask Ethan another question but was cut off by the wail of an ambulance, coming from the direction of the fire.

"Wait here," the policeman said as he ran back to move his unit.

The ambulance spiked Ethan's concern; he pulled to the curb, throwing his pickup into Park. "I gotta get in there, Dad. I can't wait around for this dude. Maybe you should stay here. The smoke is awfully thick."

George waved Ethan on, trying and failing to suppress a cough. "You go. I'll just hold you back. My asthma's been giving me trouble today, even before the smoke. I'll stay here, see what I can find out from the officer. Call me when you know something."

Ethan tossed George the keys, double-checked to make sure he had his phone, and sprinted down the sidewalk toward the fire.

"Hey, I told you to stay put!"

The officer started to follow Ethan, but fear spurred Ethan on and the pursuit ended almost before it began. The uniformed man stopped, said something into the radio strapped to his shoulder, then walked back to George in the pickup.

"That guy doesn't listen very well, does he?" the cop said, obviously displeased.

George nodded grimly. "Not when he's worried the fire might be in his building and he has elderly tenants inside."

"I suppose that's understandable, but if he gets too close, he'll be in trouble. Hell . . . *I'll* be in trouble for letting him slip past me."

"Understood, Officer."

As Ethan rounded the corner, his worst suspicions were confirmed. His two-story building was on fire. A second ambulance was parked at the end of his driveway, lights flashing.

Ethan felt physically ill at the sight of the rescue unit. He ran up as far as he could go, but a perimeter of yellow tape held rubberneckers at bay. Ethan lifted the tape and took two more steps toward the building when a firm grip on his shoulder stopped him in his tracks.

"Where the hell do you think you're going?" a deep voice boomed behind him, competing with the wail of sirens. "You know I can't let you in there."

"But you *have* to. That's my building!" Ethan tried but failed to twist away from the heavy hand.

"You have some ID?"

Now Ethan spun around to get a better look at the guy who'd stopped him. The man was in full fireman gear from the neck down, his head and face uncovered. Sweat ran down his forehead and the smell of smoke rolled off him.

Ethan pulled his wallet out of his back pocket and flipped it open to show the man, who took it out of his hands, squinted at it, and handed it back.

"Follow me."

The man didn't head toward the fire but led him to a knot of like-dressed people, congregated next to one of the firetrucks.

"Hey, boss, this guy claims to be the building's owner."

A taller man turned his attention from the clipboard in his hand to the fireman leading Ethan. "What?"

"I said, this guy might be the owner," he said, motioning at Ethan with his gloved thumb over his shoulder.

"That's right," Ethan said, stepping around the fireman who had accosted him. "What can you tell me? Is anyone else in there?" Ethan's voice was tight with dread. He could see flames shooting out a broken window in the top right unit—Penelope Jarvis's unit. Both doors stood wide open and numerous fire-hoses snaked inside.

"We've cleared the top two units," the man with the clipboard said, "and we're checking the first of the two bottom ones now."

"Were they . . ." Ethan swallowed, his throat dry from the smoke, and asked again. "Were the people you helped out of there . . . okay?"

"Too soon to tell," the imposing man replied.

"Thank God the one unit is vacant," Ethan said, pointing to the bottom right. "You shouldn't have to check in there. We're doing a remodel down there, but no one's working today."

Another siren blared—this one a loud short burst—drawing Ethan's eye down the block. It took him a minute to comprehend what he was seeing. Why was Rex's pickup parked there? Had he somehow heard about the fire, too? Had Brooke maybe called him once Jess told everyone else out at Whispering Pines what was happening?

And then he had a horrific thought.

Did Rex come in to work on the remodel today?

What if Rex was in that ambulance, speeding away in the direction of the hospital? Or what if he was inside the burning building? He scanned the growing crowd outside the crime tape barrier, hoping against hope to see his old friend there.

"On second thought, please have someone check that lower unit on the north side right away. That's my foreman's truck parked down the street. He shouldn't be here today, but that's his truck," Ethan said, pointing at the vehicle.

The fireman nodded and spoke into the walkie-talkie he'd pulled off his belt.

"They're heading in there now," the man reported back. "They couldn't find anyone in the other lower unit."

"What about the upstairs units? I saw the one ambulance leave. Are they okay? Are they seriously injured?"

"Like I said, sir, too soon to know. We'll check with the hospital here in a bit. In the meantime, don't go anywhere. I'll have questions for you soon, but right now, we just need to make sure everyone's out of there. That structure could come down at any minute.

Could come down at any minute . . .

Ethan looked on in horror as the sound of exploding glass pierced the air. This was so much worse than he'd imagined. He watched as crews of firemen hosed down the surrounding buildings.

Oh God, he prayed, *please don't let the fire spread . . .*

The phone in his pocket vibrated. It was George.

"Hey, Dad, it *is* the fourplex. And it's bad. It's really bad, especially on the side we were working on. They won't, or can't, tell me anything yet."

Ethan listened as his father told him what little the police officer was willing to share. The call had come from inside the building, from an elderly woman—probably Mrs. Jarvis. The police officer had told George she was screaming and going on. But he didn't know who or how many people were sent in the ambulance.

"Dad . . . I'm really worried about Rex. His truck is here. It shouldn't be. He was supposed to spend Thanksgiving at his older brother's. He wasn't even supposed to be back in town until tomorrow!"

A flurry of activity near the front door caught his attention. Two firemen were bringing someone out. Ethan was too far back to see the person well enough, but could tell the firemen were having to drag the limp figure out. As they inched closer, Ethan could see it was a man.

And he'd know that man anywhere.

Ethan didn't have a chance to talk to Rex before they whisked him away in the second ambulance. He'd watched as firemen hoisted his friend onto a stretcher and EMTs strapped an oxygen mask over his face. Rex was propped up slightly, his head slowly shaking from side to side. He must have heard Ethan yelling, because he looked in his direction and, just as they were loading him into the back of the ambulance, he gave Ethan a feeble thumbs-up. An EMT slammed the back doors, ran up to the driver's side, and climbed into the cab. As the rescue unit pulled away, the scream of the siren split the air.

Ethan called his dad back to update him on what little he knew. He'd hung up on George earlier when he saw Rex being dragged out of the building.

"How bad is the damage?"

Ethan squinted toward the burning dwelling, but smoke clouded his vision. He wiped at his eyes, but that made them sting even more. He'd have to wash them out later.

"I can't tell much from here, Dad. Of course, they won't let me get any closer. They said they've cleared all the units now, and they have the flames knocked down . . . at least the ones they can see."

Ethan's phone beeped to signal an incoming call. He glanced at the screen.

"Sorry, Dad. It's Elizabeth on the other line. I better take it. I'm heading your way. There's nothing more I can do here right now, and we need to go check on Rex. See if we can find out about the other tenants, too."

He took off at a slow jog while attempting to switch his phone over to his daughter's call. His lungs burned and he knew he wouldn't be able to run any faster.

He heard Lizzy say "Dad?" just as the toe of his boot caught a corner of cement where the sidewalk had heaved. He went down hard, his phone clattering away as he caught himself with his palms.

"Shit!" Ethan muttered, staying on all fours just long enough to catch his breath. The throb in his back was nothing new, but his palms stung and he felt a stab in his left knee. He felt like he imagined it would feel to swim through quicksand. He couldn't seem to move fast enough to be everywhere he needed to be.

He pushed off with his stinging hands and reached for his phone, face down on the sidewalk. He held his breath as he flipped it over, hoping it wasn't shattered. He got lucky.

Lizzy was yelling. "Dad? Dad, are you there?"

"Yeah, hon, I'm here. Sorry, I dropped my phone," Ethan said.

No need to tell her I dropped my whole body.

"Jesus, you scared me! I heard a clatter and then nothing. Are you sure you're okay?"

Ethan again started toward his pickup and George, but this time he took it slower. Lizzy must have heard the pain in his voice.

"I'm fine. But Elizabeth, the fire *is* at our fourplex. And it's pretty bad."

"I know. Matt already called and talked to Renee. He's there somewhere. Didn't you see him?"

Ethan scanned the area, but he didn't see anyone in the type of brown uniform Matt usually wore, nor did he see his patrol car. "No, I haven't seen him. I wish I had, though. He could probably tell me what's going on. They're being pretty tight-lipped."

"Was anyone hurt? Was anyone home?"

Her question set off the wrenching sound of the ambulance siren again, but this time it was in Ethan's brain. He doubted he'd ever be able to forget that sound, or the feeling of helplessness that accompanied it.

"I can't be sure. They did take some people away in an ambulance, but I'm hoping it was just precautionary. Since I can't do anything at the fire right now, I'm heading to my truck and driving over to the hospital."

Then he remembered the fireman telling him to stay put to answer some questions. *Damn.*

"Is Gramps with you?"

"He's waiting for me at my truck. Hey, Lizzy, I gotta go, okay? I'll call you when I know more. Keep an eye on the boys and try not to worry. Update Brooke for me, too, will you? I'll call you soon."

Maybe I shouldn't have mentioned Brooke to Lizzy . . .

Ethan pushed his phone back into his jeans pocket and tried to catch his breath. Between the smoky air and his run, fall, walk, talk . . . he was out of breath. By the time he reached his truck, he had to stop and bend over at the waist.

Something didn't feel right.

Before he could straighten and climb into his vehicle, someone was at his side. He could feel a hand on his shoulder and see the toes of his dad's shoes.

"Ethan . . . son . . . are you all right?"

Ethan waved him off. "I'll be fine. Just give me a minute. Too much smoke. We need to get over to the hospital."

He took the remaining few steps to his driver door but wobbled a bit. George was back at his side, a steading hand under his elbow.

"Come on, get in my side. You shouldn't be driving," George said as he ushered Ethan around the tailgate.

Ethan pulled back, frustrated at his father for treating him like a child. But a sudden pain in his chest seized him and he suffered a coughing spell, forgetting all about his dad for a minute.

I'm sure the pain will go away in a minute . . .

He let George help him into the passenger side of the truck and up onto the seat. When his dad slammed the door and came around the front, Ethan rubbed surreptitiously at his chest, now that his dad was out of sight. The air wasn't as smoky inside the truck and he was able to inhale without as much pain.

It's getting better.

George got behind the wheel and wasted no time driving over to the only hospital in town. Ethan saw him glance his way a time or two, concern etched into his face, but he didn't say anything more. Ethan appreciated the reprieve. He just needed to catch his breath and he'd be fine. He had to make sure everyone else was going to be all right.

George headed straight to the ER, as that was the most likely place to get some answers. This time George stayed a few feet from Ethan instead of taking him by the arm. Ethan had been assuring him for the past five minutes he was fine. He'd just gotten winded. It was apparent, though, that George had his doubts.

They went through the automatic doors into the waiting area. It smelled like most hospitals: a cross between strong antiseptic and cafeteria food.

"Can I help you?" an elderly woman in scrubs asked from behind the receptionist desk.

"Yes," George said, "we just came from a fire. There was a terrible fire at my son's building and we're worried about the tenants and a friend of ours who they pulled out of there."

Ethan spoke up, his voice strained. "I need to find out how everyone is."

"Are you injured, sir?" she asked, looking him up and down.

Ethan looked at her in surprise. "No, *I* wasn't in the fire."

"Smells like you were," the woman said. "Why are your hands bleeding?"

Ethan glanced down at the palms of his hands—they were smeared with blood, and he could see gravel embedded in his palms. They instantly began to sting again. *Power of suggestion,* he thought. A quick glance at his shirt showed he'd managed to smear some blood there, too.

"I fell," he said, "scraped them up. I was just in a hurry to get over here and was clumsy."

The woman looked at him over bifocal glasses. She didn't look convinced.

"Fine. Are you family?"

"This is my dad," Ethan started to explain, but she cut him off.

"Not the two of you, the ones they brought in here."

Ethan felt stupid. "Sorry, I misunderstood. No, I'm not related to any of them. But the one guy is a good friend, and he works for me. The others are all tenants in my building. I'm concerned for their welfare."

"Their welfare, or your pocket book?"

Ethan was stunned at the woman's audacity. Before he could reply, his dad said, "Excuse me, ma'am, we're just trying to get some answers. We have a genuine concern for these people. Can you tell us anything?"

Ethan couldn't believe his father wasn't chewing the woman out for being so rude. Instead he was being polite to her.

The nurse turned from Ethan to George, her face softening a bit at his request. "Even if I knew anything, I couldn't tell you much. You know . . . HIPAA and all. But since you asked so nicely," she said, looking between father and son, "I'll go check with the ER doc, see if there are any updates I *can* give you."

The woman rolled her chair back away from the reception desk and exited through a set of swinging doors to her left.

"Can you believe that woman? Where does she get off talking to someone like that? And why were you so *nice* to her?" Ethan ranted at his father.

George smiled. "I can't say why she was so snarky, but she obviously didn't seem to care for you. I thought I might try a slightly different approach. As you can see, at least I got her to go check. Now, let me see your hands, son." George grabbed Ethan by his left wrist and held up the palm so he could better inspect for damage. "Do they hurt? You need to get those cleaned up."

Ethan pulled his wrist out of his dad's hand, shaking it to take away the sting. "They didn't until she brought it up. I'll just go find a men's room, run them under some water. Keep an eye out for her, will you? Maybe she'll tell you more if I'm not around."

Ethan turned away, in search of the bathroom, absently rubbing at his chest.

George watched his son walk away. He was genuinely concerned about him. God forbid someone was seriously injured—or worse—in the fire. And now Ethan was acting strange. George didn't like how winded he was when he'd gotten back to the truck. Now he was rubbing at his chest, although George doubted Ethan was even aware he was doing it.

Could that mean . . . ?

The swinging doors opened again and the crotchety nurse was back.

"What did you say your name was? If it's Ethan, there's a guy back there asking for you."

"Ethan's my son. He went to clean up his hands. He'll be back in a second. Who is the guy? Is it Rex Forde? I know Rex was taken away by ambulance."

"Yep, that's him. They are going to admit him. You might want to leave for a while, come back in a couple of hours. They should have him settled in a room by then, and visiting hours go until eight o'clock."

"Maybe we'll do that. Can you tell me anything else? Anything about the tenants?"

She shook her head. "No, I'm sorry, sir, but I can't say."

The nurse lowered her head and started flipping through some paperwork on the desk, the gesture feeling very dismissive. George sighed and turned away, looking for a spot to sit and wait for Ethan.

The sliding doors they'd entered through a short time ago glided open again. A woman rushed in and made a beeline for the reception desk.

"I received a call that my mother, Penelope Jarvis, was injured in a fire. Is she okay? Can I see her?"

George hadn't been trying to eavesdrop, but he couldn't help but hear what the woman said. He thought he remembered Ethan mentioning a Mrs. Jarvis as one of his tenants. Now George sat forward in his chair, hoping to learn more.

Footsteps echoed down a sterile hallway. Ethan was coming back.

George nodded discreetly at him and angled his head toward the desk, hoping his son wouldn't mess up their chances of getting some answers. Maybe if this woman was related to one of Ethan's tenants, the nurse would tell her something.

Ethan caught on, saying nothing as he took the empty seat next to his dad.

George turned his attention back to the two women.

"I'm not going to 'calm down' until you tell me how my mother is!"

Didn't sound like the old nurse was being any more forthcoming with the new woman.

"What did you say your name was again?"

"Rebecca Sinclair. I'm Penelope Jarvis's daughter. I was told she was brought in here for smoke inhalation. My mother has serious lung issues, and I'm very concerned. I told her she needed to move. Move somewhere without stairs, somewhere not so dated. That old building she lives in isn't safe for her. I swear to God, if it turns out the fire was caused by something faulty in the building, that landlord will pay. He will pay dearly."

George groaned, sinking back into his chair. Ethan didn't need to hear this right now. He glanced at his son. Too late.

Ethan was already getting to his feet.

Ethan couldn't believe what he was hearing.

What are the odds . . . ? He'd had no idea.

He approached the women, neither of them paying any attention to him as the visitor tried to wheedle information out of the tight-lipped nurse.

"Excuse me," Ethan said, standing slightly behind the agitated woman.

If the woman heard him, she gave no indication. She continued to demand she be allowed to talk to a doctor.

He tried again. "Excuse me," he said again, louder this time. "Rebecca. Is that you?"

Now the woman stopped talking and looked over her shoulder at Ethan. She turned slowly to face him, looking him up and down.

"Were you at the fire? Do you know something about my mom?"

Ethan held up his hands as if to slow her down. She saw the blood budding from his palms and sniffed the air.

"You smell like smoke and your hands and knees are banged up. Were you at the fire?" she asked again.

Ethan had managed to wash the blood and grime from his hands, so he was surprised she noticed. He looked first at his hands and then at his knees. She was right. His palms didn't look too bad, but the knees in his jeans were torn and filthy.

"I wasn't there when it started, but I got over there as quickly as I could after I heard about it. I apologize for interrupting, but I couldn't help but overhear you talking to the nurse. You're Rebecca *Wilson*, right?

"I used to be. I'm Rebecca Sinclair now," the woman replied, studying Ethan's face. Ethan could see when recognition dawned. "Oh my God . . . *Ethan Richter?* It's been, what, twenty years?" She reached out both of her hands to Ethan.

He took her hands in his and gave them a light squeeze in way of a greeting. The pressure on his scraped palms caused him to flinch. "Might have been even longer than that," he said, dropping her hands. "Hey, we can catch up later—and I want to, I do—but I heard you say your mom was brought here from a fire."

"She was. And I'm scared to death. Her health hasn't been great in recent years, and exposure to a bunch of smoke is incredibly dangerous given her lung troubles."

"Excuse me, but if you two are going to have a cozy little reunion, I'm going to have to ask you to go sit down, away from my desk. I'm busy here."

Ethan glanced toward the rude nurse, but chose to ignore her.

"What did you say her name was?" he said, keeping his attention on his old friend. "I just always knew your mother as Penny Wilson."

Rebecca gave a quick laugh, although her face was still etched with worry.

"Penelope Jarvis. But when we were kids, you're right, she was Penny to you. Jarvis was the last name of her fourth husband."

Ethan's eyebrows shot up in surprise. "Fourth?"

"Like you said, we'll have to catch up sometime, but not now. Mother's story is best told over a cup of coffee, or maybe a whiskey."

Rebecca's attention was pulled away by the sound of the door opening behind the reception desk. Another nurse came into view and she whispered something into the ear of the first nurse. The crabby nurse nodded and stood.

"I'm going to go speak with the doctor," she said to Rebecca. "I'll be right back."

Rebecca nodded and turned back to Ethan. "You said you went to the fire as soon as you heard about it. Why? Do you live in the same building as Mother? *That* would be a crazy coincidence!"

Ethan slipped his fingers into the front pockets of his jeans and rocked, heal to toe.

She's not going to like this . . .

He tried not to grimace as he said, "I don't live there. I own it."

Before Rebecca could comment, two doctors approached.

"Mrs. Sinclair, can you follow us, please?"

Rebecca nodded to them but turned back to Ethan, shock and confusion in her expression.

Ethan fished out his wallet, removed a business card, and pressed it into the palm of her hand. "Call me. Let me know how your mom is doing. And we'll talk."

Rebecca nodded, the expression on her face now stony. "We'll talk, all right. I'll be in touch."

Ethan watched her disappear with the two doctors, his head reeling. Could today get any more bizarre? He walked back over to stand before his dad.

George looked over Ethan's shoulder, in the direction the woman had gone with the doctors. "Who was that?"

"Believe it or not, she's an old college friend."

"Small world."

Ethan nodded. "Very. Any word on Rex when I was washing my hands?"

George stood. "Yes. They're going to admit him. They said to come back in a couple of hours and then you can see him. He asked for you."

"All right. Let's go, then. I need to see if I have anything more than a pile of rubble left."

Chapter Nine

GIFT OF ADVICE

"Rex . . . God, buddy, you had me worried. How are you feeling?" Ethan greeted his friend, lying in a hospital bed. The kids had begged to come along, but Ethan wanted to see Rex first, see what kind of shape he was in.

Rex struggled to push himself up straighter on the bed.

"Wait, there has to be a button here somewhere," Ethan said, not wanting Rex to exert himself. He looked haggard, weak. Ethan ran his hand over the bed rail until he found the control mechanism and raised the head of the bed.

"Thanks, man. That's better," Rex said. "I can't lie. I've had better days."

"Are you hurt?" Ethan asked, but then grimaced. "Sorry, dumbass question. If you weren't hurt, you wouldn't be here. *Where* are you hurt? Was it the smoke?"

"The smoke didn't help, but I've got pretty nasty burns on my legs, too," Rex said with a cough, patting the white blanket covering him from the waist down. "Can't feel much right now. They must have me on some pretty strong shit. But I suspect it'll be a bitch when the meds wear off."

Ethan nodded and looked around the small room for a place to sit. He hated seeing Rex in that bed. His friend looked older, grayer. Both his hair and his complexion seemed leeched of color. Ethan didn't even want to think about how much worse it could have been if the firemen hadn't found Rex when they did. He spied a chair tucked in a corner and pulled it closer, taking a seat next to Rex's bed. He had so many questions.

"Rex, what were you even *doing* at the fourplex? I thought you were spending the weekend at your brother's."

Rex shifted, his burns apparently causing him pain despite his claim to the contrary. Before he could answer, there was a light rap on the doorframe. Ethan stood and whisked the privacy curtain out of the way. Two uniformed men stood there, looking at him expectantly.

"Sorry to interrupt," the taller one said, "but we need to speak to Mr. Forde. We were told this is his room."

Ethan's stomach tightened at the sight of them. What were the *police* doing here? But maybe their presence shouldn't come as a surprise. A building had burned and Rex was pulled out of the fire. They probably just had a couple of questions for him.

"Yes, this is Rex's room. And I'm Ethan Richter. I own the building. Rex works for me. And he's a friend. Can I be of assistance at all? Rex is pretty doped up on pain meds right now."

"As a matter of fact," the tall cop said, "we do need to speak to you as well, Mr. Richter. But we'd like to start with Mr. Forde, and in private, if you could leave us alone for a bit? Sit in the family waiting room down the hall and we'll stop in there when we're done here."

The officer doing the speaking seemed friendly enough, but Ethan didn't have a good feeling about this. He turned back to Rex. "Rex, these guys have a few questions for you. Are you feeling up to talking to them? Or should I ask them to come back later?"

Rex shrugged. The faraway cast to his eyes hadn't been there when Ethan first arrived.

"Actually, I'm not sure he's up to speaking to you right now," Ethan said, turning back to the officers, feeling his own heartbeat pick back up to an uncomfortable pace. Something in the officer's attitude spiked Ethan's concern for Rex even higher. His friend was hurting and he shouldn't have to deal with these jokers right now. "Can you guys wait out in the hallway while I check with his doctor first?"

Their displeasure was evident, but they stepped out of the room. They stood in the hallway, still within earshot.

Ethan pushed the call button. Five minutes later (*Thank God no one's dying in the room,* he thought) a male nurse finally appeared.

"Do you need something, Rex?" the nurse asked.

"I pushed the button," Ethan said, running his right hand through his hair. His palm was beginning to sting again. "Look, the police are here, and they want to talk to Rex, but I'm not sure that's such a good idea. He seems pretty out of it. Can you get a doctor in here to get a professional opinion?"

The nurse nodded. "As long as I'm here, let me just check on a couple things real quick, then I'll see who's on rounds."

Ethan glanced back at Rex, but his friend appeared to have drifted off. He took a seat and waited, watching as the nurse checked monitors and Rex's vitals.

His phone buzzed. It was a text from Lizzy, asking about Rex and telling him to check the local news station's app. There was a story about the fire. He sent back a text to let her know Rex was awake but groggy and he was waiting for the doctor to stop in. Then he pulled up the story on the fire.

His breath caught when he looked at the picture at the top of the post. It must have been taken shortly before he arrived. EMTs were carrying a stretcher out of the building, smoke billowing through the front door and around them. He could just make out a tuft of white hair on the stretcher. It had to be Mrs. Jarvis—Rebecca's mother. There was little chance anyone else would recognize her from the photo, but it made Ethan sick to his stomach.

Penelope might have been a thorn in his side some days, but he hated to think of how scared she had to have been when she first noticed the fire. He doubted she could have gotten out on her own. The last few times he'd run into her while at the fourplex, she'd been using a walker, which had to make the stairs up to her apartment problematic. He was having a hard time reconciling the frisky yet frail Mrs. Jarvis of today with the woman he remembered as Rebecca's mom.

He scanned the article Lizzy had sent, hoping to learn something new. There was mention of injured tenants, but no specifics. It went on to say the fire marshal had been called in for further investigation and to stay tuned for additional updates.

The fire marshal?

Again, he probably shouldn't be surprised. He wanted answers just as much, if not more, than anyone else. But the article felt like it had an ominous tone to it, almost seeming to imply foul play. Leave it up to the media to try to add hype where there was only tragedy. Ethan suspected the fire might have been caused by something electrical, or maybe even something irresponsible like an unattended candle . . . but certainly nothing malicious.

He had yet to find out anything about the two male tenants. One lived upstairs next to Penelope, and one downstairs next to the unit he was remodeling. He could only hope they weren't home at the time of the blaze.

The murmur of voices just outside of the door pulled his attention back to his surroundings. The beep and then static sound of a radio confirmed the police were still waiting outside. He hoped a doctor would get there soon.

"Excuse me, gentlemen," he heard a deep voice say, and then the curtain swayed as a man in a white lab coat entered the room.

Ethan stood and introduced himself. He quickly explained the situation to the doctor. The doctor nodded but didn't immediately comment. He checked the monitors beeping on the other side of Rex's bed and then approached Rex.

"Hello, Mr. Forde. My name is Dr. Huntley. I just checked your chart, and your boss here gave me a quick update as well. How are you feeling?"

Rex's head turned toward the doctor's voice, and his eyes opened, but he didn't respond verbally. The doctor checked his pupils and his pulse.

"I'm going to agree with you on this one, Mr. Richter. Mr. Forde here isn't in any condition to answer questions right now. They'll have to wait until at least tomorrow. His burns are pretty extensive. I'll speak with them."

"Thank you, Doctor. I appreciate it," Ethan said, extending his hand to the elderly physician.

The doctor returned the handshake, looking Ethan in the eye. He lowered his voice.

"In the meantime, you may want to call your lawyer."

Ethan watched him leave. He was right, of course. It was something he should have done already, but he'd hesitated. His main concern was the health of Rex and his tenants. The last thing he wanted to do right now was start delving into the *business*—and maybe even *legal*—implications of the fire.

The two officers came back into the room.

"We understand Mr. Forde isn't able to speak with us today. Should we find somewhere quiet to talk, Mr. Richter?" the shorter, younger of the two officers asked Ethan. He glanced at his watch. "It shouldn't take long."

"Actually, given I own the property and the damage was extensive, plus there were injuries, I'd prefer to have my lawyer present when we talk." Ethan hoped the shaking in his knees wasn't too apparent.

Why the hell am I so nervous? I have nothing to hide. It had *to have been an accident.*

But he kept hearing Rebecca's words playing over in his head, before she knew he was there as the building owner. She'd said she'd make him pay if anyone was at fault.

"Sir, you must have misunderstood. We just have a few questions for you."

Ethan shook his head. "I didn't misunderstand. I can call him right now, see if he's available this evening. Otherwise, I'll see if he can come down to the station with me tomorrow. Which do you prefer?"

The younger officer started to reply, but the older one stepped slightly in front of him, a clear signal as to who was really in charge.

"Tomorrow would be just fine, Mr. Richter. We realize it's been a very long day for you. Here's my card," he said, pulling one out of the breast pocket of his uniform and handing it to Ethan. "Call the number on there and set up an appointment. We'll try not to take up too much of your time."

With that, the man turned and walked out of the room, the younger officer following close behind.

Ethan let out a breath he hadn't realized he'd been holding. His damn chest felt tight again. He rubbed at it as he took one more look at Rex, asleep in his bed, and followed the rest of them out. He needed to swing by the house and get the phone numbers of the other two tenants in his building. Hopefully Rebecca would give him an update on her mother soon. He was worried sick about all of his tenants. All three were elderly. Celia had rented to them for years.

Marvin Miller rented the other upper unit adjacent to Mrs. Jarvis. He was hard of hearing, and Ethan didn't even know if he had a cell phone. If all he used was the land line, Ethan would have to hope another contact number was in the records Celia's lawyer had passed on to him.

Norman Westfall was the downstairs renter. He was younger, maybe mid-sixties, and had mentioned once to Ethan that he was very involved in his church. He probably carried a cell phone. Ethan just needed a number for him, too.

He'd try them both tonight, before it got much later. If he wasn't able to reach them, he'd keep trying tomorrow. He should call Matt, too, and ask him what to expect when he did go talk to those cops.

Maybe tomorrow would bring some answers and he'd be able to catch his breath again.

Maybe.

Chapter Ten
Gift of Assistance

Ethan tossed and turned, his sleep haunted by licks of fire and plumes of choking smoke. In all his years in construction, nothing of this magnitude had ever happened in any of the properties he'd worked on.

Finally, he gave up on the premise of sleep. He pulled a sweatshirt on over his bare chest. There was a definite chill in the air as he wandered out into the dark kitchen. No one had bothered to close the blinds on the sliding glass doors leading out to their minuscule apartment deck. The sky remained black, but a streetlamp cast meager light across the carpet nearest the sliding door. Dawn wouldn't lighten the horizon for three hours yet.

Looks like winter has finally arrived, Ethan thought as he leaned against the patio door, watching heavy snow fall in the courtyard. The dark beyond the reach of the streetlights made it feel like he was inside a snow globe. If this didn't let up, Lizzy was going to have a hard time getting back to school. She may need to wait one more day.

Ethan checked his phone where it lay abandoned on the coffee table. No messages. Hopefully no news was good news right now. He wondered how Rex's night was going and if his friend was getting any rest.

Ethan drew the blinds shut against the dark of pre-dawn and made his way back to the kitchen in the gloom. Glass bottles rattled in the door when he opened the fridge. The meager contents signaled the need for another trip to the grocery store. Keeping ahead of his three hungry kids was nearly impossible these days.

An unopened jug of milk stood in the back of the top shelf. He pulled it out and poured himself a glass before taking a seat. His mind raced as he sat there, alone in the dark. The old clock ticked on the wall.

Today was Sunday. Yesterday had started out as a normal day. It ended as anything but. By the time he'd left the hospital and gotten back out to the resort, those who had remained were cleaning up. He'd missed dinner but grabbed a few Christmas cookies, which had been cooling on the large island. Exhausted as he was, he and Brooke had helped Val package up the various baked goods and store them in the large freezer in the lodge.

He cringed when thinking back to his arrival at the resort. When Brooke saw him, she ran into his arms, exclaiming how worried she'd been. Lizzy walked into the room just then and caught the exchange, the hurt evident in her eyes. He'd gently assured Brooke that Rex, their mutual friend, was recuperating in the hospital, but then he extricated himself from her embrace and tried to comfort his own daughter. It had been the type of exchange he'd been hoping to avoid ever since pulling into Brooke's driveway that morning. He never wanted his kids to think he'd choose anyone else over them.

The boys peppered him with questions during their drive home. Lizzy said little after Ethan tried to assure her Rex would be all right. Rex was more than just Ethan's foreman. He was more than just Ethan's buddy. He was like an uncle to the kids. He was family.

Ethan still couldn't figure out why Rex had even been at the fourplex yesterday. He should have been at his brother's house for the Thanksgiving weekend. He'd been talking about their plans for weeks. It wasn't uncommon for some of those plans to fall through, but Thanksgiving? Hopefully Rex had still spent Thursday with his family but had simply come home early for some reason.

There were lots of pieces of the remodel at the fourplex in motion right now but nothing so pressing that Rex should have felt compelled to stop in there yesterday. In fact, Ethan made a point to tell Rex to take four days off and they'd get back to work on Monday. Apparently Rex had ignored him. Now he lay in a hospital bed, heavily medicated, with burns to his legs. That meant either the fire had been inside the unit they were working on . . . or Rex had tried to help others get out. The second scenario seemed more likely.

Ethan hadn't been able to reach either Marvin or Norman, his other two tenants. He knew one, if not both, might have been taken to the hospital by ambulance before he'd arrived at the fire. He didn't have a cell number for Marvin but did have the number for his son. That had gone straight to voicemail, so he'd left a message. Norman's phone also went straight to voicemail, but at least it was a cell. There weren't any secondary contacts listed for Norman. Ethan didn't know if he had family. He'd probably reach out to the pastor at Norman's church if he wasn't able to find out anything in the morning.

With nothing more to be done at this ungodly hour, Ethan tried to go back to sleep.

Despite it being Sunday morning, Ethan put a call in to his lawyer. Given the time of year, at least the man wouldn't be at his favorite hangout—the golf course at the country club. He might be at church, although Ethan doubted it.

"Since you can't be calling me to play a round of golf in this shit weather, I'm going to have to assume you've got an issue serious enough for you to call me bright and early on a Sunday morning," his lawyer, Steve Dodds, said when he answered Ethan's call.

"You know me well, Steve. Normally I would wait until Monday, but I *do* have a big problem, or problems, this morning. Did you hear about the fire?"

"Fire? No. We were out of town for a wedding until late last night. What fire? Are you guys all right?"

The bathroom door slammed. Someone was up.

"Hold on a sec," Ethan said.

He didn't want the kids to listen in on this particular phone call. He went into the laundry closet and shut the door, the hum of the dryer hopefully masking his words.

"The kids and I are fine. The fire was at one of my rental units. The fourplex over on Forty-second. My brother-in-law, Matt Blatso, is a sheriff, and he heard about it before I did. I got over there as fast as I could, but of course they wouldn't let me get anywhere near the building."

"Damn, I'm sorry to hear that, Ethan. It must have been a decent-size fire, then?"

Ethan absently touched his chest as he thought back to the sight of flames licking out a window and the billowing smoke. "Unfortunately, it was."

"Will it be a total loss?"

"Too soon to tell. It's possible."

"All right, then. Now tell me who you have for tenants in there, if anyone was hurt, that kind of thing. Tell me everything you can think of. Don't leave anything out."

Ethan started back at the beginning, from when Jess recognized the address as possibly being his building. He told Steve everything he could remember, including the visit from the police at the hospital and his own refusal to speak to them before he had a chance to talk to his lawyer.

"So, just to be clear," Steve said when he'd finished, "you haven't yet talked to any of your tenants directly?"

"I've tried, but I'm hitting some snags. So that's correct."

Ethan heard Steve exhale on the other end. "Honestly, that's good news. I know you're worried about their wellbeing, but stop trying to contact them. Let me see what I can find out, legally, as your counsel. We need to be very careful what we say to your tenants, particularly if any of their injuries are severe. We need to do everything we can to protect your assets."

"Jesus, Steve, can't we at least find out if they're alive? Let's be human here."

"I know, I know. I'm sorry, man, but you have to trust me on this. I'll find out what I can and try to protect you and yours. There's bound to be plenty of finger-pointing and accusations of responsibility. Now, let's compartmentalize. I need to switch gears for a minute. We might want to talk about ways to add another layer or two of protection on your assets."

Ethan sank down to the floor of the large closet, his back against the door.

Was it really less than twenty-four hours ago that he'd been so worried about getting some of their last-minute jobs done in time for the upcoming holidays? And how much his daughter's car was going to cost to fix? And how he was going to get Dylan to his after-school activities on time if Drew was working?

And Brooke? he added.

None of that was of any consequence now. Now his best friend was lying in a hospital, he didn't know if his tenants were alive or dead, and his lawyer was talking about ways to protect his assets.

"Okay, Steve. I'll try to do as you say on this. But can you please see what you can find out about my three tenants? I'll email you their names. Can we possibly meet at your office in a few hours? I need to set up an appointment for us to go down to the police station, too."

"Yes to all of that. I'll meet you at my office at, say, one o'clock. Set something up for around three with the two officers who were nosing around yesterday. I'll come with you when you talk to them."

"Thanks, Steve. Sorry to ruin your Sunday."

The lawyer chuckled on the other end. "It comes with the job. Say, Ethan, one more thing before I go. Have you given any thought to what might have started the fire? Did one of the firemen give any hints? This is going to sound heartless, but you're going to want to hope it was started by one of your tenants doing something stupid, like a grease fire or space heater, and not because one of the building systems malfunctioned."

This sucks, Ethan thought. *I'm going to have to try to dodge all responsibility if I don't want someone to swoop in here and clean me out.*

Brooke called to see if there was anything she could do to help. Ethan promised to call her if anything came up.

George picked up Drew and Dylan as they'd originally planned. He and Lavonne would take the boys to church, then out for breakfast, and then they'd deliver the lap blankets they'd made the day before. They invited Ethan and Lizzy, too, but Ethan couldn't get away and Lizzy wanted to go up to the hospital to see Rex and then get on the road back to school so she wouldn't be stuck driving in the dark. The snow quit by the time the sun rose, and it was already melting. Roads should be clear for her by the time she headed back.

Ethan appreciated his parents keeping the boys busy. Everyone was worried about Rex.

While Lizzy packed and got cleaned up, Ethan called Matt to see if he had any news about the fire. Matt told him he'd stayed at the scene for a couple of hours, helping with traffic control, but had heard very little. He was able to give Ethan a few pointers as to what to expect in his upcoming discussion with the police. He apologized for not being much help as far as the fire itself, but Ethan felt a little better after talking to him.

Once his daughter was ready to go, Ethan left for the hospital and Lizzy followed him in Rex's car. Her car was still at the shop, and Rex had insisted she use his as long as she needed it.

Rex was sitting up in bed when they got to his room, far more alert than the previous day. He smiled when he saw Lizzy. She reached over the bed rail and gave Rex a hug.

"We've been so worried, Rex! How dare you scare us like that. What the hell happened?"

Rex looked over Lizzy's head at Ethan.

Ethan knew what Rex was thinking: Lizzy sounded *just* like her mother. Stacey would have said the exact same thing—although, now that he thought about it, Ethan realized he hadn't even thought to call her to let her know Rex was hurt. He'd call her when he left the hospital.

"Slow down, Elizabeth," Ethan said, pushing a chair in her direction. "Sit here. I'll find another chair."

There was a small waiting room across the hall and down a few doors from Rex's room. Ethan grabbed a chair out of there and brought it over.

A nurse stepped in right behind him. "I need to draw blood. If that bothers you, you're welcome to step out into the hallway," she said to Ethan and Lizzy.

Lizzy paled a bit and stood up.

Rex grinned. "Hey, Lizzy, why did the vampire take up acting?"

Lizzy, who had been known to pass out at the sight of blood, grinned back. "Oh gee, let's see, Rex, is it *in his blood?* You know that only worked to distract me when I was, like . . . twelve."

With two active brothers, she'd needed distracting more than once.

Ethan pulled a few bills out of his pocket and pushed them into Lizzy's hand. "Go down to the coffee bar next to the cafeteria. I only had one cup this morning and I've got a long day ahead of me. Grab yourself whatever you like, too, and then come back. Rex will probably be ready to visit by then."

"Thanks," she murmured as she hurried from the room, eyes averted from the hospital bed and the nurse.

"I take it she isn't considering a career in medicine," the nurse joked.

"Nope, not that one," Rex confirmed. "She may *build* a hospital someday, but I doubt she'll ever work in one."

Blood and needles weren't Ethan's favorite, either, but he waited for the nurse to finish up. He wanted to talk to Rex for a minute before Lizzy came back. Once the nurse left, Ethan closed Rex's door.

"How are you *really* feeling?"

"Better." Rex sat up taller in his bed, and this time he didn't need Ethan's help. "I got some sleep last night. They're still giving me pretty heavy pain meds, so nothing hurts, but I'm nervous to be on those for much longer."

Ethan nodded. He understood. Years ago, Rex had confided to him that he'd dabbled in a few street drugs when he was a kid. He'd even spent two weeks in a rehab unit but, as far as Ethan knew, all of that was far back in Rex's past. But you couldn't be too careful.

"Be honest with your doctor. They'll figure out a way to try to manage the pain and reduce the drugs. Hey, really quick, I wanted to talk to you about one thing before Lizzy comes back."

Rex gave him a guarded look. "Don't tell me someone died in the fire? God, that would just kill me."

"No, it's not that. To be honest, I haven't been able to find out how the three tenants are even doing. I tried, but was having trouble getting ahold of people last night—and of course the hospital won't tell me anything. But this is kind of related. I talked to Steve this morning."

"Steve?"

"Steve Dodds. My lawyer."

To this Rex nodded. He'd met Steve on more than one occasion.

"I'm going to head over and meet with him here in an hour or so," Ethan said, feeling uncomfortable about what he had to say next. "But . . . he cautioned us to be very careful what we say about the fire to anyone. He doesn't want you speaking to the police until he has a chance to talk to you first. He'll call you later this afternoon, after he runs down to the station with me. If the police show up here again today, be asleep. Be groggy. Be whatever you need to be to hold them off."

Rex's head whipped in Ethan's direction, and he winced at the movement, but that didn't mask his sudden anger. "Jesus, man, do you think I have something to hide?"

Rex's outburst surprised Ethan. He'd thought no such thing.

"Absolutely not! Don't be ridiculous. Steve is just trying to figure out what happened. He said there'll be all kinds of finger-pointing going on, and he just wants us to be careful. Rex . . . he implied my business could be at risk."

Rex's anger turned to sober shock.

"I'm sorry, Ethan. I overreacted. Of course I'll do whatever Steve tells us to do. I know how hard you've worked to build up your business. It's important to you. It's important to me, too."

Ethan laid his hand on Rex's shoulder. "Thanks, bud. I know I can count on you."

A light tapping on the door caught their attention, and Lizzy's voice called out, "All clear, Dad?"

Ethan opened the door, took the large paper cup she held out to him, and stood aside so Lizzy could enter. He pulled the door shut again behind them. He wanted a heads-up in case one of those officers from yesterday showed up again unannounced.

Lizzy pulled a chair right up next to Rex. Ethan knew his daughter would grill Rex on what happened at the fire. He sat down next to them, anxious to hear as well.

"Dad said you burned your legs," she started in. "How did that happen? What were you even doing there? I thought you were out of town for Thanksgiving!"

Rex took a moment before responding. Ethan wished he could see what was going on inside his friend's head. Finally, Rex began.

"I did spend Thursday with my family, Lizzy. Mom was there, my two brothers, the kids, and a few others. We'd planned to stay through today and go to my nephew's basketball tournament. He's thirteen now and they're in a fun league. But it turned out the games weren't local."

Rex pulled at the blanket covering the lower half of his body. Lizzy noticed and carefully tugged the white coverlet up so it wasn't tight up against his legs. Rex smiled appreciatively and continued.

"Mom wasn't feeling well and said she didn't want to spend another three hours in the car just to get to the tournament. We would have had to stay in a hotel. She wasn't up for it. She asked me to take her back home. What could I say? Of course I took her, but by then, I'd have missed half of the first day, so I decided to just come home, too."

He reached for the cup of water on his side table.

"Well, good," she replied, putting a hand on his arm. "I'm glad you weren't alone for Thanksgiving."

Rex shook his head, chuckling. "Lizzy, you need to quit worrying about me. I'm fine. Your dad here keeps me crazy busy, and I'll get plenty of basketball in watching Dylan's games."

Ethan chimed in, finally able to ask the question that had been most itching at him. "But why were you over at the jobsite? I specifically told you to take the weekend off."

Rex shrugged. "I know you did. I left my damn toolbox there on Wednesday night, and I needed it to do some things over at my house. I just ran over there to pick it up."

Ethan nodded. When Rex was bored—as he probably was yesterday, his weekend plans interrupted—he liked to tinker. And for Rex, tinkering meant a drill or some such tool in one hand and a beer in the other.

"Did you see anything strange when you got there? You know, like things out of place or anything? Did you see *anyone*?" Ethan asked, desperate to have a window back in time to find some answers.

"Nah. It was quiet, except I do remember hearing a TV blaring somewhere. But I didn't see anyone. I didn't see or smell any smoke, either."

Ethan nodded again. "The television was probably Marvin. Poor guy can't hear much."

"What happened then?" Lizzy asked. "How long were you there before you saw the fire?"

Rex paused, then said, "That's just it. I remember thinking as long as I was there maybe I'd finish removing the old trim to get ready for the new cupboards in the kitchen."

Of course he did, Ethan thought. The man couldn't go a day without getting some work in.

"And . . . ?" Lizzy prodded.

"That's it. I can't remember anything else until the emergency room."

Ethan leaned forward, his elbows on his knees. "Nothing? You have no memory of the fire . . . getting hurt . . . nothing?"

"Not really." Rex's brow furrowed. "It's so strange . . . maybe I hit my head or something, because when I woke up, here at the hospital, I had a splitting headache. They checked me over when I complained about it, but couldn't find any signs of trauma to my head. They said maybe it was from the smoke. Some of that can get pretty toxic, depending on what's burning."

"Damn," Ethan said, disheartened. "I thought you might be able to shed some light on what happened over there. Maybe the fire marshal will find something. Figure out what started it."

Rex squirmed in discomfort, and Ethan realized it was time go. He had to meet Steve over at his office in thirty minutes.

They said their goodbyes, Ethan promising to be back and Lizzy thanking Rex again for letting her take his spare car back to school.

"Ethan," Rex said, calling him back from the hallway.

Ethan peeked back through the door. "Yeah, bud?"

"Sorry I can't remember anything useful. I hope to hell we can get some answers. Something . . . something isn't adding up."

Ethan nodded, reassured him, turned, and jogged down the hallway to where Lizzy was holding the elevator, waiting for him.

He hoped Steve might have some answers.

Chapter Eleven

GIFT OF THE GREATEST GENERATION

"WONDER HOW REX'S FEELING this morning," Drew said. They'd waited twenty-five minutes for a table at the most popular diner in town, and now, barely fifteen minutes later, Drew was halfway through a caramel roll that nearly draped over the sides of his plate.

"Hard to say, dear. Burns are incredibly painful," Lavonne said. "I don't know if you boys know this or not, but after your dad and aunts left home for college and whatnot, I volunteered quite a bit at the hospital."

Dylan scrunched his face up. "Really? Why would you do that?"

Lavonne waved her fork at Dylan with a teasing scowl. "What's that supposed to mean, young man?"

"I mean, don't volunteers get all the grunt work? Why didn't you just get a job there instead?"

"Child, you have a lot to learn. You can't expect to get paid for absolutely every kind of work you do. Volunteers serve a critical need. When was the last time you did any volunteer work?" Lavonne asked.

Dylan simply stared back at her sheepishly.

She put her fork down. "Don't tell me you've *never* volunteered for anything?"

"You stepped in it now, little brother," Drew said.

Lavonne turned to Drew. "And what about *you*?"

"Actually," he said, puffing his chest out, "I've had to do quite a bit this year for National Honor Society. We have to put in something like twenty hours a year to be part of the group. Most of mine has been with the Big Brother program. I spend a couple hours a week over at one of the elementary schools, hanging out with Benton. He's a pretty cool kid, but he's got some issues."

George had been watching the exchange between his wife and grandsons, knowing full well where she was going with this. "And do you have fun when you spend time with Benton?" he asked.

Drew pushed his now-empty plate away and took a sip of coffee before responding. "I do," he replied with a nod. "I can tell he appreciates it when I go see him. Last week, the principal stopped me when I was leaving. She said whatever I was doing with Benton was making a difference. The kid was behaving better in class and turning in homework, apparently. He knows if he screws up too much, he can't spend time with me. Kind of like bribing him to behave, but hey, if it works . . ."

Lavonne smiled at Drew. "Do you think you're getting as much out of the relationship as Benton is?"

"Yeah, totally. In fact, it's got me thinking that maybe I want to do something to help at-risk kids down the road. You know, like a counselor or something."

"Counselors don't make much money," Dylan chimed in. "I heard two of ours talking at school when they were monitoring the halls. You better think twice about that."

George caught Dylan's eye and gave him a slight shake of his head. "Drew, I'm proud of you for taking that boy under your wing," he said. "He's a lucky kid. Now, if you guys are done with your breakfast, we've got things to do."

"I should probably get home, Gramps—I've got lots of homework," Dylan said when they pulled out of the diner parking lot.

"Actually, Dylan, I told your dad you two would spend the day with us. *He* said you told him this morning you didn't have much homework, so I'm thinking what you do need to get done can wait until this evening." George glanced in the rearview mirror as he spoke and caught the eye roll but ignored it.

"There are some great games on this afternoon. Can we have a fire in the fireplace and watch some football?" Dylan asked.

"Maybe later. We have something to do before we can relax."

"Did you remember to throw the lap blankets in the trunk, dear?" Lavonne asked George.

"Yep. *And* I called ahead. They said we could bring them by anytime."

"What?" Dylan asked.

"Don't you remember? We said we were going to deliver all those fleece blankets you guys made out at Whispering Pines yesterday," George replied.

"Well . . . yeah . . . of course I remember *making* the blankets. But I didn't know you meant *us* when you said *we* would deliver them."

"Dylan, have you ever visited a nursing home?" Lavonne asked.

"Sure. We had to go sing Christmas carols at one every year in grade school."

"Then you know how sweet some of those residents are," she said. "How lonely they can be."

Dylan looked surprised by her question. "Not really. We didn't actually *talk* to any of them . . . you know . . . one-on-one. They're so *old*. Why would they want to talk to a bunch of kids?"

Lavonne grinned. "That doesn't make any sense, Dylan. Your *grandfather* here is old, and *he* likes hanging out with you."

"You have a point, Grandma," Dylan said, cracking up.

Lavonne reached over and jokingly poked George in the ribs. He didn't take offense, knowing she was trying to make a point.

"Tell you what, Dylan. I'm going to ask you that same question again in a couple of hours . . . after you talk to a few of the residents," Lavonne said, turning to face forward in the front passenger seat.

"You kids did a great job on these blankets yesterday," George said as they each carried a pile into the nursing home.

"I had blisters on my thumbs by the time we were done tying all these fringes," Drew said. "It's a good thing you didn't have us make *full* blankets."

An employee who introduced herself as Tina met them inside the door.

"Oh, these are *wonderful*! Thank you so much. Our residents are going to love 'em . . . all the bright colors and holiday prints. It looks like you have enough for most everyone, too."

George nodded. "I called ahead to ask how many residents you have—I wouldn't want anyone to feel left out. I was told thirty-five."

"We are actually up to thirty-six now. We had a surprise addition late yesterday when someone was displaced from their home. But don't worry if you only have thirty-five. We have a couple residents who sadly won't know the difference."

"Would it be all right if we handed them out to the residents?" Lavonne asked. "It would be fun to visit with some of them."

Tina nodded excitedly. "Oh, they would love that! Some of them never have any visitors. Don't be surprised if some are extra chatty."

"That sounds great," George said. "Anything we should be aware of before we start?"

Tina glanced around. There were a few residents in the halls, sitting in wheelchairs; two men were playing chess in front of a window. "Not really," she said. "If someone's door is shut, let's not disturb them. We can give them their blanket later. But, for the most part, we try to keep the room doors open so people don't feel too isolated." Tina brought her wrist up and checked the screen on her smartwatch she wore. "Sorry, folks, I need to attend to something. Go ahead and hand them out. And thanks again!"

Lavonne set her pile of blankets down on a nearby table. "How do you want to do this, George?"

"I think we should split up. That way we'll get done faster. I suspect they probably serve lunch before too long."

"I don't know, Grandpa," Dylan said, doubt in his voice as he looked around. "How about if we go in pairs?"

George knew exactly what Dylan was getting at. His grandson didn't want to approach the residents by himself. But that was exactly what George and Lavonne had planned earlier, and Lavonne was just playing along now.

"No way, Jose!" she said. "You reminded me the Vikings game starts at noon. If we split up, we won't miss much of it." Lavonne pointed each boy down a different hallway, gave George a discreet wink, and made her way to the chess players.

Dylan hated the idea of handing out blankets by himself.

What can I possibly say to senile old people?

Despite his reservations, he knew his grandparents weren't going to change their minds. They were trying to teach him a lesson—it was obvious. He wasn't exactly sure what that lesson *was*, but he could tell they wanted him to see one. He wasn't buying into their act.

Might as well get this over with.

Dylan walked to the end of his assigned hallway. The door to the room on the right stood wide open. He peaked around the corner and saw an old woman sitting in a wheelchair in the middle of the room, facing her window. She seemed intent on something outside.

He knocked softly and she turned his way.

"Well, hello. Come in, come in," she said, waving him in.

Dylan entered with a little wave of his own.

"Hi, uh . . . my name is Dylan. My family . . . we made these blankets. Would you like one?"

"My, that is so gracious of you, child," the woman said, a smile lighting her wrinkled face. "My name is Anne. It's a pleasure to meet you, Dylan. I would love one of those pretty little things. The weather has turned chilly."

"Which one would you like?"

"Do you have any with birds on them? I love my feathered friends." She turned back to the window. "I was just watching a blue jay when you stopped by. Blue jays are interesting creatures. So beautiful and colorful. But you must be careful, child. They can be mean, very territorial. Come. Look."

Dylan moved farther into the room to stand beside Anne and was surprised to see a beautiful blue-and-white bird at the feeder. Together they watched it for a moment. Another bird, this one brown and ordinary-looking, tried to land on the feeder, but the blue jay chased it away.

"He *is* tough," Dylan said, glancing at Anne.

Her eyes had widened amongst the web of wrinkles lining her face. Her ringlets of pure white hair bobbed as she nodded, as if to say *I told you so*. Her eyes were as blue as the bird outside.

"Well, I better keep moving," he told her. "I've got to get the rest of these handed out. Then we're gonna go watch the Vikings kick the Packers."

"Thank you again, Dylan," she said, smoothing the blanket she'd laid across her lap. "Come back and see me anytime. I'll introduce you to more of my feathered friends."

As Dylan left the room, she yelled "Skol!"

Dylan laughed out loud at the well-known battle cry for Vikings fans.

That wasn't so bad.

And so it continued. As Dylan made his way back up the hallway, he found he enjoyed visiting with most of the residents he met. One guy was cranky and couldn't hear him, but the rest weren't at all what he'd expected.

Drew was experiencing many of the same things as his younger brother.

The previous year, he'd come to this same nursing home with his American History class. Each student was assigned a resident to interview and write a paper about. He'd talked to a guy named Bud, and he hoped to be able to see him today. Bud's room wasn't in the hallway his grandmother assigned to him, but as soon as he'd given out all but one of his blankets, he made his way toward Bud's room. He could hear his own grandfather talking to a resident a few doors down. With any luck, George hadn't gotten to Bud's room yet. Drew wanted to give him his last blanket.

Drew knew as soon as he looked into the room that something was different. Gone were all of Bud's pictures on the walls and the bright quilt on the bed—the quilt Bud's daughter had made for him.

The room was stark now. There were no pictures anywhere, and the blanket covering the bed was a boring beige. A television blared inside. A man sat in a brown, velour recliner, staring at the set. It wasn't his friend Bud. The other man noticed Drew in the doorway and used the remote in his bandaged hand to mute the TV.

"Hello," the man said, his voice gravelly, as if he had a chest cold. "What do ya need, kid?"

"Hi," Drew said, walking a few steps into the room. "I was looking for Bud?"

The guy shook his head. "Sorry, no Bud in here. But I just got here last night. I haven't had a chance to meet many people."

Drew realized this must be the thirty-sixth person the lady Tina had mentioned. "Doesn't look like you've had a chance to unpack yet, either," Drew said, again looking around the spartan room.

"What? You have to speak up, son, I'm hard of hearing."

"Oh. Sorry about that. I was just noticing you don't have any personal things in here yet. Are you waiting for your things to get here?"

"Nah. Had a bit of trouble at home yesterday, but hopefully I won't have to stay here too long. Believe me, I'm not ready to hole up in one of these joints and wait for the bitter end quite yet. I've got things to do." He said all this while staring at the TV.

Drew nearly laughed. This guy reminded him of Bud. Spunky.

"Is that why your hand is bandaged? Did you get hurt?"

The man glanced at his hand. "This? Nothing to worry about. It'll heal. Now, what's your name and why you looking for this Bud guy?"

"I'm Drew. I'm here with my family to deliver a bunch of these," Drew said, holding his last blanket up. "Would you like one? We made them for the residents. It was my grandpa's idea."

"Really? Your grandfather sounds like a decent man. Let me see that thing, young man."

Drew handed the small blanket over and watched him unfold and study it and then spread it out over his lap. The bright green fleece and white tassels gave a much-needed punch of color to the room.

"I'll take that as a yes?" Drew asked with a smile. "I hope you're able to go home soon. I better go . . . but I didn't catch your name."

The man started to speak, but a phone sitting on the end table next to him gave a shrill ring.

"Sorry, this is probably my son. I have to take this. But thanks, kid! Keep up the good work."

Drew gave the new guy a wave and left the room, smiling as the hard-of-hearing man yelled into the phone. He thought the corded phone looked almost as old as the man.

Then he sobered. Bud had been old, too.

He should have kept his promise to come back and see him.

"That was actually kind of fun," Dylan admitted as they drove away. "Those old people had some great stories, and you could tell they *liked* to talk. They liked the blankets, too, but they really seemed to like the company the most."

George nodded. "I bet we could have easily spent the afternoon there and never run out of people wanting to visit. But they're heading down for lunch, so the timing was good to head out. What did you think, Drew?"

"I'm with Dylan. That was more fun than I'd expected. I was actually here with my class a couple times last year, and I was hoping to talk to a guy I interviewed for my assignment, but there was someone else in his old room."

"He probably croaked."

This had Lavonne spinning around in her seat. "Dylan Scott Richter! That is an *awful* thing to say!"

Dylan held up his hands in defense. "Jeez, sorry. Isn't that about the only way to get out of a place like that?"

Lavonne sat facing forward again. "It most certainly is not. Some people have to be there for just a short stay. Usually because they got sick or had surgery or something. They go there to heal and get their strength back, and then they can go home again."

"Actually," Drew said, glaring at his brother, "that's kind of what the guy said who's in Bud's old room now. Said he just got there last night and he hoped to go back home soon."

Lavonne nodded. Dylan just shrugged.

"I saw some kids working there," he said. "They looked like they were Drew's age. That might be kind of a cool job, later, when I'm old enough. It would be better than working in fast food or a grocery store or something."

"You think you might enjoy working with old people?" George asked over his shoulder, a twinkle in his eye.

"Yeah," Dylan said, a note of surprise in his voice. "They were *way* different than I expected."

"You know, Dylan," George said as he drove, "you aren't old enough to work there yet, but I think they have some different activities open to the public. I could check them out, and if any of them look like something I think you might like, we could go together. That might give you a better idea if you want to work there . . . down the road."

"Sure, Gramps, keep me posted. Just don't make me tie any more of those blankets. I need my thumbs for basketball."

Chapter Twelve
Gift of Protection

"Here's what I've been able to learn so far," Steve said, getting right to the point as he unlocked the door to his office building. "No one's injuries are life-threatening."

Ethan, standing off to Steve's right, sagged against the exterior brick wall, relief flooding his body. "You have no idea how glad I am to hear *that*."

"Your woman resident is still in the hospital. Sounds like she had some pre-existing lung conditions and the smoke exacerbated things."

"Yes, that's what her daughter said," Ethan confirmed as he followed Steve into his office.

His lawyer pulled up short. "Wait . . . I thought I told you *not* to talk to any of them."

Ethan nodded and sat down in one of the chairs. "You did tell me that, but I saw her before I called you. We actually knew each other back in college, but I haven't seen her in twenty-plus years. She walked into the hospital while I was there to try to see Rex."

"What else did she say?" Steve seemed exasperated.

"Well . . . before she saw me sitting there, she was threatening that whoever owns the building will pay dearly if it turns out the fire was due to some kind of building issue."

Steve slapped the manila folder he'd been carrying onto the desktop and plopped down into another chair.

"That is exactly *why* I told you *not* to talk to anyone connected with the tenants, Ethan! Did you speculate to her at all as to what might have started the fire?"

"Of course not. I'm not an idiot, Steve," Ethan spat out, rubbing the back of his neck.

"*That's* good, I guess."

"Look, it was a short conversation. They called her back to see her mother and I gave her my card, told her to call me when she had any updates on her mom's condition. So far I haven't gotten a call."

"All right, let's leave that for now, then. The guy in the other upstairs unit . . . wait, let me look up his name, I've forgotten it . . ."

"Marvin? Marvin Miller?"

"Yeah, that's it. He had some minor burns, so they treated him but didn't keep him overnight or anything. The person I talked to said they found a place for him to stay until his kid can get to town to help him find a more permanent solution, because, well—who knows when, or *if*, they can get back into your building."

Ethan was relieved Marvin wasn't badly hurt. "What about Norman Westfall? He was the downstairs tenant."

Steve nodded. "That one is more of a mystery. No one seems to remember seeing him yesterday. He must not have been home. Maybe he was away for the holiday."

"That would be good news. The only problem is . . . I don't want him to come home to a fire-damaged building without a heads-up. I do have a cell number for him, but I didn't try him again once you told me not to. Someone should call him. Do you want to try?"

Steve handed Ethan a legal pad. "Yeah, I can do that. Write his number here and I'll call him when we're done at the police station."

Ethan wrote it down and checked his watch. "Speaking of, we need to be down there in twenty minutes. Have you learned anything else yet? Like how bad the damage is? Or when I can go in there, check things out myself?"

"I don't have anything on that yet, but I did place a couple calls. Look, Ethan, you're probably going to have to be patient. These things take time. And until they rule on what they think started the fire, they're going to want you to stay out of there."

"Can they do that?"

"They sure can."

—ell—

"Thank you for coming down, Mr. Richter, Mr. Dodds. We appreciate you taking time out of your Sunday afternoon."

"I just need to get some answers," Ethan said, looking between the two officers. He recognized them from the hospital.

The older, taller one of the two motioned for them to take the two seats in front of his desk. He sat down behind the desk and the younger officer stood off to the side. Ethan was surprised when Steve knew the older cop, calling him by his first name—Karl.

"Let's start at the beginning," Karl said. "We want to get an idea of how involved you are with this particular piece of rental property—whether you know the tenants, how much maintenance has been done on the building, those kinds of things."

Ethan glanced at Steve, and the lawyer signaled him to go ahead.

"I've owned the property for two years. I inherited the building and four others from my aunt, Celia Middleton. She had a much longer history with the properties and most of the tenants than I do."

"Lucky you," the younger cop—Bob, he'd introduced himself as—said. "My aunt tried to leave me her cat. I wasn't interested."

"Celia was a generous woman," Ethan acknowledged, smiling at the thought of her. "A *successful* and generous woman. All of the properties *do* have mortgages on them, so it isn't quite as lucrative as it might sound, but they provide me with a bit of cash flow—at least in those months that I don't have surprise expenses."

"Like fires," Bob said.

"Is maintaining the properties where you spend most of your time, then?" Karl asked.

"No. Not really. I own a small construction company and I still have two teenagers at home, so I spend my time on all kinds of things."

"And did *you* find the current renters, or have they lived in the building since your aunt's time?"

"They all came with the property. I got lucky. Two of the single-family homes she passed on to me have had some vacancies. Finding decent renters is tough."

Karl crossed his arms on top of his desk, angling forward slightly toward Ethan. "But you had one vacancy in this building, too, didn't you?"

"Well, yeah, but I hadn't started to look for a new renter yet. The old guy who was in there passed away. Health problems," Ethan said. "I decided it was probably time to do a bit of a facelift to the unit before trying to rent it out."

"A facelift." Karl nodded. "Makes sense. The building was probably built back in the seventies, would you guess?"

"Actually," Steve spoke up, "we can get you the exact year, along with repair records to show Ethan's aunt, and now Ethan, have been diligent in maintaining a safe environment."

Karl relaxed back into his office chair. Ethan was starting to understand why Steve had insisted on coming with him. Ethan knew he had nothing to hide, but Steve would make sure he didn't accidently imply any negligence.

"That would be helpful," Karl conceded. "Tell me about the remaining three tenants. I realize your knowledge might be somewhat limited, but I appreciate you sharing what you know."

At Steve's nod, Ethan went on to give him a brief bio on the one woman and two men who rented from him, abbreviated as his knowledge was.

Karl nodded, then looked up from the legal pad he'd been using to take notes. "In addition to the three tenants, there was also a man found in the lower unit, the unit you're refurbishing."

"Yes, that's right. As you know, his name is Rex Forde. Rex is my foreman. He's worked for me for a long time. Going on twenty years. And he's a family friend."

"What can you tell us about Rex's background?" Bob asked as he leaned against the office wall, hands in his pockets.

Ethan shrugged. "What do you want to know? And why? Rex was there because he's overseeing the remodel project."

"We're just trying to cover all our bases," Karl said. "We want our report to be complete and thorough so we can all put this behind us. Rex was found passed out in the unit where it looks like the fire started. We're curious why he was there, alone, on the Saturday after Thanksgiving. Just seems odd. Unless you're one of those asshole bosses who makes their employees work damn near twenty-four-seven while you play."

Ethan could feel his blood pressure rising. *Who does this guy think he is, attacking me?*

Steve held up a hand. "How about we take it down a notch, Karl. You have no reason to speak to my client like that. We want to get to the bottom of this as much—actually *more*—than you do. I assure you, Ethan is a top-notch businessman who treats his employees fairly."

Karl stood up, walked over to a coffeepot in the corner of his office, and filled a Styrofoam cup with black liquid. "Anyone else want a cup?"

Bob turned his nose up at the offer. Steve and Ethan declined.

Karl walked back to his desk with his coffee. "I didn't mean to imply anything. Apologies, Ethan. I just feel bad for a guy, having to work over the Thanksgiving weekend. I've been there."

"Go ahead and give Karl some background on Rex," Steve said to Ethan. "I know what a stand-up guy Rex is. Tell these guys."

"All right," Ethan said, although he was reluctant to tell these two clowns anything personal about his friend. But if it could prevent them from going to the hospital and grilling Rex themselves, he'd try.

"I never asked Rex to work this weekend. In fact, I told him *not* to. The guy works too much as it is. He's always been a hard worker, but things changed for him about ten years ago. He was married to Gail. She was great. They were inseparable. But she died. Car accident. It was hell. I wasn't sure if Rex would get through the grief, but somehow he found a way."

"Sorry to hear that," Karl said, cradling his half-empty cup. "Did they have kids?"

"No, no kids. I never asked, but I got the impression they *wanted* kids. It just didn't happen. Now Rex spends most of his time working and driving over to spend time with his nephews in St. Cloud. He helps me out with my kids, too, especially recently. My wife and I divorced a year ago. I do most of the child-rearing. She's busy."

Bob pushed away from the wall and walked over to the bare window looking out over the parking lot below, turning his back to the room to gaze outside. "Divorce, huh? That's usually a costly venture. You sound a tad bitter. She take you to the cleaners?"

"The impact of my client's divorce on his personal financial situation is *way* beyond the scope of our discussion today, boys," Steve said, a warning tone in his voice. "Let's not make this a fishing expedition."

"Just making an observation," Bob said. "I'm speaking from my *own* personal experience."

Karl took back control of the questioning. "All right, you mentioned Rex had some issues dealing with the grief over the death of his wife. How did he handle that? Did he have any trouble with drinking? Maybe get himself some pills to help deal with the depression?"

"Absolutely not," Ethan said. "Rex doesn't drink any more than the next guy. He doesn't do drugs. Why would you even ask that?"

Karl and Bob exchanged a knowing look before Karl met and held Ethan's gaze.

"Because Rex was passed out on the floor, *drunk,* in the middle of a Saturday afternoon when the firefighters found him. Flames were crawling up the kitchen wall, near the stove, not two feet from him, and he was out cold. Now . . . doesn't that sound slightly suspicious to you?"

"I don't believe it," Ethan stammered when he and Steve got outside. He'd said as much to the officers, did his best to defend Rex, but he could see the skepticism in their eyes. They were ready to declare Rex guilty. But guilty of what? Carelessness? Or worse? "I don't—"

"Get in the car," Steve ordered, cutting Ethan off.

Ethan did as he was told, but he was furious.

"Well, you were right about one thing," Ethan said, glaring at Steve.

"What's that?" Steve asked as he backed out of his parking spot.

"There's all kinds of finger-pointing going on."

"Don't get discouraged, Ethan. Most of that in there was standard procedure. Kind of like poking a bear. Seeing if anything makes you roar. Think about it from the cops' perspective: You're the landlord. You told them you have a mortgage on the property, it barely cashflows, and you just went through a divorce. Rex's not only your employee, he's your friend. They might see it all as Rex's way of helping you out. A fire equals a bailout from the insurance company. And if the company survives, he keeps getting a paycheck. Or"—Steve shrugged—"they think maybe he's just a drunk who screwed up and accidently started a fire."

"If you're trying to cheer me up, you're failing miserably," Ethan said, slumping down in his seat. "But I admit . . . when you put it like that, I can kind of see why they might ask those things. If I watched a scene like that on some TV drama and the cops *didn't* ask those questions, I'd have turned the channel because the storyline was crap."

They rode in silence for a bit, Ethan lost in his own thoughts. Up until this point his main concern had been about his tenants and Rex. But according to both Steve and now the police, no one had been seriously injured other than Rex. Personally, he was still very concerned about Penelope. She was still in the hospital, and Ethan felt terrible that the fire had made her existing health problems worse. He prayed she'd be able to bounce back from the havoc the smoke likely played on her lungs.

As they approached Steve's office and Ethan's pickup, he had to ask the nagging questions he'd been chewing on. "Steve."

"Yeah."

"And just to be clear, I don't think Rex did this on purpose. Rex wouldn't even know how much insurance I have on the place. And the pictures those guys just showed us proved there's extensive damage in the vacant unit. Rex is lucky to have gotten out of there alive. There's a ton of work to be done to get those people back in their homes, and if they determine the damage isn't covered for some reason, I'm screwed. I could lose everything."

"Yeah?"

"Well . . . do *you* think Rex somehow caused the fire?"

Steve was silent.

"And," Ethan went on, "if you do, do you think my insurance could be in jeopardy?"

After another beat, Steve finally spoke. "You are getting *way* ahead of things, Ethan. I get why you're spooked. I do. But we'll take this one step at a time. I personally am skeptical about what they said about Rex being passed out drunk. I'll check with the hospital. Either way, your insurance company has a reputation for being fair. If they end up having to make a big payout on this, they may drop your sorry ass down the road, but if your claim is legitimate, payment shouldn't be your concern."

Ethan popped off his seatbelt as Steve pulled in behind his truck. "You have no idea how much I hope you're right. At least you got those guys to agree to leave Rex alone until tomorrow."

Steve put his car in Park and checked his watch. "Go home, Ethan. Go watch some football and try not to worry. I'll go give Rex a call and we'll get to work on all this tomorrow. I'll try Norman Westfall again for you, too. There's nothing more you can do today."

Ethan knew Steve was right.

"Thanks again, Steve. I'll talk to you in the morning. I need to go get my kids. They're going to be worried."

"Anybody home?" Ethan hollered as he let himself into the kitchen through the back door of his parents' house.

"In here, Dad!" Dylan yelled from the living room.

Ethan grabbed a beer out of the fridge, peeked into the pot of chili bubbling on the stove, and headed for the front living room. What used to be a slightly stuffy formal living room had been transformed with comfortable recliners and a new, big-screen TV.

"Dad, you missed a great game!" Dylan said when Ethan walked into the room. "The Vikes kicked butt!"

Jess and Seth were over, too. His sister pushed up out of her comfy spot on the new sofa and came over to give Ethan a hug.

"Who are you and what have you done with my sister?" Ethan asked, smirking a bit as he hugged her back. Jess was not a hugger.

"Ha, ha. Joke all you want, but I've been worried sick about you," Jess said, slugging Ethan on the shoulder before she walked back to reclaim her spot.

Ethan looked around for his youngest niece. "Where's Harper?"

"She's napping up in my old room. All the activity at the lodge yesterday wore her out."

Ethan still marveled at Jess for agreeing to raise Harper as her own. Just when his sister was getting to the point where her other two kids were off to college, along came baby Harper, the child a result of her now ex-husband's illicit affair. The baby's mother was unstable. It was a huge leap of faith on Jess's part, but as far as Ethan could tell, she was loving having a third child, even if it meant going back to the days of diaper bags and teething.

"Dylan, get up and let your dad sit down," George said. "From the looks of him, today hasn't been any easier than yesterday."

Ethan caught his father's eye. He knew his dad was sick with worry, too. The whole situation was a mess.

"How is Rex feeling today?" Lavonne asked, looking up from the blanket she was crocheting. She'd never been a big football fan, but she liked to be part of the action.

"I think he's in a lot of pain," Ethan said as he sank into the spot his son had been keeping warm. "Lizzy and I went up to see him. We didn't stay long, but we did visit with him a little. He's got some healing to do before he can get back to it."

Ethan's mind flew back to the allegations the police had made against Rex. Maybe they weren't really allegations and he was being too defensive, but if what they said was true, there was trouble ahead.

"I said lots of prayers for that poor man in church this morning. I said prayers for all of those poor people suddenly out of a home, right before Christmas."

"Gee, sure am glad I came over here to get cheered up, Mom."

Lavonne looked guilty. "I'm sorry, honey, don't mind me and my big mouth. Of course I prayed for you, too."

"Mother, quit before you dig yourself any deeper of a hole," Jess warned. "I think I hear the timer on the oven going off. Is that your bread?"

"Oh darn, I bet it is. I'll be right back."

Lavonne left the room, stopping next to Ethan to give him a quick hug. He patted her arm. *She means well,* he reminded himself.

"How bad is the damage, Ethan?" Seth asked. "Fire can be pretty destructive, and so can the water and fire retardants they use to put it out."

Ethan shrugged. "It looked pretty nasty in the pictures the cops showed me, but they won't let me in there just yet. They said they need to let the fire marshal finish his inspection and have a structural engineer make sure it's safe before they let anyone else back in there."

"I suppose you've seen your share of burned-out buildings, huh?" Jess asked, squeezing Seth's hand.

"I have," Seth confirmed. "I actually got my start in one. Back when I wasn't much older than Drew, my grandma was on the board for a historical society. By the way, your aunt was on that same board and they were friends. That's where I first met Celia. Anyways, there was a fire at this cool old theater and it couldn't be saved. They let me go in and pull out what I could. Now here I am, nearly twenty years later, still digging around in old, dilapidated buildings."

Ethan appreciated what Seth did for a living. If not for people like him, so much history would be lost.

"If they shut me down after this fire, maybe I'll talk to you about a job," Ethan joked. He hoped it wouldn't come to that.

"What are you talking about, Dad?" Drew asked. "Could that really happen?"

"I'm kidding, bud. I'm sure it'll all work out. But things are going to be a lot slower for a while. I won't have Rex to help lead the crew until he's feeling better, and I'll need to spend time clearing up this mess related to the fire. Things will get back to normal at some point, but probably not until we get past the holidays."

"Looks like Christmas might be a bit bleak this year, in terms of presents, huh?" Dylan said. "Not that I'm complaining, Dad. I'm just worried about you."

Ethan eyed his youngest. It was amazing how a tear in a family's lining, followed by a near tragedy, could make kids grow up so fast.

Chapter Thirteen
GIFT OF TRUST

THE FOLLOWING WEEK UNFOLDED much as Ethan expected it would. He spent his time between going to Steve's office, visiting Rex in the hospital, overseeing the two crews he had working on four other projects, and arguing with the authorities to let him get inside his damaged building.

He'd learned Penelope was feeling well enough to leave the hospital and was staying in a local hotel. Rebecca Sinclair, Ethan's old college friend, left him a message saying as much, but they never did connect. When he'd called her back and got her voicemail, he promised to keep her posted as to if and when her mother could move back in.

If she wants *to move back in.*

Steve was able to learn a bit more about the two male tenants. Norman Westfall had indeed been out of town at the time of the fire. He was down in Arizona, escaping the early Minnesota winter. Norman's original plan had been to come back in a week, but when Steve let him know the seriousness of the situation, he decided to stay longer.

That left Marvin. Ethan worried about Marvin. As far as he knew, Marvin didn't have any family in the area. Steve discovered the hospital was able to get Marvin a room, temporarily, at a local nursing home. When Ethan asked which one, Steve reminded him it was a bad idea for him to go see the man. While Steve wouldn't give him the name of the facility, Ethan knew he could find Marvin without much difficulty. There were only three nursing homes in town.

But he was so busy, he heeded Steve's advice—at least for now.

Brooke called numerous times to offer her assistance, but he'd been putting her off. He wasn't sure what to do about that whole situation. He enjoyed spending time with her, and the boys liked her, but he didn't see it going anywhere. He told her as much when he'd talked to her the previous evening.

"Ethan, we've talked about this. I'm not looking for a ring. I just have fun with you and your family. Think of me as a safe harbor, away from all the craziness that's your life right now. You know what they say about all work and no play, don't you?"

Ethan laughed—he knew she was right. With all this stress, he was growing old way before his time.

"Okay, you're right. I need a break. How about dinner tomorrow night?"

"Sure, that would be fun! Hey, why don't you invite Jess and Seth, too? You know . . ." Brooke grinned at him. "A double date."

When Jess brought Harper over, Renee couldn't help but ask.

"Jess . . . if you don't want to go, why did you say yes when Ethan called?" She'd agreed to watch the little girl for a few hours while Jess and Seth double-dated with Ethan and Brooke, but now she just couldn't help but express her confusion. "He'd probably understand if you just told him you don't particularly care for the woman," she added.

Jess set Harper down on the floor and watched the child totter off toward the kitchen where Matt was whistling while he did dishes.

"You trained him well, didn't you?" Jess asked, nodding her head toward the whistling.

Renee blushed happily. Having only been married since June, Matt and her sister Renee were still in the honeymoon phase. "I had nothing to do with it. He's not used to having anyone around, waiting on him, so he's pretty self-sufficient. It's great."

Jess was well past the reservations she'd originally had about Matt when he first showed up at Whispering Pines; he'd surprised Renee with an impromptu visit after they'd met on a tropical vacation months earlier. Fortunately, it hadn't taken Jess long to realize he was the real deal and the best thing to happen to Renee in a long time.

"As I was saying," Renee said, circling back to their initial conversation, "why put yourself in a situation where you're uncomfortable? Does Seth know how you feel?"

"*God*, no," Jess said, horrified. "He'd think I'm being ridiculous! When I first met Brooke over at Ethan's this past summer, and it was apparent that Brooke and Seth were friends, he teased me about asking her out." Seeing Renee's raised eyebrows, she added, "Since I was hesitant to date him at first. But I don't want him to think I'm a ridiculous, *jealous* girlfriend."

"But you *are*."

"Oh my God, shut up, would you?" Jess said, clearly sick of her sister's good-natured teasing.

"Shu-shu-shu," came Harper's little sing-song voice from the other room.

"You two better keep it down in there! Young ears pick up everything," Matt said from the kitchen.

"Great, *now* look at what you made me do," Jess said, pinning Renee with a hard look.

Renee held up her hands and laughed. "Don't blame me, sis. Now go. Since you're too chicken to be honest with our big brother—*or* with your boyfriend—you better get going. I think that's your handsome man heading this way," she said as footsteps echoed on the wooden steps on the front of their adjoining duplexes.

Jess opened the door before Seth could knock.

"Well, hello, gorgeous," Seth said, kissing the tip of Jess's nose.

Renee made a gagging noise in the background.

"Ignore her," Jess said to Seth, capturing his hand and pulling him inside. "I'm just going to kiss Harper goodnight and we can leave."

"Where is that little devil? Been a while since I've seen her."

"In the kitchen with Uncle Matt." Jess turned but was struck against her leg by a force of nature. "Or not," she laughed, scooping Harper up in her arms.

"You weren't kidding when you said she was walking everywhere. She's practically running already."

"I know! I won't know another moment's peace now for a few years."

Seth picked a discarded pink elephant up off the floor and held it out for Harper. She reached for it and Jess passed her into Seth's arms. He took both elephant and girl into the center of the living room and sunk down onto the floor amongst a collection of Harper's other toys Jess had brought over for the evening. He made a circle with blocks, pretending they were at the circus. Harper giggled when he made a trumpeting sound and trotted the elephant around the makeshift ring.

"She's eaten and had her bath," Jess told Renee as she pulled her coat on, "so it should be pretty simple. Maybe read her a story and lay her down in the playpen. We shouldn't be late."

Renee nodded, grinning down at Seth and Harper.

Jess checked her watch. "I hate to break this up, folks, but we better get going if we don't want to be late."

"But the tigers come out next," Seth complained.

Jess laughed and picked her baby daughter up off the floor, handing her to Renee.

Harper pushed against Renee, trying to escape her arms. She didn't want to stay behind.

"Just go," Renee urged, shooing them both out the front door. "She'll be fine. Kids are like goldfish—she'll forget all about you in five minutes."

The two couples met at a new restaurant downtown. Only Brooke had been there before, a fact that somehow increased Jess's anxieties about the date.

Jess watched Seth shake Ethan's hand when they arrived at the same time, then give Brooke a big hug. Jess got a small finger wave.

I hope the wine gets to the table fast.

Jess had worked hard to convince herself the whole way over that Brooke wasn't a threat to her relationship with Seth.

She's dating Ethan . . .

Seth and I are in a good place . . .

You're being too sensitive, Jess!

He wouldn't play circus with Harper and then leave us both for another woman.

She jumped when Seth placed his hand at the small of her back to usher her to their table. He gave her a warm smile and she took a steadying breath, reminding herself to relax.

Once all four were seated at a table near a window, Seth turned to Jess's brother. "Thanks for the invite, Ethan."

"Brooke suggested it, and I thought it was a great idea."

Don't worry . . .

"So, Brooke," Jess spoke up, trying on a smile of her own. "I don't feel like we've gotten a chance to get to know each other very well yet. It seems you and Seth go back, and I'm sure my brother has learned some of your life story, but I'd love to have my turn."

"Sure," Brooke said, the smile on her face seeming genuine enough. "What would you like to know?"

Jess shrugged. "Whatever you'd like to share."

"Well, let's see. I grew up in the area. I have one sister and four brothers. My sister is married, has one little girl, and my goal is to be the 'world's best auntie.' Three out of four of my brothers are married, too, and between them I've got a bunch of other nieces and nephews. But for some reason, spoiling them isn't quite as fun as spoiling my sister's kid. Sometimes sister-in-laws don't appreciate that, I guess," she joked.

Brooke paused to take a sip of her wine.

"Our parents moved south once we were out of the house, so we don't see them often. We *did* move out to California for a while, my sister and I. She actually met her husband out there. But it wasn't for me. I came back first, and then they moved back when Stella was born. Things were too expensive out there, and with a new baby, they decided it wasn't worth it."

"How old is Stella?"

"Fourteen months now. Close to your youngest daughter's age, right? Here, I'll show you a picture of her," Brooke offered, pulling out her phone.

Jess had to admit the child was darling, with raven-dark curls and big blue eyes. *Just like her aunt.* She did look close to Harper's age, too. It had slipped Jess's mind that Brooke met Harper at the Halloween party and again the Saturday after Thanksgiving when she came out to help at Whispering Pines.

"She's adorable," Jess said, handing Brooke's phone back. "I admit I do have something I've been dying to ask you . . ."

"Shoot!" Brooke said, smiling.

"How did you end up doing tile work for a living?"

"Yeah, Brooke, how did *that* happen?" Seth chimed in. Jess couldn't tell if the look on his face was a smirk or a genuine smile, if the question was a rib or genuine curiosity.

Their orders arrived just then, and as the waiter placed their meals on the table, Ethan ordered a second bottle of wine.

"Kind of by accident," Brooke began once the waiter had left, getting back to Jess's question. "I went to school for graphic design. Three years in, I met someone. This idiot's roommate's brother, as a matter of fact."

Jess looked to Seth. "What roommate?"

"Dawn," Seth replied.

Jess nodded.

"Who's Dawn?" Ethan asked Seth, clearly not following.

"You remember my daughter, Kaylee? I brought her to the Halloween party. Dawn is Kaylee's mother."

The look on Ethan's face was inscrutable. "Ah. I see."

Jess would fill Ethan in on Seth and Dawn's history another time. She wanted to keep Brooke talking now. "You dated Dawn's brother? What was his name?"

Brooke grimaced. "*Cameron.*"

"And he was *pretty*," Seth joked. Something banged the bottom of the table, making the silverware jump. "Ouch—what'd you kick me for?"

"You are always *such* a jerk about this," Brooke said with a pout.

"All right, now you have me curious," Ethan said, joining back into the conversation. "Sounds like there's a story here."

"Oh, there's a story, all right," Seth said.

"Should I just let *you* tell it?" Brooke asked him.

Jess was starting to understand where their easy banter came from. She'd been right to think there was history between them . . . but maybe not the kind of history she'd assumed.

Seth picked up his fork and steak knife. "No, go ahead. I promise, I'll shut up."

"That would be new," Brooke said. "Okay, *as* I was saying . . . I was introduced to Cameron during my third year of college. I had a class with Dawn, and we met at a coffee shop to work on a project. He picked her up. We met. And—stupid me," she said with a self-deprecating laugh, "I fell hard and fast."

"That actually sounds kind of romantic," Jess said, surprising herself.

"It might have been if he didn't turn out to be such a douche bag."

Seth nearly choked on his steak.

"Are you going to try to deny it? Stand up for your friend again, like you used to?" Brooke demanded.

Jess was starting to regret bringing up the whole subject. She tried to divert the conversation. "I'm confused. How does this all relate to you getting into the tile business?"

"It's coming, be patient," Seth said, trying to keep a straight face, but his eyes twinkled.

Brooke tried again, shooting one last glare at Seth. "Cameron *was* 'pretty,' as Seth so eloquently put it. He was cute, he was charming, and he was full of shit. It just took me *way* longer than it should have to figure out that last piece. He convinced me to quit school and go into business with him. He'd learned tile work from his grandfather. And, I have to admit, as much as I hate to, he was talented."

She paused to sip her wine, and Jess found herself irresistibly drawn in to the story.

Brooke continued, "He was also persuasive. I did it. I quit school—against the wishes of everyone in my family—and sunk what little money I had into his plan. His grandfather had a stroke and his grandma needed to sell the business. She was willing to sell Cameron everything: the equipment, the customer list, and the name. And she was fair about the price."

Brooke nodded to Ethan when he offered to refill her wine glass, taking a moment before continuing.

"At first, things went well, at least business-wise. We worked together and he taught me much of what he'd learned from his grandfather."

"She was a quick study," Seth confirmed, earning himself a grateful nod from Brooke.

"But he started to change. Got more possessive. We worked together, all day every day, and he didn't like it if I wanted to do anything outside of work that didn't include him. He always thought I was flirting with other men. One time"—she paused, then rushed on—"he even accused me of sleeping with Seth."

Jess half expected Seth to choke on his food again, but he nodded and added, "Which was complete BS, of course, since I was with Dawn at the time."

While she would never say it out loud, Jess could kind of understand Cameron's suspicions of Brooke and Seth. She'd had similar ones herself.

"What happened then?" Jess asked. "I take it you eventually had a falling out of some sort?"

"Oh, we certainly did," Brooke said. "Are you sure you want to hear this? It's kind of embarrassing."

"Not if you don't want to tell us."

"Come on, Brooke, finish the story," Seth pressed. "*He* was the loser in all of this, not you."

"Two years after we started working together . . ." Brooke said, "Cameron was arrested."

"Okay, I did *not* see that coming," Ethan said. "For what?"

"Drinking and driving. Not once, either, but twice in one month. The second time he didn't even have his license." Brooke shook her head in disgust. "I should have known. Deep down, I knew his drinking was a problem, but he always denied it. I'm just so thankful he didn't hurt anyone. Or worse."

"Did you know enough about the business to keep it running? Could you even run it . . . you know, *legally* . . . at that point?"

"I wasn't sure. But, despite everything, I'd felt like I'd found my niche. I loved the creative process and getting my hands dirty. I somehow figured out a way to keep the business going. I bought him out and he faded off into the sunset, never to be seen again." She lifted her wine glass in a joking toast. "I *hope*."

"Well, technically, he faded off to Baltimore to live with his cousin and work in a body shop," Seth said, "but we get your drift."

"Spoilsport," Brooke said. "My version sounds better. You're probably sorry you asked, Jess, but that's how I ended up in the tiling business and how I know Seth. Of course, I met your brother somewhere along the line in our day jobs, too. Ethan, how long ago did we meet?"

"Oh man, I don't know, maybe three years ago? Rex knew you before I did, suggested we use you on a few jobs."

"But enough about me." Brooke smiled at Jess. "I think it's someone else's turn to be on the hot seat."

"That wasn't as bad as I thought it might be," Jess said to Seth as they were driving back to Whispering Pines.

A heavy, wet snow was falling, and Seth was keeping a close eye on the road. "What wasn't so bad?" he asked, obviously only half listening.

"Never mind. Did you have fun tonight?"

"The food was good."

Jess turned toward Seth as he focused on the snow-covered road. " 'The food was good.' Is that all?"

"Jess, what do you want me to say?" He shrugged. "To be honest, I thought it was all a little weird."

"What do you mean?"

"Don't take this the wrong way, okay?"

Jess shifted again in her seat, staring out the front window at the snow. It was falling even harder now. "That opening doesn't usually bode well, but okay, I'll try not to take anything the wrong way. What's bugging you?"

"Ethan and Brooke. They just make such an odd couple."

That wasn't what she'd expected. "What do you mean?"

"I don't know. They just don't seem to have much in common. Ethan was pretty quiet tonight. I've known guys Brooke has dated in the past. They were all a lot more like Cameron. Loud and fun-loving. And by the way—they weren't all losers like Cameron turned out to be, either."

"Ethan can be fun-loving," Jess said, feeling defensive of her brother. "*Loud*, too."

"Hey, I told you not to take this wrong. I like Ethan, I really do. He seems like a great guy. He just has a lot on his plate right now, so I think it's odd that he's dating someone so much . . . I mean, so *different* from him."

Jess leaned her head back against her seat. "Tell me you didn't almost say 'so much younger.' That would be a bit ironic, don't you think?"

Jess felt the butterflies in her stomach roar to life. She was seven years older than Seth, and he insisted it was nothing, but their own age gap still felt strange to her sometimes.

He sighed. "I'm sorry, Jess. I know our age difference is a sore subject for you. And yes, that's what I almost said. But it's not really about their ages. It has more to do with where they're both at in life, you know? Ethan just got divorced a year ago and has three kids, two of whom are still at home, but not for long. I kind of think Brooke is at the point where she wouldn't mind finding someone and settling down. You know, have a couple kids, buy a house, get another dog. And she seems to like your brother quite a bit. But I doubt he's looking for the same thing. Unless he's looking for a new mom for the three kids he already has, which seems doubtful."

"I cannot believe you just said that!" Jess said, taken aback. "Ethan is my brother, and he is one of the most hardworking and caring men I know. That ex-wife of his took a lot from him and now she's barely acting like a mother. It's all falling on Ethan. But he is a good man."

Seth had to slow down as they caught up to a snowplow. They were on a two-lane highway and it was getting harder to see the road. She hoped he wouldn't try to pass the plow.

Seth seemed to be unapologetic. "You won't get any argument out of me on any of that, Jess. I'm just saying I think they are probably both looking for something different. Brooke is great, too. I think she deserves more."

"Why, Seth, are you *jealous*? Does it bother you that Brooke might actually *like* my brother?"

Seth eased his pickup into the passing lane ever so slightly, but glaring headlights and the blare of a horn pushed him back into his own lane. "Shit. I can't get around him. These roads suck. And don't be ridiculous! Why would I be jealous of Ethan where Brooke is concerned? It's not like that between me and Brooke. You know that."

Jess didn't respond. She wanted to believe him. It wasn't Seth's fault her own past had made it tough for her to trust a man again.

Maybe it's time to talk to someone about my *hang-ups,* she thought.

"I'm worried."

"Hmm?" Renee asked.

Jess sighed. She could tell her sister wasn't really listening. She was concentrating on their plan for the upcoming "New Year, New Beginnings" women's retreat. It was hard to believe it would be their third annual.

"I think I might have screwed things up with Seth last night."

Renee finally turned her full attention to her sister. She took off her reading glasses and set them down on the paperwork, pushing her chair back from her kitchen table. Jess could practically read the *I told you so* in her eyes. "What did you do?"

Jess squirmed under her sister's judgmental stare. "Nothing that made *Ethan* uncomfortable. He has way too much on his plate to pile any more on about his new girlfriend."

"You must have said something to Seth, then."

Jess took a deep breath before opening up.

"I'm such an idiot. The evening went well—better than I expected, in fact. Brooke did most of the talking at dinner. I asked her how she got into the business she's in—you know, running her own tiling business—and that opened a whole big discussion about an ex of hers who was the brother to Seth's roommate at the time."

"Wait," Renee said. "Seth and Brooke never dated? I thought you said they went out before."

"Technically, I think I said I *thought* they must have dated before because of how friendly they seemed. But based on their comments last night, now I don't think so. This other guy and Seth were friends. Remember me talking about Dawn, the mother to Seth's daughter Kaylee? Apparently, Brooke dated Dawn's brother. His name is Cameron. I guess it all ended badly."

Jess took Renee's nod to mean she was following so far. Renee had met Kaylee when Seth brought her to their Halloween party at Whispering Pines a month earlier.

"To be clear," Renee said, "Brooke and Seth never dated?"

Jess let out a frustrated grunt and got up from the table to pace the kitchen. "Probably not."

"So you're jealous of a relationship that's based on friendship. Jess, that's not good."

Jess groaned. "But they seem *so* friendly."

"Jess, think about it. Their relationship sounds an awful lot like one *you* personally share with another man."

Jess stopped her pacing in front of the kitchen sink to gaze out at their shared backyard, white now with last night's fresh blanket of snow. Dark green pines stood out in stark contrast, rimming the backside of the yard. The trees were dense, making it nearly impossible to see far into the woods.

Jess didn't like not knowing what was hiding out there—just like she didn't like not knowing enough about Seth's past. But really, as far as she could tell, he'd been honest with her. *She* was the one with the problem.

Renee was right, too. Jess knew exactly who Renee was referring to, but she'd never considered that her relationship with Grant Johnson might be similar to the one between Seth and Brooke. Grant was the twin brother to Jim, Renee's first husband who'd died twelve years ago. While Jess adored Grant, and would defend him against the world, they'd never had a romantic relationship. They'd considered it, but ultimately decided they valued their friendship too much to risk it.

Maybe that's how it is between Seth and Brooke, too.

"It pains me to admit this, sis, but you're right. If Seth was jealous of my friendship with Grant, I'd think he was being ridiculous. It's probably no different for Seth as far as Brooke is concerned. We don't get to this point in our lives without plenty of history behind us. No one lives in a vacuum for the first forty or fifty years of their lives." She turned from the window. "I think I owe Seth an apology."

Renee stood, dumped her cold cup of coffee down the sink, and stood next to her sister, her arm around Jess's shoulders. "I suspect you do. Seth's a great guy. He understands you're damaged goods. He'll probably forgive you."

It was a joke, but Jess hoped she was right.

Chapter Fourteen
Gift of Observations

Ten days after the fire, Rex was able to leave the hospital. He wasn't cleared to go back to work yet, but he could go home. He'd need to focus on recovery, including physical therapy.

"I don't see why you feel the need to drive me home like I'm a little kid," Rex complained from the passenger seat in Ethan's truck.

Ethan thought back to the pain reflected in Rex's face when he'd climbed into his pickup just minutes earlier. There was no way the man could drive. Rex's heavy work boots had protected his feet and ankles from the flames, but burns from his shins to above his knees would need time to heal. At this point, he was refusing to take anything stronger than over-the-counter meds to control the pain. Despite Rex's complaints to the contrary, Ethan knew this first trek home would take a lot out of his friend.

"Knock it off, Rex. Those legs have to hurt like a bitch," he said, glancing down at Rex's lower legs before backing out of his parking spot. "If they hadn't pulled you out of there when they did, you'd have more than just your legs to worry about."

"Don't even joke about that," Rex growled—but the way he squirmed told Ethan his friend picked up on what he was implying.

Tempting as it was to continue to tease Rex, Ethan decided today wasn't the day. Normally, he'd give his friend a hard time about how little he'd dated ever since losing his wife, but Rex wasn't in the mood for bantering. His wife's death had been so long ago that Ethan didn't usually have a problem teasing Rex about what he assumed was a lack of a sex life. In fact, since he found himself in a similar boat these days, he felt justified.

But not today.

"Do you have any food in your house?" Ethan asked instead. He dreaded the thought of having to make a grocery run, but he'd do it for Rex if need be.

"Unless the grocery fairies broke into my house while I've been laid up, there's about a hundred percent chance the fridge and cupboards are bare."

Ethan suppressed a sigh. "I'll run and pick you up a few things, then, after you get settled."

Rex was quiet for a moment, then he said in a sober voice, "Ethan . . . I'm sorry. I know what a burden this is on you, me being out of commission and all. If I'd have just listened to you in the first place and not gone in to do some work on Saturday, I wouldn't have been anywhere near the fire—and I wouldn't be compounding your problems now. Not only are you having to do your job *and* my job right now, you're playing nursemaid to me, too."

"You'd do the same for me, man, so don't even mention it. In fact, you *have* been doing the same for me."

Rex raised his eyebrows in a question.

"You've been a huge help since Stacey left," Ethan said. "You're even saving Elizabeth's butt right now by letting her use your spare car."

Rex scoffed. "We're not even close to even."

They rode the rest of the way to Rex's in silence. Ethan longed to ask Rex about some of the things the police had insinuated the previous week regarding his potential involvement in the fire itself, but Rex was in a lot of pain. Besides, Ethan still doubted any of it was true. Rex was a true friend, and he'd never do something so stupid as to put people's lives or Ethan's business at risk.

He wished the officers had never put those tiny seeds of doubt in his head.

When Ethan pulled into the driveway, Rex opened his door and started to climb out. "I can get it from here. No need for you to come in. Thanks again."

Despite Rex's bravado, Ethan could see the blood drain out of his friend's face as he took his first couple steps. The pain level must be getting out of control again. He grabbed Rex's duffle bag out of the pickup box and caught up with him halfway up the driveway. He wasn't entirely sure Rex was going to make it into the house without keeling over, but Ethan tried to be nonchalant as he walked beside him.

"I'll warn you, the house might be a mess. When I left, I thought I'd be home in a couple of hours, not damn near two weeks."

Rex slid his key in the door and pushed it open, leaning heavily against the doorjamb to catch his breath. The stench of rotting garbage floated out the door.

"You maybe should have thought to ask me to come over and dump your garbage before today," Ethan said, trying in vain to wave away the stink.

"Maybe you should have thought to offer."

"Touché. I'll take it out now," Ethan said, fighting the urge to cover his nose with his shirt as he entered the house in front of Rex. "Hey, when did you get a cat?"

"What the f—"

"Just kidding, bud," Ethan said, laughing. "Here—you better sit before you fall down."

Ethan pulled a chair away from the dining room table and placed it closer to the door. Rex sank gratefully into it.

"I may just spend the rest of my day right here," he said, bending down to try to take his shoes off.

"You sit there and catch your breath. I'm going to get that garbage out and open some windows.

"Ethan, it's ten degrees outside."

"Cold air is better than garbage-scented air. It'll air out quick."

Ethan headed back to the kitchen. He'd been in Rex's house plenty of times, so he knew his way around. Normally Rex was a relatively neat housekeeper.

How hard could it be to pick up after yourself?

This was why the sight that met Ethan in the kitchen surprised him so much. Besides the garbage piled high in the trash can in the corner, there was a stack of dirty dishes in the sink, an open pizza box on the island . . . and three bottles of booze on the counter. Luckily the pizza box only contained grease stains and crumbs. When Ethan tried to get the stuffed trash bag out of the garbage can, a nearly empty carton of milk tumbled out. The stench made him gag.

"You all right in there?" Rex hollered from the front of the house. "Sorry about the mess."

Ethan wrestled the bag out and tied it tight, not wanting any further surprises to fall out. He found a spray bottle of kitchen cleaner under the sink and doused the puddle of curdled milk on the floor before he took the bag out.

"You might want to consider hiring a cleaning lady there, slob boy, if your kitchen looks like that every day. How can you live like this?"

Rex put his hands up in defense. "Relax. I warned you. It doesn't *usually* look like that. I was in a hurry and planned to clean it up when I got home."

This mess didn't just accumulate overnight and you were not *in a hurry,* Ethan thought, but didn't comment out loud. *You were killing time at the jobsite instead of taking the weekend off.*

"Leave it, I'll clean it up tonight," Rex ordered, but his voice lacked conviction.

Ethan ignored him and spent the next twenty minutes cleaning the kitchen. At some point, Rex managed to make it from his perch next to the front door to the recliner in front of the television. Ethan heard the set turn on and then the muffled voices and canned laughter of a sitcom.

Ethan checked his watch—only an hour until he needed to pick up Dylan at school.

He went to ask Rex what he wanted from the grocery store, but the guy was already asleep in the chair.

No wonder he went quiet.

Not wanting to disturb him, Ethan grabbed the solitary bottle of water out of the fridge and checked the cupboards for something he could leave out for Rex to eat if he woke up and was hungry before he could get back. A packaged stick of jerky and a bag of chips were all he could find. He set them on the end table next to the water. His toe kicked something hidden under the table. He scooped up a glass beer bottle before it could roll far on the wooden floor, cringing at the noise he was making.

I'm as noisy as the nurses Rex complained about in the hospital.

He threw away the beer bottle and left as quietly as he could.

Ethan squeezed in his trip to the grocery store before he picked up his son, filling the cart. Rex's fridge may have been as empty as a typical bachelor's, but his own was as empty as the home of two teenage boys. They'd swing by Rex's and put his food away before heading back to their apartment. Dylan would probably be anxious to see how Rex was holding up, anyway.

As Ethan made his way through the mass of parents picking up their kids around the middle school, his mind wandered. He couldn't help but be bothered by the mess he'd found in Rex's house. It wasn't the empty milk cartons and dirty dishes that bothered him—he was guilty of the same some days.

It was the bottles of booze.

Maybe Rex had people over?

But that didn't sound like him. Ethan knew Rex had the occasional drink if they all went out after work once in a while, but to sit at home and drink alone—more than an occasional beer . . . Ethan wouldn't expect that of Rex. There'd been a bottle of Jack Daniels, a bottle of tequila, and a bottle of vodka on the counter, all three in varying degrees of emptiness. There was also a half-empty case of beer in the fridge.

Damn those cops, he thought. *If they wouldn't have put those thoughts in my head, I would have just assumed Rex brought the bottles home from his brother's after their Thanksgiving celebration.*

Maybe *that* was it. Those jerk cops, filling his head with unfair ideas. Ethan reminded himself he had enough things to worry about right now and that he should pull his nose out of his friend's business. There was no way Rex had anything to do with the fire. And Rex was a grown man who could take care of himself.

The blaring of a horn pulled his attention back to the school parking lot. He needed to pay attention. There were kids everywhere now, darting between cars as they made their daily escape. He scanned the area for Dylan. The kid had shot up over the last year and now stood taller than many of his eighth-grade classmates, making him easier to spot.

Dylan found him first. He flung open the door, threw his backpack into the backseat of their extended cab, and climbed in. Ethan knew the backpack was heavy—he'd lifted it himself often enough. Dylan always lugged plenty of books home, but he didn't always pull them out once he got there. He hadn't yet developed the study habits of his older brother. He preferred sports and buddies to homework, but what thirteen-year-old didn't?

"How was your day?" Ethan asked.

"Same as always," Dylan said. "Wait. No. Actually, there was a fight in the lunchroom at noon. That was pretty cool."

If Stacey had picked Dylan up from school, Ethan knew she'd have scolded their son for a comment like that. He probably should have, too, but he understood that sometimes fights could be interesting—"pretty cool"—depending on the circumstances.

"Was there blood?" he couldn't help but ask, knowing full well he shouldn't condone fighting. He'd get the details *first* and then remind Dylan it was not okay to fight, at school or anywhere else.

"Yeah, but it was just a bloody nose. No big deal."

"A bloody nose might not look like a big deal, but when you're the one bleeding, it *is* a big deal." Ethan wasn't about to tell Dylan, but he'd been in a fight or two himself as a kid. "What were they fighting over?"

Dylan shrugged. "Someone said it was over a girl. You'd think it would take more than a girl. You get in big trouble, fighting in school."

"I don't know . . . when the heart's involved, you'd be amazed at what you're willing to risk."

"Ha. Not me!" Dylan proclaimed. "Not my style."

We'll see, Ethan thought. *That's something you need to experience firsthand before you understand.*

After they'd dropped the groceries off at Rex's and eaten supper at home, Ethan wanted to run over to Celia's house to check to see if his crew had finished installing the new flooring upstairs.

There I go, he thought, *calling it Celia's again.*

Because he'd been going solo ever since Rex got hurt, not much was getting done at Celia's. Moving in before Christmas had been his goal all along, but at this rate it wasn't going to happen. He'd reluctantly contacted his landlord and extended their month-to-month lease for thirty more days. Few people wanted to move in during December or January, so he got lucky; they hadn't rented their apartment out to anyone else yet.

Both boys wanted to come along. They hadn't been there for a month. Ethan suspected they also wanted to avoid hitting the books, but he welcomed their company. He needed it to start feeling like home.

"I can't wait to get out of this apartment and into the house," Drew said when they pulled up, as if he'd read Ethan's mind. They piled out of the truck. "Sharing a room with you sucks, Dylan. No offense."

"None taken. You suck, too."

"Now that we've all established how much you each suck, why don't you drop it before someone actually gets ticked off?"

"Why'd you park on the street, Dad?"

"Because there's three inches of snow on the driveway and, instead of driving over it, I'm going to let you two able-bodied young men grab those two shovels leaning against the side of the house over there and shovel it real quick."

"*That's* why you invited us along? Slave labor?" Drew said. "I should have known."

"Hey, no freeloading around here. Everyone helps."

"Yeah, yeah, yeah," Dylan said, but Ethan was already halfway up the walk leading to the front entryway, paying them little attention.

He flipped the light on as he entered, feeling a sense of pride. What used to be a tiny, cramped entryway was now open and spacious, flowing right into a wide hallway, with a room branching off on each side and an impressive staircase straight ahead. He was happy with the balance he'd accomplished throughout the house; he'd ushered it into the modern age while staying true to the bones and leaving glimpses of the past here and there.

Celia would be proud, too.

And what kind of a contractor would I be if I didn't show off at home?

The revamped staircase was a point of pride. A smooth wooden railing was supported with black iron spindles, graceful in their simplicity. The newel post at the bottom was original, but the craftsman he'd hired to help rebuild the new staircase married the different elements seamlessly.

The updates to the main floor were done.

During the planning phase—with input from Lizzy—he'd decided to forgo a separate dining room and instead repurposed it into an office.

Maybe now I'll be able to keep up with paperwork, he thought wryly.

To the left of the staircase was a comfortable living room, and behind was the kitchen. He could picture a Christmas tree in front of the bay window overlooking the front yard, just like Celia used to do.

Next year, Celia. Promise.

He was about to go upstairs when the boys stomped through the front door. It was good to hear the sounds of family in this house again. It had been too long. Celia had lived here alone—never having had children or a husband of her own—but Ethan and his siblings had visited often. He hoped Celia would have approved of what he'd done with her house.

"Take your shoes off!" he yelled over his shoulder as he started up the stairs.

Now I'm starting to sound *like Celia.*

She'd have skinned them as kids if they'd worn their shoes in the house.

The flooring in the hallway at the top of the stairs was safe now to walk on. He flipped more lights on, expecting to see a nearly finished upstairs.

What he saw was a mess of tools, empty water bottles, and a stack of yet-to-be-installed flooring. But he supposed he shouldn't be too surprised—he'd put one of the younger guys in charge of this project temporarily while Rex was laid up. Ethan tried to keep his temper in check. The kid obviously needed more direction. He'd talk to him in the morning. Give him a second chance. But if they left a jobsite like this again, his temporary leadership role would be even shorter than anticipated.

Not much had been done over the last two days. It was frustrating to be so close but not quite done.

Footsteps pounded up the stairs.

How can two teenagers make so much noise in their socks?

"Back here, guys," Ethan hollered.

Drew made his way over to Ethan, picking his way around the mess. "You can tell Rex's not running the show these days."

Ethan grinned. "Right? I'll talk to Jason in the morning, remind him this is *not* how we do things around here."

"Other than the mess, this looks great, Dad. Do I still get this room back here?" Drew asked as he wandered down to a room he'd tried to put dibs on months ago.

Ethan followed him. "I don't see why not. Nobody's fighting you for it, right?"

"Well," Drew said sheepishly, "Lizzy wasn't thrilled to get the smallest room. But she's not gonna be here much."

Ethan sighed. "It'll be more of a guest room, I suppose, but I still want to say it's hers. I want this to feel like home for her, even if she never really lives here. Who knows where she'll end up after college?"

Or where you or your brother will go?

Drew checked out the closet in the bedroom. "This is a really big house, Dad. Are you still sure you want to live here? I'll be gone after next year, too. You could probably sell it for a lot of money."

Ethan shrugged. "Guess I might just have to fill it up with family number two, if you three are all going to desert me."

Drew gave Ethan a strange look he couldn't interpret.

"What?"

Drew shrugged. "If Brooke has her way, that's probably what she wants."

Ethan didn't laugh. "Oh God, Drew, don't even say that. I was joking. You three keep me *plenty* busy."

"I don't know, Dad. Just callin' it like I see it."

Drew wandered off, probably to find Dylan or look into the rest of the rooms on this level.

Ethan didn't move. Drew's comments threw him for a loop. The thought of a second family with a younger wife wasn't anything he'd even *remotely* considered. And if she thought that was going to happen, he'd need to set her straight.

Chapter Fifteen
Gift of a Support System

Ethan rapped on Steve's office door. His lawyer had asked him to swing by at ten o'clock Monday morning. He'd already had one tough conversation today with Jason about how not to oversee a jobsite and crew; he was hoping this conversation with Steve would go better.

Jason did not appreciate constructive criticism. No surprise.

Ethan hoped the young worker would come back after lunch. While Jason wasn't stellar, Ethan thought he might have potential and workers were tough to come by these days.

"Come in," Steve said from behind the closed door.

Ethan let himself in and took the empty chair across the desk from his attorney. "Tell me you have good news."

"I have *news*—some good, some bad. What do you want to start with?"

"You pick," Ethan suggested. He could feel a headache coming on.

"All right, the good news. You can have your building back. You're free to go in, start cleaning up, whatever you need to do."

"About damn time. They deemed it structurally sound, then?"

"They did," Steve confirmed. "But remember, based on the pictures, there was a *lot* of damage. You're going to have to go in there with an open mind and a big bucket of patience."

Ethan sighed with relief. "I'll head over there this afternoon."

"That should be fine. But I have a suggestion. Bring someone with you . . . for moral support, if nothing else."

Ethan nodded. "You're right. It can't be Rex, I know. He's not getting around very well yet, either. I've got a couple people I can call."

"Good. I've also talked to your insurance agent. You need to call him when we're done here, and he can update you on how things will work from a reimbursement standpoint. But that's also where things might get complicated. That's the bad news, by the way."

Ethan still wore his jacket, but he was getting hot. Either the heat was turned up in Steve's office or all this talk about damage and complications was making him sweat. Given the heavy wool sweater Steve was wearing, Ethan was going to guess he was the only one feeling the heat.

"Are there questions about what my insurance will cover? Are they going to bail on me now, after all these years of being a good customer? I have all my company insurance through them—my cars, my rentals . . ."

Steve shook his head and Ethan stopped. He knew he had an annoying habit of rambling when he was avoiding what someone else needed to say.

"That's not exactly the problem," Steve said. "The *problem* is that, at this point, the fire marshal's investigation has been inconclusive. They're having trouble pinpointing the origin of the fire. Don't be surprised if the insurance company drags their feet in regards to paying out on any claims until they have more assurance that this fire wasn't intentional."

"Intentional? Are you kidding me? What is wrong with people? Accidents happen. Things malfunction. Not everything is a goddamned conspiracy."

Steve said nothing. He waited for Ethan to digest the news.

"Sorry—I know you're the messenger," Ethan apologized. "And I appreciate your help. What do you suggest I do now?"

Steve drummed his fingers on the desktop. "I think you need to go see how bad things look over there. Start to formulate a plan. I know I don't need to remind you about your three displaced tenants, so the sooner you can figure out what to do with them, the better. Regardless of where things land on insurance, you'll need to cover your deductible. Have you figured out where that money will come from yet?"

Ethan felt a wave of guilt at Steve's words. Last night he'd been wandering around his new home, trying to figure out how to get his own family in before Christmas, when he should have been more focused on his tenants. At least he and his kids had a place to live that already felt a bit like home.

"I'll have to figure out the money for the deductible. But, to be clear, do I have the green light to talk to my tenants now?"

"Yes," Steve confirmed. "I'm sorry if I came across as cold-hearted before. I was just trying to protect you."

And that's ultimately what I'm paying you to do, Ethan thought. As to where the money would come from to cover his deductible . . . he hadn't the slightest. He'd need to figure that out, and soon.

"Sounds like I have plenty I can get started with, so I better get to it," Ethan said, standing to leave. "Any other words of wisdom for today, Steve?"

"Maybe, but you aren't going to like it."

"Give it to me anyhow. You're usually right about things."

Steve stood up from his desk, hands on his hips.

"Look, I know you and Rex are friends . . . but you may want to think about finding a new foreman. It's good you aren't taking him over there with you today. Depending on how this investigation goes, Rex might not be the man for the job anymore."

"You're right that Rex and I are friends, Steve, but this time you're wrong about the rest. We've been through a lot together, Rex and I, and I'm not about to end any of that because someone who doesn't know Rex is throwing around unfounded accusations."

Steve nodded, his face grim. "I hope you're right, Ethan. Just be careful that your loyalty isn't misplaced."

There were decisions to be made and lots of work to do. Ethan thought back over Steve's advice time and again as he drove over to his parents' house. He'd called ahead and knew George was home.

"I'm glad I caught you, Dad," he said as he strode into the kitchen where George was at the counter making a sandwich. "Got enough of that for me?"

"Sure, help yourself. Your mother is out, so it's just us boys. What brings you by?"

Ethan grabbed the loaf of bread and began making himself a ham sandwich. "I just left my attorney's office."

"Got news? About the fire?"

Ethan plopped his sandwich onto a plate, grabbed a bottle of water out of the fridge, and joined George at the kitchen table. His father had given him plenty of advice through the years, right here at this very table. He hoped he could help him out today, too.

"Yep. I can get back in the building now. See for myself what I'm up against and how soon, if at all, I can get my tenants back in. Steve reminded me that my tenants should be my top priority. He's right, of course."

"I'd say that's good news, son. At least you can move ahead now, instead of feeling like you're in limbo. When are you heading over there? Today?"

"Thought I'd go when I'm done here. What are you doing this afternoon?"

"Sounds like I'll be walking through a burned building."

Ethan took a bite of his sandwich, nodding. "I'd hoped you'd say that. I'd take Rex, but he isn't in any shape to be trudging around over there yet. But . . . Dad . . . the air might still bother your asthma, so you don't have to come. Mom won't like it."

George gave him a mischievous grin around a bite of sandwich. "She's not here, so if we hurry up, we can leave before she gets home."

Ethan laughed. "Really? Sneaking around behind her back is your answer?"

"It isn't 'sneaking,' son. I like to think of it more as *strategic avoidance of an anticipated argument.* In the end, I'd go anyhow, because you need my help. Best to skip the argument part altogether."

Ethan stuffed the rest of his sandwich in his mouth and cleaned up their mess. "Better not leave this out. Just so she's not pissed at *me*, too."

"Don't worry about your mother, I can handle her."

"Yeah, right, Dad. If you say so."

George grabbed his winter coat, hanging on a hook by the back door, and sat down on a strategically placed bench to put on his shoes. "Did you call anyone else to come along?"

"No, why? Did you have a suggestion?"

"Maybe. Since Rex can't join us, what about Seth?"

Ethan scooped his keys off the kitchen table. "Seth, huh? That's a good idea. Wonder if he's around."

George stepped out onto his back steps, waiting for Ethan so he could lock the door. "He'd be able to add a practical perspective. If he's free, of course. He might not even be in town."

"I'll give him a call."

Ethan's stomach rolled when they pulled up in front of his damaged fourplex. He'd driven by every day since the fire, keeping an eye on things from a distance, but now he'd see how bad it was inside.

The air was cold. Bright sunlight emphasized the soot staining the walls. Snow blanketed much of the mess that he knew lay on the ground underneath.

"Be *really* careful, Dad. There's likely lots of ice everywhere from the water they used to put out the fire. It's been below freezing most of the time since it happened. Mom will *kill* me if you fall and break a hip."

"While I appreciate your concern, son, the next time you allude to me being a feeble old man, I'll smack you up alongside the head."

"Point taken."

"Now let's get in there," George said. "Or should we wait for Seth?"

Ethan headed toward the front doors. "No—he's coming over, but he said to go ahead and get started. He'll be here shortly."

The two men approached the building, frozen grass crunching under their boots. They walked on the lawn instead of the sidewalk for better traction. Ethan could already smell the remnants of the fire, and they weren't even inside yet.

He pulled a small ring of keys out of his pocket and unlocked the front door. What had been a light-filled entryway, thanks to the white walls plus a transom over the front door, was now dim and dirty. The bright sunlight couldn't penetrate the grime. It didn't appear the flames had reached this area, but there was still damage.

"Up or down?" George asked.

"Let's start upstairs and work our way down," Ethan suggested. "Let me go first. I've got the keys."

They entered the unit in the upper south side of the building first—the unit Marvin rented. A greasy soot covered everything. The fire must have traveled up the back outer wall. A four-by-eight section of sheetrock was torn off, revealing charred insulation. Surprisingly there didn't appear to be much water damage, but the amount of cleanup necessary to make the place habitable again was mindboggling.

"You're gonna want to get a service in here as soon as possible. Specialists in this kind of thing. The worst of it appears to be concentrated in this area," George said, motioning toward the back wall. "The bedroom and bathroom have a nasty glaze of soot over everything, too, but nothing like this."

They continued to walk through Marvin's unit but didn't find much else. George flipped a faucet on, but of course there was no water. Since the furnace was shut down, the water needed to be turned off so the pipes wouldn't break.

As they continued the walkthrough, discussing the ever-growing list of things that needed immediate attention, Seth yelled from downstairs.

"Up here!" Ethan replied.

He could hear Seth on the stairs, calling up as he climbed. "Got here as quick as I could. How are things lookin'?"

"Like a big frigging mess," Ethan said as Seth entered the unit. "We've already checked out this first unit. See what you think and then find us over here."

Seth nodded and Ethan and George moved over to Mrs. Jarvis's side.

George whistled. "Damn," he breathed, taking in the damage.

"This is bad," Ethan agreed. "I was afraid it'd be worse than Marvin's unit, since they said the fire likely started in the unit beneath this one. I'm not sure if much of this is even going to be salvageable."

George again moved from room to room. Ethan took more time. Two walls showed damage. He was concerned about the integrity of the framing as well as the wiring and pipes within the walls.

Seth joined them, clasping Ethan on the back, his expression grim.

"I don't know, bud. There's some pretty serious damage in these units. Even if the shell of the building is still sound, it might be a total gut job. Soot like this is nearly impossible to clean off of things."

"I tried to prepare myself for this, but I don't know if you really can, you know? To see all of their things, so filthy and probably ruined, makes me sick. Thank God no one died in here."

There was a beat of silence where none of them spoke.

"Come on," Ethan said. "Let's go check out the downstairs unit I was remodeling. It sounds like that was where it started."

They locked up Penelope's unit and headed back down the stairs. The door was missing from the unit in question. And it certainly *did* look like the fire was concentrated near the oven: the walls, floor, and ceiling in the kitchen were scorched.

A wave of despair washed over Ethan. Seeing this now, he knew Rex was extremely lucky to have made it out alive.

If they wouldn't have found him in time . . .

Ethan left George and Seth in the burned unit. He'd inspect it more closely later. He couldn't take much more right now.

Instead, he went into Norman's unit. This last one seemed to have fared better than the others. The fire must have traveled up and over. There was smoke damage, some greasy soot, but little else.

Just as he was about to inspect the bedroom, he paused. He had the strangest feeling he wasn't alone. But he was the only one here—he could hear Seth and his dad talking next door. He moved slower, approaching the closed bedroom door with caution. He turned the doorknob and slowly pushed it open.

He froze. Someone was there in the dark, lying on the bed, unmoving.

What the . . . ?

"Who's there?!" the prone figure yelled, apparently startled awake.

"I could ask you the same thing," Ethan said, clutching his chest. "Are you *nuts*, Norman? You should *not* be in here! There's no heat or water. It isn't safe yet!"

Norman, the apartment's renter, swung his feet off the side of the bed and pushed up into a sitting position. "Goodness, Ethan, you startled me. I know I shouldn't stay in here long. I just came to pick up a few things, but I got dizzy for some reason and had to lie down. I must have fallen asleep. And then you scared the tar out of me."

"Who told you it was all right to come in here?" Ethan asked, still shocked to find the man inside.

Norman shrugged. "No one told me *not* to."

Ethan noticed an open suitcase on a chair in the corner. He sighed, trying to relax. "Come on. I'll help you get what you need, but then you need to get out of here. Your unit is in the best shape of the four, but until we can get the utilities and such up and running, and get someone in here to clean this, you can't stay."

Norman cautiously rose to his feet, as if concerned they might not support him.

"Are you sure you're okay?" Ethan asked, concerned.

"Yes, yes, I'm fine. My clothes in the drawers smell smoky, but at least they aren't covered in soot. The dresser was shut tight. I'll take them to the laundromat and pray the smell comes out. I can't afford to buy a whole new wardrobe."

Ethan didn't respond, not knowing what to say. Instead, he helped Norman add a few more things to the large suitcase. George and Seth heard their voices and came over, nearly as shocked as Ethan to see someone else inside the building.

"I thought you were talking on the phone at first," Seth said, shaking his head in disapproval.

"We nearly gave each other a heart attack," Ethan said, trying to laugh. "We're just grabbing a few things and then we can go. I've seen enough for one day."

Together the four of them locked up and went outside. Ethan insisted on carrying the suitcase for the older man.

"Can we give you a lift somewhere?" Ethan asked Norman. He looked around but didn't see a vehicle nearby, other than his and Seth's.

"That would be superb. I walked from the bus stop a block over, but I didn't have anything to carry on the way here," Norman said, gesturing at the large case now sitting on the sidewalk next to them. "If I go trudging down the street wheeling that thing, I'll look like I'm homeless."

The old man laughed, but the sound broke Ethan's heart.

Chapter Sixteen

Gift of Old Friends

Now that he'd had a chance to get inside the apartment building, he needed to see Rex again. He couldn't shake the despair that enveloped him when he saw the charred remains of the kitchen where they'd found his friend.

Rex was walking to his truck when Ethan pulled up.

"Man, you are one lucky son of a bitch," Ethan said when he reached Rex in the driveway. "I didn't realize *how* lucky until I saw that damn unit they pulled you out of."

"Hey to you too," Rex said in way of a greeting. He paused beside Ethan and shrugged. "You know me. Got nine lives."

"Not anymore, you don't. You used one or two up that day, maybe more. Where you headed?"

Rex pulled keys out of his jacket pocket and continued toward his pickup. "Physical therapy. Again. It's a legal form of torture. *And* I have to pay for it. Ridiculous."

He swung the door open and climbed in. Ethan caught the grimace of pain Rex wasn't able to mask.

"You sure you should be driving?"

Rex gave him a perplexed look. "You're kidding, right? I've been driving myself to therapy all week. Who else is going to haul my sorry ass around?"

Ethan paused. The man had a point, and if he was still trying to handle the pain with ibuprofen and nothing stronger, he was probably fine to drive.

Rex slammed his door but rolled down the window. "Sorry to rush off, but I've got an appointment. Speaking from experience, Nurse Nancy don't appreciate it if I'm late. What a battle axe, that one."

"I'll catch you later." Ethan backed out of the way as Rex shifted his vehicle into Reverse, but then he stopped.

Say it now, he told himself.

"Say, Rex . . . what was with all the bottles of booze sitting out on your counter when we got back from the hospital that first day?" He tried to play it off with a joke: "Looked like you had a party and didn't invite me."

Rex let the truck back up slowly until he was even with Ethan.

"I can't remember the last time I had a party at my house, with *or* without you," Rex replied through his still-open window.

"Things did get pretty rowdy over here after that one softball game," Ethan replied, thinking back to a late summer barbeque in Rex's backyard. But his friend was right—Rex's home wasn't exactly an entertainment mecca.

"Look, Ethan, if you're going to play detective, I'll play along. I'll be the cooperative witness. The bottles were sitting out because I'd taken them to my brother's for Thanksgiving. We didn't get around to finishing them off since Mom and I came back early, so I brought them home. Not about to leave perfectly good liquor there for them to drink without me. Sorry if I'm not a neat enough housekeeper for you."

Ethan regretted bringing it up. Rex was clearly irritated by his question. His friend didn't owe him any explanations as to how he lived his life outside of work.

"I get the message. I'll back off," Ethan said, literally taking another step back from Rex's truck. "Unless you want me to give you a ride?"

Rex started to roll up his window and back up yet again.

Ethan wrapped his fingers over the top edge of the window. Rex had to either stop or squish his fingers. He stopped.

"Thanks," Ethan said. "That would've hurt."

Rex just stared at him.

Ethan continued, "I just feel like you're still in lots of pain. Do you want me to go to therapy with you? You know, for moral support?"

Rex paused then finally nodded. "You're right. My legs still hurt like hell. That's *why* I'm going to therapy. To see if I can't do something about that. But no, I don't need a goddamn babysitter. I'll call you later."

Ethan watched his friend drive off, regretting having asked him about the booze bottles. The man was *cranky*. Maybe it was just the pain speaking.

"Thanks for letting me stop by, Rebecca," Ethan said as his old classmate opened the door of her hotel suite.

"I'm hoping you're here with good news," Rebecca said, stepping back to let him in. Her voice was still a bit guarded, but not as stony as when she'd first learned he was her mother's landlord.

"I wish I was," he replied, glancing around the set of rooms. This was a pretty swanky place. "Your mother is staying here with you, isn't she?"

Rebecca closed the door and followed Ethan into the room. "She is. She's lying down. Her stint in the hospital set her back. Since you aren't here with good news, I take it her apartment isn't ready yet?"

Ethan shook his head, feeling a deeper sense of regret than Rebecca would probably believe. "I'm sorry, Becca. They finally let me in there, and the damage *is* extensive. Some of your mother's things won't be salvageable, and what we *can* save will definitely need a good cleaning. There's greasy soot over everything. There was also some damage to a couple of her walls."

"That sucks . . . by the way, it's been a *really* long time since anyone's called me that," Rebecca said, her tone softening.

She sank down onto the small couch in the front room of the suite. Ethan didn't feel right sitting next to her, but the only two chairs both held suitcases. He remained standing.

She finally looked up and asked, "Any idea how long all of that will take?"

"I think we need to prepare ourselves. It could take months . . . maybe even until spring."

Ethan could see the despair in Rebecca's eyes.

"I need to get back," she said. "I've been away from home too long. I've been doing what work I can from here, remotely, but that option has about run its course. My boss threatened to fire me if I wasn't back by Monday. Plus, I can't afford this place much longer."

"Becca, I'm so sorry about all of this, I truly am," Ethan said. He knew his words did little to ease the dilemma Rebecca and Penelope faced, but he didn't know what else to say. "Is there anything I can do to help?"

The woman wiped at her eyes and sat up straighter. "No. It doesn't sound like you can help much, at least in the short term. We'll have to make some decisions. Right now, I'm leaning toward finding Mom another place to live. Permanently. I'm not sure she can wait months to get back in there—and even if she could, the steps might be too much."

"I understand," Ethan said, and he meant it. "Hopefully the insurance company will treat us all fairly. Your mom had renter's insurance, right?"

Rebecca stood, her stony expression back. "My mother's financial situation is none of your concern. Thank you for stopping by today with the update. We'll be in touch to let you know what we decide."

It was a clear directive to leave. Ethan wasn't sure what he'd said to turn her so frosty, but he suspected the answer to his question about renter's insurance was *no*. He started for the door. He could take a hint.

"Is that you, Ethan?" a voice came from the back bedroom.

He stopped. "Yes, Mrs. Jarvis, it's me. I just stopped by to check on you and give you some updates. But don't let me disturb your nap. Rebecca can update you later."

"Oh, nonsense. Wait a minute, I'm coming out."

Ethan glanced at Rebecca, who sighed, nodded, and went back to the bedroom, presumably to help Penelope get up.

Ethan couldn't believe the difference in Rebecca's mother. Shortly before the fire, she'd scolded him from the top of the stairs, small but feisty as ever. Now she looked frail, her thin white hair matted down around her head. She leaned heavily on her walker. Her sweater and slacks hung on her gaunt frame.

"When can I go home?" she asked, getting right to the point.

"I'm sorry, ma'am. I was finally able to get in the building to see how bad things are. Unfortunately, the damage is extensive. It'll take some time before it's safe for anyone to move back in."

"Well . . . *shit*," the old lady replied. Ethan had to bite his cheek to keep from laughing out loud. Though she looked frail, he'd be wise to remember she was still a tough old bird. If she could outlive four husbands—*If they're indeed all dead,* he amended—she probably wouldn't let a thing like this keep her down for long.

"Mrs. Jarvis, I promise we'll do all we can to get it cleaned up as quickly as possible. I'm so sorry it leaves you in a tough spot."

"Well, shit," the woman repeated, waving away his words. "Rebecca here will take care of me. It's her turn. I raised her and took care of her for eighteen-plus years, and now she can return the favor."

Rebecca caught his eye. If she was concerned he would mention her job troubles to Penelope, she shouldn't be. He would never do that.

"Mother, this isn't good news. You know we can't stay here forever."

"Of course we can't stay *here* forever, dear. It's too expensive. I'm not going to live forever, either. Hell, I'll be lucky if I live long enough to get back into my place, according to this handsome man. Say . . . didn't the two of you date once upon a time?"

This comment had both Rebecca and Ethan stammering.

"No, Mother, I've told you before. Ethan and I . . . we were just friends."

Technically that wasn't exactly true, and Ethan doubted Rebecca had forgotten. Then again, he no longer knew this woman standing next to his tenant. It had all been a very long time ago.

He remembered it quite differently. It was their freshman year of college. Ethan switched schools at the last minute, so he got paired with a random roommate. He and Ryan hit it off immediately. It would be the beginning of a fun, party-filled four years.

Ethan remembered two big dilemmas coloring his first year at college. The first was figuring out the bare minimum he had to study to pass his classes so he could stay there. The second was figuring out what to do about Rebecca. Becca had been Ryan's girlfriend since high school; they'd dated since they were sixteen. Ethan felt a strong attraction to her from the first time he met her, but he fought it. He wasn't *that* kind of guy. He'd never steal a girl away from someone else, especially a good friend.

But one night, after too much keg beer, Rebecca admitted to Ethan she had feelings for him, too. Ryan was away for the weekend, home for a family emergency. He'd even asked Ethan to "keep an eye on his girl" for him. When Ethan found himself alone in a bedroom of some frat house, staring into her eyes, he knew in his gut that this was not what his friend had in mind. They'd kissed. Only once, but it was one too many times.

After that, Ethan and Rebecca's friendship became stilted. Ethan dated a number of girls, and Ryan teased him about being a "ladies' man," joked that he must be trying to get over "the one who got away." His roommate never knew who it was Ethan was so anxious to forget.

Ethan even asked Rebecca's best friend, Stacey, out on a date when she came to town for a visit.

So much history, all so long ago. He hadn't thought about Rebecca for years, up until their chance meeting in the hospital. He'd lost touch with his old friends. As far as he knew, Stacey had, too.

"How is Ryan, by the way?" Ethan couldn't help but ask. He'd known the two got married once they finished college, but he'd noticed in the hospital that Rebecca didn't use Ryan's last name.

A shadow passed over Rebecca's eyes. "Ryan died."

That hit him like a punch in the gut. "Oh God . . . Becca, I'm so sorry. I had no idea. If I'd have known, I'd have reached out. How long ago did it happen?"

"We were still young," Rebecca said. "It was a freak accident. We were riding four-wheelers out at his uncle's farm. It was something so dumb, so seemingly inconsequential. We hit gravel and he lost control. I was wearing a helmet—he'd insisted I put it on—but there was only one. The hardest part was how it changed him. He survived the accident but never really recovered from it. He got out of bed, went through the motions, but he suffered a traumatic brain injury. In the end, he couldn't accept the man he'd become."

Ethan sat down before his legs could give out.

Suicide? Ryan?

"Look what you've done, Rebecca. You've upset the boy."

Rebecca sat down and laid a hand on Ethan's shoulder, very briefly.

"I'm so sorry," Ethan said again, still struggling to comprehend what he'd just learned. How could his friend have died and he'd never been told?

"And then you had to go and marry that man," Penelope said, her dislike of whomever *that man* was apparent in her tone. "Where did that get you? Other than divorced. If you'd have come back here, like I told you to, maybe you could have met up with Ethan again instead of that loser."

"Mother, you've said enough. Please stop," Rebecca said, standing and walking over to the door, holding it open. There was no mistaking her meaning. Ethan again started for the door, feeling like Rebecca would physically kick him out if he didn't get moving.

"You take care now, Mrs. Jarvis. Hopefully we can get all of this figured out before too long," Ethan said to the older woman.

"You better figure things out soon," she said. "Otherwise, we may need to move in with you."

Ethan knew she joked, but his mind flew to the big house Celia left him.

"Mom, stop with the kidding already," Rebecca said.

"Who says I'm kidding?"

Rebecca mouthed the word "sorry" to Ethan as he brushed past her on his way out.

"Don't worry about it," he whispered. "She's always been spunky."

"I heard that!"

Ethan pulled into the parking lot of the nursing home—the second of the three in town he'd planned on checking. He'd struck out at the first. Marvin wasn't there. Based on what Steve said, he might be at this one or the third.

Of his three tenants, Marvin was his favorite, although he'd never tell anyone else that. The man liked to visit. He didn't get out much, so when he saw Ethan, he'd talk his ear off if he got the chance. He would often talk about his wife, gone now some twenty years. He had a son and daughter, although they lived on the west coast and Ethan had never met them. His son was a firefighter—the irony of which wasn't lost on Ethan—and his daughter was a stylist to Hollywood stars. Ethan got the impression he was closer to his son.

Ethan couldn't be sure how much of the stories Marvin told about his kids was fact and how much was fiction. It didn't matter. Marvin simply liked the company.

Upon entering the sprawling, one-story building, Ethan inquired at the front desk whether or not Marvin Miller was a resident at this particular nursing home. The man at the desk took his name, asked him to wait, and disappeared around the corner, returning only a few minutes later with a big smile.

"Mr. Miller would like to see you. He's in Room 311. Right down that hall there."

Ethan thanked him and headed for the hallway, his gut filling with dread. It was the right thing to do, but still—he hated telling these folks they wouldn't be back in their homes for months yet.

A television was blaring from inside a room, so Ethan figured he'd found Marvin before he could even make out the small room number posted beside the door. He knocked on the doorjamb.

Marvin stood in front of the TV, aiming the remote at it, punching buttons. "Can't get this damn thing to turn off."

"Hello, Marvin. How are you doing?" Ethan asked, accepting the remote Marvin handed to him and clicking the television off.

"I'm doing just fine, Ethan, considering all this," Marvin said, motioning around at his spartan surroundings. The only spot of color was a small blanket laid across the foot of his bed.

Ethan eyed the blanket with curiosity. Marvin noticed.

"Some good Samaritans came around the first weekend I was here and gave me one. A kid stopped in here. Talked my ear off, too."

What are the odds? Ethan thought with a chuckle. Aloud he asked if the kid was his height or a few inches shorter. He was sure either Drew or Dylan gave him the blanket.

"Shorter. Why?"

"I suspect that good Samaritan was Drew, my middle kid," Ethan said.

Marvin shook his head. "Small world, isn't it? Is this just a social visit, then, or are you here to tell me I can move home tomorrow?"

"Why don't we find a place to sit and talk? I'll tell you what I know up to this point," Ethan said. "Do you want me to pull another chair in here, or would you rather go out to the commons area?"

"Let's go out there. These four boring walls are going to be the death of me if I don't get a break from them."

Ethan let Marvin lead the way, dreading with every step the conversation that would follow.

Once they were seated in comfortable club chairs in front of a bright set of windows, Ethan reported on his recent visit to their building. Marvin didn't interrupt, which was rather unusual for the old man. When Ethan finished, he paused, waiting for Marvin's reaction. What the man said was worse than Ethan had expected.

"Son, do you have any idea what they charge in this place? One month will deplete my savings. Where will I go? I'll be out on the streets."

Ethan took a deep breath. He didn't doubt Marvin's claim. He'd heard the horror stories of the cost of nursing and assisted-living homes. "I vow I will not let that happen, Marvin. We'll figure something out. Trust me on this. In the meantime, can your kids help you out at all?"

Marvin grunted. "Nah. I might have embellished their level of success a bit in the past. A guy wants to be proud of his kids, you know? But my son's been on disability for over a year now, and my daughter, she isn't exactly a stylist to the stars. She's more like a . . . *server* to the stars. As in, barmaid. At a titty bar in Vegas, no less. So, no, they're not in any position to help out their old man."

Ethan hated hearing the truth about Marvin's kids, although it might help to explain why he'd never met them. It didn't sound like either would be able to afford a plane ticket to come visit, let alone help Marvin pay for nursing-home care.

Ethan didn't dwell on what Marvin shared. What would be the point? And the man was clearly embarrassed to admit the truth. Instead, he tried to brainstorm options with him.

"Do you think you're able to live on your own?" Ethan asked. "That's a pretty big wrap on your right hand. Did you get burned?"

Marvin gave a brief nod, but rested his right hand in his lap and covered it with his undamaged, left arm, as if wanting to hide his weakness. "Course I can live alone. They just stuck me in here because there was nowhere else for me to go on such short notice. The smoke made it hard for me to catch my breath for a time, but I'm all right now. I'm actually paid up here until the end of the year, but I'm going to have to have a new plan figured out by New Year's, which is coming on faster than I'd wish."

"Let me start working on that," Ethan said.

Ethan knew he should be careful not to overcommit. But he didn't care. He couldn't be sure how any of this was going to turn out for any of them.

But I have to try.

Chapter Seventeen
GIFT OF OPTIONS

"ETHAN, YOU NEED TO get over here to my office right away. We need to talk."

Ethan stared at the now-silent phone in his hand. He knew Steve's abrupt phone call couldn't be good; his lawyer wasn't normally a man prone to theatrics. He tossed his clipboard full of measurements for the Klondike project onto his passenger seat and drove straight over to Steve's. His attorney's office door was ajar and no one else was around, so Ethan pushed in without so much as a knock.

"What's up?"

"They're charging Rex with arson."

Steve's words brought Ethan up short.

"I'm sorry, what did you just say?"

"You heard me right," Steve said, loosening his tie as he stood and closed the door behind Ethan. He motioned to a chair. "Take a seat. I know this isn't what you want to hear, but the police just called. They feel confident they have enough evidence to charge Rex with arson. They think he started the fire, probably in a drunken stupor, although they're unclear as to motive."

Ethan kicked the chair in front of Steve's desk in frustration. "You do know how preposterous that is, don't you, Steve?"

Steve nodded, motioning again for Ethan to sit down. "Please, Ethan, I know you're upset, but use my chairs for sitting."

Ethan spun the kicked chair around and sat, feeling stupid for his outburst. A framed photograph behind Steve's desk caught his eye. The shot was of Steve and a guy Ethan didn't know, smiling at the camera. Steve's arm was draped over the man's shoulders and it looked like they were on a golf course.

"Who's that?"

Steve glanced where Ethan was pointing. "A close friend of mine," he replied as he sunk back into his black leather office chair behind his desk, unbuttoning the top button of his dress shirt. "We've played golf together for years, ever since law school."

Ethan nodded. "You two look to be good friends. How would you feel if someone accused him of doing something terrible, something you *knew* in your gut your buddy would *never* do? How would you feel about that, Steve?"

Steve stared at the picture, silent for a moment, before turning his eyes back to meet Ethan's expectant look. "Ethan, the fact is, it doesn't matter what we think or how we feel about this. What matters is the evidence they think they have."

Ethan put his head in his hands. He needed to think. He needed to pay attention and not lose his cool. There had to be a way to prove Rex had nothing to do with the fire.

Then a thought struck him. He looked up.

"Does Rex know yet?"

"They were heading over there at three o'clock, so"—Steve checked the Rolex on his wrist—"yes, I would say he does."

Shit! Shit, shit, shit!

"Let's go then. We need to go talk to Rex."

But Steve hesitated. "Ethan . . . I think Rex should get a lawyer of his own. These things can be tricky. It would be difficult for me to defend both *your* best interests and Rex's at the same time."

Ethan noticed Steve's quick glance at the picture of him and his golfing buddy.

"What the hell does that mean? Our interests are not mutually exclusive," Ethan said, hating to admit what Steve was saying might make sense. "As his employer, shouldn't I provide legal counsel?"

"I wouldn't advise it."

"It wouldn't be the first time I didn't like your advice," Ethan said, frustrated.

Steve let out a heavy sigh. "I appreciate how tough this is to hear, Ethan."

"Do you? Do you really? I went and talked to my tenants today. Well, two of them at least. I already talked to the third, but only because he showed up uninvited. I told them it's going to be quite a while before the building is livable again. It's putting everyone in a terrible position."

"I figured you would be in touch with them. Just tell me you didn't make them any promises," Steve said.

"Well, maybe a little. Dammit, Steve, I'm *responsible* for these people. I can't just leave them out in the cold. Literally. And I feel responsible for Rex, too. He was working on *my* building when he got hurt."

"I know you want to do the best you can by all of them, Ethan. The problem is, we don't know what that means yet."

Ethan grunted. He refused to be a jerk to his tenants or his best friend, regardless of how his uptight lawyer thought he should handle things.

Rex posted bail. Or, more accurately, his brother posted bail *for* him. Ethan would have to thank him. Maybe the guy wasn't a total schmuck after all.

When Ethan called Rex and asked if it was all right if he stopped over, Rex didn't say no. He didn't say much, other than in regards to the bail.

Ethan parked in the driveway and headed straight for the front door. He pounded on it, and when Rex didn't answer, he tried the doorknob. It was unlocked.

He let himself in, yelling for Rex as he went. The house was silent. It felt empty. A flicker of motion through the kitchen window caught his eye. Rex was out back, sitting in a lawn chair, staring into space.

Ethan checked the fridge and grabbed two beers. He let himself out the back door, handed Rex one of the bottles, and sat down, saying nothing at first. The air felt frigid as they sat silently on patio chairs, watching the horizon blaze with the setting sun.

Eventually, the silence started to get to him. Ethan leaned forward, the chair creaking and the snow crunching at his feet.

"We need to talk about this," Ethan said, glancing at Rex's stony expression.

"Do you believe what they're saying about me?"

Now Ethan turned to more fully face his friend. "Of *course* not. I don't believe a word of it. Come on, Rex, you know me better than that. And I know *you* better than that, too. You would never do something like that. *Why* would you ever do something like that?"

"Enough people obviously think I would."

"How did you get out on bond so fast? I know you said your brother paid the bail, but it's only been like . . . what . . . an hour?"

Rex set the glass bottle down on the icy deck, the beer untouched.

"I know this guy. He's a lawyer. I'd called him before, when the police were asking a bunch of questions. My gut told me I better be prepared. When they hauled me in, I gave him a call and he got busy. Bryan helped me out on the financial end. And here we are."

Ethan sat back in his chair, cradling his beer between his hands. He'd grabbed them out of habit but wasn't any more interested in drinking it than Rex seemed to be.

He was surprised to hear Rex had already reached out to another lawyer. While Ethan had done his best to ignore the suspicions around Rex, his friend had taken the situation much more seriously. Luckily.

"I thought you might want to work with Steve," he said aloud.

"Nah, I thought I better find someone a bit more . . . *independent* of the whole deal."

"Funny—Steve suggested the same thing today."

"Look, Ethan, maybe you shouldn't be here. Maybe we should keep some distance until this whole ugly mess sorts itself out," Rex said, picking his beer up from the frozen ground as he stood.

At least his movements seemed less awkward.

His burns must be healing.

"Do you really think that's necessary?" Ethan asked, hurt that his friend would put this wall up between them.

"I do."

Ethan stood up as well. "I'll respect your wishes . . . for now. But I promise you, Rex, we're going to figure this out. I *know* you aren't guilty of anything—more than working too much, at least."

He turned to leave, but he paused when Rex spoke.

"I hope you still feel that way when they share all the evidence with you. Because it looks bad, Ethan. It looks really bad."

"I don't know what to do, Dad. I've got three displaced tenants and a foreman accused of arson. I've got a building with significant damage, shitty weather, and an insurance company that's dragging their feet on paying anything out. Got any suggestions?"

Ethan had headed over to his folks' house when he left Rex's. They'd always been a good sounding board for his troubles through the years—although his troubles now seemed ten times worse than ever before. Lavonne was out at Whispering Pines, helping Renee or Jess with something, so only George was home. A roast was cooking in the oven. They sat at the kitchen table, steaming cups of black coffee in front of each of them. Ethan didn't drink that beer at Rex's, and he was glad for that.

"I'll admit, things look pretty bleak right now, son," George acknowledged, warming his hands on his cup. Ethan suspected his father's arthritis was acting up again, although he never complained. "What you need to do is focus on the things you *can* control."

"It doesn't feel like I can control *anything* these days, Dad."

George shook his head. "But you can. Let's start with the building itself. Why don't you get your crew in there and start the cleanup process?"

"I've been hesitant to do that because I'm not sure if, or when, insurance will start paying. How will I pay my crew?"

"You'll figure it out, son. Let's take a step back. Worst-case scenario: insurance doesn't pay because they find some loophole like suspected arson. Now"—he held his hands up, preempting Ethan's response—"before you get all ticked off, I'm not suggesting Rex had anything to do with it. But that doesn't mean someone else couldn't have started that fire."

"But who would do that, Dad?"

"I have no idea, son. But set that to the side for now. If there is no insurance payment, what will you do?"

Ethan grimaced down at his coffee. "I haven't wanted to consider that."

"Ethan, I learned a long time ago that denial is *not* a course of action. I promise you, you'll feel better if you have a plan for the various ways this could play out. Humor me on this. *What would you do?*"

Ethan took a minute to think about how best to answer his father's question. What *could* he do?

"All right, I'll play along . . . I have a mortgage on the building that's equal to about sixty percent of the building's value, pre-fire. I can cover the monthly payments for about six months with the money Aunt Celia set aside for unexpected costs related to the fourplex—bless her soul. I haven't touched that emergency fund up to this point."

George raised his coffee in a toast to Celia. "Good. So that'll keep the bank off your back for a bit. Do you have people you could put to work on the building?"

"I don't want to pull my one crew off the rehab project they're doing for a customer out in the hills . . . but I *could* pull the ones working on my remodel project over at Celia's old house and put them on the fourplex instead. Dylan and Drew won't like it, but . . ."

George nodded. "Good. You wouldn't be bailing on paying customers that way. Your kids will understand. Your crew could shift gears and start the cleanup process ASAP. You'll also need someone in there as soon as possible to get the heat and water back up and running."

Ethan stood and rummaged around in his parents' junk drawer. There were always pens and paper in there. He sat back down and started making notes, speaking while he wrote.

"I'll call my furnace guy when we're done here. With any luck, a cleaning will be all that's needed there. The heating unit is downstairs, but on the opposite side of where most of the fire actually burned. Fingers crossed. No sense doing anything with the water until the heat is back on. Busted pipes are the last thing I need. We got lucky when that didn't happen at the time of the fire. I owe someone at the fire department a big thank-you for getting the water shut off and enough water drained out of the pipes so we didn't have further damage."

Ethan's cell rang. He glanced at the screen: *Brooke*. He'd call her later. Maybe. He really didn't have time right now.

He and his father continued talking through the logistics of getting some balls rolling.

"Outside of the building itself," George said, "it sounds like your main concerns are the charges against Rex and the tough situations your tenants find themselves in. You aren't going to like to hear this, Ethan, but the deal with Rex may be one of those things that is beyond your control. I know you want to help him. So do I. But until the officials are willing to share more, I don't see that there's much we can do."

"God, Dad . . . you know how much I hate that."

"I do. But focus on what you can control *today*," George reminded Ethan. "Tell me about your three tenants."

Ethan refilled their coffee cups and shared what he'd learned about each of their current living conditions.

George listened without interrupting, then asked, "What are you legally liable to cover?"

"I need to find that out. Man, I bet Celia could have answered your questions off the top of her head. But being a landlord is new for me. I think maybe they're responsible for the cost of cleaning or replacing their own personal contents. Hopefully they had renter's insurance. I'm not sure about their actual costs of living somewhere else while my building is uninhabitable, though . . . I'll need to talk to my insurance guy. That'll be, like, question number ninety-nine I have for him."

"Ask him anything and everything, son. We need to know. Can all three of your tenants live independently, or were their injuries from the fire significant enough that they need more help these days?"

Ethan grabbed his pen. "Good question. I think Marvin would be all right—the only injury he had was to one hand. And Norman wasn't even home during the fire, so he's fine. No injuries there. Plus, he's maybe ten years younger than the others. He's staying with a friend from church right now. Not a good long-term solution, but I'm less concerned about him. Penelope might be a different story. She had a lung condition, even before the fire. Her daughter seems quite concerned." *And pissed off.*

"Do you have any vacancies in your other rentals?"

The question gave Ethan pause. Why hadn't he stopped to consider that earlier? He *did* have one vacancy in a duplex. It was a two-bedroom unit. But the rent on that was higher than either Marvin or Penelope had been paying. He couldn't afford to let them live there for nothing. He talked through it further with George.

"Maybe you at least mention it to Penelope's daughter," his dad suggested. "If Penelope isn't able to live on her own anymore, but she isn't so bad that she needs to be in a nursing home, maybe she'll need a roommate. You just don't know without asking."

"I suppose you're right. I'll give Rebecca a call. We still haven't thought of any possible solutions for Marvin. He's paid up at the nursing home through the end of December, but after that, he can't afford to stay there. He doesn't seem like he needs to be in a nursing home at all, to be honest. There has to be a better option."

"We'll keep trying to come up with something for him. But you have a pretty good list there, son." He tapped the piece of paper in front of them, now covered in Ethan's messy scrawl. "You can get to work. You can make some calls. Does it help to feel like you have some direction?"

"Yeah. It does. Thanks, Dad. I better get out of your hair. I need to pick Dylan up from basketball practice. Drew's at work."

George checked his watch. "Tell you what, why don't I pick Dylan up and you can go get started on that list? Come back here around six thirty and we'll eat. That way you don't have to figure anything out for supper. Call Drew and tell him to come, too, if he gets off by then."

Ethan downed the rest of his coffee. "Thanks, Dad. I'm not sure what I'd do without you."

George grinned. "That's what we're here for, Ethan. Now go. Start checking things off that list of yours."

The next day, Ethan pulled into the parking lot at the coffee shop where Rebecca had agreed to meet him. They needed to talk without her mother eavesdropping in the background. He made his way inside, but she wasn't there yet, so he ordered a black coffee. As he pulled his wallet out to pay, Rebecca arrived.

"Morning," Ethan greeted her. "Let the barista know what you'd like and I'll get it."

Rebecca ordered and went to save them seats at a table near the window.

"Thanks for agreeing to meet me," Ethan said, handing her a cup a few minutes later. "I thought we might be able to have a better discussion if your mom wasn't in the next room."

Rebecca nodded as she accepted her drink. "Thanks for the coffee. And thanks for your suggestion to meet elsewhere. My mom can be . . . a bit much."

Ethan took his heavy jacket off. It was warm inside. His actions gave him an extra minute to study his old friend. She'd matured into an attractive woman. He hoped the few lines around the corners of her eyes and her mouth were etched there through years of laughter and not worry. The girl he used to know was constantly laughing. Rebecca didn't appear to be as lighthearted as she was back then. While he suspected losing Ryan and then divorcing her second husband had taken a toll, he hoped she'd had more good years than bad.

"Do we have to get right down to business," Ethan asked, "or do you have a few minutes to catch up first? It's been a long time since our mid-twenties adventures. I'd love to hear what you've been up to."

Rebecca checked her phone. "Mom is getting her hair and nails done, so I guess I've got some time. Why don't you start? How is Stacey?"

Great first question, he thought wryly.

"Stacey is fine, last I talked to her. We split up a couple years back. The extent of our communication these days is around our three kids."

Rebecca didn't look too surprised at the news of his divorce. "I'm sorry, Ethan. Divorce is tough. It's been years since I talked to Stacey, so I didn't know. But tell me about your kids."

Ethan took a few minutes to tell her about Elizabeth, Drew, and Dylan. He tried not to brag too much, but he was proud of them all.

Rebecca smiled. "It's fun to see your face light up when you talk about them. I remember how you always said you wanted a bunch of kids. I'm glad that part of your plan came true."

"Enough about me," Ethan said; he'd been wanting to hear about Rebecca and her life ever since running into her at the hospital.

"Well, let's see . . ." She sipped her drink. "As you know, after college Ryan found a teaching job and I thought I'd landed my dream job as a management trainee. Remember when we'd meet for dinner, the four of us, and talk about all the things we'd accomplish in life? We had big dreams."

Ethan did remember. They'd only stayed in touch for a year or two once they were out of school—he even remembered being at Ryan and Rebecca's wedding. While he was happy for his friends, he'd gotten sloppy-drunk that night, unwilling to admit to anyone he still felt like he'd missed out on a chance at real happiness with Rebecca. He thought he'd convinced himself years earlier that he was over her. Watching her commit to a lifetime with Ryan was like a punch to the gut.

He also remembered Stacey being furious with him that night. He'd never confessed his feelings for Rebecca to Stacey, but he'd always wondered if she suspected. After that, he worked harder on his relationship with Stacey and began distancing himself from Rebecca—and Ryan.

He took a sip of his cooled coffee, bringing his attention back to this current-day Rebecca, sitting with him in a café and talking about her past.

"I remember you getting transferred to Indianapolis," he said. "Was Ryan able to get a teaching job there?"

Rebecca nodded. "He did. He was teaching high-school economics and coaching track. I traveled a lot for work. We were renting an apartment, never sure if they'd move me again. Ryan was able to build some connections there, through work. He was happy, settling in."

"And you?" Ethan prodded.

"I was doing all right. Kind of lonely. I missed our friends and family back home." She looked up from her drink. "I missed you guys. We talked about starting a family, but I really wanted to be in a house first, you know? So we agreed I'd stay with my job for a couple more years and then make a change, maybe start trying to get pregnant."

Ethan did the math in his head. That would have been right around the same time Lizzy was born.

"Were you able to start a family with Ryan?" As soon as the question left his mouth, he realized he might have been out of line to ask something so personal. *Nice one,* he chided himself.

She didn't seem to mind the question, though. "No, we never did. A couple years turned into three. It was hard to give up the income. Ryan didn't make nearly as much teaching. And then we went home for a family wedding—Ryan's cousin. The night before the wedding we were out at his uncle's farm. There was lots of food . . . probably too much beer. A few of us took out the four-wheelers. And then it was all over. Well . . . not *technically*, but it felt like it."

Ethan reached for Rebecca's hand. She accepted his offer of support. Both took a few seconds to remember Ryan. Then she pulled her hand back with a sigh.

"I'll skip the worst of the details. I already mentioned to you that Ryan survived the accident that day, but he was never the same. The injury stole the Ryan I knew. He couldn't accept what happened, either. We tried to get him help, but in the end, he made the decision."

"Becca . . . I'm so sorry."

She met and held his gaze. "I know, Ethan. And I'm sorry I never reached out to you and Stacey. I should have. It was just a very dark time. I focused all of my energy on my work after he was gone. I traveled as a buyer for a large department store chain. Bouncing from city to city, trying to stay up on all the local trends, trying to keep my mind off things for a while. My body healed quickly, my spirit took longer."

"You were hurt? Oh God, Becca—"

Rebecca shrugged off his concern. "Compared to Ryan, my injuries were nothing. Broken collar bone, busted leg. I still have trouble once in a while with my leg, especially when it gets cold, but it could have been so much worse. Like it was with Ryan. He saved my life that day, insisting I wear the helmet. Believe it or not, in those terrible months afterward, after . . . you know, him being *gone* . . . I would get so angry with him for not putting the helmet on himself. Irrational, I know, but grief can mess with your mind."

She gazed at people passing on the sidewalk outside, lost in thought. Ethan couldn't imagine what it would have been like for her. He'd always thought the two had been a couple that could go the distance.

Funny how life sometimes has other plans.

"Anyhow, I eventually met someone, even though I wasn't looking. Gavin Sandvig. We met on a plane, both of us traveled on business. It was a long-distance relationship for the first year, and then I moved to Omaha, where he lived. We got married—against my mother's advice, as you might have gathered from her comment earlier. Gavin is older. He had kids from a prior marriage, so he wasn't interested in starting a second family. I didn't think I was, either, until I could feel my biological clock slowing. But he wouldn't be swayed. He loved his golf buddies, his travel, his gin. I was never quite sure exactly where I fell in the line-up. We split up five years ago."

Ethan didn't like the haunted look in Rebecca's eyes as she recounted how her life had unfolded since they'd last seen each other. He remembered Becca as a fun-loving, vivacious girl . . . not this serious, somber woman sitting across from him now.

"What do you do for work these days?" he asked, hoping she might have more enthusiasm around her career.

She laughed, but Ethan sensed a hint of bitterness to it. "Funny you should ask that today," she said.

"Why's that?"

Rebecca shrugged. "I quit yesterday. Called my boss and told him I'm done."

Based on her expression, Ethan suspected she wasn't thrilled about it.

"That must not have been an easy decision."

She shrugged again. "I couldn't see any other way to help Mom. She needs me *now*, and Omaha is just too far away. I proposed a plan to my manager to work remotely and cut my travel schedule. He flat out denied it. I maybe could have convinced him to give it a try, but I've worked there long enough to know it would be an uphill battle. Despite all the business I've brought in through the years, it's never enough. So . . . I decided to quit instead of fight. At least that takes some of the time pressure off for figuring out what to do with Mom. But it also magnifies our financial issues."

The knot in his stomach tightened. "I'm sorry we're all in this predicament . . . the fire has really messed things up for so many people," Ethan said, knowing he was stating the obvious but unable to stop apologizing. "Guess life is full of surprises."

"It is. And the more we learn to roll with the punches, the better off we are." After a pause, she said, "You wanted to meet today. What did you need to talk about?"

"I thought we should talk about your mom's living situation. You mentioned needing to go home soon and I wasn't sure what that would mean for Penelope. If you don't mind my asking, do you think she could still live on her own?"

Ethan could see the skepticism on Rebecca's face before she even answered.

"Look, Ethan, I know we were friends back in the day, but things are different now. You're the landlord. There was a fire in the building, so Mom needs other accommodations, at least for a while."

"Maybe I'm not *legally* responsible for helping her make other arrangements, but I want to help out my tenants where I can. Your mom rented from my Aunt Celia for quite a few years, and I know my aunt would have wanted to help. She'd have expected me to do the same."

She raised an eyebrow. "You're doing this out of the goodness of your heart, then? Not because you want to try to keep people from coming after you for being an unfit landlord?"

Ethan met and held his old friend's gaze. "Becca, you know me better than that. We used to be friends. I'm offering to try to help. If you don't want my help, I'll back off. I can let you know when the apartment is habitable again and leave it at that. Just say the word."

He gave her time to think about his offer. Eventually, she gave him a brief nod and slipped her heavy jacket off.

"I'm sorry," she said finally. "I was out of line. I can't blame you for what happened. Thank you for trying to help. Sometimes, I'm afraid I can be every bit as ornery as she is—even though I vowed never to be."

"Don't worry about it," Ethan assured her. "What options have you considered?"

"You asked if I thought she could live alone right now? Perhaps . . . but she shouldn't. She gets around all right with her walker, but she gets short of breath and that can make her lightheaded. If she fell, and was all alone . . ." She shook her head. "I hate to even think about how dire that could be."

"Do you think, with time, she may be able to get back to the point where she can live alone? Or is it time for something like assisted-living?"

Rebecca frowned. "I don't think she's at that point yet. Her doctor is relatively confident her lung condition was irritated by the smoke. Her breathing may improve. If it doesn't, that'll be a different story, but I'm optimistic. She's so damn stubborn, you can bet she'll do what she can to heal. Mom likes her space and has no desire to be dependent on *me* for longer than she has to. Heck, she's been married four times, buried two of them and divorced the other two. She's tough."

Ethan laughed. "She was only engaged to husband number two when I first met her, after your dad passed away. I wouldn't have guessed she'd go through two more!"

"I started saving my dresses I wore to her weddings just in case I'd need them again," Rebecca replied with a conspiratorial grin. "But seriously, Mom is a strong woman. She's just in a rough patch right now."

"I'm glad to hear that. Okay. So you don't want her alone for the time being. Do you have any family or friends she could stay with until her apartment is ready? Maybe by then she'll be able to live alone again."

"Believe me, I've spent countless sleepless nights trying to figure that out. There are maybe a couple of possibilities, but Mom isn't exactly *easy* to live with, so I haven't pursued them. I'm probably the only logical choice. Work was my biggest obstacle, but now that's a non-issue."

"If she were to live with you, would you take her home to Omaha with you?"

"Maybe. But she would *not* be happy about that. Mom has a group of lady friends that are super important to her. They've seen her through all her marital heartbreak. They're almost more family to her than *I* am, what with my travel schedule through the years and not living here."

"If you don't want to take her away from her friends, are you considering moving back here, then?"

Rebecca fiddled with her coffee cup, popping the plastic lid off and setting it to the side. She swirled the liquid still in the cup, deep in thought.

"I'm starting to think . . ." She stopped, sighed, then tried again, her voice stronger. "I'm starting to think there isn't anything worth going back for. Most of my friends were work friends. I have no children and no significant other. But I'm not sure where we could live until her apartment is ready again."

Ethan wasn't sure Penelope would ever be able to go back to his building, even if he *could* get it back to where it was inhabitable. The stairs were a real issue for her.

"If you're worried about your mom's lease with me, don't be. I understand if she might not be able to handle the stairs there anymore, after this latest bout with her lungs."

"It's funny—I've asked her about that, too. She *insists* she's going back. I can't figure out why she's so adamant. But she is."

Ethan chuckled. "All right, then. What if you and your mom move into a two-bedroom unit I have vacant in one of my other buildings? We could do a month-to-month lease and figure out a fair rental rate. If I could afford to let you live there for nothing, I would, but I have to pay the bills. Would that interest you at all?"

Rebecca looked surprised. "Just how many properties do you have?"

"Besides the building your mom lives in—lived in—four other rental units. Two apartments in a duplex plus two small, single-family homes. Celia left them all to me. They all came with mortgages, but they usually earn me a little more than they cost me every month."

Rebecca grinned. "Probably not worth all these headaches."

"A little hard work never killed anyone," Ethan joked. He'd had the same thoughts lately, but knew he'd appreciate having the properties in the long run. To quote Rebecca, he was just in a "rough patch" these days.

"Could we go look at the two-bedroom? In fact, would you have time right now?"

Ethan checked his watch. "Yes. Let's go look real quick. Then we can each take a day or two to think through how we might make this work. I can't imagine you want to stay in that hotel much longer. It's got to be costing you a fortune."

Rebecca drained the last of her coffee and stood up, gathering her coat. "You have no idea."

By the end of the week, Rebecca and Penelope were partially settled into Ethan's duplex. The building had no stairs, just one level with two side-by-side units. He was glad his dad pushed him to help his tenants figure things out. He was feeling better already.

Rebecca booked a flight home and arranged for a friend of Penelope's to stay with her for the three days she'd be gone. She'd told Ethan she needed to start the process of moving back home. She had a house to sell, friends to say goodbye to, and belongings to get packed and moved. Then she needed to start looking for a new job.

Ethan suspected Rebecca was feeling whipsawed by the massive changes in her life; but, based on what she'd shared with him, maybe a fresh start was just what she needed. In that respect, they were in a similar boat.

With one of his three tenants taken care of, Ethan called Norman.

"I appreciate your concern, Ethan," Norman replied when Ethan told him why he was calling. "But don't worry about me. I'm house-sitting for a friend who's in Arizona for the winter. If he gets back before my apartment is ready, I think I have another favor or two I can call in with others. Just keep me posted on how things are coming along and what we should do as far as removing any of our things that need to be cleaned and all."

Ethan assured him he'd be in touch and felt the weight on his shoulders lighten a bit more.

Now to figure out what to do about Marvin.

Chapter Eighteen
Gift of Christmas Cheer

"Are you sure you don't want to spend part of your Christmas break with your mom, Lizzy?"

Ethan and his daughter were carrying presents down from the apartment out to his truck. He worried the rift between his eldest child and his ex-wife was widening. He'd hoped by now things would be getting better between Lizzy and Stacey. They used to be close. What confused him was that now neither seemed to care too much that they spent so little time together.

"We've been over this, Dad. Mom has her new life and it doesn't include us. She tries to squeeze us in when it's convenient for her. I'm *done*. I'm done with her games."

Ethan stood back to let Lizzy shove her armful of presents into the box of the truck and then slammed and locked the tailgate. "One more trip upstairs to get the food, and then we better get over to Mom and Dad's," he said, heading back into the apartment building.

"Who's going to be at Grandma and Grandpa's?"

"Pretty much everybody, I think."

"Even Nathan and Julie?" Lizzy asked. Ethan knew his daughter missed her two oldest cousins the most, getting home as infrequently as she did. Nathan was Jess's oldest, the same age as Lizzy, and Julie was Renee's oldest. Both were in college.

"I think so. Harper should be fun, too. She's almost one now and walking all over the place."

Together they finished loading the pickup then drove across town.

"I wonder if Mom has started planning her wedding."

Ethan suppressed a sigh. *So much for not caring about what her mother is up to* . . .

With everything that had been going on since the fire, Ethan hadn't thought much about his ex; he might not have at all if the kids weren't affected by her decisions.

When they'd first separated, Ethan thought it would bother him when Stacey started to date again. He'd had no interest in going out with anyone until well after their divorce was final, but Stacey made it clear she'd be looking for someone else to make her happy immediately. He'd tried to tell her that until she started to like herself better, no one else was going to be able to help her in that department. His advice had fallen on deaf ears.

It hadn't taken him long to get over any discomfort over Stacey's antics. The only time it got to him was when it negatively impacted their kids. He hoped this claim that she was getting married again was real— and was for good—and wasn't simply a tactic to get attention.

"How are you feeling about your mom getting married again? Have you talked to her about it much?" he asked, trying to gauge if Stacey's engagement bothered Lizzy more than she'd initially let on.

She shrugged, her eyes trained on the bright Christmas lights outlining most houses along the streets. In December, darkness came early in Minnesota.

"Who knows? In case you haven't noticed, Mom doesn't seem to want to be alone at all. And besides, this guy's rich."

"Yeah, I remember you saying that. Is that his only redeeming quality?" Ethan joked, trying but failing to mask the disappointment he felt over Stacey's actions.

"I haven't been around him enough to tell. He's definitely older than you guys. Do you remember Mom's joke about marrying rich?"

Ethan didn't. "Ah . . . no."

"Yeah. She'd say, 'You can marry more money in a minute than you can make in a lifetime.' And then she'd laugh, flip her hair back over her shoulder like that snotty friend of hers always does, and say she wished someone had taught her that about thirty years ago."

"Ouch. That hurts." Ethan knew exactly which friend Lizzy was referring to, and he'd wondered if she'd been the one to encourage Stacey to walk away from their family. Not that it mattered now.

Lizzy snapped off her seatbelt as Ethan pulled up in front of his parents' home. "And you wonder why I don't want to spend Christmas with her."

The Richters loved to celebrate Christmas with the same menu, timeframes, and activities most every year. This year was no exception.

Ethan and Lizzy arrived through the back door to a full and bustling household. The whole family was there. Val was again running things in the kitchen, getting their traditional dinner on the table. Renee and Jess were setting the tables. Cousins were everywhere. The unmistakable scent of pine competed with the warm smell of baked ham. A real Christmas tree stood in one corner, adorned with handmade decorations and twinkling lights.

"Hey, Uncle Ethan," Logan said as they walked in with their arms full. "How do you like the tree I helped Grandma and Grandpa pick out from our Boy Scout lot? Pretty sweet, huh?"

"Hey, bud—let me set this stuff down and then you can show me."

Ethan set the bag of groceries on the island near Val. "I think I got everything you asked for," he said to his youngest sister, giving her a quick smile. "How have you been? I haven't seen you since Thanksgiving."

Val pushed a section of dark red hair off her forehead with the back of her hand, in which she held a wicked-looking knife. "I'm good. We're all good. I think my son wants you to go look at the tree with him, though."

Ethan saluted her as she turned her attention back to a half-minced onion and made his way over to the tree and his nephew.

"You did good, Logan. I can't remember the last time we had a tree this nice. Perfect height. Good color. And I could smell it when we walked in."

Logan beamed, puffing his chest out. "I wouldn't let them settle for just any old tree. Grandma gave up on us and went and waited in the car. But me and Gramps, we went through them all. He tried to go with a couple other ones, but they were too scrawny."

Ethan made sure he took enough time to inspect the tree. His parents had switched to an artificial tree years ago, but the fact that their grandsons were part of a scout troop hosting a tree lot would be enough to send George digging around in their basement to find the old tree stand. Anything for his grandkids.

Ethan laid his hand on his nephew's shoulder and leaned down to whisper into his ear. "Don't tell your Grandpa," he muttered conspiratorially, "but I never liked it when he switched from real trees to fake. I'm glad you and Noah convinced him to get a real tree again."

"Happy to help," Logan whispered back.

Val's boys are growing up just as fast as mine, Ethan thought, tickled to see how proud Logan was of convincing his grandpa to go back to having a live Christmas tree.

"I'm sorry I didn't have a chance to come get a tree from you, too. I just didn't get a chance to decorate the apartment this year. Next year, when we're in our house, I promise I'll come get a tree from you, all right? Will you be sure to save me a good one? Maybe even as good as this one?"

"You bet, Uncle Ethan! Mom told me about the fire at your building. I'm sorry . . . do you need help?"

Ah, the innocence of a nine-year-old, Ethan thought, touched by his nephew's offer.

"I appreciate that, Logan. I'll be sure to keep you in mind and I'll call if there is anything."

"Come and get it!" another young voice rang out from behind them. "Supper's ready!"

"We better not keep your little brother waiting. Jake isn't the most patient kid around," Ethan said, winking at Logan.

Logan rolled his eyes. "Ya got that right!"

Later, after they finished eating and then exchanged gifts, Lavonne called Ethan out into the front living room.

"What do you need, Mom? We better start loading everyone into the vehicles and get over to church so we can all sit together," Ethan said, drawing up short when he saw *another* decorated tree, this one the fake he'd expected when he first arrived, now here and still surrounded by wrapped gifts. He was surprised to see Lavonne wasn't alone in the living room, either. Everyone appeared to have gathered in the now-crowded room when he'd run out to his pickup to grab Lizzy's phone for her. "Why is there another tree in here? And what the heck are all these presents for? Didn't we just open everything?"

"Robbie, why don't you tell your uncle what you've been up to?" Lavonne suggested to the young man standing beside her. Robbie, Renee's son, was now a senior in high school and nearly a foot taller than his grandma.

"Oh, are these for another toy drive? I remember you working at one of those a couple years ago," Ethan said to his nephew.

Robbie laughed. "Not exactly. This year I thought we'd help out some *much* older kids."

Ethan just stared at him, confused.

"Come on, honey, I think you might have to spell it out for Ethan. Maybe you should have borrowed that Santa suit again this year. He's not catching on," Renee suggested to her son.

"Why would Robbie need one of Santa's suits?" Jake, Val's youngest, could be heard asking his mother.

Renee mouthed *Sorry!* to Val.

Robbie walked over to his uncle and put a hand on his shoulder. With his other hand, he motioned to the wrapped gifts under the tree. "I thought it would be cool to see what we could come up with as far as presents for the older people who lived in your building and were displaced by the fire. Everybody thought it was a good idea and chipped in. Plus, we thought maybe it would be fun if a few of us delivered them tonight. We can all go to church tomorrow morning instead."

Ethan was floored. He'd worked hard to be sure his tenants all had proper living arrangements but was ashamed to admit that he hadn't thought too much about the kind of Christmas the three of them might be having this year.

He wrapped Robbie in a big hug and attempted to stay dry-eyed. He mostly succeeded. Then he turned to the rest of his family, gathered around him.

"Were you all in on this? If so, you are *scary* good at keeping secrets!"

"Dad, you were clueless!" Lizzy chimed in. "Since when would I actually *forget* my phone in the truck?"

"You should know me better than to believe I'd simply 'forget' all those ingredients for dinner tonight, too," Val yelled from the other side of the sunroom.

"Seriously? Was that just a ploy to slow me down?"

"Totally!" Val laughed. "And it worked! These guys were still busy wrapping until about five minutes before you and Lizzy got here! Even Logan was keeping you occupied with the other tree while they got all these stacked under here."

Ethan spun around, looking for Logan, and spotted him sitting on the stairs.

"I'm pretty good, huh, Uncle Ethan?" Logan said with two thumbs up. "Sorry I couldn't talk Grandpa into two trees from our lot. That one you don't like still got put up in here."

Everyone laughed except Ethan. He cringed, knowing his mother wouldn't appreciate hearing he was dissing on her artificial Christmas tree. Logan shrugged in apology.

"You can't believe everything you hear, Mom!"

Everybody helped load the gifts into the back of Ethan's pickup while he called Penelope, Marvin, and Norman to see if he could stop by. All answered, and all were curious why he was out so late on Christmas Eve, but he assured each of them it would be a quick stop.

There were plenty of offers to help deliver gifts, but he only had room for four in addition to himself. Robbie was coming along, since he'd coordinated everything; Drew wanted to help, too, because he remembered Marvin from his nursing home visit—he'd been shocked when Ethan told him he'd recognized the lap blanket when he went to visit Marvin; and George and Matt grabbed the other two open seats. Everyone else would stay home, get comfortable, and relax after a busy evening.

Robbie shared a bit more with Ethan as they drove. Ethan was impressed that he'd taken the initiative to not only suggest they do something like this, but to also make sure it all came together in time. He'd assigned each of Ethan's sisters one of the tenants, and George and Lavonne wanted to get something for all of them. He'd even gone so far as to suggest gifts they might want to consider, everything from new pajamas and a holiday sweater, to a game or a book, even movie passes. Things they might enjoy when they couldn't be spending Christmas in their own homes.

As Ethan pulled up at the home Norman was house-sitting, Matt spoke up.

"Hey, Ethan, if you want to invite these folks out to Whispering Pines tomorrow afternoon to join the family, Renee and everyone were fine with that. Might be kind of a fun change of pace for them."

This year they were trying something new. Normally they spent both Christmas Eve and Christmas Day at George and Lavonne's house. But the kids were all getting bigger, and the house felt as if it were getting smaller.

Out at the resort, there were sledding hills and places the kids could skate on the lake. They'd all decided to head out there early in the afternoon, enjoy some indoor and outdoor activities, and wrap up Christmas in the lodge with their traditional turkey dinner. They wouldn't have been able to fit more people at George and Lavonne's, but it wasn't a problem to invite more out to Whispering Pines.

Ethan turned back to Matt as he put the truck into Park in front of Norman's. "I appreciate that. Man, you guys have thought of everything. I have no idea if they'll have other plans or be up for it, but, hell, let's invite them all."

He took off his seatbelt and started to open his door but paused. "Do you all want to come in, or are you going to hang out here?"

"We didn't come along to sit in the truck," Robbie said, jumping out his side and opening the back-passenger door for his grandfather. "Let's go, guys."

And so, it began. They took the presents out of the back of the truck that were labeled for Norman and all five of them took them up to the front door. The house looked quiet, but the front light was on.

Robbie knocked and they could hear footsteps inside. Norman greeted them all with handshakes and a grin from ear to ear. There was a fire crackling in the hearth and an old black-and-white movie playing on the television. He invited them in, surprised to see Drew and Matt carrying presents as they brought up the rear of the small group.

"This is completely unexpected . . . you gentlemen are too kind," he said, clearly touched by the gesture.

They visited for ten minutes or so but declined when Norman offered everyone a beverage.

"We'd love to stay," Ethan said, "but we have two more stops to make and it's getting late. But we're having a small gathering tomorrow out at our family's resort. We would love to have you join us if you're free."

Norman had commitments at his church in the morning, but his afternoon was free, so they arranged to have someone pick him up at one o'clock and bring him out to Whispering Pines. He was clearly excited at the idea.

"I'll come, then, as long as you allow me to treat you to some holiday cocktails tomorrow. I won't show up empty-handed," Norman insisted as he followed them all back to the front door.

As they said their goodbyes and walked out the door, Ethan smiled as he heard a young girl's voice come through the television.

"Look, Daddy! Teacher says, 'Every time a bell rings, an angel gets his wings.'"

The iconic film *It's a Wonderful Life* was still Ethan's favorite. He felt a bit like George Bailey, receiving help and love from his family and community during a time of need. The messages played out in the movie were timeless for a reason.

Hope and good can *prevail.*

Energy was high as they piled back into the pickup.

"Did you see his face? I think we made that guy's Christmas! Good job, cuz!" Drew said, reaching up from the backseat to slap Robbie on the back.

Robbie looked as excited as Norman had when he first opened the door. "Right?! This is why I think it's so cool to do special stuff for people at Christmas. Dude, we are so lucky to have this family. Lots of people, kids and adults, are alone. Or homeless. Or sick. Or whatever. When we did that first toy drive, my sister and my mom and me . . . I'd never felt like that before."

Drew nodded. "I get it. Kind of like at Thanksgiving when Grandpa made us take all those lap blankets to the nursing home. I thought it was kind of a dumb idea until we did it. But it was actually kind of cool. I met Marvin that night, the guy we're going to see next. I haven't seen him since we figured out he's one of Dad's renters."

Matt, George, and Ethan all exchanged looks but kept quiet. It was fun to hear Robbie and Drew.

Drew continued, "Robbie, ya better start thinkin' now about what we might be able to do next Christmas. This is fun. It'll be hard to top. We can't count on Dad to have an *annual* fire so we can play elves to his tenants every year. But I can help you figure out someone else to help."

Marvin was sitting out in the gathering area at the nursing home when they arrived, watching for them. He slowly stood up and walked ever so carefully toward them as they all entered the lobby.

"Hello, Marvin," Ethan said.

"I must say, it was a surprise to hear from you tonight, Ethan. You have me curious. Seeing all these folks with you, I can't imagine what brings you over on Christmas Eve."

"My nephew here, Robbie Clements, orchestrated a bit of a surprise for you," Ethan said, first shaking Marvin's hand and then motioning Robbie up to the front of the group. "Robbie is my sister Renee's son. He fancies himself a bit of a Santa Claus and thought you might be able to use a few new things this Christmas, given everything that's happened."

"Really?" Marvin asked, bewildered. "Young man . . . no one's ever done anything like that for me before. Christmas is always a quiet time for me. I figure it's a time for families and young people, not old codgers like me."

Ethan laughed, but he noticed the man was unsteady on his feet. "Do you want to go back to your room to visit or sit down out here?"

Marvin glanced around. Only a few residents were about. "Might as well stay out here. I'm tired of that tiny little room they've got me in. Can't wait to escape in a few days. Just in time to ring in the new year."

George motioned to Robbie and Drew to gather up a few more chairs, and they all sat around a large table.

"If you'd like, we can go put these in your room to open later," Matt said. He'd brought in Marvin's stack of gifts.

Marvin gaped, speechless, until he managed to say, "Those are *all* for me?"

"Sure," Matt replied. "Which room is yours?"

Drew interrupted. "Hey, Marvin, it's me, Drew. Remember me?"

Marvin took a closer look at the youngest member in their group. "Well, I certainly do. You are that nice young man who brought me the blanket right after I got here, right after the fire."

"Yep! Ethan's my dad. What are the odds? You live in my Dad's building and we didn't even know it! I can show Matt where your room is if you like."

"That would be perfect. Thank you." He turned to the others as Drew and Matt went off searching for his room. "I just can't tell you how nice this is to get a little company, on tonight of all nights. Good thing you called, Ethan, or I might have turned in already. Many of our residents left to visit families. We had a small holiday celebration here, earlier today, with the staff. Some cute little kids came in and sang for us." He shook his head. "I figured that was about all the celebrating I'd be doing."

Drew and Matt came back and joined them at the table. Drew seemed even more energized, if that were possible. "Dad, did you invite Marvin yet for tomorrow?"

Ethan shook his head. "I was just getting to that. But do you want to do the honors?"

Drew grinned. "Sure! Marvin, have we got a deal for you. Want to come out to Whispering Pines with all of us tomorrow afternoon for more Christmas fun? Someone could pick you up and bring you out."

Marvin's brow furrowed. "What is Whispering Pines?"

"It's our lake resort," Robbie chimed in. "My mom runs it. About an hour from here."

"Oh, now, I don't think so. That's awful kind of you, but I don't want to intrude. You guys have already done enough."

"Aw, come on, Marvin," Drew said. "Don't be a party pooper. It's a blast out at Whispering Pines, honest. Besides, your neighbor Norman already agreed to come. And you've met all of us. You'd know people there."

"It's completely up to you, Marvin," Ethan said, giving his son a look. "But if you feel up to it, we'd love to have you. It'll be loud but fun, with plenty of good food and conversation. I'm going to ask Penelope, too, and her daughter. In fact, we probably should get over there before it gets too late. I can call you in the morning if you want to wait till then to decide."

Marvin sat up taller in his chair. "You're going to go see Penelope now? My neighbor Penelope?"

"Sure. We have some gifts for her, too," Ethan said.

Marvin paused to think, then turned to Drew. "Any chance I can get you to do me a favor?"

"Sure, anything."

"Run back to my room and bring me that wrapped package in the top drawer of my dresser, will you, son?"

Drew stood. "Be right back."

While he waited for Drew to return, Marvin turned back to Ethan. "Would you mind giving Penelope something for me? It's not much. Of course, I didn't do much shopping at all, stuck in here as I am, but last weekend they had a gift bazaar right here. I know how much she likes krumkake cookies, so when I noticed someone was selling them I picked her up a box. Figured I'd get it to her somehow. We always get each other a little something."

Ethan grinned. It sounded like Marvin might have a tiny bit of a crush on his neighbor Penelope.

"I'd be happy to do that for you, Marvin. I'm sure she'll appreciate it."

Drew came back carrying a present the size of a shoebox, gaily wrapped in striped Christmas paper.

"They had free wrapping," Marvin said shyly.

Ethan stood as a signal it was time to go make their last stop. "What do you think, would you like to join us tomorrow?"

"Actually, Ethan, I don't have to sleep on your invite. Yes, I believe I would like to join you tomorrow. What time should I be ready?"

When the door opened, Ethan and the rest of his delivery team found themselves facing not Penelope, but Rebecca. Ethan smiled at his old friend, admiring her pretty holiday sweater in the dim light. The room behind her was festively lit by a four-foot Christmas tree, strung with multi-colored lights.

"Nice tree," he said as he entered the duplex Rebecca and Penelope were renting from him temporarily. "You got that up quick!"

"Thank you," Rebecca replied. She nodded at George. "Your father was kind enough to tell us about the tree lot his grandsons were working last week. There wasn't much left, but I've always been partial to the underdog."

Ethan looked closer. Now that she mentioned it, the tree was sporting a couple sparse spots; it still managed to transform the room with holiday cheer.

"Now if you would quit *marrying* the underdogs, you might actually find some happiness," a voice said from the adjoining kitchen.

Rebecca rolled her eyes. "And that would be my charming mother, who, by the way"—she raised her voice—"has been married twice as many times as I have been. But don't tell her I said that. Won't you all come in?"

Rebecca led the line of men through the small living room back to the kitchen.

"Can I get you a cup of coffee, or a can of pop, maybe?" she offered as they all crowded into the tiny room, where Penelope was seated at the kitchen table. It looked like their arrival had interrupted a card game.

"No, no, but thank you. We just brought a few things over for you ladies," Ethan said.

Drew and Robbie set a stack of gifts down on the kitchen table, avoiding the cards spread out on its surface.

Thank God someone thought to include Rebecca in the gifts, Ethan thought.

"Oh my goodness, whatever for?" Rebecca asked as Penelope took the top present off the pile to inspect it.

"Child, didn't I teach you not to look a gift horse in the mouth?" the older woman said, giving the package a shake. "If a bunch of handsome men want to bring me presents, who am I to question their motives?"

Everyone laughed, and Ethan caught the wink Penelope gave to George.

He explained to the women how Robbie encouraged their whole family to brighten up Christmas for the tenants impacted by the fire.

"Now *that's* the kind of young man I like," Penelope said, raising her hand to give Robbie a high five.

"Speaking of handsome men, we just came from visiting both of your old neighbors," Ethan said. "One of them asked me to give you something." He dug the gift from Marvin out of the pile and handed it to Penelope. "This one is from him, not us."

Ethan would have sworn the older woman blushed pink, a pretty contrast to her white hair. He thought he noticed a slight shift in her demeanor. Gone was the joking, slightly brash woman, replaced with a shy demeanor.

"Marvin sent this over . . . for me?"

"He did. He said you two usually exchange, and he thought you'd like this."

Penelope took care as she opened the end of the wrapped package not to tear the pretty paper. She slid the box out and then neatly folded the wrapping. Ethan didn't know if she was being careful because it was from Marvin or because this was something she always did. He glanced at her daughter. Based on Rebecca's expression, gift exchanging with a man named Marvin was news to her.

Penelope took the cover off the box and carefully removed one of the delicate cookies from inside. "Oh, yes. Krumkake. I've always loved these cookies, ever since I was a child. My mama always made the best krumkake."

She took a dainty bite of the treat; tiny pieces broke away, sprinkling the front of her shirt. "These are nearly as good as Mother's. Here, pass them around. Help yourselves."

Never ones to pass up cookies of any kind, Drew and Robbie both took one, but everyone else passed, not wanting to eat all of her present from Marvin.

George asked Rebecca and Penelope about their favorite holiday traditions, and the conversation flowed from there. When George eventually offered, both women seemed excited about their invite out to Whispering Pines the following day.

"Will Marvin be there?" Penelope asked, her voice faux casual.

"Yes," Ethan said, trying not to smile too much. "He said he thought it would be fun."

The shy little smile was back.

Matt's cell rang and he stepped back into the dimly lit living room to take the call. When he came back, he made his apologies but said they needed to run.

"Duty calls?" Robbie asked his stepfather.

"Afraid so."

"What kind of duty calls on Christmas Eve night?" Penelope asked.

"The kind that never sleeps," Matt replied with a sad smile. "I wasn't on call tonight, but the holidays can be a tough time for lots of people. They're feeling short staffed, so I better go see how I can help. But it was very nice meeting you two, and hopefully we'll see you tomorrow."

"Oh yes, you better go, then," Rebecca said. "Don't let us keep you. But thank you all again. You have no idea how much we appreciate your kindness." She showed them back out to the door—a strange experience for Ethan, being treated like a guest in a duplex he was so familiar with.

As everyone else headed for his truck, Ethan asked Rebecca, "Want me to swing by and pick you up about one?"

"Text me the address and I'll drive out with Mom. What can we bring?"

"Nothing, just come on out."

Rebecca shook her head. "Absolutely not. We aren't going to crash your holiday party empty-handed."

Ethan laughed. He'd forgotten how stubborn Rebecca could be. It used to drive Stacey nuts whenever they'd gone out as a group. "Well, if I remember right, I won't be able to change your mind on that, so feel free to bring something. Whatever you might have handy, I suppose. You aren't going to be able to pick anything up before you come out. Things will be closed on Christmas Day."

"I'll figure it out. Hey . . ." She lowered her voice. "What's up with Mom and Marvin? What was all that about?"

Ethan chuckled. "I have no idea. But Marvin was funny about it, too. I thought maybe there might be a little romance going on there."

Rebecca hung her head in exasperation, but her eyes twinkled when she looked up again and met Ethan's gaze. "Leave it to Mom. I swear that woman is unable to go more than a few months without a man in her life. I thought she'd finally given up on love, after four marriages, but maybe there's been something going on at home that I didn't know about."

Ethan nodded. "That might help explain why she was so insistent on waiting for her old apartment to get fixed up instead of finding a new place to live."

"It just might at that."

Chapter Nineteen
GIFT OF FRIENDLY COMPETITION

THE NEXT MORNING A light snow fell as the lodge at Whispering Pines once again became a hub of activity. By noon, the festivities were ramping up.

"I think you girls are on to something, moving Christmas to the Pines," Lavonne said to Renee and Jess as she watched them hustle around the kitchen, preparing the food they'd need to serve their hungry crew throughout the day.

Ethan handed a stack of stoneware from an uppermost cupboard down to Renee. "Hey, Mom, why is it always about 'you girls'? I swear, I get no credit around here."

Lavonne laughed. "Sorry, son. I think you *kids* are on to something. There's so much more room out here. And plenty to do, both inside and out."

"You need to keep hanging around with us, Mom," Jess said as she arranged a bag of frozen Christmas cookies on a large tray to thaw. They'd baked them the weekend after Thanksgiving. "You are the only one in the world that would refer to us as *kids*. Good confidence booster!"

"You'll always be *my* kids. What time are our guests arriving?"

Ethan climbed down off the step ladder and checked his watch. "Dad's picking Norman and Marvin up now. We invited Rebecca and Penelope for about one. Same with Brooke."

"Seth is bringing Kaylee, too," Jess added. "He's excited. This is the first time in four years he's had her over Christmas."

"This'll be fun, but it sounds like I'll be needing a pick-me-up," Lavonne said, standing up from the stool she'd been perched on and making her way over to the coffee pot.

Ethan noticed how gingerly she walked. "Have you scheduled that scope for your knee yet?"

"No, but I think I'll have to after we get past the holidays. I was hoping it would heal on its own, but I guess that isn't going to happen."

Renee came back into the kitchen carrying a large cardboard box.

Ethan hadn't noticed she'd left. "What do ya got there?" he asked.

Renee set the box down on the huge kitchen island. "Check these out. I found them upstairs."

She pulled out four old trophies, varying in height and all dated back to the 1950s and '60s. Three were silver, one gold, and all sat on heavy marble bases.

"Oh my God, these are great!" Jess said, picking up the tallest one. She squinted at the metal plate affixed to the base of the trophy and read the inscription out loud. " The Whopper Club Ice Fishing Derby, First Place, January 16th, 1965.' "

Renee said, "You know how we talked about having some contests today? I thought we could turn these into traveling trophies for the winners. What do you think?"

"I love it! What were you thinking, ice fishing?" Ethan asked, picking up the smallest trophy, topped with a golden fish. "I'd be up for that."

"Yep, if enough people want to. I think the kids would love it. The ice is plenty thick out there, and it's supposed to be sunny and in the twenties today. Maybe Dad would help organize it. I found a bunch of old ice fishing rods and tackle in the shed out back and had Matt pick up some frozen smelt we can use for bait."

"I'll help, too," Ethan offered. "You've got four trophies here. This one's a bowling trophy, though. There's lots to do out here, but there's no bowling alley. And it's probably too cold for softball."

Renee snatched the trophy from Ethan. "No shit, Sherlock. This ice fishing one fits, but we'll have to use our imagination for the others. I thought about using a

Sharpie to change the descriptions on these, if that would even work, but decided against it. These old things are cool the way they are."

"What other contests should we do?" Jess asked.

"I definitely thought we should have a whist tournament. Not everyone can go out and fish, but maybe we'd get some takers on that. And what about a snowman-building contest? The snow is deep enough, and it should be sticky today with the sunshine."

"Good idea!" Ethan said. "That way most everyone can participate in something. Do you think we need a fourth?"

Renee shrugged. "I told people to wear an ugly Christmas sweater, if they have one, so maybe we can all vote on our favorite."

"Works for me," Ethan glanced down at his red flannel shirt he'd thrown on earlier. "But I guess I'm not going to win that last one."

"Like *you'd* have a Christmas sweater, big bro," Jess said, laughing. "Ugly or not!"

Everyone arrived by 1:30. Some of the kids had never gone ice fishing, so that particular contest generated lots of excitement. Ethan and George decided the area in front of their beach would be best, so they sent the kids out onto the ice, forty feet from shore, with the task of shoveling the snow off an area large enough so that everyone would have a small section to themselves. The snow wasn't deep, so it wouldn't take long.

A cold snap meant the ice was plenty thick. The old manual ice auger in the shed wasn't a good option—it'd be dark before they managed to get enough holes drilled using that—so Matt called over to a neighboring resort that catered to fishermen year-round. They were happy to let him borrow a more powerful, gas auger. Within the hour, eleven lines were dropped down the drilled holes and their ice patch was littered with folding chairs, fishermen (and fisherwomen) tending their spots.

"Hey, Grandpa, what are the rules?" Robbie hollered across the ice from where he knelt next to his hole, giving his line a jiggle every few seconds. "Is it the number of fish or the total weight?"

George straightened from helping one of the younger boys secure the frozen bait on his hook. "Let's go with total weight. That way, if someone catches a northern, it'll be worth more than little perch. Because, believe me, pulling one of those big monsters out of one of these little holes is a kick! We'll fish until four o'clock. I'll run back to the lodge and get a clipboard so we can record things as we go. That way you can catch and release. I don't want to be stuck cleaning a bunch of fish when this is done!"

"I'll go grab it, Dad," Jess offered. "Just give me a second to show Kaylee how to get started."

Seth's daughter had never stepped foot on a frozen lake before, and her fascination with the whole concept of fishing through a hole drilled into ice a foot thick was evident on her face.

It didn't take long before they started reeling in small pan fish. As predicted, the day was sunny with no wind. Dave, Val's oldest, cranked up the music from his phone.

"Dave, can you play some Christmas carols?" Julie asked.

Her request was met with groans and protests.

"Nope! No way, cuz," Dave replied with a grin. "If I have to listen to another stupid carol, I'm going to lose it. Mom's been playing that crap since Thanksgiving."

George shot Dave a look of disapproval but said nothing. Everyone was having fun.

With thirty minutes to go, it was a tight race. George wouldn't share the status, but it was obvious the contest was coming down to two possible winners:

Robbie or Julie. Neither was going to give up gracefully. There was nothing like competition between siblings.

"Ethan, are you going to let these kids beat you?" George hollered across the area of cleared ice to his son. "I've only got you down for two itty-bitty perch."

"I'm not *letting* them do anything," Ethan shot back. "Guess it's just not my day. Besides, Matt and Luke aren't doing much better."

Suddenly, screams erupted.

"Oh my *God*, I think I caught the bottom of the lake," Julie cried, sending George running in her direction. He could see that her stubby ice fishing rod was bent nearly in half. She had something big on the line.

He almost made it, too, but he didn't see the slick spot where water had sloshed out of one of the holes and onto the ice, coating the surface nearby. He slipped and suddenly his momentum was sending him straight for his granddaughter.

"Look out, Julie!" George yelled, unable to veer off the collision course. Their eyes met and in that split second, he could see her struggle with the choice between self-preservation or continuing to fight the fish on the end of her line.

It all happened at once. George slid right into the chair Julie still sat on, sending her tumbling. His arms careened like crazy as he fought to stay on his feet. He knew if he went down he might never get up again. A wild fall at his age could be the end. Somehow he succeeded, grabbing for Julie's upended chair as he skidded to a stop. George set the chair back up and sank into it, fighting to catch his breath.

Julie was already back on her feet but she'd dropped her pole as she went over.

Jake, the youngest out on the ice, had been standing near Julie, cheering her on. From his vantage point on the righted folding chair, George saw the instant Jake noticed Julie's pole, now skidding across the ice in the direction of her fishing hole. George's breath caught when he saw Jake dive for the pole. The kid's quick reflexes slowed the pole, but his small hands, ensconced in snowmobile gloves, couldn't get a decent grip. Both he and the pole continued the slide toward the hole. Whatever was on the other end of the line wasn't waiting around.

Julie was much closer to Jake than George.

"Julie, grab him!" George screamed.

First the pole disappeared down the hole. Jake wasn't far behind. Julie lunged for Jake's foot, catching it and holding on for dear life. Jake made one last futile grab for the pole, his small arm disappearing down the hole.

"Jake! Get away from that hole!" George yelled, shuffling as fast as he could without falling again, over to Jake's side.

Ethan got there before George, grabbing a fistful of Jake's parka and yanking him up off the ice. His red snow boot came off in Julie's hand.

"Oh, man, I *missed* it!" the little boy cried, kicking his feet as Ethan held him suspended above the ice. Jake's right arm dripped with lake water.

Julie stood and shoved the boot back on Jake's foot, and Ethan set the boy down. Water still sloshed out of the hole, seeping toward them.

Jake started to cry. Julie put her arms around him.

"You'll be okay, buddy," she said, holding him tight. "Are you cold?"

"No!" Jake gritted out, pulling away from his older cousin. "You had a whopper on and now it got away! And your pole's gone! *Grandpa!*"

Jake was spitting mad. George knew the cold would set in any second.

"Hey, Jake, relax! It was an accident. You need to be more careful. You could have gone right down that hole if Julie and Ethan wouldn't have grabbed you." In truth, George was more scared than mad over what had just happened.

"I could *not*, Grandpa! I'm too big."

A door slammed and a woman's voice cut through the yelling.

"*Jake Patrick Davis*, what are you doing out here?! You better not be yelling at your grandfather! Get over here, *right* now!" Val, Jake's mother, was stomping her way from the lodge down to the shore, trudging through snow. She'd clearly heard the commotion, and a mother's sixth sense had told her it must be her own son causing it.

"Oh, man, Jake, you're gonna get it now," one of his brothers warned the fuming child.

Jake spun on his heel to face his brother. "Shut up, Dave. I'm telling Mom you were playing music with *swear words* in it."

George glanced from the two boys back to Val, now furiously waiting along the shoreline, hands on hips. As the adrenalin faded, he began to feel the after effects of his near fall. His knee was killing him. He'd let Val deal with Jake . . . and Dave.

He watched Dave shrug, his smirk doing nothing to settle Jake down.

Jake looked from Julie, to his grandfather, to his mom. Apparently realizing he better listen to his irate mother, he took off in her direction, a pout on his face and his arms crossed.

Julie walked over to where George stood with a hand braced against his lower back. "Are you okay? That could have been really bad."

No, I'm not okay, but I'm not about to admit it, George thought.

Aloud he said, "I'm fine, kiddo. I'm sorry if I made you lose a big one."

He bent over to grab the board that held his tracking sheet. As he slowly straightened back up, he noticed Robbie take a fish off the end of his line and slide it quietly back into the hole. He chuckled but said nothing to the boy.

"How about we wrap this up, Dad?" Ethan suggested.

George nodded his agreement. *I need to get inside where it's warm before I tighten up like a bowstring after that little acrobatic stunt.* "All right, everybody, Ethan's right. It's close enough to four o'clock that I'm going to call this fishing derby officially over. Gather up your things and put everything away. We'll meet back in the lodge for official results later."

While the fishing derby was happening outside, serious games of whist were being played inside the lodge. Norman declined the invitation to play, never having learned the game. He insisted that what he *was* skilled at was the creation of holiday cocktails, and he offered to whip up a few beverages for anyone interested. He'd even brought along a case, similar to a briefcase only larger, containing various bottles of liquor and mixes. He had plenty of takers, so Val, never one to pass up the opportunity to learn new recipes, worked with Norman in the kitchen to prepare the refreshments.

Meanwhile, the whist competition commenced with four teams situated around two card tables. Renee and Seth teamed up, since both of their significant others were outside fishing. They took on Rebecca and Lizzy.

"Liz, I wouldn't have guessed a college girl like you knew how to play whist," Renee said to her niece as Seth shuffled the deck.

"I learned a couple years ago. Two of my roommates played all the time growing up and wanted to teach me. We started holding game night for when we were too broke to do anything that required money on the weekends."

Rebecca laughed. "You sound like us, back when we were in college. We'd play cards in one of our dorm rooms. We'd even chip in what little cash we each had, find a five-dollar coupon for a large pizza, and order in. Those were the good old days. Your mom was a pretty good card player, too. Your dad, not so much."

"Wait, you knew my parents in college? I thought your mom just rents from my dad," Lizzy said, lowering the cards she'd been arranging after Seth dealt.

"You know what they say about it being a small world. Yes, Mom does rent from Ethan. She used to rent from your great-aunt when Ms. Celia was still alive. And yes, I went to college with both your mom and your dad. In fact, I introduced them. But Ethan didn't realize he was renting to *my* mother, because her last name was different, and he'd only met her once or twice when we were kids. It wasn't until we ran into each other at the hospital, after the fire, that we put two and two together."

Groans and laughter erupted from the table next to theirs.

"Ladies, do you think we can play and share life stories at the same time?" Seth asked. "Someone's gonna go out over there before we even get through our first round."

"Oh, sorry," Rebecca said, flipping over her card to indicate to the rest of her table that she was passing. The round got underway. Renee granded, but Lizzy had a strong hand and ended up setting them.

"Maybe you should've went fishing instead of playing whist," Seth teased his partner. "You might have had a better chance at a trophy outside with the kids."

"Hey, I should have been able to rely on my partner for at least a couple tricks," Renee shot back, but there wasn't any heat in the exchange, and the two laughed.

The game continued and the lead flipped between the two teams. Eventually, the score was eleven to twelve with Lizzy and Rebecca ahead. The other group was already finished. Penelope and Marvin had made quick work of Brooke and Lavonne.

"This is it," Renee said, picking her cards up off the table and arranging them. "Play it out, my dear Lizzy."

"Oh boy, getting cocky there, aren't you, Auntie?" Lizzy said, leading with her strongest suit. But it was no contest. Renee had all the aces and was long in one suit. She couldn't be stopped.

"Now what was that you were saying about fishing, Seth?" Renee asked as they stood to move over to the winner table. Seth followed her, doing a celebratory dance.

"Good game, guys," Rebecca said, taking a sip from the pink cocktail Norman had delivered to her moments ago.

"Would you ladies care to go up to the library while these card sharks battle it out for first place?" Lavonne asked, looking between Brooke, Lizzy, and Rebecca. "I asked Luke to get the fireplace going up there before they headed out to fish."

"That sounds great, Grandma," Lizzy agreed. "I'm just going to ask Norman for a refill first. This was yummy."

As Lavonne watched her oldest granddaughter head back to the kitchen, she sighed. "I feel old. My grandbaby is legally old enough to drink."

Rebecca laughed. "I can't believe *Ethan* has a daughter that old, either."

Brooke and Rebecca followed Lavonne to the stairs leading up to the library, but she stopped. "You two go on ahead of me. My knee's been giving me trouble. I need to take these a little slower."

"We don't have to go upstairs if it's too hard on your knee," Brooke pointed out.

"Nonsense," Lavonne replied. "It's feeling better with this liquid medicine."

They laughed when she held up her half-empty glass of what looked like eggnog.

The two women went up, not wanting Lavonne to feel rushed. Warmer air met them at the top of the stairs.

"Oh wow, this is something else," Rebecca said in awe as she crossed over to the large windows overlooking the lake. She glanced toward the library with its crackling fire, but the view outside beckoned to her. "Look, you can see them out there fishing. How fun!"

"It *is* fabulous, isn't it?" Brooke acknowledged, coming over to stand next to Rebecca. "Ethan brought me out here for a Halloween party and gave me a tour. And I came out here with him and his kids after Thanksgiving. He helped Renee remodel this place. They revamped it so Renee and Jess can hold retreats out here during the non-summer months. I love the gorgeous view from up here."

Rebecca glanced over at the stairs, but Lavonne hadn't reached the top yet.

"You and Ethan are dating then?" Rebecca asked the woman she'd just met earlier in the day when they arrived at Whispering Pines. She had the distinct impression Brooke was laying claim to Ethan with her comments. Rebecca wasn't sure how she felt about her old friend dating this younger woman.

"We are," Brooke replied. "We work together on some jobs. That's how we met. His kids are great."

Rebecca nodded. "I haven't really met Dylan yet. Drew came with Ethan and the rest of the guys on Christmas Eve. It was so nice of them to bring us gifts. I look forward to visiting more with Elizabeth, too. I was friends with both of her parents in college."

"Isn't that view spectacular?" Lavonne said, finally cresting the top of the stairs. "Ethan was right, I'm afraid. I'm going to have to go get my knee looked at. This is ridiculous. Come on, ladies, a warm fire awaits us."

The light was fading and people were getting hungry. But before dinner, there was one last contest. Each team would have thirty minutes to attempt to build the best snowman. When time was up, Drew would take photos of each creation with Jess's iPad. There would be voting inside, during dinner, and all awards would be given out after. For this contest, there were ten teams in all, so winning wouldn't be easy.

Jess begged off. Still chilled from ice fishing, she wanted to help get dinner set out. This left Seth looking for a partner again. His daughter had already run outside with Robbie. Ethan was trying to convince Rebecca to come out and play in the snow, so Brooke grabbed Seth by the hand and insisted they'd have a shot at the title. Renee watched people disappear outside as she poked at the boiling potatoes on the stove.

"Val and I can handle this in here if you want to go build a snowman, Jess," Renee said.

Jess didn't appreciate the twinkle in her sister's eyes. "If you have something to say, just say it," she said, hands on her hips.

"What? I just know how much you like to beat Ethan at everything. Now might be your chance. Oh, wait . . . Maybe not, since Seth already has a partner."

Val, accustomed to the bantering between her sisters, barely glanced up from the chocolate cake she was frosting. "What are you too picking about now?"

Renee caught the warning look Jess shot her way. She knew Jess didn't want her to bring up her insecurities where Seth was concerned in front of Val again, but ribbing her was more fun. "Nothing. It's just a hoot to tease Jess sometimes."

Val grunted. "Yeah, right. Maybe after another of Norman's cocktails you'll be a bit more forthcoming. You two always leave me out of things."

"You've been whining about that since you were six," Jess said. "We don't leave you out of things."

"Oh, really? Do you *really* believe that?" Val asked, dropping the frosting knife onto the countertop in frustration, brown goop causing a sticky mess. "Why is it always *Renee* you confide in? You two are like two peas in a pod. Ethan and I are just bookends."

For all their arguing and kidding around, Jess really didn't want Val to believe that.

"Val, you know we love you. We don't mean to leave you out of anything. It's just that sometimes . . . you know . . . Renee and I are struggling with similar things."

"What's *that* supposed to mean?"

Renee put the lid back on the huge vat of potatoes and pulled a stool up next to the island, taking a sip of her wine before commenting.

"Don't get all defensive, baby sis," she said. "Jess just meant our kids are older, leaving the nest . . . and God knows we've had a bit more drama in our love lives than you. You've been happily married to Luke since you were *teenagers*, and your boys are still young."

"Oh right, because living in a household with five males is such a piece of cake," Val said, looking between Jess and Renee. "My problems could *never* measure up to the drama in both of your lives."

"Is there something wrong, Val?"

Val sighed. "I guess I could just use some girl-time once in a while, but you two tend to leave me out of things."

"We never mean to do that, sis," Renee said, standing back up and walking over to Val, who was wiping at the gooey mess she'd made with the frosting. Renee hugged her from behind, laying her cheek against Val's back. "You know how much we love you."

Val finally cracked a smile. "Get off me, you idiot, before I frost you."

The hungry crew made short work of the turkey dinner. The salad Rebecca and Penelope brought was a hit. Those who could pitched in with cleanup. It didn't take long with so much help.

Renee, who could see people were getting tired, clapped her hands to get everyone's attention, yelling for the kids watching a movie upstairs to come down. It was time to hand out trophies.

"Matt and I just wanted to take a minute to thank everybody for coming out today. We hope you had as much fun as we did," she said, winking at her husband. "All right, guys. Let's get these babies handed out," she said, motioning to the vintage trophies sitting on a table to her left. "Consider these 'traveling trophies.' If you win one today, you get to keep it, put it in a place of honor at your house, whatever you want . . . but if we decide to do this again next year, bring it back. You have to *earn* the right to keep it each year."

Her explanation was met with nods and smiles from around the large room littered with her family and new friends. For just a minute, her eyes misted over. She was overcome with the blessing of it all.

How much you've changed my life since that day I was laid off, Celia, she thought.

Matt came up to stand beside her, squeezing her hand. "Come on, babe, let's get these bad boys handed out. George, do you want to start with the ice fishing results?"

Renee squeezed Matt's hand in return and beckoned her father to the front. George came up, carrying his clipboard.

"I took it upon myself, when the contest was starting, to divide the contestants up into two groups." He turned his sheet over so the crowd could see what he'd scribbled down. "I mistakenly assumed, since so many of the kids hadn't ice fished before, that those over thirty—lovingly dubbed the 'Old Farts' by yours truly, the oldest fart around—would have an unfair advantage. Mistakenly, I say, because I'm embarrassed to report to you that Luke, Matt, Jess, and Ethan are simply *terrible* at ice fishing. They were easily defeated!"

Laughter.

"But George, we were helping the kids most of the time," Luke yelled in defense.

There were boos and tongue-in-cheek name-calling.

George held up a hand to quiet the crowd. "If you Old Farts are done being poor sports, I'll announce the winners now," George said, trying but failing to keep a straight face.

"Come on, Grandpa, get on with it," Robbie yelled.

"All right, all right, settle down, everyone," George said, trying to regain control. He picked up the fishing trophy from the table. "It was a close race. In the end, it came down to Robbie and Julie. And despite a bit of a debacle on my account, I'm pleased to announce that *Julie* is the official winner of our First Annual Whispering Pines Christmas Fishing Derby!"

Julie popped up from her seat on the floor and rushed to the front to cheers and applause, grabbing the trophy from George.

"Ha-ha, suck it, Robbie!"

Val, standing behind Jake, clapped her hands over his ears, but he wiggled out of her grasp.

George walked back to his folding chair to taunts and cheers all around, and Renee headed back up front, saying, "All right, I'm going to cut you off right there, oh daughter of mine, before you embarrass me further. Next, the votes are in for the *worst* Christmas sweater of the day."

She picked up another trophy, this one sporting a silver statue of a woman posed to pitch a softball on top of a wooden pedestal. "This was originally for First Place Women's Fastpitch, awarded July 25th, 1965. Today, fifty-two years and five months later, this trophy is being awarded to *another* tough woman."

It was easy to guess who Renee was referring to. Most eyes turned to Lavonne.

"I promise all of you, I didn't purposefully set up this contest so Mom would go home with a trophy today. But, since she again showed up wearing the exact same holiday sweater she's worn every Christmas Day for the past ten years, the rest of you really didn't have a chance."

Lavonne stood from her chair and Renee handed her the softball trophy. Lavonne accepted her prize with a fist pump followed by a curtsey and a grimace. She pointed at her bright-red sweater, festooned with a large, appliquéd Santa Claus holding reins that wrapped around to her back, where they connected to Rudolph, knitted right into the pattern. She carefully danced around in a circle to show off her winning top, causing the little bells sewn into the reins to jingle.

"They don't make 'em like this anymore," Lavonne exclaimed, smiling as she again held up her trophy.

"No . . . no, they sure don't, Mom," Ethan replied, causing more laughter.

Lavonne took a seat and Renee picked up another trophy.

"Come on, Aunt Renee, who won the snowman-building contest?" an impatient Jake yelled from his position on the floor up front, where he'd moved to get away from his mother.

"You're going to have to be patient for just a few more minutes, Jake," Renee said, grinning at her youngest nephew. She couldn't get mad at him, even when he was being a bit of a brat. Jake had been the baby of the extended Richter family since birth—at least up until Harper entered the picture. He tended to hold a special place in the hearts of many.

Jake started to protest but hushed when Val warned him to remember what they'd talked about after the ice fishing episode.

"Now, where were we?" Renee asked, teasing those anxious to hear which snowman would take the prize. "Oh, yes—*cards*."

Groans from the littles.

"This year, we're lucky to have some new visitors to Whispering Pines. While the fire over at Ethan's building was awful, and put many of you in tough spots, the one good thing to come out of the tragedy is a chance for new friendships."

"And the rekindling of old friendships," Ethan hollered, raising a beer in Rebecca's direction.

"See? I told you, Rebecca—you should have dated Ethan back when you had the chance," Penelope chimed in, leaving Rebecca red-faced and Brooke looking irritated.

Renee laughed—she was used to losing control of her audience when it came to her family. "Yes, old friendships, too. Trophy number three goes to . . . and this won't be a surprise, since we all know who won the whist tourney . . . *Marvin and Penelope!*"

Enthusiastic cheering ensued.

Renee continued, "I'm not sure where you two learned how to play cards like that, but the rest of us didn't stand much of a chance. Seth, what did it take, like, four hands for them to clobber us?"

Marvin accepted the trophy but quickly handed it over to Penelope. "You keep it. That way I'll have an excuse to come visit."

This brought more hoots of laughter, but no response from the older woman other than a blush. Rebecca laid her head down on the table across from her mother in mock dismay.

"All right, that's enough from me," Renee said, searching the room. "Drew, would you come up here, please? By now, you've all had a chance to see the pictures of the amazing family of snowmen now littering the lawn next to the lodge outside. Drew kept track of your favorites and will award the victor. The winning team of two needs to figure out who gets to be in charge of the trophy until next year, or if you'll swap it in rotation throughout the year. I only hope you're as gracious about it as our new friend Marvin."

A round of applause accompanied Drew's path to the front of the room, the loudest of the cheers coming from little Jake.

"Thanks to everyone for taking this last competition so seriously. Renee and Jess, I apologize in advance if you're missing all your extra scarves and boots you keep for your resort guests. But rest assured, your army of snowmen outside are well protected from the elements."

"Not to worry," Jess said, laughing. "Renee will clean 'em up!"

Drew fiddled with the iPad. "All right, I thought I'd show you the third-place winner, second, and then first."

"Oh man," Jake groaned, his always-short attention span stretched to the limit.

Drew clicked the screen and turned it around for all to see. "Our third-place team got points for representing Kaylee's home state of Texas. Good job, Robbie and Kaylee!"

Seth called out over the cheers, "Now go take that Dallas Cowboys jersey you gave me for Christmas off your snowman and throw it back in my truck!"

"Yes, sir!" Kaylee agreed, saluting her father before fist-bumping Robbie. "But first I want to hear who won."

"Come on, Drew, get on with it," Ethan yelled from the back of the room.

"Well, it certainly wasn't you, Dad!" Drew answered. "You need to get more creative than a snowman with a red Santa hat! Now, as I was about to say, in second place—and let me go on record that the bribe of homemade lasagna was appreciated but not enough to push you up to first—is Brooke and Seth!"

"I told you to throw in your chocolate cake too, Brooke," Seth said in mock disappointment, hanging his head. "You cost us the win."

Renee, observing now from a front corner of the room, had to laugh as she watched Jake getting ever more antsy in the front row. Either the kid had to use the bathroom or he'd held out high hopes as to who the winner would be. Aloud she told Drew to end the suspense already.

Drew set his iPad down and scooped up the final trophy—the one that had towered over all the rest—and held it high in the air. "And, last but not least, the winner of our first ever Whispering Pines Snowman Escapade is . . . drumroll, please . . . *Jake and Grandpa!*"

Jake shot up off the floor and leapt at Drew, reaching as high as he could for the winning trophy, but Drew held it just high enough that the boy couldn't reach it. He put his free hand on the top of Jake's head, holding him down.

"Jake, don't you have something to say to Grandpa first?"

"I already 'pologized," Jake said as he tried to shake off Drew's hand.

George walked up front and took the trophy from Drew. He laid his other hand on Jake's shoulder and Drew stepped back. "Thanks, Drew. Jake did apologize. He got caught up in the moment and didn't mean to be careless. He's also assured me he won't yell at the rest of us the next time he's disappointed."

"I'll give that a day," one of his brothers muttered.

"Be that as it may," George said, "I'd be honored if Jake would keep our traveling trophy in his room until next year. It was his idea to build an upside-down snowman and name him Slippery Sam, modeled after my unfortunate stumble out on the ice today."

George handed the trophy to Jake and motioned for him to sit back down.

"Matt and Renee have already said it, but I wanted to add my thanks to everybody for coming out today, for participating, and basically making it a great Christmas Day! It's probably about time we finish cleaning up and head home. All this fun wears us old guys out."

"And the Old Farts!" Jess added with a laugh.

"Sure does!" Norman chimed in.

George gave Norman a thumbs-up. "Travel safe, everybody. And thanks for the great day."

Everyone got up and started gathering their things. Extra tables and chairs were put away and leftovers were taken out to vehicles. Jess and Renee would be preparing the lodge for their retreat the weekend after New Year's, and Renee appreciated that no one wanted to leave them a mess to clean up first.

Renee handed George a box of food to take out to his car. George took it but scanned the room.

"Robbie, come here please," he said when he spied his grandson talking to Seth's daughter.

Robbie made his way over to his mom and grandfather. "What do you need, Grandpa? Want me to take that out for you?"

"Sure, that would be great. But I wanted to let you know I saw what you did with that fish today."

Robbie put his arms out to take the box. "What fish?"

George chuckled. "You know exactly what I'm talking about."

Robbie set the box on his hip and grinned. "Hey, nobody wants to win because someone else got bumped off her chair."

"And nobody wants to be the reason someone loses because of their own clumsiness, either. Thank you."

"You're welcome," Robbie said with a nod, turning away to take the box of food out to George's car.

"What was that all about?" Renee asked her father.

"You're doing a great job with that kid, honey," George said, giving Renee a hug. "Merry Christmas."

Chapter Twenty

GIFT OF A COOL HEAD AND COOL HANDS

REX REMEMBERED WHEN HE used to like Christmas, back before his wife died. Gail always had a knack for making the holidays special. They loved to travel, and flights were cheaper on Christmas Eve when everyone else wanted to be home with family.

Through the years there had been beach vacations, ski trips, and even an overseas adventure where they slept in a castle. The ghosts that were rumored to share their sleeping quarters never materialized, but the food was amazing and Rex was happy to keep Gail "safe from the boogeyman" until dawn.

Now those memories were all he had to keep him warm at night.

After Gail was gone, Rex struggled with the holidays, just as so many others do after they lose loved ones. He'd often take his mom over to his brother's house and try to enjoy the festivities. He even went to Ethan's parents' house a time or two. The crowd and excitement were fun for a while, but it only magnified the quiet once he got home.

This year was different . . . worse. He couldn't bring himself to do much of anything. He'd barely managed to arrange for his niece to get his mother over to see the rest of the family. He wasn't allowed to leave town, anyway, as a condition of his bail. Ethan and some of his family had left a few messages for him leading up to Christmas Eve, but Rex hadn't called anyone back.

He kept getting calls on his cell from a number he didn't recognize, too. The caller ID appeared to be for a local number. The number kept calling and calling until he finally answered it out of frustration, ready to chew out whoever was on the other end of the line. But no one was there. It must have been coming from an auto dialer.

He'd bought a small turkey breast, intending to prepare himself a Christmas feast, but he hadn't even bothered to take it out of the fridge once he brought it home from the grocery store. Chips and beer made an easier, if less tasty, meal—and if he drank *enough* of the beer, he sometimes thought about something other than smoke and flames.

He was proud of himself on Christmas Eve. He held off on drinking the beer until after he'd gotten home from church. Attending Midnight Mass was the one tradition he'd continued after Gail died. The darkness of night, the glowing candles in the sanctuary, and the smell of incense somehow made him feel closer to his wife . . . as if a part of her was somehow still there, in the church, looking over him. He'd arrived early so he could sit in their favorite pew—the same pew they always used to try to sit in whenever they went to Mass.

Even when they used to travel over the holidays, Gail always insisted they find a church so they could celebrate the Lord's birth. And so he still went without her. This year, he'd plastered on as friendly of a face as he could muster as he left the church after Mass. A few acquaintances wished him Merry Christmas as their paths crossed on the way out to their vehicles. Those brief conversations would be the sum total of words he'd exchanged with other people for four or five days.

Never had he felt less like celebrating.

Instead of driving straight home that night, he found himself down by the river. Snow was falling. The night was silent. He ended up at the park bench where he liked to stop sometimes in the summer to drop a line in.

It looked different in the dead of night, in the dead of winter, under the glow of a bright, gold moon. He sat for a spell, but the water wasn't visible from his bench, so he made his way over to the edge of the river. Gazing down, he looked into the gap between the frosty bank and the jagged edges of ice. Water rushed by, moving too fast in this spot to freeze solid. For a brief second, he wondered what it would feel like to let himself sink into that gap. Would he feel the bitter cold for long, or would it all be over quickly?

Somewhere overhead, an owl hooted, snapping him out of his trance-like state. *What the hell is the matter with me?*

He quickly turned his back on the invitation of oblivion, knowing that wasn't the answer he sought. Back into his truck he climbed, leaving one of his favorite places on earth until he could come back when he'd feel sunshine on his back, instead of this vast loneliness.

Once home, he plucked his four remaining beers out of the fridge by the plastic ring, taking them out to his favorite chair in the front room. He surfed through the endless options on his television—his online streaming subscription a Godsend during these dark days. But nothing interested him tonight. Finally, he settled on his favorite series. It didn't matter that he'd watched every episode more than once; *Longmire* was his go-to.

Two beers in, he must have nodded off. Something woke him. His show still played, although it had flipped to another episode while he slept. His picture window stood naked, undoubtedly giving anyone outside, in the dark, a clear view in.

"Shit," he muttered, pushing up out of his comfortable chair to close the curtains. He scraped his shin on the old magazine rack, a shot of pain radiating up from his tender new skin. He limped over to the window and yanked the curtains shut, pulling too hard on one side. The rings on top started to let go and the curtain sagged, no longer completely covering the window.

"I'll deal with that in the morning," he said to the empty room. "Time to get my sorry ass to bed."

Ethan couldn't remember the last time he'd had as much fun as he did on Christmas Day out at Whispering Pines. Helping the kids ice fish, getting to know his tenants better, and reconnecting with Rebecca made the day all the more special.

Lizzy also seemed to enjoy the day. He'd worried she'd think it was lame. Seeing her jump into the whist tournament was a surprise. Both Rebecca and Brooke commented to him, individually, that they'd enjoyed visiting with her.

He'd also been right not to worry about his boys enjoying the day. It was a relief to get to spend the entire Christmas weekend with all three of them and not have to share them with Stacey. She'd have them for New Year's Eve, much to their horror. Teenagers and college students saw New Year's as a time to party with friends.

Maybe next year.

Ethan knew he got the better part of the bargain this year.

His only regret—only niggling worry throughout the days of festivities—centered on Rex. He worried his friend might have been sitting home alone. Ethan tried to contact him numerous times to invite him over, but the stubborn cuss wasn't returning his calls. Rex would have known why he was calling and made a point to ignore him.

Ethan always gave his construction crews the week off between Christmas and New Year's, with pay. It usually wasn't too much of a financial burden on him because he planned ahead for the expense all year, but he hoped this year he wouldn't regret it; his cash flow was already taking a hit with Rex out of commission and the fourplex unlivable.

Regardless, Ethan never considered taking away the pay. His longer-term employees had come to rely on it. It would all work out.

But maybe now, with Christmas behind them, he'd be able to talk Rex into lunch. The kids were off doing things with friends, affording him a rare free afternoon.

"Well, I'll be damned. You *are* still among the living," Ethan replied when Rex picked up after three rings. "Merry belated Christmas, pal."

"Same to you," Rex replied. "Have fun?"

"We did. Thanks for asking. You could have, too, if you'd have bothered to answer my calls beforehand." Ethan's comment was met with silence. "Did I lose you?"

"Nah, still here. I was kind of tied up. Glad you had fun. I worried the kids might be off with their mother."

Ethan held the phone between his ear and his shoulder as he dumped thick cleaner into the toilet bowl.

Should have made the kids clean for an hour before they left the house.

"They have to go with Stacey for New Year's. I got 'em for Christmas this year."

Rex barked out a short laugh—a sound Ethan hadn't heard since before Thanksgiving. "Bet they're not too happy about that. About New Year's, I mean."

Ethan grabbed his phone so he wouldn't drop it in the toilet as he reached for the scrub brush. "You are very right about that," he confirmed.

"What the hell are you doing? One moment I can hear you and then it gets all garbled," Rex complained.

"Scrubbing the damn toilet."

"Fun."

"Yeah. But someone's got to do it, and I didn't tell the kids to do it before they scattered in all different directions. I need to get out of here before my fingers start to prune from too much housework. Lunch?"

Another beat of silence.

"Look, Ethan, I told you, I don't think that's a good idea right now. Until this mess gets straightened out, we probably need to keep our distance. But thanks for calling. Glad the kids had a fun Christmas."

Click.

Ethan dropped his phone on the laminate countertop, swearing. He made quick work of cleaning the rest of the bathroom, fueled by frustration over Rex's stubbornness.

Rex drove him nuts—especially when Ethan knew his friend was right.

Stashing the cleaning supplies under the bathroom sink, Ethan walked back down the hallway, searching through his phone for Steve's number. He hadn't talked to his lawyer for a week, given the holidays. He didn't know if Steve was taking time off, but he figured he'd try him.

After just the second ring: "Hey, Ethan, have a nice Christmas?"

"We did. How about you, Steve?"

They exchanged pleasantries for a minute and then Ethan got down to business.

"Do you have any updates since last time we talked?"

He thought he could hear Steve shuffling some papers. He might have caught him at his desk.

"Actually, I got a copy of the police report on Rex's arrest just this morning. I haven't had a chance to read it yet. Do you want to stop over this afternoon? Give me time to read it first and then I can share the highlights with you?"

"I could. Or would you want to grab lunch? My turn to buy," Ethan offered. He had to get out of this tiny apartment before he went crazy.

Steve laughed. "Hell, if you're buying, I'm not about to pass that up."

After their dishes were cleared away, Steve pulled an envelope out of his jacket's inside pocket.

"Anything in the report?" Ethan asked, nodding at the white envelope.

Steve unfolded the report. "Most of it we already knew. Some of it we didn't. Let's see . . ." Steve again fished around in his jacket, pulling out a pair of glasses.

"Why don't you just let me read it?" Ethan suggested, holding out a hand.

"Hold on. God, you are impatient."

Ethan wanted to retort that his patience had been tested now for over a month, but instead he sat back in his chair, arms crossed over his chest, and waited.

"Basically, I'd agree they have enough to take a harder look at Rex. I'm not sure they have enough to make the charges stick if this goes to trial. I think they'll need to get more in order to actually convict. But this gives them a way to keep talking to Rex, pressing him for more details. Things we already knew—they found Rex on the floor in the lower unit where the fire started, unconscious, a mostly empty bottle of Jack sitting next to him. One of the firemen reported smelling alcohol when they picked him up to pull him away from the flames—though how he smelled alcohol through all the smoke and his own helmet, I don't know. Regardless, here is where we start to learn some new stuff. Based on the burn patterns on the floor and up the wall, they are confident an accelerant was used to start the fire."

Ethan was afraid of that. "Can they tell what the accelerant *was*?"

Steve shook his head. "Not definitively, at least according to this. They also found the remnants of what looked to have once been a pile of rags. May have been used to fuel the fire."

"Where?"

"On the countertop."

Rex had helped install that new countertop a few days before the fire. Ethan didn't believe for a minute he'd use the surface to start a fire.

"Is there anything specific in that report that implicates Rex, other than his physical presence?"

Once again, Steve shook his head. "Not inside. Oh, other than a comment about a boarded-up window in the unit. That might have been done to slow detection."

"*No*. That's wrong. Someone on my crew accidently broke that window a few days earlier. I helped board it up myself until we could get a new sheet of glass installed."

Steve lowered the report to the table and looked across at Ethan.

"Sorry," Ethan said, rubbing the back of his neck. "I know you're just the messenger here."

Steve consulted the report one last time, then folded it up and stowed it away in his pocket.

"The last thing it talks about is what they found in Rex's truck. There were some empty cans of Bud Light on the floor of the backseat. In the pickup box, they found two bottles of paint stripper, a bottle of turpentine, and a bag of rags. All things that are a bit damning when found at the scene of a potential arson case."

"Also, all things a contractor needs when cleaning up old woodwork and cabinets in a remodel," Ethan pointed out. "Was his truck locked?"

His lawyer shrugged. "It didn't say. Why?"

"Just wondering," Ethan replied. "Rex doesn't usually drink Bud Light."

Both men sat quietly for a minute while the waiter asked if there would be anything else and dropped the check on the table between them. As promised, Ethan grabbed the check.

He stood to leave once the waiter was gone. "Thanks for meeting me, Steve. And thanks for the updates. For the record, I still know there's no way Rex did this. And I'm going to do everything I can to prove it."

Steve stood as well, folding up his reading glasses. "I understand why you feel the need to do that, Ethan. I'm sure I'd feel the same way if I were in your shoes. Just be careful. The last thing you want to do is make things *worse* for Rex."

Ethan stopped at the grocery store after lunch. He'd need to feed the kids for two more days until Stacey picked them up. Since it was another mild winter day, he thought hamburgers on the grill would be a nice break from pasta or pizza.

The apartment was still empty when he got home. He'd been going over and over in his mind the things Steve told him were in the arrest report. He wasn't impartial, he knew, but he couldn't see how those things would be enough to prove beyond a reasonable doubt that Rex started the fire. But he couldn't just rely on his gut. He needed to help convince the police that Rex was innocent.

He'd just sat down at their small kitchen table with a pad of paper and a pen when a loud buzz cracked through the air. He walked over to the intercom. One of the kids must have forgotten their keys.

"Yep," he said as he pushed the button.

"Ethan, it's me, Brooke. Can I come up?"

Surprised, Ethan pushed the second button to unlock the security door down on the first floor. Brooke's timing was good—she knew Rex. Maybe she'd have time to help him brainstorm.

He opened the door just as she was about to knock. "Hey," he said in greeting, a smile spreading over his face as he took in her appearance and caught a whiff of something fresher than the usual stale air of the apartment hallway. "This is a nice surprise. Come on in."

Brooke brushed past him with a smile of her own.

"I saw your truck parked outside and thought I'd drop in. Hope you don't mind. I had lunch with my sister and niece, but it was Stella's nap time so they went home. Back in the day we'd have spent the afternoon shopping, but that isn't any fun with a cranky toddler in tow." She looked around. "Where are your kids?"

Ethan stepped forward as Brooke slipped her jacket off. "Here, I can take that for you. They're all out and about, somewhere. I think Drew had to work at two. They've all had enough family time."

Brooke handed him her red coat but stepped closer as she did so. She put her hands on his waist and smiled up at him. "Thanks for including me in your fun day out at the lake on Christmas."

Ethan smiled down at her, seeing the invitation in her eyes. For the first time in a couple of weeks, no one else was around. He dipped his head for a kiss. What started out as a quick greeting started to heat up. He pulled back.

Focus on Rex!

Stepping away, he motioned to his notebook on the table. "I'm glad you stopped by. I was going to call you."

Brooke glanced at the table. "Good . . . but why? What are you working on?"

"I just came from lunch with my lawyer. He updated me on Rex's arrest report."

Brooke's smile slipped off her face and her shoulders drooped. "Poor Rex. I can't stop thinking about him. The whole notion that he had anything at all to do with the fire is ridiculous. How's he feeling?"

"Physically? Better, I think, although it's been a while since I've seen him. Speaking of ridiculous . . . he's insisting we not spend any time together until this all gets figured out. I did talk to him on the phone earlier today, though. He said the burns are better. He's still going to physical therapy. He's not cleared to work yet."

Brooke pulled out a chair and sat down. "What about emotionally?"

"That seems to be a bigger struggle."

"How can I help?"

Ethan grabbed two bottles of water out of the fridge and set them down on the table, taking the seat across from Brooke. "I'm not sure. But your timing is perfect. Maybe you could help me brainstorm on what we might be able to do to prove that Rex is innocent."

He filled her in on what Steve shared over lunch. She listened carefully, adding her thoughts as appropriate.

"Wait, did you say Bud Light? Rex doesn't drink Bud Light, does he?"

Ethan rubbed the corner of his mouth in thought. "Not very often. I thought that was kind of strange, too. I remember he and Gail used to drink it. She was always on him about trying to be healthy and watch his weight. Not that *any* beer is great, but she did what she could. But ever since . . . you know . . . I've just seen him drink Budweiser."

Brooke shrugged. "Maybe he either ate too much or he was feeling nostalgic—you know, missing her. He seems to do that a lot, doesn't he? And remember, this was Thanksgiving weekend."

Ethan nodded. "That might be why. It's probably nothing. Anyhow, I thought maybe I could do some digging of my own. Talk to people who know Rex, maybe get some character witnesses lined up in case he needs them."

Since Brooke worked with many of the same people as Rex and Ethan, and since Rex didn't do much *other* than work, together they built a list of people Ethan could talk to. They worked on it for an hour, until Ethan noticed the light dimming outside. He pushed back from the table, stood, and stretched his back. It'd been giving him trouble again.

"That's probably enough for today. I thought I'd grill up some burgers for the kids when they get home. Want to stay for dinner? I'm sure I have enough."

Brooke stood, too. She came around behind Ethan and started to massage the spot in his lower back that he was trying to rub but couldn't quite reach.

"We'll see. How about a back rub first?"

Her strong fingers were already loosening the knot in his spine. He placed both hands on the table and leaned forward, giving her a better angle. "I'll give you an hour to quit that."

"Why do you have so much trouble with your back?"

Ethan glanced over his shoulder. "That obvious, huh? I'd like to blame it on work, but honestly, it's bugged me ever since I played football."

"Ah, the glory days," she said with a laugh. "I could do this better if you'd lay down."

Ethan straightened and turned back to face Brooke and his living room. He glanced at the old couch but knew his tall frame wouldn't comfortably fit on it. The floor looked like torture. His bed was the best option . . . but he wasn't sure he wanted to go there.

Up to this point, he'd held off on getting intimately involved with Brooke. But, *damn*, those hands of hers. And it had been a long time since he'd been with anyone. Maybe he was being a prude.

Or maybe all she really wants to do is give you a massage, idiot.

"About the only place I fit is my bed," Ethan said, searching her eyes for a hint as to what she was thinking. She smiled back at him, but he couldn't read her.

Deciding to stop overthinking it and see where things led, he took her by the hand and ushered her down the hallway. He closed the door to his sons' messy room. (He hadn't dared enter it when he was cleaning earlier.) Lizzy had been sleeping on the couch, so her suitcase was stowed in a corner of his bedroom, along with a pile of pillows and blankets.

"Give me just a minute, will you?" he asked as he sat down on the edge of his bed, fiddling with his phone. He used the tracking app to check on the location of each of his kids. It looked like Lizzy was at the mall, Dylan was across town at his buddy's, and Drew was at work. He didn't need anyone walking in when he had a girl in his room.

"Do you have any baby oil?" Brooke asked, pushing the sleeves of her sweater up out of the way.

Ethan dropped his phone onto his nightstand and laughed. "You're kidding, right?"

Brooke shrugged and watched him closely. He felt like she was sizing him up too.

Sticking with the premise of what brought them into his room in the first place, Ethan flipped over and laid diagonally, face down, on his bed. His feet hung off the edge.

"It's awfully quiet in here," Brooke observed. She used her phone to start some music, keeping the volume low and setting it down next to Ethan's.

Shit, shit, shit, he thought as he lay there, tense and waiting, his forehead resting on his wrist and his face buried in his comforter. Maybe this was a bad idea.

The bed dipped further from their combined weight as she sat next to him and started to massage his lower back. He'd thrown on a decent shirt before meeting Steve for lunch, and it was still tucked in his jeans. His belt added yet another layer. He laughed quietly, a nervous edge to it, as she attempted to navigate around all the clothing.

"What?" she asked, her hands momentarily paused. "Is this helping at all?"

Ethan rolled to his side, half sitting up. "Yes, but it'd feel better if my damn belt and shirt weren't in the way. But I feel like a teenager, waiting to see if you'll dare to reach under them." He paused. "Why does this feel so awkward?"

Brooke grinned back.

"Oh, I'll dare . . . if you want me to," she said, gently tugging at the front of his shirt.

He didn't stop her hand. He held her gaze. Once the front of his shirt was free, he helped her out by untucking it the rest of the way and unhooking his belt. He tossed his belt onto the carpet and assumed his previous position.

He could have groaned out loud when her cool hands came in direct contact with the skin of his lower back. In fact, he wasn't sure that he didn't when he heard her give a nervous giggle.

Maybe I'm not the only one finding this awkward . . . or pleasurable.

They stayed like that for a time, Brooke massaging his back, the tension seeping away. It was good to feel a woman's touch again.

Brooke's hands started roaming farther, and now Ethan started to feel a different kind of tension. He sat up and slid his body over so they were sitting hip to hip. He brought a hand up and turned her face toward his, catching her up in a kiss. One of her hands traveled up over his shoulder and into his hair.

They both froze at the sound of keys in the door out in the kitchen.

"Oh, crap!" Ethan whispered, panic sluicing through his body. "Quick—get in the bathroom! Wait a minute before you come out!"

Brooke held a hand over her mouth in an effort to stifle a giggle. She slipped from the room and into the bathroom, gently closing the door. Ethan snatched up his belt, buttoned his shirt, and jammed the tail of it back into his jeans. He finger-combed his hair and tried to walk nonchalantly back out to the kitchen.

Lizzy had dropped her keys on the table and hung her purse on the back of the chair Ethan had sat in earlier. She barely glanced at her father, but Ethan saw her take in the other handbag, hanging in a similar fashion on one of the other chairs.

"Oh . . . hi, Dad. What are you up to? Is Rebecca here?"

This stopped Ethan cold.

"Rebecca? Why would Rebecca be here?"

Now his daughter *did* look at him. "Maybe because there's a woman's purse hanging here that I don't recognize."

Dammit if he didn't feel his cheeks burn. Ethan's mind searched for a plausible explanation. *Deflect!* was all he could come up with.

"Oh, that's Brooke's. She stopped by and was helping me brainstorm about Rex's case. You know, since we all work together and stuff. She's in the bathroom." He picked up his notebook and tried to look like he was studying his notes. Maybe mentioning Rex would be enough to distract Lizzy. When she remained silent, he continued. "I was just going to start making some burgers for supper and invited her to stay. You don't mind, do you?"

Lizzy gave him a long look. "Dad. I'm not a child. You don't have to pretend you weren't back in your bedroom with a woman."

Ethan, momentarily speechless over his daughter's audacity, started to deny it, but Lizzy spoke over him.

"*I'm* not a child, but Dylan *is*, and he was just getting dropped off in the parking lot when I walked in. You might want to rebutton your shirt—the right way this time—and turn that music off back there if you don't want to scar him for life."

Ethan glanced down at his shirt, mortified. *How could I be so careless?*

Based on the expression on Lizzy's face, she didn't find any humor in the situation either. He knew if he'd walked into the apartment and found *her* in a similar state, he'd have been furious. She had a right to be angry. He quickly fixed his shirt as the doorknob turned.

"What's to eat? I'm *starving*," Dylan moaned as he dropped his backpack next to the door and kicked his tennis shoes off. "You are never going to guess what I saw today!"

"You wouldn't believe what *I* saw either," Lizzy grumbled as she walked across the kitchen and opened the fridge.

Ethan hoped he could trust her to keep his indiscretion from Dylan.

Chapter Twenty-One
Gift of Generosity

Brooke hadn't stayed for dinner. Once Lizzy showed up, followed closely by Dylan, she begged off, claiming to have another commitment. Ethan thought Lizzy did a fair job at not making Brooke feel awkward. She pretended nothing was up when Brooke joined them in the kitchen. She didn't go out of her way to be friendly to Brooke, either, but Ethan supposed that would have been expecting too much. It wasn't like he was in any position to scold her for her behavior.

Dylan, on the other hand, was excited to see Brooke—no surprise there—and had even tried to convince her to stay for burgers.

Ethan didn't mind that she'd left. He was still feeling awkward about what happened. He also wanted to talk to the kids, alone, about an idea of his that would impact all of them—or at least the boys. Now that they'd each polished off two burgers, he wanted to catch them before they all scattered again.

"I think I have a solution for Marvin's housing situation but I wanted to talk to you three about it first," Ethan said, looking around at his three kids, all crowded around the miniature kitchen table.

"What did you come up with, Dad?" Drew asked. Ethan knew Drew had been concerned about Marvin, asking him every day where the elderly man would go, since he needed to be out of the nursing home by the first of January.

"I had to get creative. Marvin is getting low on cash after spending a month in that home. Do you guys have any idea how much one of those places cost?"

"Not exactly, but probably more than college," Lizzy offered. "Glad I'm almost done there, too. I can't afford *that* place much longer, either, even with yours and Mom's help."

Ethan laughed. "Exactly. You can kind of relate, Lizzy. Believe me when I say nursing homes are crazy-expensive. I'm not charging Marvin rent while he's out of my building, obviously, but he would need quite a bit more than a normal month of rent if he had to sign a new lease somewhere else. Besides, he still says he wants to come back once our building is ready."

"So what's your idea," Dylan prodded, glancing at the clock on the wall. Ethan knew his son's favorite show was starting soon.

"I'm getting to that. Chill, Dylan. This is important. It worked out great to have Penelope move into one of our vacant units in another building, but I only had one opening. For some reason I kept asking myself, 'What would Celia do?' Remember how Aunt Celia always helped people out when they were in trouble? And then she passed much of her money and possessions on to us with the expectation that we'd do the same?"

All three kids nodded patiently.

"Well, then it struck me . . . why not invite Marvin to move in with us?"

"With *us*?" Dylan asked, his voice incredulous. "Dad, we only have two bed-rooms, and Lizzy said that couch hurts her back. It would probably *kill* Marvin. Unless you're giving up your bed? And even then, I still think that would get awfully crowded."

Lizzy and Drew stared at Dylan as if he'd sprouted a second head.

"Seriously, dude, you need to think before you talk," Drew said, shaking his head. "He's talking about *Celia's house*, not the apartment, you idiot."

Dylan's mouth opened for a brief second, then he said in defense, "But Celia's house isn't ready yet. If it was, *we'd* be moving in there."

Lizzy put her fingers in her mouth and let out an ear-piercing whistle. "Both of you! Shut the hell up and let Dad talk."

Ethan wasn't sure if it was the blast of a whistle or the cussing, but it proved effective.

"That may have been overkill," he said with a grin, then went on. "Like Drew said, I meant Celia's house. But we all need to work on calling it *our* house. Celia wanted us to live there, make it our home. She never intended for it to be a shrine to her. That's why I was comfortable making the big renovations. If we'd have stayed on schedule, we probably would have either been in there by now or close. I know the upstairs isn't ready for us, but I'm hoping we can all move in within a couple months. But the main living area is done."

Lizzy was nodding. "You're right, Dad. I think this could work. Since you took your daughter's brilliant advice and turned that small powder room into a full bath with a shower and moved the door so you don't go in through the kitchen, everything he needs is really right there on the first floor."

"Would you use one of the other rooms, like the study, as a bedroom for Marvin?" Drew asked.

"Yes," Ethan confirmed. "He'd have access to the kitchen and a bathroom. What more could he need? Far better than the place he's in now."

Dylan suggested they bring down Aunt Celia's bed from where they'd stashed it in the attic when they'd cleared everything out to start the construction. "You might need a couple extra guys to get it back downstairs. That thing was one of those fancy deals where you push a button and the top part of the bed goes up or down. It was heavier than a mother."

Dylan saw the look on Drew's face.

"What?"

"Dylan, don't you remember Aunt Celia died *in* the house *in her sleep?* She probably died on that bed. That is just wrong. We shouldn't make anybody sleep on that mattress. I'm trying to be mature about living in the house, and I'm all right with it, but there are lines that shouldn't be crossed."

Dylan looked from his brother to his father, eyes wide.

"Oh, for God's sake, Drew, she didn't die in that bed," Ethan said. "She hadn't been feeling well and so she was sleeping in a recliner in the living room. Your grandfather got rid of that chair immediately."

"Oh . . . really?" Drew looked relieved. "Here I've been freaked out about that bed being in the attic this whole time. I thought it was kind of cold for you to keep it."

Ethan stood and started clearing the dirty dishes. "So, other than a potentially haunted bed, do you three have any other concerns? Liz?"

"Nope, I think it's a great idea. Celia would have approved."

"Thank you, honey. I like to think so. Boys?"

Dylan seconded Lizzy's vote.

"Who would have guessed Marvin would get to move into our new house before *we* would?" Drew asked. "I hope *he* thinks it's a good idea."

"Absolutely not," Marvin said after Ethan shared the basics of his idea with the older man the next morning.

A bingo game was in full swing in the large commons area, so they were back in Marvin's room. Two cardboard boxes lay open at the end of his bed, ready to be used to pack up his meager belongings.

"Why not?" Ethan asked, shocked at Marvin's response. He'd expected it to be an easy sell.

"I'm a proud man, Ethan, and I don't take handouts. Now, don't misunderstand me—I appreciate everything you've done for me since the fire. But this is too much. I will not move in with your family."

"We don't even live there yet, Marvin. The main floor, where you could stay, is all finished. There's a small bathroom and a kitchen, and we'll convert the study into a bedroom for you. It's just temporary, until the fourplex is livable again."

The confusion on Marvin's face told Ethan he wasn't explaining himself well enough.

"Celia left me her personal residence when she died, along with some rental properties, including the building you live in *and* the one Penelope is staying in now. You remember Celia, don't you?"

Marvin rolled his eyes. "Of course, I remember Celia. She wasn't a woman one could easily forget. A friend of hers would come over with her twice a month and we'd play bridge. Penelope made it a foursome."

"Good. Then you know Celia was always helping people out. And she expected us to do the same. She drilled that into all of our heads since we were kids. I'm trying to carry out Celia's wishes. Are you going to make that impossible for me to do?"

Marvin shifted uncomfortably in his chair. "Well, no, I guess I didn't think about it like that. You and your kids . . . you aren't going to live there?"

"Actually, we *are* going to move in before too long. But the upstairs, where all the bedrooms are, still needs some work done before we can move out of our apartment."

Marvin considered this. "I'll need to think about it."

Ethan sighed. "Marvin, normally I'd love to give you all the time you need to think about it, but in this case, you need to be out of here by the day after tomorrow. Unless you've come up with some other options since we last talked, I'm afraid I'm all you've got."

Marvin nodded but said nothing.

"Tell you what. Why don't I run down to the cafeteria and see if I can't get us a cup of coffee? Give you a minute to think about it in peace and quiet. Would that help? How do you take it?"

"Yes, why don't you do that. Black."

Ethan nodded and slipped out of the room. He felt bad for the poor guy. None of this was Marvin's fault. His two kids couldn't—or wouldn't—help. If he refused to come to Celia's, they were back to square one and Ethan was out of ideas.

He didn't rush back. The pot of coffee in the cafeteria was nearly empty. An aide noticed Ethan looking and said he'd brew a fresh one. Ethan appreciated the offer and checked his emails while he waited. Steve had sent him a note, basically telling him he didn't have anything new but was heading out of town for New Year's. He'd be in touch the following week.

Ethan wished *he* could drop everything and leave town for a vacation. The extent of his New Year's celebration might end up being hors d'oeuvres at his Uncle Gerry's annual bash. While he loved his family, and appreciated his dad's brother inviting him, partying with the seventy-plus group sounded a bit too conservative, even for him. Maybe he should give Brooke a call.

"Your coffee is ready, sir," a woman in a hairnet hollered to him from the front of the kitchen.

Ethan put his phone away and accepted two paper cups of fresh black coffee from her.

"Appreciate it," he said with a wink, catching the woman's blush as he turned away.

He could hear Stacey's voice in his head. *"You'd flirt with the goddamn Pope if he was a woman."* Technically he wasn't flirting, but she might have had a point.

Marvin was standing at the solitary window in his room, looking outside. A birdfeeder stood to the right of his window. Ethan caught a flash of red as a cardinal swooped in.

"I managed to rustle up some fresh coffee," he said.

Marvin turned around and reached for the cup with his left hand. The bandage he'd worn on it when he first arrived at the nursing home was gone, but now Ethan could see the damage. It was nearly healed but would probably always sport a pink scar. The hand shook a bit.

"Why don't you sit down and I'll give it to you?" Ethan suggested, nodding to the chair.

"Give me the damn coffee, Ethan. I'm not an invalid."

Properly chastised, Ethan handed Marvin the cup.

"I do appreciate your offer, Ethan, and I've thought about what you said. You're right. I don't have any other options at this point. I'll stay in Celia's home, and I'm grateful, but I have two conditions. No, wait—*three* conditions. First, I'll pay you the same rent I'd be paying you at the fourplex."

Ethan started to protest, but Marvin shut him down with a hard look.

"Second, I'd like to help a bit at Celia's. There must be something I can do to make myself useful so you can get your family moved in. And third, this is only temporary. If you aren't able to get the fourplex fixed up within a couple months, three at most, I'll figure something else out. I don't want to overstay my welcome. But for now, I'll gladly take you up on your offer."

Ethan reached out and shook Marvin's right hand.

Now he just needed to figure out what he could let Marvin help with at the house. There had to be something.

The old man certainly won't be able to haul the bed down from the attic.

"I can see why you guys liked to come up here when you were kids," Lizzy said, looking around the large attic at Celia's house. "If there wasn't so much junk up here, this would be really cool."

Ethan surveyed the vast open space, following Lizzy's eyes as he reached the top of the narrow wooden staircase. "Back then, there wasn't all that much up here. Believe it or not, we used to ride our bikes up here in the winter when we were young. You know, like training-wheels-on-the-bike young. Not ten-speeds, obviously."

He turned at the sound of a scuffle below.

"Hey, guys, knock it off! Somebody's going to get hurt."

More footsteps pounded up the stairs as Drew and Dylan raced to see who'd get to the top first.

"You boys are worse than a three-year-old," Lizzy said, disdain in her voice. "Where's that bed you were talking about, Dad?"

Ethan wandered farther into the crowded room. One of these days he'd need to get this place cleaned out. He felt guilty for making such a mess up here.

"Guys, do you remember where you put the mattress that came out of Celia's room?"

Drew nodded off to his right. "Yeah, it's leaning against that wall over there. See?"

Ethan saw . . . and groaned. Getting it over to the stairway was going to take all four of them. Boxes and other old furniture littered the path between here and there.

Dylan sneezed. "Man, it's *dusty* up here!"

Ethan turned at the chiming of the old doorbell. "Now what?"

"Dylan, go look through the window and see who's down there," Ethan said, motioning to the small double-hung window on the front of the house.

Dylan plowed his way toward the window, knocking a box over as he went. From the clatter it made, the box must have held old pots and pans.

"Be careful!" his sister yelled.

"It's Brooke!" Dylan said as he pressed his face up against the icy glass, excitement in his voice.

Ethan dug in his back pocket, catching his daughter's eye roll. "Liz, be nice." He pulled out his cell and sent Brooke a text:

We're up in the attic. Door's open. Come up.

"Let's see if we can't clear some kind of path so we don't kill ourselves getting that mattress over here," Ethan directed. The kids started doing what they could, restacking boxes, making a tunnel of sorts.

"Hey, Dad, look at this cool old trunk over here," Lizzy said, disappearing as she crouched down behind a tall stack of boxes. "I *love* this blue color."

Ethan knew exactly what Lizzy had discovered before he'd even reached her side. The old wooden trunk was large, its flat top scratched and worn; the faded blue still reminded him of a trio of robin's eggs he'd discovered in his favorite climbing tree when he was ten years old.

"Ah, yes, the infamous blue trunk. We used to play with this all the time as kids. We'd play restaurant up here. I'd be the waiter, Val would be the chef, and Renee and Jess the customers. This would be our table. They'd sit on old books or whatever they could find as makeshift chairs."

Dylan snorted as he came over to see what they were looking at. "You guys were lame."

Ethan shrugged. "We were little kids in the pre-screen age. We had to entertain ourselves somehow."

"Touché."

Lizzy lifted the lid and the heavy hinges groaned in protest. "Hey, there's stuff in here."

"Yes, it's full, and you have to be careful with that stuff. It's really old. Celia used to keep that thing locked up, but your Aunt Jess and I opened it up last summer when we were looking for some of Celia's old paperwork."

Lizzy nodded as she carefully laid the lid open. "I'm surprised you had the key."

Ethan laughed. "Technically we didn't. But Seth managed to snap the old padlock open somehow."

"I'll be sure to keep Seth in mind if I ever need to do any breaking and entering," Lizzy replied.

"Hello?" Brooke called from the bottom of the attic steps. "You guys up there?"

Dylan walked over to the top of the stairs. "Hi, Brooke! Come on up. We could use an extra set of hands."

Brooke jogged up the steps, her footsteps clattering on the wooden treads. She joined Ethan and Lizzy by the old trunk, looking around as she did so. "This is a great space up here! What are you guys doing?"

"We're supposed to be moving this beast downstairs for Marvin, but these guys are just screwing around," Drew said as he tried to lift the corner of the mattress to test its weight.

"Relax, Drew, give us a second. There's some neat stuff in here," his sister shot back as she carefully lifted some kind of off-white fabric out of the trunk. "Oh my God, this is *gorgeous*." The excitement in her voice was enough to pull her brothers over closer to see what she'd found. "It's an old wedding dress," Lizzy declared as she held it high in the air. "Whose was it, Dad?"

Ethan could only shrug again. "We're not sure. When we found it last summer, Jess thought it was really cool, too. We asked Dad, and even Uncle Gerry, but they didn't know either. There was so much going on at the time, we decided to just put it back in the trunk for now, for safekeeping. There are a couple of other things in there, too."

Brooke reached for the old gown. "Here—I can hold it, Liz, while you see what else is in there."

Lizzy carefully handed it to the other woman and dropped back down to her knees to see what other treasures the old trunk held. "Oh *wow*," she said, pulling out another ivory-colored garment, this one smaller but every bit as fancy with its lace and tucks. "Is this what I think it is?"

Dylan looked at the old dress, his face screwed up in an odd expression. "A mini wedding dress, like for a doll or something?"

His sister shook her head. "Good guess, bro, but I think it's a christening gown."

"A what?" Dylan asked.

"Babies sometimes wear christening gowns when they get baptized," Lizzy explained. "I bet that's what this is."

"That was our guess, too, Liz," Ethan confirmed. "But again, we don't know who this stuff belonged to."

"These pieces are exquisite," Brooke said, a look of wonder on her face as she fingered the wedding dress. "Don't you just wonder who the beautiful bride was who wore this, decades ago? And how many little babies were christened in that?"

Something about the look on Brooke's face, the longing in her eyes, made Ethan extremely uncomfortable. "Come on, Liz, put that stuff away now. We have work to do. We need to get everything set up for Marvin today and get him moved over here tomorrow morning. Then your mom is picking you up at noon, so we need to get this all done."

Lizzy sighed. "I hate to put these gowns back in that old trunk. Do you think they're safe up here?"

"We decided they'd been safe up here for God knows how long, up until we found them last summer, so they should be all right for a while yet. I hate to take them downstairs now. Maybe after we get all moved in and settled, you can bring these down and hang them in your closet," he conceded to Lizzy. "But for now, take pictures if you want, and then you and Brooke can get them put back in there, carefully, while we muscle this mattress downstairs."

Lizzy carefully folded the smaller of the two gowns and laid it back inside the trunk. "Looks like there are some other little baby things in here, too. But I'll check them all out another day. And we should probably figure out a place for this trunk downstairs. There's too much history around it to leave it up here, Dad."

Chapter Twenty-Two
GIFT OF CLARITY

THE NEXT DAY ETHAN left the apartment while it was still dark, to squeeze in an early-morning workout. With everything going on, he hadn't been to the gym in weeks. His back was bugging him every day now. Maybe another yoga class would be the answer, although he was still uncomfortable about the process of contorting his sizable body into all kinds of bizarre poses. Lizzy had suggested he try it earlier in the year, and the stretching *did* give him some relief. Plus, if he was going to be dating now, he didn't want to let himself get flabby. He hadn't worried about that kind of thing while he was still married.

But even more than worrying about his looks, he needed an outlet for the stress. He didn't want another episode like he'd had on the day of the fire. For a minute there, he'd been afraid he was having a damn heart attack. It hadn't happened again since, but it was past time he started taking better care of himself.

It was seven by the time he got home. He was surprised to find Drew in the kitchen, awake and brewing coffee, so early.

"Who are you and what did you do with my son?" Ethan joked.

Drew poured Ethan a cup of coffee, along with one for himself. Ethan got a kick out of his son's morning habit. He didn't think Lizzy even drank coffee yet, unless it was one of those fufu drinks that cost five bucks. Not Drew. He took his straight-up black.

"I thought I'd help you get Marvin moved this morning, at least until it's time to leave to go with Mom," Drew said, handing the cup to his father. "I was wondering if Marvin might want to stop over at his apartment to grab a few more things he might need."

Ethan leaned an aching hip against the countertop. "That's a good idea. He had me bring a few things once I could get back in the building, but I'm sure there's more he could use. He may even want to get started cleaning some of his things."

Drew nodded. "I could help him with that. He'd just have to tell me what he wanted done."

Ethan sipped his coffee and studied his son.

"What?"

"It's great that you want to help Marvin. And I'm sure he'll appreciate it. I'm just curious *why* you want to help him."

Drew shrugged. "I guess I just think he's a good guy. When I first met him, we were delivering those blankets we made at Thanksgiving. He'd just gotten there, after the fire. When I walked in his room, I'd expected to see someone else."

Ethan furrowed his brow. "Who?"

Drew was silent for a while as he took a bowl out of the cupboard, filled it with cereal, and sat down at the table. After a few bites he said, "Last year, we went to that same nursing home for a class I was in. We each picked a resident to interview for a paper. I interviewed a guy named Bud. He was great. I always meant to go back and visit him . . . I even told him I would. But I never did. I thought I'd have my chance when we went back there with Grandma and Grandpa."

"And let me guess . . . Bud wasn't there anymore."

Drew nodded, looking down. "When we got out in the car afterward and I told them the same story I'm telling you, Dylan said Bud probably died. He said it all smartass-like. I didn't appreciate it. But I knew he might have been right."

"I'm sorry, Drew. He might have passed away, but maybe he was able to go back home. Some residents can do that, you know. Like Marvin's doing."

Drew let his spoon clatter in his bowl. "Dylan was right. I couldn't even remember Bud's last name, so I dug out my old paper when I got home and looked him up online. Found his obituary. Even recognized his picture. It sucks that he died. But it was interesting to read about his life. He told me all about his family and his business for the interview. But he never told me he went to war. He was a soldier. Dad, why wouldn't he have talked about that with me?"

Ethan pulled out a chair and sat. "A lot of people won't talk about their experiences when they come back from war, son. My guess is that's why your friend didn't mention it. Those poor soldiers saw some horrendous things. Things they'd rather leave in the past."

Drew nodded. "I think that's why I want to help Marvin. Obviously he isn't Bud, but he kind of reminds me of him, you know? And Marvin's still here. I can help him. Kind of make up for not going back to visit Bud. Bud did admit he didn't have family close and never had visitors. I know Marvin's kids don't live around here, either."

Ethan checked the time. "Come on, let's get going. I told him I'd pick him up at eight. He needs to be checked out by noon. Are you packed to go to your mom's?

"I *can* be in five minutes. I'll be right out."

There'd been no sign of movement from the other two kids, so Ethan left them a note. On the drive over to the nursing home, Drew brought up Rex.

"Dad, I know you don't like to talk about it, but Lizzy and Dylan and I talked, and we're really worried about Rex. How's he doing? Have you seen him?"

Ethan sighed as he navigated a left-hand turn. "I haven't seen him, but I did talk to him a couple of days ago. He had good news about his burns. Said those are healing. He still has to go to therapy and he can't come back to work yet, but he's feeling better."

"That's good. But why hasn't he come around at all? He can't possibly think we'd believe he had anything to do with the fire . . . does he?"

Ethan considered how best to respond. He didn't want to cause any long-term damage to his kids' relationships with his best friend. He couldn't very well come out and tell Drew that Rex didn't want to spend time around them right now.

"I just think, between his physical therapy sessions and working with his lawyer, he doesn't have a lot of time. He's trying to rest, and sleep more, so he can heal faster."

Based on the look Drew gave him, Ethan doubted he was buying his story, but he dropped it. It helped that they'd just pulled into the parking lot at the nursing home.

They parked and walked into the building, greeting the individual at the front desk. The aide recognized Ethan. "I'm sure Marvin will be happy to see you two this morning. Head on back."

Marvin wasn't in his room, but his two boxes, taped shut, waited on the now-stripped bed. Ethan had a moment of panic seeing the bed like that. Had something happened?

Don't be ridiculous, he scolded himself.

"Come on," he told Drew. "I bet he's down in the cafeteria for breakfast."

As they were leaving the room, they nearly ran into a woman in a brightly colored nurse's top. "Hello," she said. "Are you here to collect Marvin?"

"We are," Drew said. "Is he down eating?"

"He is. He was actually a bit out of sorts this morning. I'm not sure if he was nervous about leaving or what, but I told him to go ahead and I'd get his things ready. I just threw his bedding in the laundry. He should be about ready."

"Thank you for doing that," Ethan said. "We'll go see if he's done with breakfast. Is there any paperwork to be taken care of, or do we just take him?"

She laughed. "He's taken care of all that, so he's free to go. I'll miss him, you know. He hasn't been here long, but he's so friendly. It's cute how he talks about going home to his apartment." She dropped her voice and leaned toward Ethan. "I think he misses his neighbor friend."

Ethan frowned at something she'd said. "You do know he isn't going back to his apartment yet, don't you? It isn't ready."

The nurse seemed surprised by this. "I guess I just assumed he was going home. Where is he going, then?"

"He's coming to live with us for a bit. Well, not technically *with* us . . . but at our house. We haven't moved in yet. I'm sorry, it's a bit complicated and you probably don't care."

The nurse shook her head. "No, I *do* care what happens to our residents when they leave here." She did seem sincere. "Was Marvin comfortable with your plan?"

"Honestly, not at first, but he came around. It isn't like he has many options. This place is too expensive, given he doesn't really need nursing care, and his old apartment is still being renovated because of the fire."

"That might explain why he wasn't acting like himself this morning . . . oh, but I'm sure he'll be fine. Good luck to you."

Ethan led Drew toward the cafeteria.

"Dad, maybe this isn't such a good idea. What if Marvin isn't up to being alone?"

Ethan was having the same second thoughts. "I'm sure he'll be fine. We'll get him all settled and I'll try to check in on him a few times a day. What's the worst that could happen? It's not like he's going to burn the place down or anything."

Both Ethan and Drew groaned at his ironic, poor choice of words.

The worst had already happened.

Marvin seemed fine when they found him at breakfast. He said his goodbyes to the people at his dining table, and not twenty minutes later Marvin's things were loaded in Ethan's truck and they were headed for the fourplex. He did want to stop to see his apartment and pick up a few things when Drew suggested it. He didn't seem "out of sorts," as the nurse had warned—at least not to Ethan.

"Marvin, I want you to be prepared. It's a *mess* inside," Ethan warned him when they pulled up to the fourplex. "If you'd rather stay out here and just tell us what you'd like for us to bring for you, we can do that, too."

Marvin regarded Ethan from the passenger side. Drew was in the back.

"Please don't coddle me, Ethan. I'm a grown man and I know my limits. Let's go."

Marvin pushed open his door and was walking up the driveway before Ethan even had the truck in Park.

"Get out there with him," Ethan hissed over his shoulder at Drew. "There's lots of ice. Make sure he doesn't fall. But for God's sake, be discreet about it!"

Marvin might have been fast, but Drew was faster. Ethan nearly chuckled as he watched Drew slip up next to Marvin before the old man got far. He hoped this wasn't a mistake.

He met the other two at the door, keys in hand. Ethan hoped they'd be able to get back to work on this place, after New Year's. Weeks had already passed since the fire and little had been done. He needed to get busy so his tenants could get home. There was so much to do before that could happen.

Upstairs, Marvin let out a low whistle when he walked into his apartment.

"You weren't kidding when you said everything was going to need a good cleaning, were you?" Marvin commented as he made his way farther into his unit. "Everything has this gritty soot on it."

"It does," Ethan agreed, looking around again grimly.

Drew walked through the rooms. He hadn't been in the building since before the fire, and even then, he'd never been in Marvin's unit. After he'd checked it all out, he came back to his older friend's side. "This is going to take some work," Drew said. "Here, Marvin, that was a long walk from the truck and the air is really cold and stale. Why don't you sit down?"

Drew pulled out a kitchen chair and wiped it off with a paper towel before slipping it behind Marvin, who sank down onto it with a sigh.

"Thank you, Drew. For all my tough talk, maybe I am just a pathetic old man. I'm feeling pretty overwhelmed at the moment."

Ethan's chest constricted as he saw the pain swimming in Marvin's eyes. Ethan had felt overwhelmed the first time he walked in here, too, and this wasn't even his home. It had to be so much worse for Marvin.

"Marvin, I promise we will help you in whatever way we can. And if you decide you don't want to come back here, I'll completely understand."

Drew crouched down so he was eye to eye with the man. "I want to help, too. Put me to work. What would you like to bring over to the house now? And then, after you have some time to think about it, if you want me to start hauling some of your things to the laundromat or whatever, I'm at your service."

Marvin laid a hand on Drew's shoulder.

"Sure wish I had a grandson like you, young man."

"Tell you what. I can be your surrogate grandson."

By noon, Marvin was settled in at Celia's house. As they set him up, he'd went on and on about how nice everything looked.

As Ethan was leaving, Marvin stopped him at the door.

"Ethan, I want you to know I've never lived in a home this nice. I appreciate you offering to let me stay here for a bit, and I promise you I will be the perfect house guest."

"Just promise me you won't throw any wild parties," Ethan said as he shrugged into his winter jacket.

Marvin laughed. "Oh, if only I'd have the energy for wild parties."

"Go ahead and make yourself at home. I'll swing by to check on you tomorrow. You have the phone I got for you, right? If you need anything at all, don't hesitate to call. I taped a list of phone numbers in three different places, but you keep that phone in your pocket, all right? My number is there, and so is Drew's and Rebecca's."

Ethan had to hand it to Drew. Picking up a cheap burner cell phone for Marvin had been a stroke of genius. There wasn't an active landline in the house and Marvin didn't own a cell phone.

"Don't worry, Ethan. I'll be fine and I'll take good care of your beautiful new home. Say, I may be too old and tired for wild parties, but what about you? It's New Year's Eve! Is there a party on your agenda tonight?"

Ethan laughed. "My kids would probably disagree with you on that—I think they consider *me* too old as well. But no, no wild party tonight. I do have a dinner date, though."

Marvin crossed his arms with a nod and a knowing grin. "A dinner date, huh? Who's the lucky lady? That pretty young thing you introduced me to out at Whispering Pines?"

"Why, yes, in fact. I'm taking Brooke out tonight."

"Well, you go and enjoy yourself while you can. Live it up! Life's too short not to have fun." Marvin started to turn away as Ethan walked toward the door to leave, but he stopped. "Oh, and say, if things don't work out with that young filly, a good friend of mine would be particularly tickled if you gave *Rebecca* a call sometime."

Ethan watched Marvin walk away. Why did the old man's comment suddenly make him feel uneasy about his date tonight?

And why did everyone keep bringing up Rebecca's name?

"Wow," Ethan said, the site of Brooke when she opened her door, making him forget his own name for a minute. She looked good. She looked *damn* good. "I think I'm underdressed."

Ethan looked from his date, wearing a shiny silver something that left her shoulders bare and didn't cover much of her thighs . . . down to the black jeans and gray sweater he'd donned for the occasion. Her heels were so high, the top of her head was well above his shoulders now. He was wearing his *good* jeans, and the sweater was new, but now he wished he'd worn a suit to be up to par with her outfit.

"Don't be silly," Brooke said, grabbing Ethan by the hand and pulling him inside. "I just threw this old thing on because it's fun to dress up for New Year's. It's freezing out there. I'll grab my coat. Our reservations are in half an hour, right?"

"Right," he said, watching her sashay down the hall and open up the closet. No other term other than *sashay* would do justice to that little show she just performed.

A cold nose pushed against Ethan's hand.

"Hey there, Ginger, how you doing, girl?" He dropped down to his knee to pet Brooke's Irish setter. He tried to keep the dog from brushing against his dark clothes—he didn't want to be underdressed *and* covered in dog hair.

He was happy for the distraction. And their dinner reservation. He suspected her choice of outfits had been more purposeful than she let on.

God, she looks sexy . . .

Seeing her looking like that, knowing there was no chance of one of his kids walking in, had his mind going down a path he'd sworn he'd avoid tonight. It would have been easy to pick up where they'd left off a few days earlier, when Lizzy surprised them at the apartment. They could usher in the new year together, from her bed, and no one would be the wiser.

But he'd already made up his mind. He had been wrestling with what to do about Brooke for weeks and had finally made a decision. She was an amazing girl, but he didn't think he could continue with this *thing* they'd started. She might be sensing his ongoing hesitation, but she wasn't going to make it easy for him to walk away.

"Does the dog need to go out before we go?"

Brooke shut the closet door and walked back toward the front door, wrapping what looked like a long, black silk scarf around her shoulders. "No, she's been out."

Couldn't she just wear a practical parka instead of this classy little doohickey? She'll freeze. No, she isn't going to make this easy on me at all.

They made small talk on the drive to the restaurant. Ethan filled her in on how things went with Marvin.

"I admire you for what you're doing for him, Ethan," Brooke said as she laid her hand, clad in black leather in deference to the elements, on his thigh.

He twitched at the contact.

Get a hold of yourself. Just because she looks sexy as hell tonight doesn't mean you need to act like a horny teenager.

He resisted the impulse to remove her hand. Instead he tried to ignore it.

"Why's that?" he asked, nearly forgetting what they'd been talking about.

"Most people wouldn't go out of their way to help a tenant like you're doing, not to mention letting a near-stranger move into your newly renovated home, before you're even living there."

Ethan considered her comment. She was probably right.

"If you'd have met my Aunt Celia, you'd understand."

"I wish I *would* have met her. By the way all of you talk about her, it's obvious she was one hell of a woman. Even Seth still talks about her, and they weren't even technically related."

"She was amazing . . . no one quite like Celia."

They drove the rest of the way in silence, Ethan lost in his own thoughts. It was tough to find a parking spot—the place was packed. Given the crowd, Ethan feared they'd have to wait, but their table was ready and waiting. He'd never been to this particular restaurant. It wasn't somewhere he'd have taken his kids.

Or his wife. He was starting to see he'd made very little effort in recent years to do things that would have made Stacey happy. The realization didn't make him feel any better.

Brooke ordered a bottle of wine. Ethan looked around. It was a nice place, with white linen on the tables and fresh flowers and candles on the tabletops. All the tables were full. Ethan spotted more than one man in a suit. Many of the women were in fancy dresses, but none of them could compare to Brooke.

In the years they'd worked together, how had he not appreciated how pretty she was? He'd always thought she was cute, but tonight she looked gorgeous.

Like she's on a mission.

Ethan feared, deep down, that *he* was the target of her mission. He'd tried to ignore the fact that they were in two very different points in life. Yes, their fifteen year age gap still bothered him some, but it wasn't the sheer number of years that was the problem. Despite all her assurances that she wasn't looking for anything more, he wasn't so sure. She might even believe it herself, right now, but he'd seen her eyes light up when she held that old wedding gown from the trunk in Celia's attic. And when she talked about her little niece, Stella. She clearly loved hanging out with the toddler. She also enjoyed spending time with Ethan's older kids. She joked about being the "world's best aunt," but he suspected it wouldn't be long before having kids of her own would move up her priority list.

He wanted that for her. She was a great person. He just wasn't—and that was a very emphatic *wasn't*—the man to give her that. He had his hands full with his own three kids and was *way* past the point of ever considering any more.

"You're awfully quiet tonight," Brooke said as she laid her menu down. "Everything all right?"

He gave her a half-hearted smile. "Just a lot on my mind, I guess."

Dinner was . . . *pleasant.* The food was exceptional and he worked to keep the conversation light. They talked about mutual work friends, what they each wanted to accomplish with their businesses in the coming year, and Ethan's frustration over how slow the cleanup at the fourplex was coming along. Any time the conversation started to get personal, he steered it in another direction.

When they got back into the truck after relaxing over dessert, Brooke invited him to her place. There was not one doubt in his mind that if he kept his mouth shut, he'd spend the night and their relationship would change—in the wrong direction, he'd decided.

When he pulled into her drive, he got out and helped her down. He walked her up to her door, holding her hand to prevent her from falling on the ice in her ridiculously high heels . . . but he suspected she misinterpreted his touch.

She unlocked the door and stepped inside, looking back at him expectantly.

"You're coming in . . . aren't you?"

Ethan nodded.

He brushed past her and could feel her eyes on him. She was likely confused, feeling as if he were sending mixed signals. Hell, he *was* sending mixed signals. She was a beautiful woman and they were all alone in her empty house on New Year's Eve. He couldn't fault himself for wanting to pick her up and take her upstairs.

But he knew that would be a mistake. It wouldn't be fair to Brooke, and it wouldn't be fair to him. Spending time with her had been fun while it lasted, but he needed to set the record straight. It would be better off that way, for both of them.

She'd pulled her heels off just inside the door, massaging her feet as she did so. Ethan saw her glance his way a time or two. She didn't seem to know what to do next. Once she was barefoot, she unwrapped the silky shawl from her shoulders and draped it over a nearby chair, smoothing the fabric with her hands.

Ethan sensed she was beginning to feel his hesitancy.

"Would you like some wine?" she offered.

"No, I better not. How about hot chocolate?"

Now she laughed. "Hot chocolate? Well . . . all right, but first I better let Ginger out. She's going crazy in her kennel downstairs."

"Tell you what—why don't I take care of the dog and you make the cocoa?"

Brooke was seated on a stool at the island in her kitchen when Ethan came back in with her dog. She didn't look at him at first, sitting there with her hands wrapped around a mug.

Ethan pulled out the stool next to her. He took a sip of his cocoa.

"Mmm . . . good. But it's missing a little something," he said, finally earning a glance from her. "Got any marshmallows?"

She smiled. "I have marshmallow creme, if that'll work?"

"Sure," he said, standing back up. "Where is it?"

"There's a jar in the fridge. My niece likes peanut butter and that stuff on little triangles of toast when she visits."

Ethan laughed, breaking the tension. "That sounds like something a favorite aunt would feed her little princess niece," he said, opening the door to her refrigerator.

His breath caught at the sight of a crystal bowl of big red strawberries sitting on the top shelf. Two champagne flutes were chilling next to the fruit.

Shit.

He didn't mention the items, so obviously prepared in anticipation of a romantic evening. He scanned the shelves for the jar but didn't see it. He moved cartons of sour cream and yogurt out of the way on a lower shelf, finally finding the jar . . . right next to a bright-pink-and-orange sippy cup.

With a steadying breath, he carried the jar back to where Brooke sat nursing her cocoa. Ethan couldn't help but notice how her silvery dress rode high on her thigh.

Better get this over with before I change my mind.

"Brooke, where do you see yourself in five years?" he asked as he settled back on his stool.

She set her mug down and swiveled to face him. "I'm going to be eating those strawberries alone tonight, aren't I?"

Her forwardness always managed to take him by surprise, but he forged on. "'Fraid so."

"We can't just keep this fun? Casual?"

Ethan shook his head. "Guess I'm not a casual kind of guy. But, seriously . . . do you envision having kids of your own someday?"

Brooke shrugged. "Sure. But I have time."

"Take it from someone who feels like his kids were all toddlers yesterday, but now at least one of them is two inches taller than me—time flies way faster than you ever think it will. Nothing is more important to me than my kids. I want you to have that, too."

Brooke took both of Ethan's hands in hers and looked deep into his eyes. "I can have that someday. It doesn't have to be right now. I know you don't want to start a second family."

Ethan brought both of Brooke's hands up and lightly kissed the knuckles on each one before releasing them. "I'll be holding you back. I'm sorry, Brooke. I don't want to do this anymore. I'm going to head home now. I hope you understand. Thank you for joining me for dinner."

Brooke slid off her stool, pulling her slinky skirt back down to where it belonged. She gave him a small smile that didn't quite reach her eyes. "I can walk you out."

"No need," Ethan said, standing up. "I know the way. Happy New Year, Brooke."

Ginger meandered over and sat at Brooke's feet, looking between the two of them. Brooke absently rubbed her silky head as she watched Ethan go.

As he turned to leave, he heard her say, "Hope you like strawberries, Ginger, girl."

Chapter Twenty-Three
Gift from a Wise Man

"All right, well, thank you for calling me back, and give me a call if you think of anything else that might be helpful," Ethan said, hanging up and dropping his phone into his jean pocket, just as the apartment door burst open and his kids piled through carrying pillows and duffle bags.

The recently cleaned kitchen floor became a dumping ground. But he didn't mind. He was glad they were home.

"Hey, kids, did you have fun?"

Lizzy shot him a look. Dylan grumbled as he headed straight for the fridge, pulling up short at the pizza sitting on a cardboard round on the counter, only one piece missing.

"Didn't you eat?" Ethan asked, trying to get someone talking. He hoped the weekend hadn't been a complete bust.

Drew opened the door to the closet, tossed his jacket inside, and shut the door. "If you can call it eating," he said, turning back to his father. "Mom and *Gregory* took us to some fancy place for 'brunch.' " He used his fingers to put the word *brunch* in air quotes. "I didn't know it was possible to ruin perfectly good scrambled eggs, but they managed it. Can we have some of that pizza?"

Ethan nodded. He'd hoped the kids would enjoy the holiday weekend with their mom. He hated that they dreaded those visits, and it didn't sound like this most recent one was any better than previous weekends. Ethan could remember when Stacey's main focus in life was making sure her kids were well taken care of and having fun. But now . . .

Dylan helped himself to another slice. "I've been starving for three days," he complained. "Mom and Gregory are on some health kick. Do you know they did not have one can of pop or a bag of chips in that house of his? And it was *New Year's*, for God's sake!"

Ethan knew this would be Dylan's personal kind of hell—no junk food in sight.

"What did you do to celebrate New Year's Eve?"

Lizzy snorted from where she'd jumped up to sit on the counter. "I wouldn't call anything we did *celebrating*."

"Get your butt off the counter, Liz," Ethan demanded.

She jumped down with a sigh, saying nothing.

"I know you were supposed to bring dress-up clothes. What were those for?" he asked her.

"Mom made us go to some stupid party at Gregory's neighbors' house. I think we were the only ones there under forty. Oh, except for the staff, walking around with fancy little mushrooms and shrimp on silver trays."

Based on their expressions, her brothers agreed with her about the party being "stupid."

"It doesn't sound *that* bad," Ethan said—although he'd never enjoyed parties like that, either.

"Trust me, it sucked," Drew said. "Mom made us *mingle*, but when we couldn't take it anymore, she convinced Gregory to let the three of us walk home. It was only a couple of blocks. The best part of the night was watching Netflix after we got back. They didn't even get home until after we went to bed, and that was after two."

Lizzy, banned from the counter, dropped onto one of the kitchen chairs. "I found it ironic how they came stumbling home, drunk, making all kinds of racket. Didn't fit well with their 'health kick' theme for the rest of the weekend."

"Was any part of it fun?" Ethan asked, more and more disappointed.

"Gregory's house is amazing," Lizzy said with a shrug. "There's that."

"I'm sorry you guys didn't have more fun. Aside from that, how was your mom? Does she seem happy?"

The boys looked to Lizzy, as if expecting her to answer on their behalf. Something told Ethan this wasn't the first time they'd discussed the topic.

"No, Dad, she doesn't seem happy. She seems edgy, high-strung. Kind of like she's walking on eggshells. We don't know if she's trying to impress this guy, or what. She puts on a good act, but we weren't buying it. The boys and I talked about it, when they were still at the party, and we think you need to talk to her."

This caught Ethan by surprise.

"What do you mean, 'talk to her'? Guys, the extent of conversations I have with your mother these days all pertain to you three. It's not like she calls me up and asks me for dating advice."

Lizzy sat forward with her elbows on the table, chin resting in her hands. Ethan hated her look of dejection, but he didn't know what he could do about it.

Why has Stacey become so self-centered? As parents we all have to do some sacrificing to keep the peace. Hell, I sacrificed a night with Brooke.

"Your mother is going to do what she's going to do, guys. She stopped listening to me a long time ago. Hopefully, once she gets the stress of another wedding behind her, things will find some kind of new normal between the four of you. Or . . . five, if you count Greg."

Dylan, having already wolfed down two slices, grabbed another piece. "If you guys want any of this, you better take some," he said to his siblings, then turned to Ethan. "Dad, don't let him hear you call him that. I called him Greg once, and he was very quick to let me know that wasn't his name. I don't think *Gregory* likes us much. His two kids are grown and gone, and I get the feeling that's how he likes it."

"I wish Mom had a girlfriend she could talk to," Lizzy said. "I just don't think she's happy. It's like she's chasing these things she thinks she's always wanted—you know . . . money, nice house, someone to do the housework. But it all feels so . . . *superficial.* Do you think maybe Rebecca would talk to her, Dad?"

"Rebecca? Honey, Rebecca and your mom were friends back when we were all kids, but they haven't talked in years. I don't see how she could help."

His daughter shrugged. "Just a thought. Hey, how was *your* New Year's? Did you do anything fun? How was your date?"

Dylan perked up. "Date?"

"I went out for dinner with Brooke. We had a nice time."

"Not exactly a ringing endorsement of your evening, Dad," Drew pointed out.

Ethan set the remains of the pizza on the table. "Have at it, Lizzy and Drew, before Dylan eats it all."

Lizzy asked as she came over to grab a slice of pizza. "Is this thing with Brooke getting *serious*, then?" She wriggled her eyebrows at him.

"No, kiddo, it isn't. We're in completely different places in our lives right now. I decided to end it before it went too far."

Ethan hoped Lizzy caught on to his "too far" comment. He didn't want his daughter thinking he slept with someone he'd only casually dated.

Dylan, on the other hand, was not happy at his father's news. "Aw, Dad, why'd you have to go and do that?" his son whined. "I like Brooke."

Ethan nodded. "I know, bud, and I *like* her, too. I just don't *like*-like her. Know what I mean?"

"Actually, it's probably good you broke it off," Drew chimed in. "By the way Brooke was looking at that wedding dress you showed us, up in Celia's attic, I'd bet she wants to be a bride someday. And I'd prefer it if *both* my parents didn't get married off again this year."

Ethan choked on the drink of soda he'd just taken.

"Believe me when I tell you, Drew—when I tell all *three* of you—that's *not* going to happen. I suspect I'll live out the rest of my days unmarried, living only to drive the three of you nuts. No more weddings for me."

Lizzy dropped her pizza onto the table. "Now you're starting to sound like Rex, Dad. Destined to live out the rest of your lives as bachelors."

Ethan ripped a paper towel off the roll and tossed it to Lizzy. "Use that. Don't be a slob. Speaking of Rex, I was heading out the door for him as soon as I was done eating when you guys got home."

"Can I come with? We never get to see him anymore," Dylan complained.

"I'm not actually going to see Rex. I'm going to see if there's anything I can do to help his case. We all know there's no way Rex started the fire at the fourplex. I need to find a way to try to prove that. I thought I'd start by talking with all the different people we both know—you know, like our workers, Rex's family, a few mutual friends. I have no idea if it will help, but I don't think it could hurt. So, no, Dylan, I need to do this alone. I'm meeting three of the guys on our crew who were working at the fourplex with Rex the week before the fire. I'm going to buy them a beer. But I'll see if I can't line something up with Rex next weekend."

"All right. I guess that'll have to work," Dylan conceded.

"I bet you all have homework you haven't touched yet, and you're heading back to school soon."

"Not me," Lizzy said. "But I'm meeting a friend downtown. We're on semester break anyway, so I don't have homework. But the boys—*they're* a different story."

Dylan groaned through a mouthful of pizza.

"I'll be home in a couple hours," Ethan said, snagging the last piece of pizza. "Boys, clean this up and then get going on your homework. And Drew, pick your jacket up that you threw on the floor in the laundry room when you got home—yeah, I saw that. You weren't born in a barn."

She came back to visit Rex in his dreams, something she hadn't done in a long time. During the day, he struggled to remember her face, her voice. But she'd come to him while he slept. Like she used to. After the accident.

Rex was self-aware enough to know this was a slippery slope he was on. He'd gotten into trouble with alcohol before. After Gail died, getting drunk and slipping into oblivion every night helped him get through the long, lonely days. But when it got to the point where he couldn't wait to get off work, to get home and crack open a beer, he knew he'd let it go too far. He got help then. He'd done it quietly, on his own, and he didn't think anyone even knew he'd gone back to his old AA group.

As a younger man, before he'd met his wife, his life looked different. He'd hated his father. The man was a raging alcoholic, abusive to their family, especially Rex's mom. Rex was only nineteen when his dad wrapped his car around a light pole. The impact killed him instantly. All Rex felt was relief. Relief that his father hadn't killed anyone else that night, and that he'd never be able to hurt anyone else, ever again.

While his father was still alive, Rex had felt obligated to live at home after high school. He'd feared that if he left, one day he'd get a call that his mother was dead. Rex needed to stay there to protect her.

Life got better after his father was gone. Rex and his brother helped their mom sell the house and move into an apartment. She was finally happy. She was free to work at a job she enjoyed, free to come and go without worrying about saying the wrong thing and ending up in the emergency room.

Rex went to trade school and worked construction. He rented a place of his own. Thinking back now, his memories from his early and mid-twenties were cloudy at best. He'd finally been at a point where he didn't feel responsible for anyone other than himself. He did his best to block his dead father from his memories, working hard during the day and going out most nights. He made a decent income, thought little about the future, and spent most of his money on trucks and motorcycles.

He never thought about his dad these days—or at least he *hadn't* until that Jarvis woman made her stupid comment about seeing a ghost.

He couldn't remember exactly when the partying went beyond alcohol and into the drug scene. Someone in their circle probably found themselves short on cash. Rex never reached the point where he was dealing, but he did use street drugs on occasion. What was the harm in it? It wasn't like anyone was waiting at home for him.

That all changed the night he met Gail. Rex remembered watching her walk into the bar with a giggling, already-tipsy group of young women. He wasn't normally shy around the opposite sex, but it took him half the night to get up the nerve to ask her to dance. She hesitated, but one of her friends pushed her into his arms. After two fast songs, the band slowed it down.

"Please, dance one more with me," he'd begged her, a hand over his heart.

And there began a new chapter in his life; the best chapter.

But that particular book nearly slammed shut before it even began. It didn't take more than one date for Rex to realize Gail was different from any of the other women he knew. She was a recent college grad, working as a high school math teacher and an assistant girls' basketball coach. She had big dreams and was already working toward achieving them.

She liked Rex, thought he was fun, but she didn't have the time or desire to hang out in bars and throw her money away, as Rex was inclined to do. After one rocky month of dating, Gail gave him an ultimatum. Change his ways . . . or she walked.

Once Gail opened his eyes to so many more possibilities, he was terrified of losing her. He vowed to give up the drinking and clean up his act. Gail never knew about the drugs. That would have been a deal-breaker.

But despite his best intentions, giving up the alcohol wasn't as easy as he'd expected. During a tearful heart-to-heart, the couple discussed Rex's struggles. Gail helped him see that he was likely an alcoholic. Alcoholism is a disease, she explained, a disease he realized his father had suffered from. Rex agreed to get help if it meant keeping Gail.

He'd found sobriety with her help, and maintained it . . . until he lost her.

He used to treat himself to an occasional beer while she was still alive, although Gail was never too happy about it. But when she died, he shattered, turning to alcohol in his grief. When the drinking started impacting his work, he went back for help, and didn't touch the stuff for another five years.

By then, he'd thought he had everything under control again. He could handle a beer now and then, but it never went beyond that. And he'd nearly succeeded, too—or at least he thought he had, until he woke up in the emergency room after the fire.

The police told him they'd found beer cans, both full and empty, in his pickup truck. He didn't remember where the beer came from. It wasn't his usual brand. They also said they found a bottle of Jack Daniels sitting on the floor next to him when the firemen pulled him out. He couldn't remember buying that, either.

Maybe he *didn't* have things under control.

His relief when Gail returned to his dreams morphed into terror when she was the one on the floor, surrounded by flames. When he tried to reach her, the heat became too intense.

"Why did you do it? Why are you killing me again?!" she screamed at him, the terror in her voice jolting him awake.

By the angle of the sun slanting through his bedroom window, he'd slept past noon and missed his therapy session at the hospital—again.

He swung his legs off the bed, careful not to rub his healing skin against the mussed bedding. He shuffled to the bathroom and straight into the shower, hoping to wash away the despair Gail's visit had brought.

Had he done it? Was his subconscious trying to reveal the truth?

Was Gail trying to help him again?

He'd been so sure it was all a misunderstanding. Never in a million years would he do something like that to Ethan. Ethan was one of the most important people in the world to him, certainly his closest friend.

But he'd been having what he thought might be blackouts. Small snippets of time, lost to him. It had been happening even before the fire, although he'd told no one.

He needed to get out of the house. His fridge was pathetically empty, and the walls were closing in on him. He found his jeans on the back of the chair in the corner of his bedroom. He shook them out, cursing himself for forgetting to throw in a load of laundry—again. He pulled on an old T-shirt he dug out of the bottom of a drawer and threw his flannel on overtop.

Even pushing a cart through the grocery store was depressing. He cared little what he ate these days and couldn't remember when he'd last cooked a decent meal for himself. He watched a woman pick out a bundle of bananas and place them in her own cart. Gail would have made sure there were fruits and vegetables in his cart, not just chips and bologna like he had now. But she wasn't walking down the aisles with him like she used to.

She'd never again walk the aisles with him.

Why did he even bother? Food would probably rot at his house, anyway.

He walked away from his cart, leaving it abandoned in the middle of aisle four, right in front of the canned vegetables.

"Screw this," he murmured, making his way to the exit.

A woman carrying a child shot him a look of exasperation.

"Sorry," Rex said, louder this time.

And he meant it. Why had he even left the house with this nasty cloud hanging over him? That woman and her child shouldn't have to be exposed to his vile mood.

His stomach growled as he drove away, so he turned into a local dive bar known for their fish and chips. He needed food.

He paused inside the door, his eyes trying to acclimate themselves to the dim interior after the afternoon sunlight outside. But he knew what it would look like before his eyes could even take it in. It would look like every other hole-in-the-wall where pathetic drunks went to drink away their sorrows during the middle of the day. And it smelled just as bad.

Rex took a stool at the bar. There were only a few other patrons there, given it was three o'clock in the afternoon.

"What can I get ya?" the woman behind the bar asked. From her gravelly voice and hard eyes, Rex suspected she'd spent most of her life in front of booze bottles and pathetic drunks like him.

"Plate of fish and chips," he replied. "And a Budweiser."

She nodded, pulled a pencil out from behind her ear, and scribbled out a ticket, walking back to what looked to be the kitchen area.

While he waited for his beer and food, he glanced around but didn't see anyone he knew. Why would he? This wasn't somewhere he normally hung out, and most everyone he knew was working on a Tuesday afternoon. Like he used to. He pulled a plastic dish of peanuts closer.

The woman returned and set a bottle of beer in front of him. "Food will be out in a minute."

Rex nodded. He wasn't in a hurry. He didn't want to go home. What for?

He turned at the sound of metal scraping across a wooden floor. An old man hoisted himself up onto the stool next to Rex, huffing at the exertion. He glanced in Rex's direction, nodding a hello to him. From the watery look in his eyes and his red, bulbous nose, Rex thought the man might be a regular.

"Hey, Marge, I'll have what he's having."

"Hold your horses, Hank, can't you see I'm busy here?" The bartender held up two bottles of whiskey she'd been using to restock the shelves.

"She likes me," the old man joked to Rex. "She just doesn't realize it yet."

"I heard that, Hank," the woman shot back, clanging the bottles into place. She brought over a second beer and set it in front of Rex's new neighbor. "How 'bout you? Need another?"

Rex nodded, trying to ignore the old man. He'd come in for peace and quiet, not to listen to some old jabber-mouth. He took a hard pull on his first bottle and set the empty aside, wrapping his hand around the cold one she set in front of him.

"Old lady kick you out of the house, too?" Hank asked, using his beer bottle to point at Rex.

Rex sighed. Who was he to judge this guy? Hell, if he didn't quit drinking so much and get back to work, he'd *be* this guy.

"Nah," he replied. "Mine died, so she doesn't give me much trouble anymore."

"Well, shit, sorry to hear that, man."

The two sat quietly for a few minutes, watching the television in the corner.

"My wife didn't really kick me out either," Hank confessed, staring down at his naked ring finger. "She gave up on me a long time ago."

Rex nodded. Life could be damn lonely sometimes, on that he could agree with the old man.

"If it wasn't a woman that drove you in here in the middle of the afternoon," the old man went on, "what brings you in? Don't think I've seen you in here before."

"Just here to drown my pain, I guess, same as every other loser in here."

Hank looked around the shadowy bar then back at Rex. "I know those guys over there, and you're right, they *are* losers. As am I. But you, my friend, you don't look quite as bad off as the rest of us. What's got you so down?"

Rex sighed again. He'd talked to no one about his situation—other than his lawyer, and that guy didn't count. He took a deep breath and shared the ugly tale with this stranger sitting next to him. Everything from waking up in the emergency room, to the charges, to his own self-doubts. It felt cathartic to say it all out loud.

Hank said nothing immediately after. He motioned to Marge to bring him another beer, then turned back to Rex.

"Sounds like you've been dealt a raw deal. What are you going to do about it?"

"What am I going to do about it?" Rex asked, bitterness creeping into his voice. Before he could say more, his phone vibrated in his pocket. He pulled it out and Lizzy smiled up at him from his screen. He read her text:

Thinking about you, Rex.

He nearly set his phone down when it pinged again:

Hope you're doing ok. Hang in there.
It'll work out. I believe in you!
Love ya
- Lizzy

Hank peered over at the phone in Rex's hand. "Cute kid. Yours?"

Rex pushed his second beer away as Marge brought his food. "Put that in a box for me, would you? I gotta go." He peeled two twenties out of his wallet and tossed them on the counter. "Get my new friend here a meal, too."

Rex turned back to Hank. "She's not mine, but she's my best friend's daughter, and she's like family to me. And I'm done disappointing her. Thanks for reminding me I don't have to just sit back and take this."

Rex clapped the older man on the shoulder as he took the take-out container from Marge.

He was done feeling sorry for himself.

True to his word, Ethan talked to everyone he could think of over the next week. He compiled a list of their names, contact information, and summaries of their comments. He stopped at Steve's office to hand them over.

"Look, Steve, before you say anything, I know you aren't Rex's lawyer. But you are *my* lawyer, and I pay you to help *me*. And helping Rex helps me too. Please, just read through all that, and if anything jumps out at you that you think might be helpful to Rex's case, let's figure out a way to get it to Rex's lawyer."

Steve shook his head at Ethan but took the folder. "I wonder if Rex knows how lucky he is to have a friend like you," he said as he glanced through the pages in the folder. "This was a lot of work, talking to all these people."

Ethan shrugged. "He'd do the same for me."

"I hope you're right. I haven't exactly been sitting back, relaxing, while you've been out interviewing potential character witnesses," Steve said, sitting down behind his desk and motioning to Ethan to take a seat. "I talked to Rex's lawyer just this morning."

Ethan sat, curious.

"It seems the police are digging deeper into Rex's background," Steve said, tapping on his keyboard. "I made some notes after I hung up with the guy. They're particularly interested in the accident that killed Rex's wife."

"Rex's wife?"

"Yes. Do you know the story?"

"Of course I know the story. Gail was my friend, too."

"Were you aware there was a relatively new life insurance policy on her at the time of the accident?"

This gave Ethan pause. "No. We never talked about *life insurance*. Rex was crushed by what happened. He felt responsible. But he wasn't. There was an investigation, which I think they have to do anytime there's a death like that, but it was deemed an accident. A lawyer encouraged Rex to think about going after his car manufacturer because Gail's seatbelt seemed to malfunction, but he ultimately decided to let that go. It would be difficult to prove, and he just couldn't face a court battle with all he was going through."

"Maybe he decided the half a million he got from the life insurance company was enough help to get him out of debt with his bookies."

Ethan wasn't following. "What the hell are you insinuating, Steve?"

Steve held his hands up in defense. "I'm not insinuating anything. I'm just passing on what his lawyer told me. They're digging deeper to make sure there wasn't insurance fraud in Gail's death. Because if there was, it sets a precedent."

"What precedent?"

"He might have done something similar here, with the fire at your building."

Ethan shot up out of his chair. "That is pure bullshit."

He stormed out, just barely catching his lawyer's last words.

"I hope you're right, Ethan. I certainly hope you're right."

Chapter Twenty-Four
Gift of a Clean Break

"I'm sorry I can't go out for lunch with you and Ethan today," Seth apologized. "I've been wondering how he's doing with his building, cleaning up after the fire. Things were in tough shape over there."

"I understand," Jess said into her phone while trying to wrestle Harper into her winter jacket. "Duty calls."

Harper twisted away and Jess wasn't able to keep her phone cradled between her ear and shoulder. It fell into her lap. She could hear Seth talking but needed to deal with the baby first.

"Hold on, Seth," she yelled, hoping he'd guess what was going on. "Come here, Harper. We need to get you bundled up so we can go see Uncle Ethan."

Harper screeched in protest, pulling away and crawling toward the front door.

At least she's heading in the right direction, Jess thought.

"Sorry about that, Seth," Jess said once she'd picked her phone back up. "What were you saying?"

"Let me guess . . . Harper is going out for lunch with you?"

"She is. And with any luck she'll take a catnap on the way to the restaurant. She's being a little pill today."

"Why don't you leave her home with Lauren? Or did she head back to college already?"

"She had to leave this morning. I'm trying not to be down about it, but I miss her already."

Seth's sigh came through the phone as static. "Sorry, babe. I know it isn't any fun to say goodbye to the kids. It was hard to put Kaylee on the plane back to her mom, too."

"I know. But what are you up to today, then? Are you on the road?"

"No. Actually, Brooke had already asked me to meet her for a quick bite."

While she felt like she'd finally accepted that her boyfriend and her brother's girlfriend didn't have the kind of history she'd once imagined, Jess hadn't expected a meeting with Brooke to be the *thing* he needed to deal with instead of going out to lunch with her and Ethan.

When she didn't immediately respond, Seth filled the silence on the phone. "Jess, we've been through this. You're not still worried about Brooke, are you?"

"No, I'm not. You just surprised me. That's all. She wanted to meet with you? I wonder why. Doesn't that seem odd?"

"She must need some help with something work-related. I can't imagine any other reason she'd want to see me. It'll have to be quick, too, because I have a customer coming out to the shop at 1:30. But hey, you better get going or you'll be late. And so will I. I'll call you later, okay?"

"Sounds good. Tell her hi for me."

"Will do. Love ya," Seth added before signing off.

Jess smiled as she shoved her phone in the outside pocket of the diaper bag and scooped Harper up from where the child was standing up against the front door.

"Let's go see what Ethan's up to."

"Thanks for meeting me, Seth. I hope I didn't pull you away from anything."

Brooke was waiting for Seth inside the door at Hammers, an aptly named local deli that served lunch to mostly construction and factory workers. They ordered subs and potato salad, taking their trays to a corner table that just opened up. The place was packed.

"You made it sound important. What's up? Wait, let me guess. Tell me you have a lead on some fabulous old building that's being renovated and needs me to sweep in and save history from idiots that favor *progress* over architectural treasures."

Brooke laughed, but Seth could see the tension around her eyes.

"I'm afraid this has nothing to do with old buildings, or a special tile I'm hunting for, or anything even remotely connected to work."

"All right, so what's up?" Seth asked, keeping his voice neutral. He could picture Jess, giving him that *I-told-you-so* look he'd come to know well. He hoped Brooke wasn't about to prove Jess right in her suspicions.

"I need some advice."

"Advice? The last time you came to me for advice was when you were having trouble with Cameron. And since you finally managed to get that loser out of your life, I've been left out in the cold." Seth smiled, but his attempt at humor fell flat.

"And I've always appreciated your advice," Brooke said, "even when I didn't listen to you. I've always been able to come to you with my guy troubles. You tell it to me straight."

Seth took a bite out of his sandwich, waiting for Brooke to get to the point. He sure as hell hoped she wasn't going to ask for advice where Ethan was concerned. When he'd mentioned some concerns he had about Ethan and Brooke's relationship to Jess, she hadn't appreciated his point of view. Brooke probably wouldn't either.

Brooke fiddled with her napkin, her sandwich untouched.

Seth put his own sandwich down. "Look, Brooke, if you brought me here today to talk about Ethan, I'm going to have to pass. With him being Jess's brother and all, I'm keeping my nose out of your business with him. Go talk to your sister or someone. Not me."

"There isn't much to say as far as my relationship with Ethan goes . . . other than I think that's over." Brooke's eyes suddenly began welling up.

"Since when?" Seth asked, surprised. He didn't think Jess knew about any trouble between Brooke and Ethan.

"Since New Year's Eve. We had a nice dinner and then I invited him over. The kids were with their mom. He came over, but he didn't stay long. He said he was afraid us seeing each other was a bad idea, that we were in two very different places in life right now, and he didn't want to hold me back."

Seth's respect for Ethan clicked up a couple notches. He didn't disagree with the man's insight, even if it wasn't what Brooke had wanted to hear.

"He might have a point there, Brooke."

Brooke threw the napkin she'd been twisting between her fingers across the table at him. "Do you have one romantic bone in your body, Seth? God, you are so matter-of-fact sometimes, you piss me off."

"What are friends for?" Seth said, tossing her napkin back. "Eat your sandwich. You can't waste all that food."

"Fine." She took one bite of her sandwich, glaring at him as she chewed.

"I'm confused, Brooke. Did you invite me to lunch so you could take all your frustrations related to men out on me, as your token male friend, or was there another reason you called?"

Brooke swallowed and took a drink of her water before responding. "For the record, I have more guy-friends than just you. *Rex* is my friend, too."

Seth sat back in his chair, crossing his arms. "Yes. Yes, Rex is your friend, too. But I suspect he has bigger issues to deal with right now than your love life."

"Yeah, he does," Brooke admitted. "All right. Enough of the BS. I really did have something I wanted to talk about with you. Some*one*, actually. You're the only one I could talk to about this."

Seth waited, hoping she'd get on with it. He needed to be out at his shop in thirty minutes.

"Cameron called."

Nothing else she could have said would have surprised Seth more.

Cameron? As in the *Cameron, the guy who nearly ruined her life?*

"What did he want?"

"He wanted to see me."

"To see you. As in, you should jump on a plane and go out to see him in Baltimore?"

Brooke sighed. "Please don't take that tone. Talking to you about him was probably a mistake."

"Too late, friend. You brought me into this. Now, spill it. How long have you been talking to him and what the hell does he want this time? Have you forgotten how bad things got the last time you let him into your life?"

"What do you mean, you broke it off with her?"

"Don't look so shocked, little sister," Ethan replied. "You told me yourself that you didn't think Brooke was someone I should be dating."

"I did *not* say that," Jess hissed at her brother, trying not to raise her voice and disrupt the other lunch patrons. She'd already been struggling to keep Harper quiet; she didn't want to be one of those mothers who let her kid ruin other people's meals.

Ethan laughed. "Actually, you kind of did. Maybe you didn't come right out and say it, but you might as well have when we were all out at Whispering Pines at Christmas. Remember, you made some comment about how Brooke seemed to love babies, and how she'd probably want some of her own sometime soon? You gave me that look, and I knew *exactly* what you were getting at."

"What's with all of you saying I have a *look*? I do not have a look."

"The hell you don't, sis. But listen, you were right. I have way too much going on in my life right now to even think about dating. And even if I did have time for a relationship, it probably shouldn't be with Brooke. If I'd been super into her, I could get past the whole age-gap thing. But the fact would still remain that she seems to want a family of her own and I already have one. I don't want to be one of those schmucks who just holds her back. Because I have no intention of starting a second family . . . ever."

Harper picked that moment to let out a squawk and throw a smashed handful of crackers onto the carpet.

"Never say never, bro. Sometimes life throws you an unexpected curveball," Jess said as she reached over to stop Harper from throwing another cracker on the floor. She took Harper out of the high chair and handed her to Ethan.

Ethan smiled at the little girl in his arms. Harper smiled back and seemed to settle down, at least for the time being. He looked back at Jess. "You know what I mean."

Jess nodded, studying her brother. "When did you say you called it quits with her?"

"Last week. On New Year's Eve."

"That's a little cold. Couldn't you have picked a non-holiday to break up with her?"

Leave it to Jess to voice the very thing he felt the guiltiest about. He knew he didn't have any business dating Brooke right now, but his timing *had* sucked.

"I know. Not my best moment. But what's done is done."

"Interesting," Jess said as she rummaged around in the diaper bag for her wallet.

"I'm getting lunch. I invited you, so it's my treat," Ethan said. "*What's* interesting?"

"Seth couldn't come to lunch with us today because he had to meet Brooke. He assumed it was work-related. Maybe, based on what you just told me, it wasn't about work after all."

"I guess. I have no idea."

Harper, surely tired of being confined, arched her back in an effort to escape.

"I think we've asked her to be a little lady for about as long as we can expect to," Ethan said, standing with Harper. He picked the check up off the table. "Ready?"

Jess nodded. "Yes, let's get out of here. It's nap time. But are you sure you're all right? Do you feel bad about Brooke?"

Ethan shook his head. "No, other than I think she was hurt and it was poor timing on my part. I never meant to hurt her. She's a good person. Honestly, I haven't even thought too much about it since. Sounds cold, I know, but I'm much more concerned about Rex and getting my tenants back into their apartments."

Jess followed Ethan and Harper to the hostess's podium and waited while he paid. When they reached the door, she held out her hands to take the baby.

"You need to take care of yourself, big brother. You are under an awful lot of stress lately. I don't like it."

Ethan had just hauled a charred cabinet out of the lower unit at the fourplex and heaved it over the side of the dump bin sitting in the driveway when Brooke pulled in.

Uh-oh . . .

"Hey, Ethan."

"Hi, Brooke. This is a surprise. What's up?"

She took her time as she approached, hands in the back pockets of her jeans. She kicked a chunk of ice into the grass with the side of her work boot.

"Got a minute?" she asked.

"I can take a break. Do you want to go inside?"

Brooke looked around. It was a cloudy January day and a brisk wind made it feel even colder.

"Yes, it's freezing out here. Maybe you can show me what you're dealing with, too," she suggested.

He turned and headed for the front door. He could hear Brooke walking behind him, her boots crunching on the frozen ground.

Wonder if this visit is business-related . . . or something else?

He sensed it was something else.

He held the door open for her. She entered and stood on the landing, unsure whether to go up or down. Ethan headed downstairs, toward Norman's unit.

"There's the least amount of damage in here. Let's go in for a minute and you can tell me what brings you by."

He felt guilty entering Norman's apartment when it wasn't strictly necessary—especially with someone else—but he'd make it quick. He turned to face Brooke, watching her as she seemed to struggle with where to start.

"Sorry for just dropping in unannounced like this, Ethan, but I needed to talk to you."

Ethan nodded, keeping silent as he waited to see why she'd come.

"I've thought a lot about what you said the other night. You know, about how different we are and how you think I want a family and I should be dating someone who wants the same thing instead of pretending that I don't."

Ethan shrugged. He hoped she wasn't about to try to get him to change his mind. "I still believe that," he said.

Brooke nodded, turning her back on him and walking the perimeter of Norman's small kitchen. "I was so mad at you that night, after you left."

"I'm sorry, Brooke. I didn't mean to hurt you. Part of me wishes I never would have brought you to that damn Halloween party back in October. I value your friendship. You're a good person. I hope I haven't screwed all that up."

Brooke walked back to stand right in front of Ethan, closer than he'd have preferred, but he held his ground, waiting to see what she would do next.

She slugged him. Not hard and not in anger, but on the shoulder, as a friend might do.

"I was mad at you, but I'm not anymore. I came by today because I wanted to thank you."

Ethan rubbed his shoulder where she'd connected. She might be small, but she packed a punch. "Thank me? For what?"

"For finally making me admit to myself that I *do* want a family of my own. And I'm not getting any younger, so if that's what I want, I better start acting like it."

"Brooke, I'm glad I helped you with that self-realization, but I'm serious when I tell you that isn't what I want.

Brooke slapped her forehead. "For God's sake, Ethan, I'm not here to beg you to *impregnate* me. Get over yourself!"

Ethan felt relief mixed with embarrassment. This was the Brooke he knew. The one he liked. "Got it!" he proclaimed, shying away from another potential shoulder-punch. "I'll never again make that assumption."

"See that you don't," Brooke said, stepping closer and reaching her arms around his waist for a hug.

Ethan, thoroughly confused by now, returned the hug for a second and then stepped back, out of Brooke's embrace.

"Now that we're both on the same page," she said, "I just wanted to let you know I might be gone for a while. I know you wanted me to work on that project with you over on Fifth, but you're going to have to find someone else."

"Where are you going?"

She flashed an enigmatic smile. "To see a friend. I'll call you when I get back to town."

And with that, she was gone.

Ethan shook his head. *I'll never understand women.*

Chapter Twenty-Five
Gift of a Woman to Talk To

Rebecca tossed her book down on the couch when the doorbell rang, welcoming the interruption, regardless of who was at the door. While she loved her mother dearly, living together came with its challenges. Plus, Rebecca wasn't used to having so much free time on her hands. Now that the holidays were over and she was at least partially settled, she needed to start looking for work before she went insane.

"Well, hello, Elizabeth," she said, surprised but happy to find Ethan's daughter standing on their stoop. "What brings you by? I thought you'd be back to school by now."

She'd actually been thinking about the girl quite a bit lately, after spending time with her out at the Christmas party at Whispering Pines. Her spunk and her smile had reminded her of Ethan, while at the same time she sensed an air of vulnerability in the girl, something Lizzy's mother had struggled with back when they were school-age friends.

"Hi, Rebecca," Lizzy said as she stomped snow off the cute ankle-high boots she wore. "I'm heading back now, actually, but I thought I'd see if we could talk for a few minutes first."

"Sure, come in, come in," Rebecca said, standing back out of the way. "Do you start classes tomorrow?"

"Tonight, actually. I have a night class."

Rebecca glanced at the heavy clouds on the horizon. The forecast had been for more snow.

How do parents do it? she wondered. *I'd be worrying constantly.*

"I hope you don't mind me dropping by like this. It's kind of spur-of-the-moment."

"No, not at all. Come on, let's sit in the living room. Mom's taking a nap in her room. Can I take your coat?"

Lizzy shook her head and visibly shivered. Rebecca thought it might be a combination of cold and nerves.

"No, I'll just be a minute," the younger woman said, slipping her boots off and taking a seat on the couch.

"Is everything all right? Is your dad okay?"

"Yeah, Dad's fine. I think he's working over at the fourplex now."

Rebecca waited, unsure as to what might have prompted Lizzy to come see her.

"Dad doesn't know I stopped," Lizzy said as she rubbed her hands together. "But there was something I wanted to talk to you about. You know, woman to woman." Lizzy tucked her right foot up underneath her.

The girl's fidgeting was starting to make Rebecca nervous. "Sure, what is it?" she prompted, wondering why the girl picked her for some girl talk instead of her own mother. Not that she'd always wanted to talk to *her* mom about things when she was Lizzy's age..

Lizzy took a deep breath. "I wanted to talk to you about my mom. You guys used to be friends, right?"

"We did, but we lost touch after college. Ryan and I—my husband at the time—we moved away for my job."

Lizzy nodded. "I appreciated you telling me about your college days and how you met my parents when we talked at Christmas. That's actually why I stopped by."

"I'm sorry, Liz, I'm not following."

"I think my mom could use a friend right now."

"What do you mean?"

"Remember how I told you she moved to Minneapolis when her and my dad split up?"

Rebecca nodded. She'd been surprised when Lizzy was so forthcoming about her parents' breakup when they'd visited out at Whispering Pines. Ethan would be embarrassed if he knew what all his daughter had shared with a virtual stranger.

"Mom's changed quite a bit over the last two years. We used to be close, her and I. Really close." The hurt was evident in Lizzy's voice. "But then, it was like she didn't only leave Dad, she kind of shut herself off from us kids, too. I mean, the boys still have to go spend a weekend or two with her each month, but Dad is pretty much a single parent these days. I can go see her if and when I want to, since I'm an adult now. Honestly, when I do go, it's to try to make it more bearable for my brothers. Mom's boyfriend—I mean *fiancé*—is kind of a prick. I honestly don't know why she even bothers to have us spend time with her. We're all miserable when we do—including her, I think. I don't think Gregory likes us."

While Rebecca couldn't remember the last time she'd actually talked to Stacey, Lizzy's description of their family dynamics was difficult to hear. She even thought she could relate to what Lizzy was describing. After her own dad died, Penelope married a man Rebecca could barely tolerate. It wasn't the same as Lizzy's situation, but she had an idea as to how the girl was feeling.

"I'm really sorry you don't feel as close to your mom anymore, Lizzy. That sucks. But people do move on and get remarried after divorce. Maybe, with time, you guys can all find your way back to each other. Though I'm not sure how I can help."

Lizzy shrugged, but her eyes filled. "It isn't the idea of Mom getting remarried that bothers me. I know people get married again all the time. I just think she's in a bad place. She always used to joke about wanting a completely different life, a life where she didn't have to constantly worry about money. She never had a career of her own. I thought part of the reason she left Dad was because she hated being so dependent on him. But now, I'm not so sure. Now she's with this guy who doesn't seem to treat her anywhere near as well as Dad did, and she's jumping right into marrying him?"

Rebecca sighed. Again, she'd lived through her own mother's multiple trips to the altar; but she'd never worried that her mother wasn't treated well. Penelope wouldn't have stood for that. Thinking back, she did remember sometimes feeling frustrated with Stacey's tendency to allow herself to be treated like a doormat, especially by guys she'd dated before Rebecca introduced her to Ethan. She used to argue with Stacey about it all the time.

She waited for Lizzy to share how she thought Rebecca might be able to help. Maybe Lizzy just needed another woman to talk to, since she didn't feel like she still had that with her mom.

"Do you think you could talk to her?" Lizzy asked. "I know you were close once."

"Oh, Lizzy, that was a very long time ago. It's been over twenty years since we even exchanged Christmas cards. Have you tried talking to *her* about it?"

Lizzy sat forward on the couch, eyes pleading. "Kind of, but she shut me down right away. Please? Can you try? What could it hurt?"

"Did you tell your Dad you were going to ask me to talk to Stacey?"

Now Lizzy looked sheepish. "No . . . I asked him to call Mom and try to talk some sense into her, but he said he didn't think it was his place. When I asked him if he thought *you'd* talk to her, he didn't think that was a good idea, either. But I couldn't stop thinking about it. I'm really worried. I think marrying that guy would be a huge mistake. What harm could a phone call do?"

What harm, indeed? Rebecca wondered.

She thought back to her senior year in high school, when she and Stacey had been the best of friends. They used to tell each other everything. They had each other's backs. Once they headed off to college, though, things got more complicated. They weren't as close. But the two definitely shared a history. Of course, there was Ethan to consider, too. In the short time she'd become reacquainted with him, she'd come to appreciate how important his children were to him.

If there was a chance she could help either of her two old friends avoid more heartache, maybe she should try. While she didn't like the idea of getting involved, she also hated seeing the hurt in Lizzy's eyes.

"I'm not at all sure this is a good idea . . . but if you want to give me your mom's number, I'll give her a call. Don't get your hopes up, honey. Your mom might not open up to me. Remember, it's been a really long time."

Lizzy stood and dug a slip of paper out of her pocket, handing it to Rebecca. "I was hoping you'd say that. And I know it might not do any good. But I needed to at least ask."

Ethan rang the doorbell and waited. He probably should have called ahead, but when the local cleaning service called to say they had an unexpected opening in two days, he had to move fast. When he'd first called the service, they sent someone out to the fourplex to assess what needed to be done, but they'd put him on a waiting list because they were busy with a big job at a local hospital. When they called back, they said they could get the apartment in the upper north corner cleaned in a day, but he'd need to clear out as many of the personal effects as possible.

He'd need Penelope—or at least Rebecca—for that. He hoped one of them would be available.

The door swung inward. "Well, *hi*, Ethan!" Rebecca said, surprise registering on her face. She had a towel wrapped around her hair and wore a robe.

"Hi yourself. Do you always open the door in the middle of the afternoon wearing a bathrobe?" Ethan teased.

Rebecca laughed and stepped out of the way to let him enter. She pulled the towel off her head and shook out her shoulder-length hair, the wet tendrils dampening her robe. She didn't seem bothered to have Ethan see her with disheveled hair and no make-up. He caught glints of silver in her dark-blond hair that he hadn't noticed before. "To be honest, it's not often the doorbell rings in the middle of the afternoon around here. Although you *are* the second Richter to ring our doorbell this week."

Ethan turned back to face Rebecca as she shut the door, towel now draped around her neck. "The *second* Richter?"

"Yes, Elizabeth actually stopped to see me on her way out of town. The afternoon she went back to school."

Ethan narrowed his eyes, thinking back to Lizzy's earlier comment that maybe Rebecca could talk to Stacey. He hadn't thought his daughter would actually put Rebecca up to it. "Let me guess . . . she wanted you to talk to her mother? I'm sorry—I didn't think Lizzy was serious about that when she mentioned it."

A sound, some kind of squeaking or rolling, came from the kitchen. Penelope stepped into view. "I thought I heard your voice out here, Ethan. What brings— Rebecca! Why on *earth* aren't you dressed? For God's sake, is that your bathrobe?"

Rebecca threw her hands up. "You guys, I just came from the gym and I took a quick shower. I wasn't expecting company. Give me a second. I'll go throw some clothes on and be right back." She left the room in a huff.

Penelope came farther into the room, having to lift and place her walker with each step, as it wouldn't roll on the carpet. Ethan took a step toward her, intent on helping, but she stopped him with a glare.

"Don't even think about it. I am just fine. Come on. Sit here in the living room and tell me what brings you by. Do you have news about my apartment? Because that damn daughter of mine is starting to get on my last nerve."

Ethan chuckled. He suspected the feeling was mutual.

"Things are coming along over at the fourplex. Not as quickly as I'd hoped, but we *have* been able to make some repairs. That's actually why I stopped by. I needed to talk to you about your things."

"What about my things?" Penelope's voice rose with anxiety. "Don't tell me somebody broke in there and stole my stuff?! You've been keeping that door locked like I told you to, haven't you?"

"Mom, quiet down," Rebecca called as she came back into the room. Her wet hair was clipped up high on her head, and she'd put on jeans and a torn sweatshirt. Ethan couldn't help but notice how good she looked. She could pass for thirty-five instead of the near-fifty he knew her to be. He'd always thought she was pretty, and the years hadn't diminished that. "What's the matter?"

"Ethan just said someone broke into my apartment and stole my stuff!"

Ethan caught Rebecca's eye before she could respond to her mother, giving a discreet shake of his head. He could tell by the way she relaxed that Rebecca caught his meaning.

"Now, Penelope, that isn't what I said at all. I stopped by today because I've lined up a service company to come in and try to clean that nasty soot and other damage caused by the fire. They can do a better job if we get as much of the smaller, personal items out of their way as we can. I was wondering if maybe Rebecca could come over to your apartment with me today or tomorrow and help me do that. I don't want to do anything with your things unless either you or Rebecca are there. It might need to be Rebecca, because there's still quite a bit of ice outside, and we had to take the railing down on the stairs going up to your apartment to do repairs."

"Oh, well, that's a relief," Penelope said, sinking back into the recliner she'd lowered herself into. "Why didn't you say that in the first place?"

Ethan wasn't about to argue with the woman, but he could understand why Rebecca was getting worn out. Penelope seemed ornerier than usual.

"I'd be happy to help," Rebecca said, tucking her feet beneath her on the sofa. "I've been wanting to get over there and start going through Mom's stuff, but I was waiting until you told me I could."

"I'm not dead yet, Rebecca!"

Rebecca dropped her face into the crook of her arm where it rested on the back of the sofa.

Ethan tried to keep the conversation going. "That would be great. When would work for you?"

The doorbell rang again.

"What is this, Grand Central Station?" Penelope asked.

"No, Mother, it's Gladys. Remember, she was coming over today to help you do some physical therapy," Rebecca said, standing to get the door. "She'll be here for an hour, and then your friend Judy was going to stop for a visit." Rebecca turned back to Ethan. "*Now* would actually be a good time."

"Thank you for the excuse to escape," Rebecca said as Ethan drove back over to the fourplex. "I love my mother dearly, but sometimes she drives me bat-shit crazy."

Ethan laughed. He knew Penelope was harmless, and her bark was worse than her bite, but he could concede that she would be tough to live with. "Thank you for agreeing to do this on such short notice."

They rode in silence for a bit. Rebecca reached down and turned up the radio when a good song came on. She sang the words quietly. Ethan enjoyed the easy sound of her voice.

As he pulled into the driveway and again parked behind the dumpster, he thought he better warn Rebecca about the state of the place. "I know you've been anxious to get in there, but there were some structural issues I had to take care of before I let you back in."

"Structural? As in, 'the place could fall down' structural?"

"No," Ethan assured her as he climbed out of the truck. "Nothing like that. But there was one wall that had to be shored up, and then the electrical and some of the plumbing had to be replaced in part of your mom's unit. That's all done now. The next logical step is to clean things up as much as possible and see what still needs to be replaced because I already know we can't save it all. I'm sure the carpet will have to come out, the walls will need to be painted, and more."

"I guess Mom is getting that remodel just like you promised. She told me you probably wouldn't get around to it until she was dead and out of there, just like the poor fellow downstairs."

Ethan led the way in. "Ha! She said the same thing to me. Guess *something* good came out of all this." He warned her to be careful going up the stairs. Once inside Penelope's apartment, he turned to her. "Are you still thinking your mom is going to be able to come back here and live alone when this place is ready?"

Rebecca didn't immediately answer. Instead, she walked over to the wall of family photos in the eating area.

Eventually, she turned back to Ethan. "I have my doubts."

Two hours later, they locked up and took three last tubs out to Ethan's truck. They'd already brought out a few other loads. Mostly clothing that Rebecca wanted to try to launder. She'd toss what she couldn't get clean.

As they drove away, she called her mother's cell. Penelope assured her she was enjoying time with Judy. Rebecca could stay out "all damn night" if she wanted to.

"Well, in that case," Ethan said when she'd hung up, "how about if we grab dinner quick before I take you back? Dylan is over at a friend's house, studying, and Drew is at the girls' volleyball game."

"That sounds fun. I think both Mom and I could use a break from each other. And I've been craving pizza."

Ethan liked Rebecca's suggestion, even though they'd been eating plenty of it lately, so they drove to his favorite local pizzeria and got right in. Since it was a weeknight, it wasn't crowded. They enjoyed a pepperoni and mushroom pizza—much as they had back in their college days, she reminded him—and talked.

When Rebecca excused herself to use the bathroom, Ethan checked his phone. No one needed anything. It felt good to relax. And spending time with Rebecca felt easy.

"What are you smiling about?" she asked when she got back to the table.

Ethan shrugged. "I was just thinking about how long it's been since I've had a relaxing meal and enjoyed good conversation with another adult."

Granted, he didn't add, he'd had a nice meal with Brooke on New Year's, but there hadn't been anything relaxing about it.

Rebecca smiled as she pulled her chair back up to the table. "I agree. This is nice."

"And, not to spoil the mood," Ethan said, "but . . ."

"But you're going to spoil the mood, aren't you?" Rebecca said, a mock serious look on her face.

"Maybe a little. I've been wanting to ask you about Liz's visit."

Rebecca sighed. "Of course you have. And I've been trying to avoid it."

"That bad? I'm sorry if Lizzy put you in an awkward position."

Rebecca waved away his apology. "Don't be silly. I'm a big girl. Your daughter came to me because she wants to help her mom. There's no harm in that. I know she *acts* like she doesn't care about her mother these days, but I'm sure you know as well as I do that isn't really the case."

"It isn't?"

"Ethan, of *course* it isn't. There are few bonds in life stronger than the one between a mother and daughter."

He grinned at her. "Even if you drive each other bat-shit crazy?"

"Actually, I think that's *why* we drive each other so crazy. Because no one else's opinion matters quite as much. We want what's best for each other, no matter what. I mean, as irritating as she can be about it—and she sometimes has a crass way of sharing it—my mother is almost always right. But"—she picked up a fork and brandished it—"if you tell her I said that, I'll have to kill you."

"You don't think Lizzy and Stacey's relationship is damaged beyond repair, then? Because I thought Lizzy was ready to write her mother off for good."

Rebecca laughed, still holding up the fork like a weapon, and her laugh was as infectious as ever. Ethan couldn't help but join in.

"What are we laughing at?" Ethan said, unable to keep a straight face.

"Men can be so obtuse."

"And what the hell is *that* supposed to mean?"

Rebecca reached across the table and clasped his hand. "I'm sorry. I just understand now why your daughter came to me. There are some things only another woman can understand. Don't take it personally."

Ethan turned his hand over so he could hold Rebecca's. "Thank you for shedding some light on this whole deal. I've been worried."

Rebecca squeezed Ethan's hand and then pulled hers back, taking a drink of her soda.

After a beat, she said, "I actually *did* call Stacey after Lizzy stopped by."

"You did? Did you talk to her?"

Rebecca shrugged. "For a few minutes. It was a pretty stilted conversation. I didn't know what to expect, you know? It's been a long time. But she was pleasant enough. Lizzy had already told her I was back in town and that she'd met me out at Whispering Pines at Christmas. She didn't seem completely shocked when I called. Surprised, maybe, but . . ."

"Did you talk to her about Elizabeth? About the boys?"

"Let's just say I tried. But anytime I mentioned the kids, she got pretty evasive. She told me about her fiancé and some charity work she's doing. But then she suddenly had to go. It sounded like someone walked in. Maybe her guy-friend."

Ethan nodded. "I appreciate you trying. That had to have been a tough call to make. Kind of awkward."

"It was. I can't really tell much from such a short conversation . . ."

"I hear a 'but' there," Ethan prompted.

"*But* something did sound off. Even though it had been a long time since I last talked to Stacey, and we probably have nothing in common anymore, I'm worried."

Ethan rubbed his hand over his face, suddenly bone-weary. "I'm worried, too. But, hey, thanks for trying."

"No thanks necessary," she said, gathering her purse up off the chair beside her. "I really better get back. Judy was going to leave at seven, and it's almost seven thirty already."

Ethan nodded and together they made their way back out to his pickup. He opened her door and gave her a hand up. He kept her hand in his a second longer, meeting her eyes.

"Thank you for trying to help Elizabeth."

"You're welcome, Ethan. But I'm not sure how helpful I was."

Chapter Twenty-Six
GIFT OF CHARITY

IT WAS HARD FOR Rex to believe two months had passed since he'd walked out of that dive bar in the middle of the afternoon. He'd vowed to stop wallowing in self-pity and get back to the business of living. He hadn't wanted to end up like Hank, spending his lonely days on a barstool, handing out free advice to other drunks.

He was still living under a cloud of suspicion, but his lawyer assured him he was making progress on Rex's behalf. In the meantime, unable to sit home and do nothing, he'd taken on a few handy-man jobs around town. There was never a shortage of people looking for help. He could be as busy as he wanted to be. He'd have preferred to go back to work with Ethan, but they couldn't even consider that until he was cleared.

The evenings and nights were the toughest. He missed Ethan and the kids; since Gail had died, he hadn't realized just how much of his life had been filled by the Richters. They'd reached out to him, but he was still keeping his self-imposed exile. Until they had answers, he'd keep his distance. While he was *nearly* convinced he had nothing whatsoever to do with the fire, there was still that small kernel of niggling doubt, buried deep in his brain.

But maybe today would be the day he'd finally start to get some answers. His lawyer had called and asked him to meet him at the police station. The cops wanted to talk to him *again*. While Rex didn't see the point, his lawyer assured him it might be worth it.

Slushy roads meant the long winter might finally be giving up its grip. The promise of spring boosted his spirits as he drove to the police station. He didn't even mind the spray of muck that pelted the side of his vehicle when a semi passed him on Main.

Once inside, he headed for Karl's office.

Rex rapped on the doorjamb with his knuckles, and Karl waved him in. Karl's partner, Bob, was there again, too.

"Morning," Rex greeted his lawyer as he sat next to the man.

"Thanks for coming down today, Rex. We just had a few more questions for you. I know this thing has been languishing for a bit, and I apologize for that," the older man in uniform said from behind his desk.

Rex doubted his sincerity. "We've been over what little I can remember about that damn fire so many times now, I don't know what else I could possibly tell you," he said, unable to keep the frustration out of his tone.

Rex's attorney made a little motion with his hand, signaling to Rex to be quiet. Rex let out a huff but sat back in his chair.

Fine, I can keep my mouth shut—until we see what this guy wants this *time.*

"Rex, what can you tell us about your car accident back in 2006?"

Rex tried to hold his facial features neutral and relax his shoulders—despite the fact the man's words set every cell in his body on edge. He'd been warned this topic would probably come up.

"What do you want to know?"

"We understand this is painful for you to talk about, Rex, and I'm sorry to have to bring it up. We just need to fill in a few blanks."

Rex looked to his lawyer for guidance. The man gave him a small nod of encouragement. He rubbed his jaw as he debated where to start. He struggled every day to *forget* the accident; now they wanted him to dredge up the past again.

Keep it short. Get this over with.

"My wife and I were going to visit family. I was driving. It was November eleventh of that year. It was misting out and the sun was setting. The highway cut through a grove of trees and the pavement was littered with leaves. All of a sudden, when we came around a bend, something was in the road. Everything happened at once. I tried to steer around the three deer, but my front right quarter panel clipped one of them. The tires skidded and there wasn't much shoulder. We slid off the road. I had to turn the wheel hard to avoid the wall of trees ahead, and the pickup rolled."

Rex paused, the horrendous scene again flashing through his mind. It was always in slow motion. He shut his eyes against the inevitable ending, but nothing could stop the horror from playing out.

Karl's voice snapped him back to his chair in the police station. "How many times did your truck roll, Rex?"

But he couldn't answer. He couldn't speak. "Rex, I know this is difficult. How many times did your vehicle roll?" the man repeated.

Rex opened his mouth. "They told me it probably rolled one full time and then stopped on its roof."

"They?"

"Yeah, the officers on the scene. I blacked out. Had a nasty lump on the side of my head. I must have slammed it against my side window. When I came to, I was disoriented. My seatbelt was holding me in place, upside down."

"And your wife?"

Rex looked away from the pasty-faced man watching him expectantly, letting his eyes go to the window and stare at the bare treetops beyond the stuffy office.

"She wasn't there."

"What do you mean, she wasn't there?"

"Come on, man. You're going to make me go through the whole damn thing again? You've obviously read the report. You already know the answer. *My wife was thrown out of the truck.* When I reached out for her, she wasn't there. Her door wasn't shut tight, and I remember seeing her seatbelt just hanging there. I couldn't get my belt unhooked. My right hand was busted up. Someone stopped to help. An old guy. My window was blown out. I remember him trying to calm me down. Told me help was on the way. Somehow, I managed to crawl out of my belt and through my window, but the old man stopped me from running to the other side of the truck, from trying to help Gail. To this day, I don't know how he was able to hold me against that truck, but he did. He'd seen my wife's body when he ran up to us . . . didn't want me to see her like that—"

Rex had to stop to catch his breath. The feeling of helplessness was always the worst part. Like his feet were stuck in quicksand and he couldn't get to her. He couldn't help her.

"After that, things got crazy. Sirens, people in uniforms . . . but none of them could do the one thing I needed them to do. No one could save Gail."

Karl nodded; for once the sincerity in his eyes looked real. "Was your trip that day planned, or spur-of-the-moment?"

Rex took a deep breath, relieved to move away from the grizzly details of the accident itself. "Planned. It was our nephew's birthday."

"And did you usually drive when you went in the car with your wife?"

"Usually. Not always. Why?"

Karl glanced down at a notepad on his desk. He didn't answer Rex directly. "Was your wife wearing her seatbelt that day?"

"Of course. She always wore her seatbelt. For all the good it did her."

"But you said she was thrown from the vehicle. Wouldn't her seatbelt have kept her in place, like yours did?"

"You would think, wouldn't you? She must not have latched it right or something. Or it malfunctioned."

"Malfunctioned. Huh. Did you ever pursue that? You know, like check to see if seatbelts were a problem in that type of vehicle?"

"Come on, man. You know I did. I'm sure all of this is right there in that file on your desk." Rex motioned to the manila folder lying in front of the other officer, who'd been silent the whole time.

Karl waited. Rex waited.

Finally, Rex's lawyer intervened. "As you can tell, reliving this is very difficult for my client. I've allowed this questioning, but I have to warn you, it is awfully far removed from the reason Rex is facing legal issues right now."

"We're almost done with this." Karl turned his attention back to Rex. "So, Rex, when your wife died in the accident, did you receive a life insurance payout?"

Rex stilled. He didn't like where the discussion seemed to be headed.

"I did. It took a while because they needed to investigate the accident."

"And how much money did you receive?"

"For the record, I don't think that's any of your damn business," Rex bit out. "But since you insist on delving into my own personal hell, I'll tell you so we can get this over with. My wife's life insurance policy was three hundred thousand dollars. Same as mine would have been if the tables had been reversed."

"And what did you do with the money, Rex?"

Rex looked to his lawyer.

"You don't have to answer that if you don't want to, Rex," the man said as he sent a warning glance at the cop.

"Screw it. You're obviously digging for an angle here, but I've got nothing to hide. I didn't do anything with the money at first. I didn't want it. I hated it. I let it sit there, in the bank, for a few years."

"Is the money still there, Rex? In the bank?"

"Nah, it's gone."

"Do you care to elaborate?"

"I gave it away."

"You gave it away? All of it? Who did you give it to?"

"That's none of your business."

Karl waited. Patience was obviously something he had in ample supply.

Rex did not.

"Look, my wife was a much better person than any of you assholes. She'd done a lot of charity work for organizations that helped research cures for childhood cancer. Her brother died from leukemia when he was three. I gave it all to St. Jude's." He paused, swallowing the stone in his throat. "She'd have liked that."

Karl pushed back from his desk and stood. "Come on, Bob, let's give these guys a minute."

Bob stood and the two men left the office, closing the door behind them.

"You did good, Rex. I'm sorry you had to talk about all of that again. I think the thing they were getting snagged up on was the life insurance. I bet they're confirming your story right now about giving it all away, if they haven't already done that."

Rex dropped his head into his hands and rubbed at his gritty eyes.

This merry-go-round has to stop.

Aloud he said, "I'm getting *so* tired of this. If they're going to throw my ass in jail and throw away the key, I wish they'd just get on with it. Let's have the damn trial already."

His lawyer nodded and was just about to say more when the door opened again. The officers resumed their seats.

"Rex, I'm sorry for any inconvenience we've caused you over the past few months. While we're still convinced someone set that fire over at Richter's four-plex, we don't feel we have enough evidence to convict you in a court of law. We are dropping all charges against you, effective immediately."

Rex wasn't sure he'd heard the man correctly.

"You're dropping the charges? Just like that?"

"Yes. However, we do have some additional questions for you."

"I need to speak to my attorney in private," Rex said. "Do you have somewhere we can go?"

Karl stood up again with a sigh. "Five minutes."

The officers again left the office.

He turned to his lawyer. "What just happened?"

"I think they were probably getting pressure to move this thing along. Their evidence against you was too circumstantial. I'll be sure all the proper paperwork is filed. But, Rex, this is good news."

"Should I answer any more of their questions, or can I just go home? I am *so* done with this bullshit."

"I suggest you give them just a little more of your time. See what they're up to now. And then maybe you can put this whole ugly experience behind you."

Rex sighed, but he had to agree.

When they came back this time, they carried four paper cups of black coffee.

"Thought you might need caffeine," Karl said, settling back down. "All right, I know you're anxious to get going, so I'll cut right to the chase. Tell me what you know about your boss's financial situation."

Rex ignored the cup of coffee. "Excuse me?"

Karl shrugged. "*You* may not have set that fire, but someone did. We need to keep exploring all possible avenues."

"Now you want me to throw Ethan under the bus?"

Karl repeated his question, ignoring Rex's.

Rex took a deep breath. "As far as I know, Ethan's doing all right. It's not like he shares his checking account balance with me."

"To the best of your knowledge, was he keeping up with expenses at work? Any issues with late payments to subcontractors or employees?"

Rex shook his head. "Not to my knowledge. Look, I'm his foreman, not his bookkeeper. My paycheck showed up every two weeks, just like it was supposed to. I'm sure everyone else's did, too, or they'd have bitched to me about it."

Karl nodded. "And he recently went through a divorce, right?"

"It's been a couple years now. But Ethan never said much about the money as far as Stacey and their split went. Husband worked hard, wife got bored at home, felt underappreciated, took off. End of story. Not that unique."

"Would you say the divorce put undue stress on Mr. Richter?"

"I'm not a goddamn shrink. Divorce is painful. Hard on the family, on the kids. So, yes, it's been a stressful few years for Ethan, but he's managing."

"Do you think Ethan had anything to do with the fire?"

Rex glared at the cop. "Absolutely not."

Ethan was elated when Rex called him to let him know the charges had been dropped and he'd like to come back to work.

"Are you serious? Rex, I can't tell you what a relief this is. Steve's been telling me this might happen, since they hadn't moved ahead with scheduling a trial date. I was afraid to get my hopes up. God, man, this is such a relief," Ethan repeated.

He'd been arguing with his lumber guy about a damaged shipment when Rex called. If he was coming back, *Rex* could talk to the guy. He had a way of connecting with some of their more difficult vendors. Maybe now Ethan could start to catch up. Things were backlogged and money was tight as he waited for his insurance to pay. He needed his righthand man back on the job.

"Can you start right away? Tomorrow?"

Rex barked out a laugh. "You sure you *want* me back, Ethan?"

"Hell yes, I want you back! Why wouldn't I want you back? For the record, I never believed one word of that bullshit about you having anything to do with the fire. There was no way you could have done it."

Ethan wished they were having this conversation in person instead of over the phone. Rex didn't respond.

"You still there?"

"Yeah, man, I'm here," Rex said. "There is one thing, though. I know the fourplex needs a lot of work, but if it's all right with you, I'd rather not go back there. Can you handle that one, and I can oversee other projects you've got going? Hell, I don't even know where everything is at, project wise, since I've been out of the loop so long."

Ethan couldn't say he was surprised by Rex's request. Having witnessed the firemen pulling Rex out of the smoking building, he understood his friend's hesitation to go back.

"No problem, Rex. If you can get things back on track elsewhere, I'll handle the fourplex. I'm just glad to have you back."

It was good to be back.

Rex brushed crusted snow and ice off his grill in the backyard and fired it up. He couldn't stomach yet another frozen pizza for dinner. Besides, he had reason to celebrate. Tonight's dinner would be grilled steak and a baked potato. Then he needed to get a good night's sleep.

Back on the job tomorrow, he thought, watching the sun set. *Finally.*

"Back on the job," he said aloud, his breath crystalizing in the cold air.

He'd waited three long months to be able to say that. Just this morning, he hadn't known when, or even if, he'd ever be able to say that again.

His burns still gave him some trouble, but they were healing. The scars would remain, but hopefully the pain would continue to fade. His body was healing, but the toll the fire and subsequent accusations had taken on his psyche might prove more difficult to leave behind.

What I wouldn't give for a beer right now . . .

It might take the edge off the apprehension he felt over going back. But he knew that if he let himself have one, it could easily turn into two, three, or more. He couldn't afford to be hungover on his first day back.

He enjoyed his steak, watched television, and turned in early. He planned to meet Ethan for breakfast at 7:00 the next morning. Rex always headed to work early. Ethan couldn't usually get in much before 8:30 because of his boys, but he was making an exception this time. He'd assured Rex that Drew could get Dylan to school. Which was good—they had lots to go over.

—— *ell* ——

Rex must have dozed off, but something woke him shortly after midnight. He laid there in the dark, listening to the subtle night sounds of the house, frustrated because he knew getting back to sleep would likely be a problem based on how little he was sleeping lately.

Now was the time, in the still of the night, that the demons came to haunt him. Not *real* demons, of course. These were demons in his mind that taunted him, like nails on a chalkboard. They made him question so many things from his own past.

Had his hate toward his father tainted him for life?

Had the accident that killed Gail been his fault?

Would she still be alive if he'd hit the damn doe head-on instead of trying to miss her?

What really happened that day at the fire during the block of time missing from his memories?

In an effort to stave off the inevitable assault of conscience, Rex left the warmth of his bed and headed for his kitchen. Maybe a bowl of cereal would distract his brain. He pulled on an old pair of sweatpants draped over the end of the bed, not out of modesty—there was no one else to see him—but against the chill.

Why is it so damn cold in here?

He had his answer soon enough. His back door was open a few inches. The outer storm door was closed but did little to keep the cold out.

"What the hell?" Rex said, jogging over to the open portal. He snapped the back light on and leaned out the storm door—he wasn't about to go outside in his bare feet. Nothing looked out of place. A fresh dusting of snow on the back patio lay undisturbed.

He remembered balancing a full load in his arms earlier, when he'd brought his steak in from the grill. He'd pushed the door shut with his foot. He must have forgotten to actually lock it before he went to bed. Something had caused him to wake up . . . but wouldn't there be tracks in the snow if something—or someone—other than his own carelessness was behind the open door?

Now he was wide awake, and a bowl of cereal wasn't likely to be enough. He stood in front of his kitchen cupboard where he stored ibuprofen and the variety of medications they'd sent home from the hospital to help manage the pain. He'd avoided taking most of it, leery of it all. He rummaged through the bottles, searching for one in particular. He pulled the small bottle of sleeping pills from the back, squinting to read the label.

"Shit . . . if I take one of these now, I'll sleep until noon."

If Gail had been there, she'd have told him to drink a glass of milk instead of taking a pill, then at least *try* to go back to bed.

Her years of mothering him had left their impact. He pulled a glass off the shelf above the pills, emptied the milk carton into it, and drained the icy-cold beverage before heading back to bed.

Thirty minutes later, he remembered why he'd never listened to that particular advice when Gail used to give it to him: milk never helped him sleep. He tossed and turned while the Sandman alluded him.

The demons were back, likely brought on by that cop's irritating questions.

He was standing on the side of that fateful road again, the one he visited so often in his nightmares. His blue truck was on its top, farther down the embankment. He could see himself inside of it, hanging upside down. He fought the desire to look, but it was no use. His eyes searched her out—his Gail, crumpled along the side of the road, blood streaking her beautiful face. Not far from her, the big doe sprawled on the blacktop, bleeding, her neck obviously broken. Rex wanted to do something, *anything*, to help his wife. But his feet felt insubstantial and they wouldn't take him to Gail's side. A flicker of movement drew his eyes to the edge of the woods where twin fawns stood. The young deer seemed to be waiting, glancing between the doe and the shelter offered by the grove of trees. They raised their heads, sniffing the air. Smoke. Rex could smell it now, too. What was burning? A crackling behind him spooked the skittish deer away. Rex slowly turned; he didn't want to take his eyes off Gail, but he needed to find the source of the smoke. He jumped back—bright flames licked up from the ground in the tall brush right behind him. He could feel the heat on his face. There, partially obscured by the smoke, was a man, walking away. "Stop!" Rex yelled. Maybe the man could help Gail. The man stopped and looked over his shoulder, locking eyes with Rex—

"Ethan!"

Rex woke himself up with his own scream. His room was still dark, but his alarm clock read 6:10 a.m. It would go off in five minutes.

He untangled himself from his twisted sheets. His blanket and comforter were puddled on the floor, a testament to his last tortured hours of sleep.

At least he'd slept.

Coffee. I need coffee.

Chapter Twenty-Seven
GIFT OF SCENT

REX WAS ON HIS second cup of coffee by the time Ethan walked into the truck-stop diner at five minutes past seven.

"Been here long?" Ethan asked, tossing his jacket onto the bench in the booth and taking the seat across from Rex. A waitress placed a steaming cup of black coffee in front of him before Rex even had a chance to answer. "Thanks, Bev. I'll have the usual."

"Course you will," Bev said, grinning at Ethan before she topped off Rex's cup from the coffee pot she held in her other hand. She made her way back toward the kitchen.

"If things don't work out with you and Brooke, you might be able to take old Bev out on the town," Rex said, blowing on his cup before he took a sip.

"You *are* out of the loop, aren't you? Things *didn't* work out with me and Brooke."

"Huh. Really? Can't say I'm that surprised. You are a bit *old* for her," Rex said.

If he hoped to get a rise out of Ethan, Ethan wasn't taking the bait.

"That I am, friend, that I am. For the record, I pointed that out to her on more than one occasion. In the end, I think she finally realized I might have a point. She wants to have a family of her own someday, and I already have one."

"How did she take it?"

"She came around. Seemed all right the last time I talked to her. But that's been a few weeks ago now. She said she was going out of town for a bit. I needed to find someone to take her place on the Sonnet job."

"Where'd she go?"

"I have no idea," Ethan said.

Bev arrived with two large plates of eggs, hash browns, and toast before he could say more. Not that he knew much more. He was just relieved to be out of that awkward situation. He liked Brooke and wanted to keep her as a friend. He just didn't want to date her.

The two men ate their breakfast, the conversation turning to work. Ethan updated him on the status of their current projects, who'd quit while Rex was out of commission, and the one guy he'd hired. They'd need to add a couple more to one of the two crews Rex would be back to overseeing.

"Jason didn't work out then, huh? Shame. I thought the kid had potential."

Ethan pushed his now-empty plate away. "I did, too. And I gave him more chances than he deserved. The final straw was when I put him in charge over at Celia's. Not a huge amount of work left to get done, only two other guys working over there for him to keep an eye on, but it was a disaster."

"It happens. Some of these young guys have had it too easy. From the sounds of things, I'd have fired his ass, too."

"Speaking of Celia's, I need your help with the last push to get things wrapped up over there."

Rex wiped up the last of his eggs with the corner of his toast and tossed his napkin on his plate. Bev, ever efficient, made the plates disappear and refilled their coffee again. Ethan barely noticed her.

"I'm surprised you guys haven't moved in yet," Rex said.

"Me too. But you know how it goes. When something has to give, it isn't going to be a customer's project that gets put on the back burner. But we do have one person living at the house already."

"Come again?"

Ethan laughed. "I'm sure you'll think I'm crazy, but I let Marvin, one of my displaced tenants from the fourplex, move in to the main level. The poor guy had nowhere else to go. He was resistant, but he's certainly loving life over there now."

Rex shook his head, smiling. "I never knew your aunt very well, only met her a couple times, but based on stories I've heard, I think you're turning into her. An honest-to-God bleeding heart!"

Ethan shrugged, saluted him with his coffee cup, and grinned. "What can I say?"

"And you're right. I *do* think you're crazy," Rex added, "but it doesn't matter what I think. As long as he stays out of the way so we can get things finished over there, I don't care if he becomes a permanent houseguest for you. Let me guess . . . he's using your new office as a bedroom."

"That he is. But seriously, I think you'll like him. He's an interesting old dude. He and Drew hit it off. I also think there might have been a little hanky-panky going on between Marvin and the lady who lived next to him in the fourplex."

Rex guffawed. "Since when did you become such a gossip? Jesus, you're snooping into your renters' love lives now? Dating has *changed* you."

"Hey, you learn things about people when you suddenly feel responsible for them after the building they live in nearly burns down—with them in it."

Rex sobered at the mention of people inside the burning building. He'd been one of those people, and it hadn't been funny at all.

Ethan noticed. "God, I'm sorry, bud. I shouldn't joke about that. Most of that's behind us now. All three tenants are okay, the building is starting to get back into shape, and I've got you back to help."

"Just not to help at *that* building."

Ethan raised his coffee cup again. "Right."

It was almost as if he'd never been gone. Almost.

Rex slid back into the rhythm of the work, although it wasn't a smooth slide. The men (and the two women) on one of the crews said they were glad to have him back. He ran a tight ship, but he was usually fun to work around and was regarded as fair. He had their respect. Unfortunately, he knew he was testing their level of respect more than usual, possibly even putting it at risk. He wasn't getting much sleep at night and the exhaustion was hurting his disposition during the day. Maybe he'd come back too soon. His left leg would start to ache before he was halfway through the day.

Even though he wasn't sure he believed the fire had been arson, he found himself watching everyone closely. In his mind, a cloud of suspicion hung over everyone now.

In the past, he'd often go days without seeing Ethan. Now the man kept popping in, making up excuses for stopping by, most of which Rex thought were BS.

What was Ethan so worried about?

When Ethan asked him to field calls for him from both a plumber and a sheet-rocker because he wouldn't be able to pay either of them for another week, Rex's uneasiness grew.

Maybe Ethan's money troubles were bigger than he'd thought.

"People have been slow to pay," Ethan replied when Rex asked him about it. When he pressed Ethan for more specifics, Ethan didn't offer any. "You keep the crews running, get the jobs done, and I'll worry about getting the bills paid," was all he'd said.

So why am I the one calling your subcontractors?

Rex tried to let it go. Throughout the years that he'd worked with Ethan, there'd been lean years and better years. He wouldn't be surprised if this turned out to be one of the leanest. God knew they hadn't had a strong start.

Tomorrow he should be able to give Ethan and his kids the green light to start packing. The old Victorian was nearly ready. The guy helping him install the tile around the tub in the kids' bathroom had already left for the day. Rex was about to call it quits, too. He was supposed to go to his AA meeting but wasn't feeling up to it; he'd much rather go get a beer and a burger, then head home to hopefully get some sleep.

The tile saw, set up in the hallway outside the bathroom, had been giving him trouble. Brooke had done all the other tile work in the house, and he sure wished she'd stuck around long enough to finish the job. His left hand was killing him from when he'd slipped earlier and dropped a heavy box of tile, jamming his index finger when he grabbed for it. He was able to finish the surround, but he'd lost twenty minutes cleaning up shards of busted tile and his finger was swelling.

He'd felt off all day. It was as if his brain wasn't quite engaged in his efforts. He was going through the motions but wasn't getting any of the normal satisfaction he usually felt from a job well done.

He checked his watch. The meeting would start in twenty minutes. He was feeling vulnerable enough that he knew if he skipped the meeting, he wouldn't be able to avoid the temptation to stop at O'Kelly's on the way home.

After dumping the dustpan, he checked the backsplash one last time, flipping off the bathroom light when he was comfortable things looked straight and balanced. The tiles would set overnight and in the morning he'd clean it all up. He headed down the stairs and went back to the kitchen to grab his thermos off the counter.

"Hey, Rex. Can I interest you in a fried-egg sandwich?" Ethan's houseguest asked. He stood next to the new stovetop, spatula in hand.

"Hey, Marvin. I appreciate the offer, but I need to be somewhere in ten minutes."

"You are a busy man, Rex. Is Ethan working you too hard? You seem to be favoring that leg of yours," Marvin commented, pointing toward Rex's sore leg with the spatula.

"Nah, it's not Ethan. I just think I'm not quite back to a hundred percent yet. But it'll come. You have a nice evening. I gotta run."

Rex scooped up his thermos and let himself out the back door. Ethan had been right about Marvin. He seemed like a decent-enough fellow. Anytime Rex was at the house, the main level was neat and tidy. Marvin was always up for a chat—almost to the point where Rex wasn't able to get his work done. Once he even invited the older man to help him install the clothes rails in the upstairs closets. The man was obviously bored and happy to have something to do.

But tonight, he didn't have time to stay and offer the man a diversion with conversation or a companion for dinner. He had someplace to be.

Marvin could get used to living in a place like this. He knew he'd likely have to leave soon. Ethan's foreman mentioned he was only a couple of days from wrapping things up, which meant the family could move in soon. According to Ethan, he was free to stay until his old apartment was ready, but Marvin had concerns about that.

He'd been adamant about going back to the fourplex, but only because of Penelope. That woman added spice to his days. She was a stubborn one. They'd argue about everything, from politics to the many bizarre combinations of letters she'd claim were actually words when they played *Scrabble*. Things were too quiet when she wasn't around.

He'd made a point to visit her and her daughter a couple times each week while they all waited for things to get back to normal. The fire had set Penelope back, that was for sure. She was getting some of her strength back, but he didn't think she'd be able to handle the stairs at their old place anymore. And if he lost his neighbor, the apartment didn't hold as much appeal for him either.

They'd discussed things when Rebecca wasn't around, trying to think of other options. Marvin was relieved when Penelope admitted she wanted to keep him as a neighbor. But his friend now had to think about her daughter, too. Rebecca stuck close to her mother, obviously worried about her health and safety. Marvin thought she was being a bit over-protective but knew it wasn't his place to say anything.

He'd give it time, see how things played out.

Finished now with his egg sandwich, he took his plate over to the dishwasher. He was a bit of a slob in his own apartment, but he tried hard to keep things pristine here. Ethan and his kids deserved to move into what felt like a brand-new place. He wasn't about to mess that up for them.

Now what should I do? he wondered, looking around the homey yet modern kitchen.

His favorite gameshow was on. Might as well see if he knew any of the answers tonight. He left the light on over the kitchen sink and made his way back to the family room. He suspected Ethan and his family would have years of fun back here once they were settled. Pointing the remote at the massive television screen, he held his breath, always a bit nervous as to whether or not he'd get the new-fangled beast to work. Drew had patiently taught him which buttons to push and which ones to avoid, but the last time he'd messed it up, he'd had to wait two days until one of the guys working upstairs was able to fix it for him.

It must be his lucky night. *Wheel of Fortune* came on, the sound of the clicking of the wheel chasing away the silence in the otherwise empty house. Marvin sat in the La-Z-Boy positioned with a perfect view of the set. Someday this would be Ethan's favorite chair.

The puzzles were tough, but Marvin was happy to see the young math teacher win $30,000 at the end of the show, her husband rushing up onto the stage and twirling her around in his arms.

Oh, to be young and in love again, Marvin thought wistfully. The old saying that youth was wasted on the young felt truer than ever to him now, as he sat alone in someone else's house, passing time.

His show ended and he flipped through the channels. He wasn't in the mood for the shows in hospital settings (too much suffering) or the crime shows (too much violence).

He sighed. Why couldn't he find something decent to watch on television when he had over a hundred channels to choose from? Marvin clicked the set off, pushed himself up out of the chair, and made his way back through the kitchen, turning lights off as he went. Guess he'd settle for a book tonight. When he'd mentioned to Drew that he enjoyed reading, the boy had brought him down a box of books from the attic. Apparently, Celia used to like similar books as him.

As he passed through the front living room and crossed in front of the staircase, he paused.

What's that smell?

Something smelled hot. Marvin, an electrician in his much younger years, hadn't smelled that particular odor in a long time. Not even at the fire at his apartment. Burning wires had a particular stench to them. He flipped the lights on over the staircase but saw nothing out of the ordinary. He started to flip the lights off again, sure his imagination was in play, when he heard a sizzling sound.

"Damn."

Now he had to go upstairs and make sure there wasn't a problem up there. He eyed the stairs with trepidation—so many more steps than the short flight in his apartment building. He'd made the trip up before, but it wasn't easy, and never when he was home alone.

Pop!

That did it. One hand grabbed the impressive banister, his other checking his pant pocket to make sure he had his phone on him. He scooted up the stairs, his nose leading the way.

Ethan wasn't surprised to find Marvin in the kitchen the following morning. The Sunday paper he'd brought for the man, days earlier, was spread across the island in front of him.

"Sorry, Marvin—I could have picked you up today's paper when I filled up with gas this morning."

Marvin glanced Ethan's way, over the top of the glasses resting low on his nose. "Appreciate that, Ethan, but the weekday paper has gotten so thin. I'm glad you didn't waste your money. Say, how are things coming along? Are you close to being able to move in here?"

"I think we're pretty close. Rex said he hoped to finish the tile in the boys' bathroom yesterday. Once that's in, there's just a few items left to check off the list. He's supposed to meet me here this morning to see if we can wrap things up. We moved the two fellas who were helping him here on to different projects. I'm surprised he isn't here yet, actually. He's usually ahead of me in the morning."

"Nope, not yet."

Ethan pulled another cup out of the cupboard. He hadn't unpacked all the dishes here yet, but he'd stocked a few things for Marvin to use. He poured himself a cup from the old Mr. Coffee on the counter.

"Look, Marvin, I don't want you to feel at all uncomfortable when we start moving more of our things in here. Like I've told you before, you're welcome to stay as long as you need to—until I can have your apartment back in good shape."

Marvin folded the newspaper closed. "I've been thinking about that. I'm not—"

The slamming of the back door cut Marvin's words off. Rex made a racket as he came in, kicking heavy boots off onto the mat in front of the door and carelessly plunking his metal thermos down on the new granite countertop.

"Jesus Christ, Rex, take it easy," Ethan ordered, picking up his foreman's battered old thermos to check the counter underneath it for scratches. He glanced at Rex, now hanging his heavy work coat on one of the hooks lining the back entryway. The man looked terrible, like he hadn't slept.

"Rough night?"

No reply, but the bloodshot eyes he pinned Ethan with spoke volumes. He brushed past Marvin and Ethan with little more than a grunt, heading for the stairs.

He left the unmistakable odor of stale beer in his wake.

Ethan watched Rex's retreating back, then turned back to his house guest. "Marvin, I'm serious. Don't worry about us moving in here. It'll all be fine. We can talk later. I need to . . ." He gestured toward where Rex had stormed off, and Marvin nodded in understanding.

Ethan left Marvin in the kitchen, following Rex as he stomped his way up the stairs. His friend was obviously in a shitty mood this morning, but coming to work smelling like the floor of an old bar was *not* acceptable. A couple of the guys had talked to him about Rex's surly attitude, too. He'd planned to give Rex some space, some time, to get back in his groove again. But he couldn't let the man act like this.

"What the hell?"

Something in Rex's tone set Ethan's teeth on edge and he took the last few stairs two at a time. He hurried to Rex's side where the man stood in the hallway, just shy of the kids' bathroom.

"What?" Ethan asked, trying to see around Rex's big body in the narrow space. He placed a hand on Rex's shoulder and physically turned him enough so he could see what Rex was staring at. "What happened here?"

Ethan looked from the wall, to the worn-out tile saw he'd told Rex to throw away six months ago, and back to the wall again.

"How the hell should I know?" Rex shot back.

Ethan threw his hands up in disbelief. "You should *know* because you were in charge here. And weren't you the last one to leave last night.? Are you going to tell me that wasn't there when you left? There's a burn mark on the wall, but the saw is unplugged. I'm not buying it, Rex."

"What . . . now you're calling me a liar?!"

"I'm not calling you a liar, I'm just trying to understand how something like this could happen and how you couldn't know!"

Rex turned to more fully face Ethan, fury emanating from him.

Ethan took an involuntary step back. He'd never seen Rex so mad.

A shrill whistle cut through the tension.

"Ethan! Come here!"

Ethan spun on his heel at Marvin's demand and strode back to the top of the stairs.

Is everyone losing it around here?

"Marvin, I have a bit of a situation up here. Can it wait?"

Marvin was at the foot of the stairs with one hand on the newel post, looking up. "I may be able to shine a bit of a light on that situation, but I'm not up to all those stairs this morning. If you and Rex would quit hollering at each other for a minute and come down here, I'll fill you in."

"You'll what?"

"Just get your sorry asses down here, would you?" Marvin ordered, shaking his head and walking back toward the kitchen.

He looked back at Rex, still maintaining his hostile stance in the hallway.

"We might as well hear him out. Come on," Ethan said, nodding toward the stairs and heading down, assuming Rex would follow.

He followed. Marvin, not able to move as fast as the two younger men, was just crossing through the kitchen into the family room when they caught up to him. They all sat down.

"I take it you boys noticed the burn mark on the wall in the upstairs hallway?"

"Matter of fact, we did. But how did you know there was a burn mark? Did you go upstairs?" Ethan asked.

Rex remained silent, his expression stoic.

Marvin sat back against the sofa, rubbing at his thigh.

"Last night, after everyone left, I had myself some dinner and then watched my show," the older man began. "Never can guess them damn puzzles. Once Pat and Vanna signed off, I flipped through the channels, but there was nothing good on. I really like old westerns, but all these new-fangled cops-and-robbers shows on television these days aren't worth my time."

Rex moved to interrupt, but Ethan shushed him.

"Decided to turn in early and read," Marvin continued. "Drew brought me down some of Celia's old books. That boy of yours is a gem, Ethan."

Ethan nodded. "That he is, Marvin. But, Marvin, how did you know about the burn?"

"I'm getting to that," the man said, although Ethan wished he'd get to it quicker. The way Rex was twitching, he looked like he might have another rude outburst, and Ethan didn't want Marvin to be on the receiving end of *that*.

"I turned everything off in here and headed back to my bedroom. As I was passing by the stairs, I thought I smelled something. I used to be an electrician, see, and I was afraid of what that smell might mean. Then I heard a popping noise and knew I had to investigate."

"Marvin, you went upstairs by yourself? That probably wasn't a good idea," Ethan said, concern in his voice.

"There was no time to do anything except head upstairs to see where the smell was coming from," Marvin countered. "Must have been adrenalin, because I was up those stairs in a flash. When I got to the top, I could see sparks down the hallway. You can figure out the rest."

"Was the saw plugged in?" Ethan asked.

Now Marvin looked at him like he was an idiot. "Of course the saw was plugged in. How else do you think it could spark? I unplugged it, quick as I could, and made sure there was no *actual* fire. I hated the thought of you having to deal with *another* fire, Ethan. Could you imagine?"

Ethan couldn't believe what he was hearing. "Marvin, I hate to think what might have happened if you hadn't smelled it right away. Thank you, man!"

"Well, luckily I did, and there was no real damage. You probably owe a prayer of thanks to the Big Guy," Marvin said, pointing to the ceiling.

"And to you," Ethan said, getting to his feet. "Would you excuse us for a few minutes, Marvin?"

Marvin nodded, glancing between the two men but saying nothing more.

"Rex, outside. Now."

Ethan refused to look at his foreman as he headed for the back door. He didn't even bother to grab a jacket. The ten-degree temperature barely registered as he walked out to his truck. He leaned against the box and waited for Rex.

Eventually, Rex came out, wearing his boots and jacket, old thermos in hand. Gone was the fury, replaced with resignation, now etched deep into the lines of his face.

"For what it's worth, I'm sorry."

"Sorry?" Ethan said, clenching his fists at his side, trying to rein in his fury. "Sorry? Your carelessness could have burned this house down. *Celia's* house. That she entrusted to *me*. Hell, Marvin could have been hurt . . . or worse!"

Ethan pushed off from the side of his truck, turning his back on Rex and taking ten steps down the driveway and back, still fighting to control his anger.

"Didn't I tell you to throw that damn saw away? We *knew* the cord was frayed and decided it wasn't worth fixing it again."

Rex, who'd been staring at the house, turned back to Ethan, one eye shut against the glare of the morning sun. "We did. I hadn't gotten around to it yet. When Brooke bailed on the tiling upstairs, I thought I'd go ahead and use it since it was still out at the shop."

"Do not make this *Brooke's* fault," Ethan spat out.

"I am in no way saying this is Brooke's fault," Rex said. "This is one hundred percent my fault. My irresponsible actions could have again resulted in disaster. It wouldn't have been the first time. But it will be the last—at least as far as you're concerned, Ethan."

Rex turned and started to walk toward his own pickup. Ethan grabbed his arm, but Rex jerked it away and kept walking.

"What, that's it? You're just going to walk away?"

Rex stopped and turned back around to face his old friend.

"Yes, that's exactly what I'm doing. I shouldn't have come back. I'll let you know where you can send my last paycheck."

Chapter Twenty-Eight
Gift of Good Intentions

"Your foreman just up and quit on you?" Rebecca asked. "I thought you guys were . . . like . . . *best friends.*"

Ethan took his eyes off the road to glance over at her for a second. "We were. I mean, we *are.* God . . . these past few months have been insane. I don't know what the hell I'm doing anymore."

Ethan's frustrated declaration hung in the air.

"Ethan . . . we don't have to do this today. It sounds like you have too much going on to leave town right now."

"No. This is important, too. Besides, Stacey and what's-his-name are expecting us."

Rebecca laughed. "Tell me you haven't *really* forgotten his name. Because *I* don't know it, and we can't very well arrive at his house and call him Mr. What's-His-Name."

Ethan grinned. Rebecca had become his one solid touchpoint in all the craziness that made up his life these days. He was lucky to have her with him for this trip. "Gregory. The dude's name is *Gregory,* and *don't* call him Greg. Apparently, he doesn't *answer* to *Greg.*"

Now Rebecca laughed even harder. "I wonder where Greg and Red are going to take us for dinner."

Ethan burst into laughter. No one had called his ex-wife "Red" since their college days. She'd had an unfortunate episode with a home hair-dye kit, and despite ending up with hair that was more of a bright orange than red, the nickname stuck. Stacey never did see the humor in it.

"Oh, I just *dare* you to call her that today," he said, wiping at his eyes so he could see the highway. Traffic was getting heavier as they got closer to Minneapolis. At least the weather was behaving. They needed to make it home yet tonight. He'd never leave the boys alone overnight, at least not until they were out of high school. As far as he was concerned, that was just asking for trouble.

"Tell you what," Rebecca said between hiccups, "if dinner is a disaster, I'll just work the word 'red' into the conversation and that'll be my signal for us to bail. If we're discreet enough about it, she might not even catch on."

"You are rotten, you know that, don't you?"

It felt good to laugh. It had been far too long since Ethan had much laughter in his life. He sobered. Thinking about all that had happened brought Rex back to the forefront of his mind.

"I know that face," Rebecca said, her own smile fading. "Do you want to talk about it?"

"What you said earlier, about Rex being my best friend? You're right. He is. But that's why I was furious with him the other day at the house, when Marvin told us what happened. It was so careless of him to leave that old saw plugged in . . . he could have burned Celia's house down, maybe even killed my tenant. But maybe I was too hard on him. After all he's been through . . . I know Rex would never purposely do anything to hurt me. To hurt my kids. He's like an uncle to them. The cops put Rex through hell, accusing him of arson like they did. He didn't deserve that."

He glanced at Rebecca again. She'd always been so easy to talk to. She gave him a small smile.

"Thank you."

"For what?" she asked.

Ethan shrugged. "For being such a good listener. Not just for me, but for Elizabeth, too. Your idea of going to talk to Stacey, to try to figure out what's going on with her and see if there's a way we can help her and the kids have a better relationship . . . that was a very kind thing for you to suggest."

Rebecca nodded and then looked out her side window. "We all used to be so close. Stacey was my friend for a long time. She helped me stay sane when my dad died, when Mom got whacko for a while. That's what friends do. They stand by each other, even when things get tough."

Ethan glanced over his shoulder, put on his blinker, and pulled out to pass a slow-moving semi. "You're right. So, then, let me ask you . . . was I too much of an ass to Rex? Am I the reason he took off like that?"

"Based on what you've told me, I doubt it. Your reaction doesn't sound out of line to me. Nearly losing a *second* building to fire would make anybody a little nuts."

Ethan pulled back into the driving lane once he was beyond the semi. It was starting to drizzle and he had to turn his windshield wipers on. Drizzle in Minnesota in late March could make for tough driving conditions; he hoped it was just a small storm cell moving through.

"But this is *Rex* we're talking about. I don't know how I'd have gotten through these past couple of years without all his help. Hell, he practically kept my business going for me some weeks, when it was all getting to be too much with the kids and the divorce. I shouldn't have gotten so pissed off."

Rebecca reached into her purse and pulled out a small bag of chips. She tore it open and offered him some. "Have you tried to apologize?"

"Yeah. I gave him a day to cool off and then called him. He didn't pick up. I drove over to his house but he wasn't home. There weren't any tracks in the snow in his driveway either. Honestly, I'm worried. Rex's had more than his share of heartache. And he struggles with the booze, I think because of some of the things he's had to live through."

Ethan helped himself to a few chips and went on to tell Rebecca about the accident that took Gail's life.

"That's awful," Rebecca said. "I know how hard living through the death of a spouse is, but to add guilt on top of it because you were the one driving . . . that's gotta be pretty tough to come to terms with, accident or not. You'd always second-guess yourself. Wonder, if only you'd done something differently . . ."

Ethan reached over and squeezed Rebecca's hand. Her pain over her first husband's death was evident in her voice. Ethan hated the fact that his old college friend was gone, too.

"How did we go from laughing our heads off a few miles back to this depressing conversation?" Ethan asked, reaching over and searching for something on the radio.

"You're right. We need to cheer up. But before we do, what are you going to do about Rex?"

Ethan found a station playing music from the '90s.

"I might give my brother-in-law a call, see if he has any ideas."

"Matt?" Rebecca asked. She'd met him out at Whispering Pines on Christmas Day.

"Yeah. I already called Rex's family. None of them have heard from him. It's not like him to take off. I honestly don't think he'd do something really dumb, I'm not worried about that. But I do think he might need help. I hate to think of him off somewhere, alone, maybe drinking too much and holing up in some fleabag motel."

"Do your kids know he's gone?"

Ethan sighed. "Not yet. That is one conversation I do not want to have. I'd like to at least find out where he's at first."

Together they found Gregory-Not-Greg's house with Rebecca's phone app using the address Lizzy gave them. They waited for Stacey to buzz them in through the gate flanking the front of their neighborhood. Grand homes sat back from the road on large lots. They turned the corner and searched for the right house number.

Ethan let out a low whistle when he spied the place. "I guess Elizabeth wasn't kidding."

"About what?" Rebecca asked as she craned her neck to stare up at the impressive façade in front of them.

"She said her mother was working to snag a rich one. Looks like she pulled one in."

Rebecca snorted. "Money can't buy you love."

Ethan glanced her way, curious if maybe she'd experienced something similar, but he didn't want to pry. He parked his pickup next to the black BMW sitting in the driveway.

"Ready?" he asked.

"No, but we came all this way," she said, winking at Ethan as she stepped out of the truck.

And down she went.

Ethan hurried over to her side, nearly falling down himself on the icy driveway. "Bec, are you all right?!"

She was already getting to her feet by the time he reached her side. She waved him away and, incredibly, seemed to be laughing. "I'm fine. Just clumsy."

Ethan slid his foot back and forth on the pavement, testing it. "No, it's not you. There's a fine glaze of ice on here. Must have had rain or drizzle come through here, too." He glanced at the clouds above. They looked harmless now. He hoped they'd stay that way. "Here, take my arm," he insisted, holding it out for Rebecca.

She patted it but didn't grab on. "Thanks, but no thanks. I don't need to meet my old friend after all these years hanging on to her ex's arm."

He chuckled as she took tentative steps past him, heading for the ornate front door. She made a valid point: Stacey had always been jealous of Rebecca. While Ethan had never admitted it to anyone, Stacey had always correctly assumed she was his second choice. He shook his head, thankful for his years with Stacey despite everything that had transpired. They'd enjoyed some good years during their marriage, and, of course, their three kids were the greatest blessing of all.

Rebecca rang the doorbell as he joined her on the front step. Chimes sounded inside like church bells. They waited.

"I hope we have the right house," Rebecca said, glancing around.

"It's the right house," Ethan assured her. "She's just letting us wait for a minute."

Sure enough, a minute or two later, a lock clicked open and the door swung inward. Stacey stood just inside, seemingly unsure as to how to greet her old friend and her ex-husband.

Rebecca broke the ice. "Stacey, it's so good to see you," she said warmly, holding out her hands to the other woman.

Stacey hesitated, but then squeezed Rebecca's hands, offering a small smile. "It's good to see you, too, Rebecca. I was certainly surprised to hear from you the first time. And then when you called back to suggest we *meet* . . . well, I wasn't sure what the point was. It's been a long time."

The two women stood awkwardly, hands still clasped and the door still wide open.

Ethan cleared his throat.

"Oh. Hello, Ethan," Stacey said, dropping Rebecca's hands and motioning for them to come in. "Did you have any trouble finding the place?"

"No," he replied, not paying much attention to Stacey as his eyes roamed the impressive room. He knew quality when he saw it, and he was looking at it now.

"Should we sit down?" Rebecca asked, clearly attempting to dispel the unpleasant atmosphere.

"Actually, why don't I grab my coat and we can go?"

Rebecca looked around. "Go? Isn't your fiancé coming with us? I was hoping to meet him, too."

"He was planning to join us, but his plane was delayed. He's on his way home from a business trip. If he gets in early enough, he'll meet us at the restaurant. Otherwise, he sent his regrets for missing you."

"I bet," Ethan muttered—not as quietly as he'd intended.

"What?" Stacey demanded, her demeanor suddenly ice-cold. "Ethan, if you have something to say, please just say it."

"I've got nothing, Stacey. Let's go then. I need to get back to the boys tonight."

He could see her hesitate, as if trying to decide whether or not his comment was meant as a dig or not. (It was.)

She didn't comment. Where had the woman he used to know gone?

She picked up a long wool coat hanging over the back of a nearby chair and slipped it on, scooping a purse off the floor next to it. Her high heels *click-clack*ed across the highly polished floor. "I have reservations for five o'clock at Sal's. I thought we'd eat early so you can get back on the road at a decent time. Why don't you follow me over there? That way you can head out of town straight from the restaurant."

She held the door open for Rebecca and Ethan to exit and then locked it. She hurried toward the black BMW, head held at an odd angle, as if she could smell something in the air. Ethan started to warn her, but before he could get the words out, one of her high heels slipped on the ice. She didn't fall, but she executed an ungainly slide-and-stumble combination, stopping only when her body connected with the black vehicle.

Ethan bit back a laugh—she'd kill him if she heard it.

"Wow, that was close. Be careful," she said over her shoulder as she yanked her driver's-side door open and got in. She turned the engine over and was already backing out before Ethan and Rebecca were even in the pickup yet.

"What the hell is she in such a hurry for?" Ethan asked, quickly clicking his seatbelt into place and making sure Rebecca was settled before throwing the truck in Reverse. He didn't want to lose the BMW; he didn't know where the restaurant was located.

"I wonder if that story she fed us about Greg was even true . . ." Rebecca speculated. "She's acting as if she wants to get out of here before anyone sees us. Maybe she didn't even really tell him we were coming."

Ethan glanced in his rearview mirror at the imposing house they'd just left. "You might be right about that."

Rebecca was quiet as they drove. Ethan sensed she had something to say but was holding back. When he glimpsed over at her, the way she was looking at him confirmed his suspicion.

"Do you remember *why* we came all this way, Ethan?"

"Yeah, for the kids. So?"

"Right. For the kids. So . . . how about you work a little harder to be nice? If she's on the defensive, you're likely to do more harm than good."

He was about to deny her accusation, but instead he paused. She was right. Somewhere along the line he'd fallen into the nasty habit of automatically trying to push Stacey's buttons. He needed to stop if he wanted to help Stacey repair her relationship with their kids. And he *did* want that. Even if it meant pretending to be nice to his ex.

"Sorry . . . you're right. I'll play nice."

"And don't say anything more to her about her guy-friend. Honestly, it's probably better if we can talk to her alone, without him here."

Ethan sped up to get through a yellow light before it could turn red. If he lost sight of the BMW, Stacey might just disappear into the night, and they'd have wasted their time.

"Good point. The kids are convinced Greg doesn't like them."

"Gregory," she said with a smirk. "Did you see the wedding pictures on the side table in the living room back there? If those are his kids, they're grown and married off already."

Ethan nodded. "Drew said *Gregory* has older kids of his own."

Rebecca sighed. "If Stacey is set on marrying this guy, and he doesn't like her kids, this is going to be an uphill battle."

— ℓℓℓ —

Dinner was pleasant enough. The three of them kept things civil. They reminisced about their time together in college. Stacey acted appropriately shocked and saddened when Rebecca told her about Ryan's accident and his later suicide.

Her fiancé never called.

After the dishes were cleared, the women enjoyed an after-dinner cocktail and Ethan ordered a decaf. Rebecca mentioned again to Stacey how much she'd enjoyed visiting with Lizzy.

Stacey's disposition shifted suddenly. "Why are you talking to my daughter?"

Rebecca looked taken aback by the bite in Stacey's words. "Oh . . . I don't know. They've just been friendly conversations. I first met her out at Whispering Pines when Ethan invited me and my mom to join them out there for Christmas Day. We'd been displaced by the fire and Ethan invited all the tenants to spend the holiday out there. It was nice."

Ethan noticed how Rebecca left out the part where Lizzy stopped over to see her before going back to college. He was glad for Rebecca's omission. Stacey would have shut down. But this way, Stacey seemed to relax when told it was the fire that had put Rebecca near her kids.

"I never had any kids of my own. You are so blessed," Rebecca said, trying to keep her tone light. "Do you see much of Lizzy? I know she's not too far from here, being at the U of M."

Stacey looked between Rebecca and Ethan. He could almost read her thoughts. She was trying to decide whether or not Rebecca was being sincere.

"I *am* blessed. It's just been hard, you know, since . . ." Stacey glanced at Ethan and then at her phone, still sitting ominously quiet on the table next to her. "I've been so busy moving down here and planning a wedding. It's been crazy. But when it slows down, we'll all be able to spend more time together, I'm sure."

Ethan just *had* to ask about Gregory. He chose his words carefully, so as not to put her defenses up. "Stacey, how does Gregory feel about the kids?"

Her eyes widened a fraction and she didn't immediately respond. She picked up her cordial and took another sip of the dessert liquor.

"Honestly, he's still a little uncomfortable around them. He has two grown children of his own, but they were mostly raised by his wife—I mean, *ex*-wife. Plus, he travels a lot. But I'm sure it'll all be fine when he gets to know them."

Ethan chewed on the inside of his cheek, biting back the words that wanted to spring to his lips.

Rebecca intervened. "I guess that's understandable if he's never been around teenagers much. They *can* be overwhelming."

Stacey gave her old friend a grateful look.

Ethan was starting to understand Lizzy's concern about Stacey. She seemed high-strung, edgy. He could already tell this wouldn't be solved in just one conversation. He decided to try a different tactic.

"Stacey . . . I'm worried about the kids."

This caught her attention. "Why? Have they been acting out? Is someone in trouble?"

"No, not exactly. They're all doing fine in school. Dylan's playing basketball and Drew got a part-time job. He even has a date for prom. But you probably know all that already."

Based on the confused look on her face, Ethan couldn't tell if she'd actually known any of it.

"They're doing all right," he continued. "But they miss you. They're worried you might be moving too fast with this guy."

Stacey started to speak, but Rebecca jumped in.

"It's nothing against your fiancé," she said, pulling Stacey's attention away from Ethan. "My mom remarried after Dad died, and I remember I was dead-set on disliking the guy before I even met him. It's natural. I'm sure Gregory is a perfectly decent man. It just takes time. These things can't be rushed."

After a pause, Stacey asked, "Did you eventually come to like the man your mom married?"

Ethan suspected she really wanted the answer to be *yes*. But, based on his knowledge of Penelope's history, he also suspected she'd be disappointed by the real answer.

Rebecca sighed. "I wish I could tell you I did. But she chose poorly that time, and the marriage didn't last long."

"*That* time?"

"Mom's been married four times."

Stacey nearly toppled over a water glass as she reached again for her drink. "Four times?" She gave a nervous giggle then quickly drained her drink.

"Four times," Rebecca confirmed. "You knew Dad. She divorced number two and number three and sadly buried number four. *That* was a shame. I liked number four."

Stacey sat back, a hand over her heart. "But you didn't care for husband number two *or* number three?"

"I'd be lying if I said I did. They were hard men—men who could provide for her—but neither were warm or ever cared about her family. Mom finally wisened up the last time. He was a keeper."

Ethan's phone buzzed and he pulled it out. Dylan had sent a text asking when they'd be home.

"It's already seven. Stacey, thank you for going out for dinner with us. I do think it's important that we work harder to make things as easy as we can for Elizabeth, Drew, and Dylan. You and I are over, but they are still *our* responsibility. They miss you. If there is ever anything I can do to help, please let me know."

Stacey busied herself with her coat. When she finally met his gaze again, her eyes were glassy. "Thank you, Ethan. That means a lot. I do miss them. I'm sorry if I've been remiss in my mom duties lately. I promise to work on it. In fact, I'll call Lizzy tomorrow. See if she wants to do some Sunday shopping with me."

"That would be nice, Stacey. I'm sure she'd appreciate it."

Ethan took care of the bill while Stacey and Rebecca said their goodbyes. If the money didn't start flowing better at work, he might have to stop automatically paying for everyone's meals. Maybe he should have let Stacey pay. She certainly appeared to be living in style these days.

He watched his ex-wife climb into her high-end car and drive away. He'd gotten over their failed marriage some time ago, but the loss of their family unit still weighed heavily on his heart.

As he and Rebecca walked back to his pickup, she offered to drive. "It's been a long day, and you drove us here."

"Thanks for the offer, but if you don't mind, I'd prefer to drive. The trip home will go faster if I'm driving. If you're tired, go ahead and nap. I'll get you home safe and sound."

They talked a bit more as they left the bright lights of the city. Rebecca thought Stacey looked good, but she worried she wasn't truly happy. She voiced many of the same conclusions Ethan had already reached.

Eventually, Rebecca quieted down and dozed off, leaving him to his own thoughts.

He was glad they'd gone to see Stacey, but he'd done what he could for now as far as his children's mother was concerned. She was a grown woman and would do what she wanted to do. He could only hope she'd want to work on building a better relationship between their kids and Gregory, since she seemed intent on blending their families.

He'd continue to do *his* best to keep their kids happy—with or without her. Unfortunately, their kids were going to be furious with him when they learned Rex had taken off after an argument he had with him on the job. So much for keeping them happy.

His mind wandered back to his fight with Rex. He'd been so furious with his friend when he saw that burn on the wall. Not just because of what it could have meant. If Marvin hadn't saved the day . . .

But it also brought up all the doubts and misgivings he'd felt about the earlier fire. They still didn't have answers as to who started that one.

Damn you, Rex, for making me harbor doubts still . . .

He noticed the lights outside the big Cabela's store on the east side of Rogers, just off the interstate, when a steady sleet began to fall, instantly coating his windshield. Tail lights flashed bright red ahead as drivers hit their brakes. He took his foot off the gas, hoping to slow his momentum enough to avoid touching his own brakes; brakes and ice made for a deadly combination that could send them into a tailspin or the ditch faster than Ethan could blink. He flipped his defroster and windshield wipers on high in an effort to clear his view. He swore softly when he had to carefully apply the brakes to avoid rear-ending the cars ahead of him. Traffic up ahead was at a standstill. He fishtailed a bit but managed to pull it straight, then had to angle slightly onto the shoulder to avoid a collision.

He expelled his pent-up breath, thankful, yet anxious to be stopped on the side of I-94.

Rebecca popped up straight in her seat, awakened by the commotion. "What was that you said about getting me home safe and sound?" she asked, glancing around.

"That may prove a bit more problematic than I'd thought," he said, keeping a close eye out on the vehicles behind them.

That's when he heard it: the crunching of metal, the blare of horns, and a grating sound—as if something was being dragged across the concrete.

He made a decision, gunning the engine and taking the ditch. Thanks to a relatively dry winter, there wasn't much snow. He kept going, rough as it was, the two of them bouncing around in their seats. Behind them, chaos reigned. Rebecca whipped her head around to watch the scene unfold while Ethan fought to keep the pickup on all four wheels.

"Oh my God, Ethan! Those cars are piling up. Some are getting flung this way!"

"I was afraid of that," he gritted out, still fighting to control his truck.

He was skirting alongside a fence now, running parallel with the highway. He could see an off-ramp ahead and had no intention of stopping, if he could help it, before he got them away from the pileup.

Rebecca grabbed hold of the handle above her door but said nothing more.

"Hold on . . . almost there," he advised, and pushed the gas a little harder to climb back up the embankment and slide up onto the exit ramp. Thankfully, no one was on it—at least at this point.

Rebecca turned to look down the ramp and groaned.

"What?" Ethan said, intent on keeping his vehicle on the slick road surface.

"A semi is on its side right before the off-ramp. Cars can't get past it."

"We aren't going any farther tonight. These roads are *way* too treacherous," Ethan said as he very slowly turned onto the road that would take them into Rogers. "We'll find a hotel and wait until they get that mess cleaned up down there and the ice taken care of. It'll take a while."

"But what about your boys?"

"They'll be fine. As soon as we find a place to stay, I'll call and have them go over to my folks' to spend the night. Unless it's too icy there. If that's the case, I'll just have to trust them to stay alone."

Rebecca finally let go of the handle she'd been clinging to as if for dear life and relaxed back into the seat. "Looks like you're going to keep your promise to get me home safe and sound. Later than we thought, but safe nonetheless. That was a hell of a gutsy move back there, Ethan. Thank you. You might just have saved our lives."

"I don't know about *that*, but at least we didn't have to deal with a banged-up truck and possibly spend a night stuck out there on that highway." He spied a decent looking hotel and turned toward it, still moving slowly in deference to the ice. "Hope they have rooms for us."

"Yes, sir, we have a few rooms left," the desk clerk confirmed when they made it to the front desk. "Would you like a room for just the one night?"

Ethan hesitated, glancing at Rebecca. Based on the sleet storm outside, others were sure to be coming, needing a place to stay. "One?"

Rebecca jumped in. "Yes, one room for one night. Thank you."

Ethan pulled out his wallet and the clerk secured them a room.

"We offer continental breakfast from six a.m. until 10:30, and checkout is at eleven. Enjoy your stay!"

As Ethan took the keys and they turned away, three more parties came through the main doors, stomping muck off their shoes and shaking ice off their hair and clothes.

Must be getting worse out there, he thought.

Ethan and Rebecca stepped into the empty elevator.

"Rebecca, I'm sorry. I hope I wasn't too presumptuous back there. I just thought it would be selfish of us to take two rooms when they didn't have many left and lots of people are going to be looking for places to stay in this storm."

She smiled and shook her head. "No worries, Ethan. I could read your mind. It was the right call. Again."

Just then the lights flickered and the elevator jerked to a stop.

"Oh hell . . . you've got to be kidding."

Rebecca let out a nervous laugh. "I remember when you would have given anything to be stuck in an elevator, alone, with me."

Her words caught him completely off guard. Here he was, trying to be all chivalrous, and she started to *tease*? Plus, she was dead right—back then, he *would* have given anything.

"I'm sorry. That was in bad taste," she said, misunderstanding his lack of response.

Suddenly, he welcomed the dark. He reached for her hand, brushing against some other body part in the darkness. Before he could try again, the lights winked back on and the elevator shuddered back to life.

Their eyes met and held. He noticed she was gripping her purse with both hands.

The elevator stopped on their floor and the doors slid silently open. Ethan looked over Rebecca's head into the hushed, dimly lit corridor. Rebecca continued to watch him and didn't move to exit the elevator. When the doors started to slide shut again, Ethan reached around her to push the button. He had no intention of riding up and down in the elevator all night, especially if the storm was threatening to knock out the power.

His movement snapped her into action. "Oh God, that would have been scary to be stuck in there with no power," she said, laughing nervously.

The stain on her cheeks told Ethan she was probably mortified at her earlier comment. *Or apprehensive to be alone in a hotel room with me.* He smiled at her, attempting to convey to her that he'd be the perfect gentleman. *Even if it kills me.*

They found their room. Ethan could feel the tension and suspected Rebecca did as well. She took the key from him and opened the door. As Ethan followed her in, he wasn't sure if he should be relieved or disappointed to find two queen beds inside.

"You better call your kids and your folks."

"Ah, yes, thanks for reminding me," Ethan said, pulling his phone out. "Damn . . . it's almost dead."

"Here—I have a charger in my purse," she said, digging in her handbag and pulling one out. "We probably better charge them in case the power goes out for good."

Ethan plugged his phone in and made the calls while he watched Rebecca open the curtain to look outside. The darkness was nearly impenetrable. He decided to call to check on Lizzy, too. As it turned out, she was studying in her dorm room, oblivious to the winter weather outside.

"Everyone's settled. What about your mom?" Ethan asked, suddenly remembering that a friend had come over to stay with Penelope while they were gone; but she probably hadn't intended to stay the night.

"Helen is probably fine with staying, she lives alone, but I'll call to let Mom know we're stuck and make sure everything is fine back home."

Ethan used the bathroom while Rebecca checked on her mom. When he came out, he asked, "I don't suppose you have any toiletries in that bag of yours, do you?"

Rebecca laughed. "Sadly, no. But I bet we could get a few necessities down at the front desk. We should have thought to ask. I did see a bar of soap and a tiny bottle of shampoo in the bathroom."

Ethan nodded and glanced at the clock between the two beds. "It's not even nine yet. What do you want to do?"

He hadn't intended for it to be such a loaded question.

Rebecca held his gaze for a second but then looked away, scooping the key card off the credenza and waving it in the air. "Why don't we go down and see if they have some toothpaste for us at the front desk, and maybe even see if we can get a drink. I saw a restaurant attached to the hotel."

"Great idea," Ethan agreed, relieved for the reprieve. He picked her purse up off the bed and handed it to her.

Even *that* felt somehow intimate.

The front desk only had a few things left by the time they got down there. Rebecca tossed the toothpaste and shaving supplies into her purse. They followed posted arrows to a lounge and ordered wings and beer.

The tension faded away once they were out of the hotel room, and they once again enjoyed a lively conversation, discussing everything from politics to favorite movies. After two beers each, they switched to water, but neither were in a hurry to go back upstairs. Eventually, the conversation looped back to the early days of their friendship.

"You might not have realized this—or, maybe you did—but I had a huge crush on you in college," Ethan said. He'd probably regret the confession later, but he'd kept it bottled up inside for too long. "If Ryan wouldn't have been such a great guy, I'd have told you that a long time ago."

"Oh, Ethan, that's just the beer talking."

He laughed. "I've only had two beers. I'm a grown man. It's not the beer talking. It's time you knew. To me, you've always been the 'girl who got away.' Although, technically, I never had you in the first place, so I guess that's not entirely accurate."

"I've always known," she said softly, a slight smile curving her lips as her fingers frayed the soggy edges of the napkin under her water glass.

Ethan wasn't sure he'd heard her right. She seemed hesitant to look at him now. There'd been that one night, one night when he let his defenses down, but never again. He was sure she'd forgotten about that long ago. She'd always stayed true to Ryan, and he'd never pushed. He wasn't that kind of guy.

"You've . . . always known?"

Rebecca nodded, still staring into her icy water glass. "But you were such a good friend to Ryan."

He chuckled. "Even when it damn near killed me."

This drew a nervous giggle out of Rebecca.

"Stacey was always jealous of you. Did you know that?"

She shook her head. "I had no idea. We never gave her any reason to be jealous. She never said anything to me."

"No, we didn't. But I think, deep down, she always felt like she was my second choice."

Now Rebecca met his gaze, held it. "Was she?"

He paused, took a drink of water. "Yes, at the time. But I did everything I could to convince her she was wrong—because I *did* love her."

She nodded. "Sometimes I used to wish you weren't so noble about it all. Remember when we'd all go swimming at the lake in the summer? It was so much fun. Ryan didn't always come because sometimes he was at work. But even when he wasn't there, you'd barely look at me."

Her words took him back to sunny days spent floating around in a friend's speedboat, surrounded by pretty girls in bikinis. He'd always thought Rebecca was the prettiest of them all, but he'd been careful not to let her catch him looking.

Ethan shrugged. "I barely looked at you because I was worried if I did, I wouldn't be able to look away. You'd have been able to tell exactly what I was thinking."

He jumped when Rebecca reached across the table and ran a finger across the knuckles of his right hand, wrapped around his water glass.

"And what *were* you thinking, exactly?"

He wondered if she could actually hear the thumping of his heart, it was beating so hard now.

"Do you really have to ask?"

Rebecca laid her hand on the check their waiter had dropped off earlier. "Maybe you could show me."

Could he? Did he dare? What if all those years of wanting, of denying, had built up unrealistic expectations?

For the second time that night, he decided to throw caution to the wind. The first time had saved them from a collision. This time might just wreck him. But he'd hate himself if he didn't at least take the chance, now that she seemed to be offering. There might not be another one.

He stood and held a hand out to her, testing her. Had she meant it?

She gave him that little smile again—the one he'd never forgotten—and slipped her hand in his. She took care of the bill and together they wandered back toward their room, hand in hand, not talking. When they got off the elevator on their floor, he tugged her toward the large glass windows overlooking the front of the hotel, streaming with rivulets of water and ice. All was dark, quiet.

"Are you sure?" he whispered to her. They both knew what they'd do if they went straight back to their room. He didn't want either of them to have any regrets later.

"I'm sure. Ethan . . . we've set our feelings for each other off to the side for the sake of everyone else for far too long. I never thought I'd get this chance again."

She meant what she said; he could see it in her eyes.

The storm outside couldn't hold a candle to the turmoil he felt building in himself. He felt like an inexperienced kid again, full of nerves, as she led him by the hand back to their room. Once inside, both hesitated. After an awkward pause, Rebecca reached into her purse and pulled out two toothbrushes and the tube of toothpaste from the front desk.

She held them up, smiling.

He so appreciated the easy nature of this woman. He snatched one out of her hand and headed into the bathroom to brush his teeth. She followed, squeezing paste onto her toothbrush then handing him the tube, telling him about the time she'd accidently grabbed her mom's ointment rub and smeared it on her toothbrush, realizing too late what she'd done. They hip-bumped each other as they vied for space in front of the sink. Rebecca laid a washcloth out and they placed their toothbrushes side by side.

Ethan moved behind Rebecca and she turned to face him, her hands on his chest and her back to the bathroom vanity. He lowered his head and captured her mouth with his, something he'd dreamed of doing for as long as he could remember. The minty taste of her mouth wiped all conscious thought from his mind. He lifted her up and set her bottom on the countertop. They deepened their kiss, taking their time.

It didn't matter that they were now nearly fifty instead of nearly twenty. They'd long ago resigned themselves to the fact they could never be together. Now the years fell away, and they were simply Ethan and Rebecca, finally exploring the feelings they'd tried so hard to ignore.

He pulled her closer and she wrapped her legs around his waist. He lifted her up and carried her out of the bathroom, ignoring the twinge in his shoulder, that constant reminder that he wasn't a kid anymore.

Tonight, he was going to get to be a kid again, with the girl of his younger dreams.

He eased her down on the closest bed, confident now that they'd have no need for the other one. He watched her face as his hand moved slowly up under her shirt. Her soft smile was all the permission he needed. When he wanted to see what he was caressing, he lifted her sweater up and over her head, his breath catching at the sight of her small breasts ensconced in delicate white lace.

"Can we turn off the light?" she whispered as he bent his head to kiss the *V* between the satiny cups.

"But I've waited so long to see you like this," he said, raising his head to meet her gaze.

"Ethan, please. I'm nervous enough as it is. Let the darkness be our friend." She giggled. The hand she ran over his back felt more confident than her voice sounded.

He reached over and clicked off the light. He'd do anything this woman asked of him. She was every bit as beautiful, both inside and out, as he'd always known she'd be.

Finally, after all this time, he'd get to know all of her.

He woke up to an empty bed, an empty room. Had it all been a dream?

No—that was Rebecca's coat next to his on the chair across the room. And the other bed was still perfectly made. He rolled over and paper crinkled under him.

Went to get breakfast. Be back soon. I left the razor and shaving cream in the bathroom for you.

He got out of bed with a sigh. A shower sounded perfect. He shut the bathroom door, lathered his face, and scraped away the stubble. Then he brought the sample-size bottles of shampoo and conditioner and sliver of soap from the vanity into the shower. He used them sparingly so Rebecca would have some, too. He was just about to turn the shower off when the bathroom door opened.

"I certainly hope that's you," he said. "And I hope you brought food."

Rebecca peeked around the shower curtain with a grin. "I did bring food. If you're starving, it's in the other room. Or, if you'd rather help me reach this troublesome spot on my back before we have breakfast in bed, give me a minute and I'll join you."

"The food can keep," he assured her.

Chapter Twenty-Nine
GIFT OF FAMILY SUPPORT

ETHAN FELT AS IF he'd fallen into the deep end of a huge pool, and if he stopped treading water for even a minute he'd sink. *Everything* would sink. He was back to managing the two construction crews on his own. Any time he could devote to working on the fourplex became even more sporadic. Other than Norman's unit, none of the other apartments were even close to inhabitable yet.

He kept reminding himself to take things one day at a time.

Other than one text from Rex giving him a PO Box where he could send his last paycheck, there'd been no communication. Ethan finally had to sit the boys down and update them on what was going on. He was having to work later and later. Plus, he was tired of being evasive when they inquired about Rex.

He caught them as they were finishing up breakfast, before they left for school. He gave them an abbreviated summary of the incident that had transpired at their new house.

"That doesn't sound like Rex. I can't believe he'd just take off like that," Drew said.

Dylan was quieter than usual.

"I'm sure he's fine. But there's something you should know about Rex. I've never mentioned it before, but I think you're old enough now to handle it. Rex has struggled on and off with alcohol through the years. I'm afraid he might have relapsed. Maybe even went to get help. That's the only thing I can think of that would explain his behavior."

Dylan looked up. "Why didn't you ever tell us this before, Dad?"

Ethan shrugged. "It wasn't my place to talk about those dark periods in Rex's past. Because I thought that's where they'd stay—in his past. But now I'm not so sure."

"What are you going to do now?" Drew asked.

"What *can* I do? Rex is a grown man. He quit and left town for a while. I don't have any real reason to suspect anything bad has happened to him. For now, we wait. He'll come back when he's ready. His mom's in town and he has his house. He wouldn't just take off and never come back."

"You're probably right," Drew acknowledged. "I'm sorry he left you, too. I get why you're so uptight these days."

Hearing it laid out in those terms really sucks, Ethan thought, but he only nodded. He wasn't the only one who'd lost important people these last couple of years. First Stacey, and now Rex, had walked out on not only him but the kids, too.

"I'm sorry if I've been short with you guys and not around as much as I should be. Hopefully this is just temporary. Now, we better get going if you don't want to be late for school."

Drew stood and dumped the extra milk in his cereal bowl down the drain. "Was Lizzy still planning to stay at school over her spring break?"

"Last I heard. Why?"

Drew shrugged. "I bet she'd like to come back to help, even if it's only for a week. Have you told her you're on your own again?"

Ethan pulled his Carhartt jacket on and took his truck keys from the hook next to the door. "I haven't mentioned Rex's leaving to her yet. It wasn't really something I wanted to get into over the phone."

But Drew's idea had merit. Ethan remembered Rex's comments from earlier in the winter, reminding him how much Lizzy enjoyed working in the business with him. Right now he'd take any help he could get, even if it was only for a week. Neither boy had time to spare, what with Drew's job and Dylan's ball schedule, but having Lizzy for a week would certainly help.

"Dad, Elizabeth is an adult now. Call her," Dylan said. "Haven't you always taught us that family helps family? I know that's one of Grandpa's favorite sayings, but I've heard *you* say it, too."

Lizzy was frustrated when Ethan told her about Rex. "Aren't you *worried* about him?"

"Liz, of course I'm worried about him. But he made it perfectly clear he needed some space. I didn't mention this to your brothers, but I think I'll give Matt a call and see if he has any ideas how I might find him."

"Do it. You probably should have done it right away."

Way to make me feel worse, kid.

"In the meantime, I'm swamped at work. Any chance I could talk you into coming back here next week, over your spring break, to give me a hand? I know you said you thought you'd better stay there and study, but I'm honestly getting a little desperate here."

"Hold on a sec, Dad."

Ethan could hear shuffling over the phone. The background noise he'd been hearing faded away.

"I just stepped outside. The school union is busy today. I guess I could come back, if you think it would help."

"Honey, I *know* you could help. You'd still know some of the crew, although we have some new ones, too. I could use help both at the jobsites and with my paperwork. I'm behind on getting things over to the accountant."

He heard Lizzy greet someone else. A friend must have walked by. "Sorry. Honestly, Dad, that sounds like more fun than hanging around here and working on my capstone project. It's almost done, anyway. I hadn't planned to come home because I didn't know what I'd do all week. Most of my friends are traveling somewhere for spring break, and I knew you guys would all be busy at work and school. Too bad the boys don't have spring break the same week I do."

"This year I'm *glad* your brothers have the last week of March off. I'm going to put them to work, moving into Celia's. I want to be out of the apartment before April Fools'."

"Okay, I take it back—I'm glad I'm not off the same week." Lizzy laughed. "But seriously, I'll come home to help you. I've missed it. Working with you, I mean."

Ethan was thrilled she was coming home. He'd welcome her help—but even more than that, it would be good to see her again.

Before they hung up, she made him promise to call Matt about Rex, but before he could call his brother-in-law, his phone rang.

"Hi, Becca," he said. "What are you up to today?"

"Hey, Ethan. I'm glad I caught you. I actually have to cancel our date tomorrow night. I'm sorry."

Ethan was sorry, too. They'd managed to meet a couple times since they'd gotten back from their road trip, but he'd been so busy, all they'd managed was a quick coffee and one lunch date. He wasn't ready to let anyone else in on his and Rebecca's new level of friendship. After the intense feelings stemming from their night together, he was feeling unsure of where they stood. He'd hoped to talk to her about it when he took her out for a quiet dinner.

Now that wasn't going to happen yet.

"I'm sorry to hear that," he said. "Did something come up?"

"Yes. I actually just got a phone call from my realtor. Someone put a bid on my house."

"That's great, isn't it?"

Rebecca paused before replying. "I *think* so. I guess it kind of scares me. It feels more, you know, permanent. Like I'm severing the last ties to my old life. Sometimes I worry that I'm going backwards, moving home and living with my mom at this stage in my life."

He could hear the anxiety in her voice.

"Try to remember that you didn't move home because you *had* to, okay? Well, maybe you kind of had to, but it wasn't because of anything you'd done. Your mom needed you and you stepped up and made some hard choices. Don't forget, you were feeling unhappy in your old life and you thought this might give you a chance at a fresh start."

She gave a tentative laugh. "You're right. Thanks for helping me keep my head on straight. You've always been good for that."

"I hope I'm good for more than that," he replied. He could picture her, probably curled up on the couch at home, talking quietly so her spunky mother couldn't eavesdrop. "But why does an offer on your house mean you have to cancel for tomorrow night?"

"The offer is contingent on me being able to close quickly. I need to fly home and figure out how fast I can get all my things moved out. I'll have to put some things in storage. And honestly, I need to take a week or two, by myself, to make sure this is what I really want. I hope you understand."

Little alarm bells were going off in the vicinity of his heart—what did she mean by "this"? moving here? their relationship?—but he knew his best option right now was to be as supportive as possible. The last thing he wanted was for another woman he cared about to accuse him of not helping her live the life *she* wanted, as Stacey had done when she'd left him. He couldn't afford to screw things up with Rebecca. She meant too much to him.

"I understand," he said, careful to keep his tone light. "What about your mom?"

"I just talked to her about it. She assured me her friend is available to stay for a few days."

"Oh, good. I know you would be nervous, leaving her alone."

"That's another thing," Rebecca said, her voice now barely above a whisper. "Mom isn't getting much better. I need to decide whether or not I want to sign up for living with her for the duration, or if we need to explore other options.

Other options would get really expensive, really fast. I might need to get back to work sooner than I'd thought."

Rebecca's comments reminded Ethan that he wasn't the only one with lots of moving parts in his life right now. His old friend also had plenty on her plate. He couldn't rush things.

"Be sure to tell your mom to give me a call if she has any trouble at all while you're gone."

"I'll do that. And don't be surprised if she actually calls. She loves to keep in contact with handsome men."

"You think I'm handsome, do you?" Ethan teased, glad to be back on what felt like safer ground.

"I've never gotten tired of looking at you," Rebecca shared, causing Ethan's heart to skip a beat. "But seriously, Ethan. Thank you for being so understanding."

"Not a problem, pretty lady. Thanks for calling, and travel safe. Call if you need anything and I'll see you when you get back. Can I get a raincheck for dinner?"

"Of course."

Ethan called Matt to ask him about Rex. When Renee heard her brother was on the other end, she took the phone from her husband.

"Hey, what's the deal? You never call me anymore, but now you're calling *Matt*?" Renee teased—although Ethan knew her well enough to know she was slightly put out by his lack of communication lately.

"Sorry, sis, things have been crazy."

"Are you doing okay?"

"Keeping up has been tough lately, since the fire, but we all go through crazy stretches, right? I just happen to be in one of mine right now."

"Are you guys busy this weekend? Can I at least feed you?"

Ethan thought back to his canceled date. "Actually, I might take you up on that. Lizzy should be getting home tomorrow morning. She changed her plans and is coming home for spring break instead of staying at school. If you feed me, you feed my kids. Are you up for an extra four mouths?"

"Absolutely," Renee said. "In fact, Julie is going to be getting home, too. Why don't I check with the rest of the family, and whoever can come tomorrow night, come on over. I'll throw in a couple of roasts and make a big thing of mashed potatoes. Do you want to bring a salad?"

"If I can pick one up at the deli," Ethan replied.

"*Please* do," Renee shot back. "That sounds safer than something you'd throw together in that kitchen of yours."

"Ha-ha. Funny. We'll see you tomorrow, then. Put Matt back on the phone."

She heard Renee yell for Matt. "Sorry, he had to go up and get dressed. He's on duty in thirty minutes."

"That's fine then. Don't bother him. Will he be there tomorrow night?"

"He will, unless something comes up. Do you just want to talk to him then?"

"Sure. Sounds good. See you tomorrow."

Ethan had one more thing he had to do before he could call it a week: Steve, his lawyer, had asked him to stop by the office. He checked on his crews at two jobsites first, then drove over to Steve's. He hadn't heard from his lawyer for a few weeks and hoped he'd have good news.

He didn't.

"What do you mean, they want me to show them my financial records?" Ethan demanded. "What do my financials have to do with the fire?"

But he knew the answer before he even said the question out loud.

"Look, Ethan, I warned you this might happen. Now that they've cut Rex loose, they need to make sure they cover any other bases before they formally close the case. Cops don't often like the idea of leaving cases unsolved."

"Now they're on a witch hunt?"

"I understand why it feels that way," Steve said, "but this is pretty standard stuff."

"Do I have a choice?"

"You could refuse to cooperate, but I wouldn't advise it. It would send the wrong message. Besides, they could probably just file a warrant and get at it anyhow. If you have nothing to hide, give them the damn records and let's try to get all this behind us."

"*If?*"

"Sorry—poor choice of words."

"Steve, this is getting ludicrous. The longer they drag this out, the more it's costing me. My fourplex is sitting empty. I'm still having to pay the mortgage, pay the utilities, and I've got no tenants to help with the cash flow. Some days I wish the damn thing would have just burned to the ground. That might have been easier."

Steve sat back in his office chair, arms crossed over his chest, silent. He finally said, "Give them what they want, then, and make all this go away."

"I hope it's that simple. My buddy Rex took the brunt of their ineptitude for so long, it really screwed him up."

"What do you mean?"

Ethan regretted mentioning Rex's name. No one else needed to know about Rex's impromptu departure. "Never mind. Do you have a list of what they want to see?"

Steve rummaged around on his messy desktop and pulled out an envelope. "Here you go. Let me know if you have any questions. And I'm sorry this is taking so long to get resolved. I know it's a burden for you. I wish there was an easier way."

"Nothing's easy anymore," Ethan said. He took the envelope from Steve and left. He knew the frustration he was feeling was due to more than just the ongoing investigation. Steve was just doing his job.

One day at a time, old man.

Ethan felt some of his worries slip away as they pulled up to the lodge at Whispering Pines. Here everyone had his back, and if he needed help all he had to do was ask. Which was exactly what he planned to do if he could catch Matt for a minute.

Someone suggested snowshoeing, so after supper, those who wanted to go strapped on old wooden snowshoes Robbie had found in the shed and headed out. It was dark, but the moon was bright. With any luck, spring wasn't far away. This might be their last chance to try snowshoeing until next winter. Ethan stayed behind, along with most of the adults. Snowshoeing sounded like a lot of work after a big meal.

Once the dinner mess was cleaned up, those not going out to snowshoe headed up to the library to enjoy a fire and comfortable chairs. This was the next best thing to a bonfire; it would be a few months before they could sit around one of those.

Ethan hung back, catching Matt's eye and nodding toward the kitchen. Once they were out of earshot of everyone else, Matt asked Ethan why he'd called earlier and apologized for having to leave before they could talk.

"No problem. I was just calling to pick your brain about something."

"Okay. What's up?

"I think you've met my buddy Rex once or twice, haven't you?"

Matt grabbed two beers out of the fridge. "Yeah. He was there that time we all went out and played darts. How's he doing? He was the guy hurt in the fire, wasn't he?"

Ethan nodded. "Not so good. I mean, his burns are better, but I don't think he's pain-free yet. He isn't the type to complain. He did get cleared to come back to work."

Matt offered one of the beers to Ethan and popped the top off the second can. "That has to be a relief for you, having him back. I know Renee said you were stretched awfully thin while he was gone."

Ethan opened his beer and took a swig. "Let's just say the relief was short lived. That's what I needed to talk to you about."

"All right. What's going on?"

"Rex came back, jumped right into working full-time. I told him he could ease his way back in, but that isn't Rex's style." Ethan could almost see Matt shift into his sheriff-mode as he talked. "The guys were glad to have him back. At first, at least. Normally Rex gets along well with the crew. But he was ornerier than a snake. I chalked it up to him still being pissed at the false accusations that he had something to do with the fire. Maybe the physical pain was still there, too. I thought it would pass."

"I take it that didn't happen?"

Ethan took another drink of his beer. "No. Things went from bad to worse. It all came to a head when we had an incident over at Celia's. Rex made a dumbass mistake and nearly caused a fire."

"You're kidding? *Another* fire?"

"I know. I could hardly believe it myself. I beat him over to the house one morning and was talking to Marvin. You knew he was staying at Celia's, right?"

Matt nodded.

"Rex came in, stinking like stale beer and spitting-mad about something. I'm still not sure what." Ethan went on to tell him about finding the burn mark upstairs, the ensuing fight, Marvin's intervention, and Rex's subsequent exit. "He quit. He said he'd get me an address where I could send his final paycheck. It was a PO box. Not exactly helpful for figuring out where he went."

Matt, always a good listener, took in Ethan's story without interrupting.

"What do you think?" Ethan asked when he'd finished. "Should I be worried?"

Matt scratched at his jaw—something Ethan had noticed him do when he was deep in thought. "Hard to say. The man's got a right to quit—even to leave town, if he so chooses—without giving you any explanation."

"I know he does . . . but this is *Rex* we're talking about here. He's never done anything like this before. Never acted like this before. The only other time I ever saw him so upset was when he was struggling, after the accident."

"What—the fire?"

"No, this was years ago." Ethan went on to explain what had happened to Rex's wife.

"That's brutal," Matt said, shaking his head. "People don't always recover from trauma like that. Do you think he blames himself for her death?"

"Probably on some level. Right after it happened, Rex was a mess. But he got help. When things get too bad, he has a sponsor he calls. Even before he married Gail he'd gone to AA. Rex seemed to have come to terms with things. But the fire changed everything. He hasn't been the same since."

"Ethan, I have to ask. Do you think he might have had something to do with the fire? Could *that* be why he's acting so out of character?"

Ethan dumped the rest of his beer down the drain. It suddenly tasted bitter, nasty.

"Honestly, Matt? I've had moments when I doubted his innocence. The evidence looked pretty damning. But no, I know now that was just because I was feeling overwhelmed and the cops were putting bullshit in my head."

"Then how can I help?"

"I don't know that you can. Do you have any ideas as to how I might look for him? You know, just to make sure he's all right?"

Matt rummaged around in a drawer and pulled out a pad of paper and a pencil. "You have an awful lot on your plate right now. Why don't you give me some information about Rex? You know, name, address, phone number, vehicle, that kind of thing. I'll do some digging and let you know what I find."

Ethan took the pencil and started jotting the information down. "Thanks, Matt. You have no idea how much I appreciate this."

"Look, I get it. If Rex was my friend, I'd be worried, too. I'm not sure if I'll be able to figure anything out for you, but I'll give it a shot."

"Can we keep this just between us?" Ethan asked. "The kids are already concerned about him. I'm trying to play it down. They know he took off, but the boys don't know I was going to get the police involved—even if it's family."

"You got it," Matt agreed. "Now, we better get upstairs before they send someone down looking for us. I know Renee wanted to pick your brain on some things she wanted to do on the new house, and she won't let you leave until she's convinced you she's right."

"Is she?"

"Right? Aren't they always, Ethan?"

Ethan laughed. "You *are* still in the first-year honeymoon phase, aren't you, man?"

Chapter Thirty
Gift of a Memory

Their house was finally ready.

"I still don't see why we couldn't have started moving out of the apartment when Lizzy was home for spring break two weeks ago," Dylan complained as he and Drew wrestled a mattress down the stairs of their apartment building.

"We've been through this, bud," Ethan said, following behind them with the collapsible bed frame from his room. "I needed her help at work. She helped me get a bunch of bookkeeping done so I could finish up at Celia's. The house wasn't ready yet two weeks ago. Now it is. The three of us can handle this without her. Our apartment isn't that big."

"Weren't you giving Aunt Jess a bad time about helping us move, too, since we helped her last summer?"

"Dude, shut up and pay attention," Drew huffed as the top corner of the mattress snagged on the ceiling at a turn. "Harper was puking this morning. You expect her to bring a sick kid over here? We could get all this over to the house in a day if you'd quit your whining."

"And then another day to clear out the storage unit," Dylan countered—although Drew's refusal to complain along with him took the wind out of his arguments.

Together they continued to transfer load after load of their things from the third-level apartment into Ethan's twelve-foot enclosed trailer. They'd already delivered one full load over to Celia's.

They wolfed down sandwiches and chips for lunch. Dylan would have preferred McDonald's, but Ethan refused to navigate the drive-thru with the twelve-footer attached. Besides, the more food they ate out of their old kitchen, the less they had to transfer to the new house.

They were just debating how best to get the old couch out the door and down the twisty stairway when there was a knock at the door.

"It's open!" Ethan yelled.

George walked in carrying a plate of cookies. "Your grandmother thought you boys would appreciate some treats today."

"Yes," Dylan groaned, the promise of his grandma's cookies more than enough to pull his interest away from the couch. He took the plate from George, pulled the plastic wrap back, and snagged a cookie, the fresh scent of the baked goods wafting out.

"I'm not letting you lift anything, Dad," Ethan warned his father. "But it's good to see you."

"I figured I could still help. I can either stay down in the trailer and help get it packed as tight as possible to save you from wasting trips over to the house, or I can help direct up here. Where would you rather have me?"

Drew helped himself to a cookie. "We could use you downstairs, Gramps. We didn't do so great with the first load, and a lamp fell over and busted on the trip over. Besides, the televisions probably need to go down after we get the couch out of here, and someone should stay down there with the trailer so no one takes off with our stuff."

"No one's gonna steal our stuff, dufus," Dylan said.

"Wanna bet?!"

They got back to work. George took up his post downstairs, manning the door, directing the placement of the bigger items in the trailer, and keeping an eye on things. With his help, they were able to fit more in this time. The four of them jumped in Ethan's pickup when the trailer was again full.

"Good work, guys," Ethan said as he pulled out of the parking lot. "We should be able to get the rest from the apartment with one more load and be done this afternoon."

"And then another day of this tomorrow, moving everything out of storage," Dylan grumbled.

A cell phone went off. It was George's.

"Hi, Val," he said, greeting his youngest daughter. "Yeah, we're heading over there now with another load. Should be there in fifteen minutes." He paused, listening. "Sounds great. I'm sure they'll appreciate it. See you in a bit."

Ethan glanced at his father. "What's she up to?"

"On her way over to help," George said. "She talked to your mother. She's put out you didn't call her to help in the first place."

"I didn't want to bother anybody with this. Figured the boys and I could handle it. You guys helped so much, moving us out of the house last year. But that's great she's coming over."

He stopped at a red light and turned his body to better see his sons in the backseat. "She'll keep you boys moving!"

At their groans, he spun back around and continued on toward Celia's when the light turned. His baby sister would keep them all moving.

Val missed her calling. Should've been a drill sergeant.

"I expected to see Marvin today," George said as Ethan unlocked the front door at the house.

"Nah . . . when I told him we were moving in this week, he said it was perfect timing since he was going to be at a friend's for a few more days. He wouldn't get in the way here."

"Out of town?"

Ethan took a heavy box Drew brought through the door and headed back toward the kitchen with it. "I don't know, Dad. I didn't think to delve into his personal business. Jeez, you're starting to sound like Mom."

George laughed. "Other than my morning coffee buddies, it's mainly your mother I talk to these days. Guess she's rubbing off on me after fifty-plus years of marriage."

"Yeah. I can tell. You seem to be implying I haven't been around much lately. She's good at those kind of guilt trips. Sorry if you're feeling neglected. I just have a lot going on these days."

George tossed his jacket over the back of a nearby chair. "I'm not *implying* anything. I know you've got your hands full, Ethan. You just need to remember to ask for help when you need it."

"Hello?! Where you guys at?"

"Speaking of help, more has arrived," Ethan said, rolling his shoulder to ease the ache as he headed for the front entryway to greet his youngest sister.

Val stood just inside the doorway, kicking off her shoes.

"Oh, Ethan, this is *fabulous*. You've done so much since I last stopped by! I can't believe how you opened this up!" Val cried, gazing around the now-open foyer in awe.

"Here, give me your coat and I'll give you a quick tour," Ethan said, taking her jacket and laying it overtop his father's. He needed to get some hangers in the new front hall closet. They were packed away somewhere.

Together, Ethan walked his father and sister through the first floor of what had been George's sister's home. George had stopped over more recently than Val, so he'd seen most of this already.

"Didn't he do a great job?" George said, clapping Ethan on the shoulder. "I'm proud of you, son."

"I'd kill for a kitchen like this," Val groaned as they entered.

The kitchen was Ethan's favorite room in the house. He'd pulled in some favors with his cabinet guy, and the tile backsplash was amazing. The tilework made him think of Brooke. She'd done all of it for him on the main floor, from design to installation. He felt a twinge of guilt when he realized he hadn't even talked to her in over a month. He probably owed her a call.

"We may need to rotate and have Thanksgiving here next year," Val said, running her hand over the smooth granite of the large center island. "I could whip up a *feast* in here without too much trouble."

Ethan laughed at the look of bliss on Val's face. "First you'd have to convince Mom that we don't always have to have it at their house."

"Good luck with that," George snorted.

"Can we get some help out here?!" Dylan yelled from the front of the house.

Ethan hustled in their direction, George and Val close behind.

Once Ethan helped the boys maneuver their old couch through the front door, he pointed at the stairs. "Drew, you wanted to keep that old beast for your future dorm room, so take it up to your bedroom. There isn't a spot for it down here," he said, pointing up the large staircase. "And do *not* scratch the floors on your way up. That left leg is busted, so the end is sharp."

He saw the look of disgust Dylan shot at his brother, but the two picked the sofa back up, one on each end, and headed for the stairs.

"Oh, to have strong, young backs again," George said, watching his teenage grandsons lift the heavy furniture with relative ease.

"Right?!" Ethan agreed, rubbing at his shoulder. "Come on, I'll show you the upstairs."

They ascended the steps slowly, giving Drew and Dylan time to get the heavy old piece of furniture up ahead of them, and listened to them grumble at each other the whole way.

I'll need to take them out for a decent meal after all this, Ethan thought, watching his boys. They'd worked hard all day.

Val continued to exclaim over the updates Ethan had made to their aunt's previous home. "You really brought the beauty back to this old place, bro."

Ethan truly appreciated his sister's comments. He *had* worked hard, and was proud of the results.

"Did you do some last-minute painting up here?" George asked, sniffing at the air as they walked down the hallway toward the boys' bathroom.

"Yes, well . . . about that," Ethan said, trying to decide how much to tell his dad about the near-disaster with Rex. Something in Ethan's tone must have caught George's attention; he stopped and glanced back at him. Ethan sighed and told his dad and sister everything.

"And he just took off?" George said, shaking his head. "That doesn't sound like Rex."

"I know. I'm worried. But don't say anything around the boys, okay? They know what happened, and they're worried too. I'm trying to downplay it around them."

"Understood," George said as Val ran her hand lightly over the freshly painted portion of the hallway wall.

"Dammit, Dylan, Dad is going to have your *ass* for that one," Drew yelled at his brother from the other end of the upstairs hallway.

"They must have picked up that language at school," Ethan said with a sigh, spinning on his heel to go inspect the damage.

Val called after him: "Good try, bro!"

"Too bad Val had to go home," Dylan said between bites of his hamburger. "But it was nice of her to come over to help. Getting those pictures hung up in my room made a big difference."

Ethan nodded. "And she was the perfect person to finish unpacking the kitchen. Marvin will appreciate having more than a few dishes to work with when he gets back."

Drew picked the tomatoes off his burger before digging in. "I was bummed he wasn't around today. Do you know when he's coming back, Dad?"

Ethan plucked Drew's discarded tomato off his plate and took a big bite out of it.

"That is *disgusting*," Drew laughed.

"You don't know what you're missing," Ethan replied with a wink. "As far as Marvin goes, I'm not sure, but I bet he'll be back when you guys get home from your mom's."

Dylan dropped his half-eaten burger onto his plate. "Do we *really* have to go this weekend? It's the end of our spring break, and all we've been doing is working on this move. We weren't supposed to have to go over there until the week after."

"Dylan, quit your whining. No one likes to listen to that," George said, scowling at his grandson.

"Sorry, Grandpa . . . it's just so *boring* at their house."

Drew's cell phone went off. "Speak of the devil. It's Mom. I can call her back later."

It was Ethan's turn to scowl. "Don't blow her off, Drew."

"Dad, we're eating. Don't you always tell us not to answer our phones at the table?"

Drew's phone stopped ringing.

Ethan sighed. "Finish up and go call her back." He was determined not to let his sons disrespect their mother.

The phone vibrated a second time. Ethan glanced over. Stacey again.

"You better take it. Go out in the entryway. You can finish when you get back. She must need something."

Drew scooped his phone up and pushed back from the table. He answered it as he walked away.

Ethan turned to Dylan. "When your mom called and asked to switch weekends, she said she had something fun planned for you guys. Something with Gregory. She said she really wants all of you to get more used to each other."

"Great," Dylan said, rolling his eyes but saying nothing more.

"I plan to spend the weekend getting settled in the house. You aren't missing anything."

"Actually, I *am*, Dad. I had plans with the guys. But I guess that doesn't count for anything these days."

Ethan pushed his plate away, his appetite gone. The older they got, the more difficult this would be with him and Stacey living in different towns.

"I heard your cousin Nathan has been doing some neat stuff over at that old bookstore he started working at last fall," George said.

"Jess mentioned he was really liking his new job," Ethan replied, picking up on the line of conversation and appreciating George's attempt to change the subject. "What's he been up to?"

George wiped his mouth and draped his napkin over his plate. Before he could elaborate, Drew came back to the table, his face white.

"What did Mom want?" Dylan asked, giving Drew a strange look.

"Is everything all right, Drew?" Ethan asked. "Did your Mom need something?"

"Oh, man . . . she didn't sound good at all," Drew said, sitting back down in his chair. "I could barely understand her at first. She had to put Lizzy on."

"Wait, your sister is with your mom?"

Drew nodded. "Mom called her first, after it happened."

George was seated next to Drew. He put a steadying hand on Drew's shoulder. "Why don't you back up a minute. Is your mother ill? Or hurt?"

"I thought she might be at first, she was crying so hard."

"Dude, spit it out," Dylan said impatiently. "What's wrong with Mom?"

"I guess her and Gregory split up."

"What? You're kidding," Ethan said, surprised at Drew's news. He felt an odd combination of relief and sadness. Relief for the kid's sake, since the impending marriage had felt destined for pitfalls, but sad that Stacey was so upset. He'd hoped she'd finally found something to make her happy.

"Lizzy said it was true. She's helping Mom get a hotel room for tonight. She said Mom told her they had a big fight—Mom and Gregory, I mean—and he called off the wedding, just like that. Said he wasn't ready to saddle himself with another family."

"The bastard kicked her out?" Ethan said, shocked. Stacey might not be his favorite person these days, but he didn't want to see her hurt again. Now that he'd had a minute to process the news, he really wasn't that surprised about the breakup. Something had seemed off in regards to Gregory when he and Rebecca visited Stacey.

"No, Lizzy said Mom didn't want to stay at the house tonight. I guess he took off and she could have stayed in the house, but she didn't want to."

"Did she call you to change plans for this weekend?"

Drew shrugged. "I guess not. She still wants us to come. By the end of the phone call, she'd calmed down some. Said she needed us around her right now. She'll pick us up on Friday at five, just like she talked to you about, Dad. I guess she just thought we'd want to know about Gregory."

She needs the kids around her right now?

Ethan's sympathy toward his ex-wife was already wearing thin. She just couldn't seem to flip things around to where she was more concerned about the kids than herself. What kind of mother called her teenage son in tears because she just broke up with her boyfriend? The news could have waited until she pulled herself together.

Poor Lizzy . . . she's probably taking the brunt of it all.

"And you thought the weekend was going to suck because of *Gregory*," Drew said to his younger brother. "Now it's going to be a whole lot worse, if Mom's bawling her eyes out all weekend."

Dylan got home from basketball practice at a quarter to five on Friday afternoon.

"You better get your butt upstairs and grab your stuff," Ethan said, pointing his son toward the stairs. "You know how she gets if you guys aren't ready to go when she arrives."

Dylan dumped his backpack on the kitchen island. "I'm *starving*. Can't I eat something first? Where's Drew?"

"Drew got home four minutes before you did, and he smelled like french fry grease. I told him to drop his work uniform in the hamper and take a quick shower. How he can stink that bad after a two-hour shift flipping burgers is beyond me. And no, you don't have time to eat anything. You can let your mother take you out for dinner. She's not going to make you wait until you get back to Minneapolis before she feeds you."

"Fine," Dylan said, "but if I pass out from starvation, it'll be on you."

Ethan watched his youngest stomp out of the kitchen. He'd thought his daughter owned the crown for "most dramatic." Elizabeth might have to pass the crown on to Dylan if he kept this up.

The doorbell rang. Ethan glanced at his watch, surprised Stacey was early, but more so that she was actually coming to the door. She usually waited in the car for the kids.

Maybe she wants a tour. Or a shoulder to cry on. She's not *getting that from me.*

"You should have told me you were coming early," Ethan said, irritated as he yanked the door open.

It wasn't Stacey. Rebecca stood at his front door, holding a casserole dish.

"Well, hello," Ethan said, shocked to see her standing there. He glanced over her shoulder to see if Stacey had arrived yet. "This is a nice surprise."

Rebecca turned slightly to look at the yard and driveway behind her before turning back to face Ethan. "Expecting someone? If I'm interrupting, I can go."

"No, no, don't be silly," Ethan said, reaching for her hand and gently pulling her in. She didn't yank her gloved hand away, but she only let Ethan hold it for a minute before pulling it softly away. "Stacey is due anytime to pick up the boys. And you aren't going to believe the news I have in that arena."

Both boys came stomping down the stairs as Rebecca came in. They dropped their bags at the foot of the stairs.

"We thought Mom was here," Dylan said, hand over his heart. "I threw stuff in so fast when I heard a car, I think I forgot to grab underwear. I'll be right back."

Drew shook his head as he watched his brother run back up the stairs. "He is *not* borrowing any of mine. Gross. Hey, Rebecca. What are you doing here?"

Ethan nearly cringed. He could usually count on Drew to be polite.

"I brought over a housewarming gift," Rebecca said, holding up the casserole dish.

"Cool," he replied. "I can put it in the kitchen if you like."

"That would be great—thanks, Drew," Ethan said. He wanted to warn Rebecca that Stacey might not be in the best of moods when she got there, but he didn't want to do it in front of Drew. As far as Drew knew, Rebecca and Stacey hadn't seen each other in years—if he even remembered they'd been friends years ago.

Drew took the white CorningWare dish from Rebecca's outstretched hands. "Should I put it in the fridge?"

"Yes, thank you, Drew, that would be great," Rebecca replied.

A car door slammed outside as Drew left the entryway. He stepped closer to Rebecca and spoke softly. "You should know that Stacey and Gregory broke up earlier this week. She might not be in the best of moods when she gets here."

"You have *got* to be kidding," Rebecca whispered as she pulled the thin gloves off her hands and stuffed them in her jacket pocket. "I told you something wasn't right there."

Before she could say more, the doorbell rang again. Since she was closest to the door, Rebecca opened it. Ethan watched Stacey look from him to her old friend and back again. A light blush crept up her cheeks—a sure sign she was upset.

"Rebecca," Stacey said, nodding at her old friend, but her voice held no warmth. "What are *you* doing here?"

Drew came back just in time to hear his mother's question. "She brought us food. Wish we had time to stay and have some. Smells delicious. Dad, I put it in the fridge, but it was still kind of warm. You guys could just throw it in the microwave after we leave."

You're not helping, kid, was all Ethan could think.

"Dylan, you about ready? Your mother is here," Ethan yelled up the stairs, trying to get them out the door as quickly as possible to minimize the damage. Ethan recognized the look on Stacey's face. It never boded well.

All was quiet upstairs.

"Hold on, ladies. I'll be right back. Drew, run down to the basement and grab that box down on the bench with Lizzy's name on it. She wanted me to send it with you guys this weekend."

As Drew ran off, Ethan, painfully aware he was leaving the two women alone together, hurried up the stairs and toward Dylan's room. "Dylan, your mom is waiting. What are you doing?"

"In here, Dad," his son answered him from the laundry room at the end of the hall.

"Hurry up. You know she gets mad when you keep her waiting. What are you doing?"

Dylan straightened up from the hamper he'd been bent over and digging in.

Ethan groaned. "Don't tell me you were going to dig dirty underwear out of there to take for the weekend."

Based on the guilty look on Dylan's face, that was exactly what he was doing.

"That's *disgusting*, dude." Ethan opened the door to the cabinet above the washing machine and pulled out a plastic bag of Hanes underwear. "These are new, take these. And for God's sake, do your laundry when you get home so you don't have to go to school in dirty underwear on Monday."

Dylan caught the bag with a grin. "'Kay. I'll be right down. I just need to go to the bathroom quick."

Ethan sighed. He'd better get back down to Rebecca and Stacey. No telling what his ex might say, given her current mental state. He was about to turn the corner at the top of the stairs when he pulled up short at the sound of Stacey's voice.

"I should have *known* you'd try to horn your way into my family," she hissed. He had to assume she was talking to Rebecca.

Shit, shit, shit.

"Stacey, don't be ridiculous. It's a *casserole*, for crying out loud."

"And my daughter went on and on about how *great* you are. Look, I'm only going to say this once. *Stay away from my family.* You don't belong here. They are *my* kids, not yours. Got that?"

Shit, shit, shit, shit!

"Dylan's almost ready," he said loudly as he descended the stairs, as much to announce his presence as anything. Both women watched him come down the stairs, Stacey making little effort to hide her anger. The look on Rebecca's face was harder to read.

As Ethan reached them, Drew came up from the basement, carrying his sister's box, and Dylan took the stairs down two at a time.

"Ready?" Drew asked his mother.

"Almost," she said, her face softening as she smiled at her middle child. "Why don't you boys go get in the car? I'll be out in a minute. I need to talk to your dad for a sec."

Dylan scooped up both his and Drew's bags from the floor, and they both left through the front door.

"I think I'll be going, then," Rebecca said, turning toward the door.

Ethan caught her hand, pulling her back. "No, wait. I don't want you to go yet. Would you mind waiting in the kitchen? It's back through there." He didn't care if he sounded a bit like he was begging. He couldn't let her leave without talking to her first, in private, after what he'd overheard Stacey saying to her.

Rebecca sighed. "All right. I'll wait for you there."

Feeling better at the opportunity to make amends with Rebecca, he turned to Stacey.

"Was that really necessary?" he asked her.

"What?"

"I overheard what you said to her. That was totally out of line."

Stacey stared at Ethan, saying nothing.

"You sent the boys out. What did you need to talk to me about?" Ethan asked, deciding to let the other go until he'd had a chance to talk to Rebecca first.

"I just wanted to let you know that we won't be driving to Minneapolis tonight."

This surprised him. "What do you mean? Where are you going with the boys?"

"I rented a suite at the new hotel downtown. Dylan mentioned plans with his friends tomorrow, so I thought I'd let him do that. Hopefully Drew will help me look at a couple of townhomes."

"Townhomes?"

"Yes. I'm sure Drew filled you in on my current situation. As you know, Gregory and I've decided not to get married. That means I need a new place to live. I'm taking your advice and putting the kids first. But let's be honest. Elizabeth is graduating in a couple months and will be off somewhere to start her career. She doesn't need me close. But this back-and-forth is hard on the boys."

Ethan knew he wasn't going to like what she was about to say.

Please, no . . .

"I'm moving back to town."

Shit, shit, SHIT.

Ethan hurried back to the kitchen the minute he closed the door behind Stacey. He'd deal with her later. Right now, he needed to talk to Rebecca.

He found her sitting on the couch in the family room, staring up at the pictures of him and the kids that his sister Val had arranged on the built-in shelves.

"I'm so sorry, Rebecca. She was totally out of line back there," Ethan said, taking a seat next to her. "I can't believe she spoke to you like that. And she's such a hypocrite. After everything she's pulled over the past two years, she should *not* be giving you a hard time."

Rebecca shrugged. "She wasn't *that* far out of line. I'm sure it does seem like I'm moving in on her family, at least from her perspective."

"All you've done is try to help Lizzy figure out how to deal with the changing dynamics with her mother. You've barely spent any time with the boys. I think her bitterness is rooted deeper than the kids. Please, try not to let it bother you."

Ethan didn't like the vibes he was getting from Rebecca. The smile he'd always loved was nowhere to be seen. She was somber. Resigned, maybe.

But resigned to what?

He tried a different tactic to lighten the mood. "Thank you again for bringing food over. Should I heat it up?"

"No, you can eat it later, or save it for when the kids get home," she said, capturing both of Ethan's hands in hers. "Ethan, we need to talk."

"I do not want to hear those four little words from you tonight. They sound ominous."

"Ethan, I've felt so torn since we got back from our road trip. Please don't misunderstand me. That night was very special to me, and I'll hold it close in my heart forever. But I can't do this."

"This?"

"Yes—*this*. You and me. Not now. Maybe the time will just never be right for us. It never was when we were younger. Ryan was always between us. Now it's Stacey. And your kids. Your kids need you right now. They've been through a lot, and they need some stability."

Ethan felt as if an elephant was sitting on his chest. He pulled his hands out of hers. "Rebecca, the kids like you. They'd be perfectly fine with me seeing you, dating you."

"If you're so sure, why haven't you talked to them about it since we've been back?"

He leaned back against the sofa. "Honestly, I wanted to talk to you first. I'm not even sure what this is between us. I'd hoped we could talk about it at dinner, but then you had to cancel. I want more with you, Rebecca, I really do, but I wasn't sure how you felt."

They sat in silence for a short beat, each trying to sift through their complex feelings.

"The offer on my house fell through," Rebecca said with a sigh. "And I got a tempting job offer. I ran into someone when I was back in Omaha—I worked for her fifteen years ago—and she made me an offer I'd be foolish to pass up."

Ethan laid his head back on the pillowed sofa and rubbed his face.

After a moment, he asked, "But what about your mom?"

"Funny you should ask that. Have you heard from Marvin lately?"

Ethan pulled his head back up and looked at her. "Not since he left to visit a buddy of his. He said he didn't want to be in the way here while we were moving in, but I expect him back soon, maybe Sunday. Why do you ask?"

"Mom wasn't expecting *me* back until tomorrow. Imagine my surprise when I got home early and found her eating breakfast with the 'friend' she'd arranged to stay with her while I was gone."

He suddenly caught on to what she was implying. "You have *got* to be kidding me."

"Not kidding."

"Well, that sly dog," Ethan said, leaning forward to rest his elbows on his knees.

"Not only was Marvin staying with Mom while I was gone, the two of them have actually concluded that perhaps he should move in with her. I'm sorry, Ethan, but neither feels they can go back to your fourplex anymore. The stairs have become problematic. Mother assures me she'll be perfectly fine with Marvin. To quote her, I'm 'free to get back to my own life now.' "

Ethan turned to face his old friend. "But, Rebecca . . . none of this means you have to move back to Omaha. We can figure out something that works. I don't want to lose you."

She smiled sadly. "You're sweet. You've always been so very tempting to me. But I'm nearly fifty years old. I'm tired of drama. I've had enough heartbreak to last me a lifetime. I've decided I'm not going to let myself be vulnerable again."

Ethan could feel the fight slipping out of him.

She didn't want him.

"I hate this, Rebecca."

"I know, Ethan."

Chapter Thirty-One
Gift of Goals Achieved

ETHAN WALKED THROUGH THE upper southern unit at the fourplex, his footsteps echoing through the empty rooms. He drew in a deep breath, testing the air for any lingering smell of smoke. All he could smell was the fresh paint he'd finished applying at midnight the night before.

After Marvin paid Drew and Dylan a crisp hundred-dollar bill each to pack up his things at the fourplex and move them over to Penelope's, Ethan had pulled out all the old carpet and installed new laminate throughout the apartment. Today he could see the upgrades to the flooring were worth it. He doubted anyone walking through here now would spot any evidence there'd been a fire in the building six months ago.

The building was *finally* almost ready for renters. When Rebecca left, again taking the piece of his heart she'd always owned, he'd tried to deal with the pain by doubling down on work. He'd sworn off women and tried to convince himself he was perfectly happy alone. The fourplex benefited from his singulary focus.

As he closed the door to Marvin's old unit and entered Penelope's, he felt the shield he'd so firmly put in place around his heart the day Rebecca walked out of his life slip a little. That awful weekend after she'd thrown their new chance at happiness away—despite their lost years and the intense feelings they'd both admitted to experiencing in that hotel room—he'd made some tough decisions.

He'd slept little that night. Then he spent the better part of the next day unpacking. By late afternoon, his stomach rumbled, reminding him a man couldn't survive on coffee alone. He remembered sliding the casserole Rebecca had brought over the day before into the oven and wandering from room to room in his new home, allowing himself a few minutes to admire what they'd been able to accomplish with the remodel while his dinner reheated.

Celia . . . you'd approve of the updates to the house.

The home was spacious, renewed; it could once again be a gathering place for extended family. And when everyone else was busy with their own lives elsewhere, he'd enjoy living here—despite the fact it was too big for just one person. Celia lived here alone but managed to lead a full life. He'd do the same.

Maybe it was the six-pack of beer he'd allowed himself to consume as he ate too much of Rebecca's casserole and then parked his butt in front of the television, but as he flipped blindly through the channels he allowed himself to just . . . *feel*. Feel the pain over losing people so important to him.

Rex was gone. After so many years of helping each other through difficult times, his friend had walked away with barely a word. Rex's absence left a bigger void in Ethan's days than he ever would have guessed.

His wife had left him. He could see now, through the benefit of hindsight, that it wasn't Stacey so much that he missed but their happy family of mother, father, daughter, and two sons.

He'd thought he could casually date, once the shock at the crumbling of their marriage wore off, but his experience with Brooke proved otherwise. He wasn't that kind of guy anymore.

Then Rebecca fell back into his life. Had he grabbed too hard at the chance of something more with her? Had he scared her away, letting things move too fast?

He'd never know now. But he could do things differently going forward.

He was done with women. They'd caused him nothing but headaches. He needed to focus on getting his business back on track and helping his kids navigate these transitional years in their own lives. No more dating. No more distractions. The Richters were finally able to settle into their new home. Now they needed to all get on with life.

The closing of a door below pulled Ethan out of his own head and back into the fourplex. He had a small crew hard at work, gutting the lower unit where the fire had started. He'd left that for last, thinking he'd get things cleaned up for Norman, Marvin, and Penelope first.

Norman was planning to move back in the first of June. His apartment was ready, but he was out of the country on a mission trip with his church. Now that Marvin and Penelope had decided to make other arrangements, he'd list these two units for rent soon. And he'd use this window of time to get the last unit ready to rent as well.

He walked through Penelope's old unit. The walls needed one more coat of paint in the living room, where the damage had been heaviest. The new flooring would go in here next week. He remembered Penelope's prediction, months back, when she'd accused him of waiting until they took her out "feet first" before he'd remodel this unit.

Thank God she'd been slightly off in her prediction. She *had* gone out feet first, but not exactly how she'd implied she would, months earlier.

Something on the countertop that divided the small kitchen from the rest of the combination dining and living area caught his eye. As he walked closer, he could see it was an envelope, the word *Mom* scrawled across it. He recognized Rebecca's handwriting. He ran his finger over the simple word, remembering how he used to beg Rebecca to let him study her notes for their Chemistry lab.

The card must have gotten missed when she was moving her mother's things out. Maybe someone found it when they were pulling the carpet. He felt a bit like a voyeur as he slid the card out of the envelope. It was a pretty birthday card, the corny message inside something he could hear Rebecca reading out loud, and meaning every word. He read Rebecca's handwritten letter to her mother on the left-hand side of the card. Her words would have given her mother, and now him, a small glimpse into her daily life. There was no date on the card, so he had no idea how long ago she'd written it. The life she described sounded similar to his own. Lots of focus on work, nothing too terribly fun to report.

But hey, he thought, *that's life, isn't it?*

As far as he knew, Rebecca was back in Omaha now. He hadn't spoken to her since she'd walked out that night.

He shoved the card back into its envelope and put it in his back pocket. He'd try to remember to give it back to Penelope the next time he saw her.

Ethan stood at the head of the table and clinked his glass to get everyone's attention. Conversation slowly died away and family and friends turned their attention to him.

"We just wanted to take a minute to thank everyone for joining us today. Stacey and I are both so proud of Elizabeth, and having all of you at her graduation makes it all the more special."

Ethan raised his glass in a toast, and shouts of congratulations and encouragement echoed around the table for the new college graduate. Lizzy, sitting between Ethan and her boyfriend Hunter, blushed and fanned her fingers in acknowledgment.

"And for those of you who don't yet know, I'm thrilled to announce that my daughter has agreed to move back to town and join me in the family business."

More catcalls from around the table.

"Just make sure he pays you fairly, dear," Lavonne encouraged her eldest granddaughter from the other end of the table.

Lizzy leaned forward and gave Lavonne a thumbs-up. "I got it covered, Grandma, but thank you!"

"I just don't understand why she doesn't want to move home, too. We have a perfectly good room for her," Ethan said, still standing and addressing the whole group.

"Dad, I think eight to ten hours a day together might be more than enough," Lizzy joked.

Ethan supposed she was right, although the fact she'd rented an apartment across town with the boy sitting next to her still irked him.

"And that would mean we'd have to share a bathroom with her, Dad," Dylan tossed in. "I think having her in her own apartment a few miles away is just fine."

His comment earned him a playful sneer from his sister.

"All right, all right, don't you two get going now." As the noise settled down, Ethan took a more sober tone. "Seriously, we're thrilled you've accomplished everything you set out to do up to this point in your life, Lizzy . . . and here's to a day to celebrate all your hard work!"

Following another round of cheers, Ethan sat down. They'd disturbed the other restaurant customers long enough. Individual conversations resumed around the table.

He glanced at Stacey, sitting at the other end of the table, talking to Val. His ex never did apologize for what she'd said to Rebecca that day, even when Ethan demanded she do so. He was trying to let it go for the sake of the kids, but since she'd moved back to town he was having to see her more often, and she was grating on his nerves. He was being particularly careful not to show his true feelings today. He didn't want anything to detract from Lizzy's special day.

Matt and Renee were seated to Ethan's right, and Drew was on the other side of Renee.

"I heard you have your first prom next weekend, Drew," Renee said to her nephew. "Who's the lucky lady?"

"He finally manned up and asked Holly out," Dylan chimed in from across the table.

"Holly? As in Holly *Larson*? Jenny and Bob's daughter?"

"Yep," Drew acknowledged, but he didn't elaborate.

"Drew's been crushing on her since he was a little kid."

Ethan shook his head as he eyed his youngest son. Dylan was always more than willing to share facts his older kids kept to themselves. "Dylan, you know some day all your smartass comments are going to come back to haunt you when *you're* the one dating, don't you, son?"

Dylan shrugged. "Won't bother me."

Drew snorted.

"Did you get a suit or a tux?" Renee asked Drew.

"A suit. That way I can probably wear it again next year, when I'm a senior."

"Well, I think that's great that you're going, *and* that you asked Holly. She's a sweetheart. Is she still singing?"

The conversation continued between Renee and Drew. Matt leaned toward Ethan and quietly mentioned he had news. A quick glance around the table showed everyone else was talking and paying them no attention.

"Did you find Rex?" he asked his brother-in-law, keeping his voice equally as low.

"I did. And you were right. He checked himself into a rehab facility a few hours away."

"Did you actually talk to him, or just locate him?"

"I talked to him. *Saw* him."

Ethan paused when someone on the wait staff reached in to take away his plate, then turned back to Matt. "You should have called me. You didn't have to drive out there to see him by yourself."

Matt assured him it wasn't a problem. He and Renee had driven over to check out a few pieces Seth was pulling out of an old resort; he'd thought they might want to use them out at Whispering Pines.

"The facility was only about thirty minutes farther, and I'd called ahead. Rex was willing to see me."

"Renee knows, then?"

"She does, but she won't say anything."

His sister, who must have sensed they were talking about her, glanced Ethan's way and winked at him when he caught her eye.

He smiled back. "I know she won't. I'm not worried about that. How was he?"

"You know, he seemed okay," Matt said. "I don't know him well, of course, but he said he felt like this time he was going to be able to do it. He doesn't want to keep getting caught in these downward spirals. This last one scared him, and he knew he needed to get away and focus on getting better. I got the sense he felt guilty for leaving you in a lurch like he did."

"You don't know what a relief it is for me to hear this," Ethan said. "Is he coming home soon? Or can I go see him?"

Matt shrugged. "I don't think he wants to rush it. And no, he doesn't want any visitors. He told me he called his mother not too long ago so she knows where he is and that he's all right. He'll come home when he's ready."

Ethan glanced over at his daughter, laughing at something her boyfriend, Hunter, was saying. He may take her aside and give her an update on Rex later—she'd been particularly worried—but he wouldn't say anything to anyone else.

"Thanks, Matt. I owe you one."

"You don't owe me anything. I'm just happy to help."

Ethan noticed the table had been cleared, and some of the kids seemed to be getting restless. He stood up.

"Thanks again, everyone, for coming. I bet they could use our table, so if everyone's finished, we can head out."

Lizzy thanked everyone, too, and mentioned she and Hunter were going back to Ethan's to relax and watch a movie. Anyone who wanted to join them was welcome.

As the family started to disburse, Ethan suggested to Renee that maybe some of the adults wanted to hit the lounge for a nightcap. While he went to pay the hefty bill for everyone's meal, Renee got busy directing traffic.

Ethan slipped Drew a twenty-dollar bill. "Here's some gas money. Make sure all the kids get over to our house in either your car or Lizzy's. We won't be late."

Stacey hugged each of her three kids goodbye and followed Ethan toward the hostess's podium, stopping him before he could pull out his credit card. "This was nice, Ethan. Thank you for arranging it. It was certainly easier than having everyone over to your house, and they couldn't have all fit at my apartment. Can I help pay part of the bill?"

Ethan was surprised at her offer, even slightly touched, but he knew she was likely strapped for cash these days. "I appreciate the offer, Stacey, but I've got it. Did you want to join us for a nightcap?"

Stacey glanced over at their group but shook her head. Despite invitations, none of her extended family had joined them. They'd never been close. At least her parents had sent a gift for Lizzy.

"Thank you for the offer, but I think I'll head home. I'll be in touch."

Ethan watched as his ex-wife turned away and left the restaurant alone. He was relieved she wouldn't be staying, but he felt a twinge of something—pity, maybe—that she'd go home alone while the rest of them continued to celebrate and enjoy Lizzy's accomplishments.

Her choice, he reminded himself.

"Come on, Ethan, we're in here," his sister Jess said as she met up with him on her path from the restroom to the lounge area. "Stacey isn't going to join us?"

"Not tonight."

"Thank *God*," Jess replied with a snort. "I've had about enough of her today."

He smiled. It felt good to have people in his corner.

Renee arranged everyone remaining around two high-top tables. His parents were there, along with Val and Luke, Renee and Jess's significant others, and Nathan, the only one of the kids who was over twenty-one other than Lizzy.

"Thanks again for coming, everybody," Ethan said to the now-smaller group. "I could tell the kids were starting to get antsy in there."

"It's been really fun, Ethan," Jess chimed in. "Thank you for dinner. And with the kids all occupied, maybe we can really catch up now."

"Right?!" Lavonne said. "I can't remember the last time you all made it over for Sunday dinner to our house. Was it Thanksgiving? I remember when it was a weekly event!"

A few of them exchanged guilty looks. Sometimes things just got too hectic.

"I'm glad you two were able to make it," Ethan said to Val and her husband, Luke. "Decided it was easier without the kids, huh?"

Luke laughed. "Can you imagine those four, sitting first through a college graduation and then a nice dinner? No. That would have been nothing but stressful for us. A babysitter seemed like a better idea."

"No kidding," Val said, holding up a sweating glass of beer. "I *needed* this."

"Well, I'm glad you could make it," Ethan said, clinking his beer glass with hers. "Hey, thanks, by the way, to whoever bought this."

"Dad bought the first round," Renee shared.

"Thanks, Dad. Sorry I haven't been over for a while."

"I understand, Ethan. I'm just glad you got moved in to Celia's old place."

Conversation continued around the tables, everyone catching up on everyone else's lives.

"Dare I ask how the fire investigation is going, Ethan?" Matt asked. His question quieted the rest of the group. "Is everything settled?"

"Nearly, I think. The cops have been digging deep, first into Rex's personal business and now into mine. In fact, Steve, my lawyer, wants me to stop by on Monday. Hopefully he'll tell me we can put all this business behind us."

"That would be great, son," George said. "I know it's been a tough year for you, but summer is right around the corner and things seem to be looking up."

"Thank God," Ethan agreed. "I could use a break."

"Speaking of breaks, I've got an idea," Luke said. "Anybody up for a camping trip?"

"Camping trip? It's still early May," Val chimed in. "Isn't it too cold?"

"Hell, I didn't mean we should pack up the sleeping bags and go *tomorrow*, Val."

"Well, *sorry!*"

Ethan chuckled at the banter between his sister and her husband. Val could be a handful, but Luke had always seemed to be a good fit for her.

"As I was saying," Luke said after shooting his wife a look. "It's been a long winter. Ethan said it himself—he needs a break. I think we could all probably use one. I've been tinkering with our old camper this winter. I put new beds in and replaced the water heater and the fridge. She's almost good as new. And we've got an old guy at work who bought a new RV with the intent of driving it around the country with his wife when he retired next year. Turns out she had other plans—left him for his *cousin*."

"Ouch!"

"Now the poor guy says he's going to stick around and work for a few more years. His unit just sits in storage. If enough of us wanted to go, I bet I could convince him to let me borrow it."

Ethan considered Luke's suggestion. He'd been too busy to make any summer plans yet, but he liked the idea of a camping trip. "What if we made it a guys-only camping trip? You know, take the boys, too? Would you ladies be offended?"

"Not in the slightest," Renee chimed in, earning nods from her sisters and mother. "You boys go and have fun. Maybe we'll do something later without all of you."

"*Now* you're on to something," Val agreed. "Luke, take the older three. They'd have fun. Jake would be a handful, so he can stay with me."

Luke's idea was gaining traction. "What about Memorial Day weekend? Would that work for everyone?"

Ethan decided he'd make it work. A weekend with these guys, plus his sons, sounded fun. "I'm in!"

George nodded. "As long as I get a bed with a mattress, I'm in too."

Jess turned to Seth. "How about you? You up for a weekend with these guys?"

Seth raised his own beer. "Absolutely! I haven't been camping in years. How about you, Nathan?"

"If I can get it off work, I'm in."

That just left Matt.

"Matt? Is that sister of mine going to give you a break from wrapping up the work on your new house? I know that's getting close to when you'd hoped to move in."

Matt looked to Renee, who shrugged. "Far be it for me to be the cause of you missing a weekend of scratching, farting, and fishing with these fine men."

"Hey, now, I'm offended!" Luke laughed.

"Oh, shut up, you are so *not* the least bit offended, because you know it's *true*," Renee joked. "And Matt doesn't need permission from me to go camping with you idiots."

Matt laughed. "I'm in the same boat as Nathan. As long as I'm not on duty—and since I'm the boss, that should be easy enough to arrange. Count me in."

"That settles it," Luke said, raising his glass. "I'll call my buddy up tomorrow and make sure we can use his RV. Some of the boys can sleep in tents if it's decent outside, and if not, we can all squeeze inside to sleep."

Planning continued through a second round of drinks. The ladies started discussing their own plans for a girls' weekend later in the summer.

Ethan nursed his own beer, passing on a second. It'd been a great day, but he still needed to drive home.

He'd watched his oldest child walk across the stage and receive her college diploma. They'd had a great celebration with family, and he'd learned his best friend was indeed safe and on the mend. Now they were planning what he could envision would evolve into their first ever Memorial Day weekend guys' camping trip.

Things were definitely looking up.

But hey, he thought, *that's life, isn't it?*

Chapter Thirty-Two
GIFT OF HELP

HE WAS EARLY. DYLAN and Drew wouldn't be long. Not with the prospect of their first frisbee golf match of the season planned for one o'clock.

Ethan pulled into the empty lot on the backside of the park. A month from now, this lot would be packed, but since it was only mid-May, there would likely still be plenty of mud on the course. Mud never stopped his boys.

He got out of his truck and wandered over to a park bench overlooking the river. Ethan and Rex had fished down here often through the years, especially when the kids were younger. Young shoots of perennials, popping up through black soil, dotted a nearby flower bed. Bunches of tulips lining the rim of the bed were already in full bloom, their vivid reds and yellows complementing the bright green spring grass. A tang filled the air and the river gurgled. Some years this river would be roaring with the spring melt, but not this year. If they didn't get rain, the river would probably be low and stagnant by late summer.

Ethan's phone rang, pulling him out of his musings.

"Richter here. What do you got, Steve?"

"Hey, Ethan. Yeah. I just wanted to give you a heads-up that the department returned all the records you'd provided to them."

"Anything I should be worried about, or can we finally put this thing to bed?"

"They reported back to me that they didn't find anything disconcerting and have concluded you had nothing to do with the fire either."

"About damn time. So that's it then?"

A pause.

"Steve? It feels like they've turned over every conceivable rock."

"I know. They've assured me you're free to go about your business, and you should have no more issues with your insurance or anything."

"But . . . ?"

"They're just going to give it a little time before officially closing the case."

"Why?"

"They still feel there was criminal activity. They don't know who, or why, or really anything other than the damning evidence that the fire was intentionally set. If they know more, they aren't telling me."

"What do I do now?" Ethan asked, squinting against the brilliant sunlight reflecting off the water as he stood near the riverbank.

"Forget about it. You've done what they've asked. Let them do their work and do as they say: go about your business. If I hear anything more, I'll let you know."

After some cursory goodbyes, Ethan cut the call and shoved his phone back in his pocket. Steve meant well, but Ethan needed the dark cloud hovering over him for the past six months to completely dissipate. He needed closure. He walked back to the bench and sank down onto it.

"Criminal intent?" he said out loud.

The only response was a bird chirping in a nearby bush.

A new, unwelcomed series of thoughts niggled their way into his brain.

Rex didn't start the fire, but the police were sure *someone* did. All this time, Ethan had assumed his friend had been in the wrong place at the wrong time. A victim of circumstance.

What if . . . ?

Ethan hated to even let the thought fully form in his mind.

What if someone was actually targeting Rex? Could he be mixed up with something he shouldn't be? Doubtful . . . but is it possible?

A silvery fish jumped out of the roiling surface of the river out in front of his bench then flopped back down into the water, leaving a circular ring of ripples traveling outward.

Or what if . . . what if Rex wasn't the target? What if the fire was set to hurt or kill one of my tenants? Or . . . what if it's me *someone's after?*

Ethan rubbed at his chest. That damn tightness was back again.

This stress was going to kill him.

But still his mind whirred. He was suddenly glad the police weren't quite ready to quit digging. Maybe the threat wasn't over yet.

He heard his kids coming before he could see them. He stood and walked back to the blacktopped parking lot as Drew pulled in, windows rolled down and music playing.

"Hey, guys," Ethan greeted his boys, glad for the distraction. "Tell me you remembered the discs."

Drew parked and Dylan got out, shouting over the music, "Pop the trunk, dude!" He walked around to the back of the car and pushed the trunk lid open all the way, pulling out a backpack, discs strapped to the outside and undoubtedly filling the inside.

"Back in the day, we used *one* frisbee to play catch," Ethan said, shaking his head at the size of the bag Dylan threw over his shoulder. But he couldn't give them too much grief. He'd given them some of those discs as gifts this past Christmas.

"Dad, you sometimes *lose* more than one of these discs in a single round."

"I wouldn't if some of the holes didn't run right along the river."

"But what would be the fun in that?" Dylan teased.

Drew got out of his Chevy, beeped the locks, and headed for the first tee. "If you two are ready to shut up and play, let's go. I have to work at four."

They crossed the spongy grass, Drew leading the way. Dappled sunlight spotted the ground, but it was cool under the treetops.

Dylan offered Ethan a disc. "Age before beauty, Dad."

Ethan grunted as he stepped onto a cement slab. He attempted to wipe some of the mud off his boots before his throw, but just succeeded in spreading the mud on his pant leg. He could already tell this was going to get messy.

"Let me show you how it's done, boys," he said with a wink as he wound up. He orchestrated some fancy footwork, showing off a bit, and let his disc fly as he neared the edge of the pad. His front foot slipped in mud and he had to jerk his body hard to stop himself from going down.

"Oh *shit*, that hurt."

Ethan bent over, gulping in air. He felt short of breath. He must have pulled something.

"Dad, you okay?" Drew asked, stepping toward his father.

Ethan held his arm out. "I'm fine. Just give me a minute. I think I wrenched something."

"Why don't we forget about this today?" Drew suggested. "It's pretty muddy out here."

"Yeah, good idea," Dylan said. "Come on. We'll try again next week."

Ethan took another deep breath and tried to straighten. Intense pain radiated out from his chest. Things got fuzzy and he fell to one knee.

"Dad! What's going on?" Dylan screamed, panicked.

Ethan heard Dylan, but his son sounded far away. Underwater. He fought to stay upright but eventually had to allow himself to sit down on the damp grass.

Someone's arm rested on his back.

"I think I should call for help," Drew said, his voice steadier than Dylan's, but Ethan was dimly aware that his eldest son sounded scared.

Ethan didn't blame him—he was scared, too. While he hated to make a scene, darkness was closing in. He nodded in agreement, letting his body sink back to a prone position in the damp grass.

The wail of a siren echoed through his mind or through the air, or both, and suddenly he was standing next to his pickup, thick smoke in the air. The speeding vehicle whizzed past him. Up ahead, Rex was prone on a stretcher, motioning to him frantically as he was loaded into the back of another emergency vehicle.

"Dad? Dad, can you hear me? Help is here."

Ethan felt his eyes flutter open. A clear blue sky gleamed through the treetops above. Damp cold seeped along his back.

The wailing sound cut off. Doors slammed.

"Over here!"

Who're you yelling at, Dylan? he wanted to ask but couldn't.

Then it dawned on him.

His chest . . . his chest hurt like hell.

Those sirens were for him this time.

"Mom, quit fussing over me. I'm fine," Ethan insisted as Lavonne tucked the blanket tighter around his feet and asked him for the umpteenth time if she could get him anything. "Would you stop?"

"Ethan, you are not *fine*. You had a heart attack yesterday."

"A *mild* heart attack," he insisted. "I don't see why everyone is making such a fuss."

"Trust me, when your son is lying in a hospital bed, recovering from something like this, the words 'mild' and 'heart attack' do not belong in the same sentence."

Ethan sent a pleading look to his father, seated in a stiff recliner in the corner of Ethan's private hospital room.

"Lavonne, let Ethan rest. *I* could actually use some water, though, and I'm not going to drink his," George said, motioning to the pink plastic cup sitting on Ethan's table tray. "Would you go down and grab me one? Here's a couple bucks."

Lavonne let out an exasperated sigh. "Don't you go minimizing this now, George. Ethan has to start taking better care of himself. He's trying to do too much."

"I know, dear, and we'll try to figure out how to help him out with that. But now, go. The kids are due up here in an hour and Ethan needs to get some rest."

"Fine," she said, squeezing Ethan's foot through the thin blanket before heading out the door.

Ethan let his eyes drift shut. "Thanks, Dad."

"Not a problem, kiddo. Why don't you rest a bit? I'll read my book."

Ethan nodded, allowing himself to relax. *Just for a minute . . .*

The metallic sound of ball rollers pulled his eyes open. Shadows filled the room and he noticed his dad was no longer sitting in the chair in the corner. A nurse strode past the now-open privacy curtain, her white shoes barely making a whisper on the tiled floor. She slipped her glasses on, the chain looping them around her neck keeping them handy, and checked the monitors off to his left. She was all business. If the steel-gray of her hair was any indication, she'd been doing this same routine for a long time.

"What time is it?" Ethan asked. His voice sounded weak, even to his own ears. He must have slept longer than he'd intended.

The nurse glanced at the wall behind Ethan's head. "Nearly six. How are you feeling?"

How am *I feeling?* Ethan wondered. He didn't feel any pain, but he was bone-tired.

"Just tired, I guess. Evening or morning?"

"Six p.m. Are you up for company? Visiting hours will end at eight, but you have quite the crowd in the family room."

Ethan sighed. He wished they'd all quit fussing over him. His family had been streaming in and out ever since yesterday afternoon. They were all busy people. They shouldn't be putting their lives on hold for him like this. He was going to be just fine.

"Yeah, sure. Maybe I can convince them all to go home."

The nurse stopped what she was doing to turn her full attention on Ethan. "Do you have any idea, young man, how many people up here have *no one* stopping to see them? No one worrying about them? You're damn lucky you have people who care about you."

The woman continued to eye him, hands on her hips, as if expecting a reply.

What could he say? He *was* damn lucky. He'd best remember that.

"I apologize. No one likes a whiner. Please, send them in."

The nurse nodded, her stern demeanor fading as she offered him a wink and small smile before turning away.

All three of his kids came in, along with, surprisingly, Stacey. She hung back, along the wall. It was her first time up to the hospital.

"Thanks for bringing the kids up, Stacey," Ethan said.

She approached his bedside and gave his hand a squeeze before pulling hers back. "You gave us quite the scare, Ethan. Shame on you."

He returned her small smile.

"Sorry about that. But the boys did great, calling in the cavalry like they did. The doctors say any permanent damage is minimal, due in no small part to their quick thinking."

Drew and Dylan exchanged looks, shuffling uncomfortably at the foot of Ethan's bed.

Lizzy bent over and gave Ethan an awkward hug. He could tell she was struggling with all of this.

"I'm going to be fine, honey," he assured her, patting her hand when she pulled back.

"I just . . . I can't stop thinking about what would have happened if you hadn't been with Dylan and Drew. What if you'd been alone?" She wiped an unshed tear away and stifled a sob. "I'm going crazy thinking about it."

Stacey put her arm around their daughter, offering moral support.

"Well, the good news is that didn't happen," Ethan said. "The doctors and nurses have been great, and they've already started taking steps to help me prevent this in the future. Now, enough of this talk. Don't you boys have homework?"

The five of them continued to visit for a bit longer and then Stacey insisted they head home and let their father rest.

Shortly after they left, there was a soft knock on his partially closed door.

"Come in," he said, remembering his nurse's earlier comments about appreciating his flood of visitors. It meant plenty of people cared.

Renee peeked around the corner. "Hey," she said.

"Hay is for horses," Ethan shot back with a grin.

"I can see you're feeling better."

"I am, thank you very much. I hope to break out of here tomorrow."

Renee nodded, pulling a spare chair up to the side of his bed. "Good. I can imagine lying in that bed sucks."

Ethan nodded. He was glad it was just Renee this time. He needed to talk to someone about where his mind went the previous day while he was sitting in the park, waiting for his sons, before the heart attack. He hadn't wanted to mention any of his new concerns about the fire to his folks. They were already worried enough.

"Renee, I can't stop thinking about the fire."

His sister crossed her legs and leaned closer. "The fire? I thought most of that had worked itself out. I know you mentioned the police were looking into your finances, but I'm sure you don't have anything to worry about there."

Ethan picked at a small hole in the white blanket covering him from the waist down. "I don't. And the police have said as much, too."

"Well then, maybe you need to try to put all of this behind you."

He looked up and held her gaze. "The police are still convinced the fire was intentionally set. Renee, what if one of us was targeted? On purpose? I've been so intent on helping to clear Rex, maybe I was missing the bigger issue. *Why* would someone start the fire?"

She eyed him thoughtfully. "That's . . . *interesting*. And scary as hell. Would you mind if I talked to Matt about your concerns? He would have come up with me tonight, but he's on duty."

"Please do. I'd appreciate his expertise. Just don't say anything to Mom and Dad."

Renee assured him she would be discreet, and their conversation moved on to other topics. Ethan suspected she was trying to distract him from his worries. A bell rang, indicating visiting hours would be ending in fifteen minutes. She glanced at the clock.

"Damn. I didn't realize it was so late," she said, standing.

"I slept most of the afternoon," Ethan said. "Don't worry about it."

"No, that's not what I'm worried about. You have one more visitor. Came up just as I was leaving the family room. She asked me to let you know she was here . . . and to ask you if you even wanted to see her."

"She?" For some reason, he wondered if it might be Brooke. Seth had mentioned when he'd stopped up earlier in the day that she was coming back to town. He hadn't talked to her in months. But what Renee said truly caught him by surprise.

"Rebecca."

Ethan was surprised the monitors weren't going whacky, bringing the nurses and doctors running in, the way his heart was pounding. He'd tried to keep his emotions from reflecting in his face at his sister's words, but based on the smirk she gave him as she left the room to send Rebecca in, he was afraid he'd failed miserably.

Rebecca? What's she doing here?

Last he'd heard, she was back in Omaha, getting acclimated to her new job. At least, that was what Penelope had told him when he'd casually inquired a week or so ago.

Rebecca didn't come in quietly as Renee had done. She hurried through the door and came straight to his side. "Ethan, are you all right? I've been a nervous wreck, ever since Elizabeth called me. I jumped in my car and headed this way as soon as I heard."

Ah, Lizzy. Well, that answers one *question.*

"You are a sight for sore eyes, Rebecca," Ethan said, holding out a hand to his old friend.

Rebecca looked from his outstretched hand to his eyes, as if searching for something. She must have found it, because she grabbed his hand and leaned over him.

He sat up straighter, as best he could, and wrapped his arms around her. He must have knocked one of the sensors loose, because a monitor started beeping. He ignored it, not wanting to let her go. He could hardly believe she was here.

He could feel her body shake, causing him to pull back. Tears leaked down her cheeks, although she made no sound.

"Rebecca, I'm fine. Don't worry. But I am glad you're here. *So* glad."

She glanced over at the monitors, an incessant beeping filling the air.

"Don't ever scare me like that again," she said, fumbling behind her with one hand for a chair, holding tight to his hand with her other.

"I'm with you on that one," he said, offering her what he hoped was a reassuring smile. "The last couple days haven't exactly been a walk in the park. No pun intended."

"What happened? Lizzy just said you had a heart attack and she was scared to death."

Ethan cringed inwardly. The fact he'd scared his family and friends made him feel ill. He went on to explain what happened at the park with the boys. He left out the part about his new concerns in regards to the fire. She was upset enough.

After he'd done what he could to assure her he was going to be all right, he tried to turn the conversation in another direction. He didn't give a damn about himself. He'd be fine. He wanted to know how *she* was. Why she'd driven all this way to see him.

"I've tried, Ethan. Really, I have. I thought life would be simpler if I went back to Omaha and immersed myself in my new life. But I was wrong."

Ethan wasn't sure if he dared hope she was about to say what he so desperately wanted to hear. "How were you wrong?"

She brought his hand up to touch the side of her face with it, fingers still clasped tightly together. She turned her head slightly to kiss the back of his hand.

He felt a tear fall against his skin, where her lips had touched him.

She took a deep breath and brushed her tears away with her free hand. "Life is too short, and we've waited *way* too long to be together. I want to try. To try to make it work with you." A nervous laugh escaped her. "To hell with everything else. I should have learned a long time ago not to take love for granted."

"Damn," he whispered.

"What?" she asked, alarm in her voice.

"If I'd have known a heart attack would have brought you running back to me, I might have told you about the chest pain I was having the day I first saw you again at the hospital, after the fire."

She released his hand and gently laid her own on his chest. "You moron."

Chapter Thirty-Three
Gift of an Inquisitive Mind

Renee and Jess still needed to get things ready for their last retreat of the season, scheduled for the following weekend. They'd lost focus when Ethan suffered his heart attack, but he was on the mend, and they were running out of time. Val emailed them her menu and a grocery list, so they walked over to the lodge kitchen to see what they already had on hand. Renee was just about to update Jess on their brother's condition when Matt and Seth walked in.

Harper, playing on the floor near the women, pushed to her feet and took quick, albeit slightly shaky steps over to Seth, grasping at his pant leg. He bent down, picked her up, and tossed her softly into the air. Harper giggled then settled against Seth, tucking her face against his neck.

"Hey, you little stinker," Matt said, feigning hurt at being ignored. "Seth, just so you know, when you aren't around, *I'm* her favorite."

"Don't take it personally. You don't get up with her when she has an earache at night either," Seth said, rubbing the toddler's back.

"One time, *one time*, you get up with her and you think you should be crowned for sainthood," Jess said, dropping her towel on the island and walking over to the men. "Hello, Matt. Hi, hon." She kissed Seth and then dropped a peck on her daughter's cheek. "I wasn't expecting to see you tonight."

"I got back a day earlier than I thought. There wasn't as much salvage in that building over in Hutchinson as I'd hoped. I'm not going to bid on it."

"I'm sorry if it was a waste of time."

Seth moved to hand Harper to Jess, but the little girl wrapped her arms tightly around his neck.

"I can see I wasn't the only one who missed you," Jess laughed.

Matt walked over to help Renee as she reached for a big tin of tea off a high shelf. He took it down for her but held it behind him until she greeted him with a kiss.

"Guess we're all feeling a little shell-shocked after yesterday," Renee said. "You two would normally never kiss us in front of *witnesses*."

"That isn't true!" Matt said, a mock hurt expression on his face. "I kissed you in front of nearly everyone we know."

"That was our *wedding*, Matt. That hardly counts."

Matt grinned at her and earned himself a second kiss.

"It's been a long weekend," he said. "If you ladies are done working for the night, why don't we go upstairs and relax? I can start a fire. It's chilly in here. You might want to turn the furnace up a bit. Seth was asking about Ethan, and I thought you could give us all an update, Renee, since you were there a bit ago."

"Sounds good."

Seth nodded, turning to Jess. "Should I lay her in her playpen over there or bring her up with us?"

Jess laid her head on Seth's chest to peek at Harper's face. "Might as well bring her up. I can tell from the look on her face she's not ready to settle down yet. She'll just scream if you try to put her in there."

Everyone headed upstairs. Renee pulled two picture books off the lowest library shelf with the hopes Harper would entertain herself, even though she refused to let Seth set her down, so they could talk. Matt got a small fire going.

"Thanks, babe," Renee said. "That feels good. It's still getting cold at night, isn't it? You guys are brave to go camping in a couple of weeks. I hope you don't all freeze to death."

"We'll be fine," Matt reassured her, standing up from in front of the now-crackling fire, wiping his hands off on his jeans. "So how was Ethan?"

"Better. Didn't seem quite as tired. He thinks they'll release him tomorrow. I told him to call if he needed a ride."

"But will he go home?" Jess asked her sister. "I don't like the idea of him home alone, or even just with the boys. They did great yesterday in the park, but . . ."

"Well," Renee said, a twinkle in her eye, "maybe he has a *friend* willing to go stay with him for a day or two, until he's stronger."

This caught everyone's attention.

"Don't tell me *Brooke* is back," Jess said, "wanting to step in and play nurse-maid!"

"No," Seth said. "She's coming back, but not until next week."

Jess snapped her head in his direction. "How do *you* know?"

"Relax, Jess. She called the other day. She was upset and just needed someone to talk to."

"Let me guess . . . her old boyfriend dumped her again, just like you predicted he would, and now she's coming running back to you for comfort."

Renee looked between Jess and Seth with exasperation.

"Jess, if you want to have another one of your jealousy fits, can you hold off on that, please, until you're in the privacy of your own home? Now, do you want to hear who I think might be willing to nurse our brother back to health or not?"

Jess took a deep breath.

Matt chuckled. "Oh, I don't know, Renee. Jess is kind of fun to watch when she's mad."

"Shut up, Matt," Jess hissed at her brother-in-law. "I trust Seth, he knows that. It's *Brooke* I don't trust."

Seth said nothing, but Renee heard him grunt while he helped Harper turn a page in her book.

Renee paused, checking if they were done picking on each other.

"All right, Renee, I'll bite," Jess said, turning her attention back to her sister. "Who's hanging around our big brother these days? I don't think Rex's back, and besides, if it was him, you wouldn't be acting so squirrely. Like you have some big, juicy secret."

"It's *Rebecca*."

"Rebecca?" Jess said, a questioning look on her face. "As in his old college friend Rebecca? The one who came out here at Christmas with her mom?"

"Exactly."

No one said anything for a moment.

"I didn't know they were an item," Seth said, shifting Harper from one side of his lap to the other. She was starting to fuss. It was almost her bedtime.

"I'm not sure if they are," Renee said with a shrug. "But she was acting awfully strange when I ran into her in the hallway at the hospital, just before I went in to see Ethan. It was getting late. She wondered if I'd mind asking him whether or not she could stop in and say hello. It struck me as odd. When I asked Ethan, *he* acted funny, too. I predict there's something going on there."

"Huh," Matt said. "Okay. Good for him, I guess. But what are the doctors saying about his heart?"

"God, you are so *not* a romantic, Matt," Renee said, frowning at her husband.

"I can be romantic when I want to be," he replied, giving her a tawdry wink, to which she rolled her eyes and laughed. "Also, I'm more worried about his heart than his love life. I'm practical by nature."

"To a fault," Renee agreed. She then went on to tell him the little bit she knew about what Ethan had been told might have caused his heart attack and what he needed to be careful about going forward.

"Probably good things for all of us to keep in mind," Seth said.

"True," Renee said. "Oh . . . there was one other thing Ethan mentioned when it was just him and me in the room. He's still worried about the fire."

"About Rex maybe being involved, you mean? I thought he was cleared but then took off and Ethan was ticked at him," Jess said.

Renee updated Jess and Seth on the trip she and Matt had taken to find Rex, on Ethan's behalf.

"Renee . . ." Matt said, that one word clearly a warning to watch herself.

"Honey, I know Ethan wouldn't mind me looping these guys in." She knew from the look her husband gave her that he wasn't convinced. She'd have to deal with him later. "Seriously. He just made me promise not to say anything to Mom and Dad. He said I could talk to you, Matt. He probably won't care if I talk to Jess and Seth about it, too."

"It sounds like the guy is getting the help he needs. Why is Ethan still uptight about it?" Jess asked.

"The police are still insisting they're convinced there was criminal activity behind the fire at Ethan's fourplex. Even though they've said now they don't think either Rex or Ethan were behind the fire—anymore, at least—they won't close the case."

"This whole thing just really needs to go away. It's putting a lot of stress on Ethan," Jess pointed out. "I wish there was some way we could help him."

Conversation died away, everyone lost in their own thoughts.

"Maybe we *can* help," Renee said eventually.

Matt, seated next to her, his arm behind her on the back of the loveseat, played with a tendril of her hair. "What, are you going to play detective now? Don't you think, if there were easy answers, the professionals would have already thought of them?"

Renee shrugged. "I'm married to a professional, aren't I? Let's just brainstorm. You know, fresh eyes and all. Ethan is worried maybe he or Rex, or maybe even one of the tenants, was the target of an arsonist."

"You're right. I'm sorry. Sometimes the answers can just be elusive," Matt said. "Brainstorming. I'm in."

For the next hour, they did just that. They talked through all the different options they could come up with, on the off chance something clicked.

"I still think it was a bunch of kids, screwing around," Jess said. "Didn't Ethan mention something about a broken window in that lower unit they were remodeling? I bet kids broke in there and were drinking or smoking pot or something. Maybe Rex surprised them and they got scared. Did something stupid."

"Maybe . . ." Matt said, but he didn't sound convinced.

"We've met the three tenants," Renee pointed out. "There is no way I'm going to believe they had anything to do with it or that anyone would want to hurt them. They seemed perfectly harmless."

Seth, who'd been relatively quiet—perhaps because he now held a sleeping Harper in his lap—held up a finger. "What happened to the fourth tenant? Why was that lower unit empty?"

Renee said, "I think Ethan said he died a while ago. Ethan decided that since the unit was empty, he probably needed to give it a facelift before he rented it out again. The interior is pretty dated. That's why he was remodeling it."

Matt nodded. "Makes sense."

"What was the tenant's name?" Seth asked. "You said he was a guy?"

"I have no idea. If Ethan said it, I don't remember."

"Smith," Matt said. "T. Smith."

Renee spun to face her husband. "What? How do you know that?"

"I don't know it for sure," he said. "But I saw it on the mailbox."

Renee broke into a grin. "You are seriously *hot* when you break into lawman mode, you know that?"

"Oh, for Christ's sake, Renee," Matt said, blushing slightly. "I don't know why I noticed that, but I did."

"This guy, whoever he was," Seth said, "probably had absolutely nothing to do with it, since he died long before the fire. But if we're just grasping at straws here, maybe we could see if we can find anything out about him. And the other three tenants, for that matter. I know all three of them appear to be harmless senior citizens, but who knows what skeletons people have lurking in their closets?"

He followed up on his comment with a pointed look at Jess.

Renee noticed the exchange. "Good point, Seth. Look at all the skeletons that came flying out of my dear ex-brother-in-law's closet when the doors got blown off."

"Touché," Jess agreed. "My laptop is downstairs. Just a sec, I'll go grab it."

"If she has a blanket down there, grab that too, will you?" Seth asked.

Jess grinned at him as she pushed up out of her comfy chair and headed downstairs.

"Don't you think the police would have already looked into this T. Smith dude since he used to live there?" Renee asked Matt.

"Hard to say. They might not have thought about it, since the guy's been dead for a while."

Jess wasn't gone long. "How hard can it be to find something out about a guy with the last name Smith?" she joked as she walked back into the room. She shivered. "Man, it's cold when you get away from the fire."

"Here—can I see?" Matt asked, holding out his hand.

"Sure, have at it. I wouldn't know where to start." Jess handed him her computer.

Everyone sat quietly while Matt plinked away on the laptop. The crackling of the fire and soft snores from Harper were the only other sounds.

Renee glanced around the room, happy to be right where she was, with these very people. Visiting Ethan in the hospital—her dear brother who had been the bane of her existence as a child and then one of her staunchest supporters as an adult—following his unexpected brush with death reminded her how very lucky they all were to have each other.

"Well . . . I'll be damned," Matt whispered.

Renee had been so relaxed in the warmth of the fire, she wasn't sure if she'd dozed off. Her husband's comment snapped her attention back.

"Did you find something?"

"Maybe, hon. Maybe."

Matt didn't have time to research his suspicions until Monday afternoon.

He'd found an obituary for a man by the name of Theodore Smith, dated June 16, 2017, who'd lived in the area. He was seventy-two years old at the time of death and, according to the obituary, a veteran and retired postal worker. His wife had died six years earlier, but one daughter was listed as the surviving next of kin.

It seemed plausible Theodore could have been Ethan's deceased tenant. It wasn't the obituary that piqued Matt's curiosity—they knew a man had died—as much as an article he stumbled across when he dug deeper into Theodore Smith. But before he went down what could turn out to be nothing more than a distracting rabbit hole, he probably needed to talk to Ethan to find out if Theodore and the former tenant were one and the same.

Renee had called him late morning to let him know she was giving Ethan a ride home from the hospital. Matt debated whether or not to even bother Ethan with his idea, but he knew no one wanted answers more than his brother-in-law.

He called ahead.

"Hello, Matt. Renee said you were working today. Tell me you aren't calling to check up on me, too. Don't you have better things to do? People who need saving?"

Matt laughed. He knew he'd be ornery, too, if he'd been laid up in the hospital for a couple of days with people fawning all over him.

"Actually, I wanted to visit with you about something related to the fire. But I know you just got home, so if you need to rest, it can wait until tomorrow."

"I've been *resting* for two days, and they tell me I need to *rest* for another couple before I can start getting out among the living again. I may go nuts from all this *resting*. So please, if you have something to distract me, loop me in."

"Is there anyone there with you?"

"On and off, yes. Drew stopped home after school to change for work and to check up on me. Rebecca was here, but she offered to go pick Dylan up from spring baseball practice. And Lizzy's been in and out. Needless to say, she's got her hands full at our work with me out of commission. Damn, I could sure use Rex about now. I'm sure he doesn't even know I'm laid up."

Matt felt a twinge of guilt. Ethan was probably right. How could Rex know about Ethan's heart attack? He should have thought to call the man on Ethan's behalf, but it never crossed his mind with all the commotion. Not that Rex could have done much, if he was still in the treatment facility. He made a mental note to call Rex soon.

"Where do you keep your rental records? You know, for the buildings Celia passed on to you?"

"Those are actually here. I keep my records for my construction business over at our shop, but the paperwork for the rentals is in the house. I wanted to keep them separate, since the two businesses are unrelated. Why do you ask?"

Matt glanced at his watch. "I'm wrapping up here for the day. Mind if I stop over before I head home? This might be a long shot, but I think it's worth at least checking into. I'd rather just come over and fill you in, instead of explaining it over the phone. That work for you?"

"Sure. Come on over."

On his way over to Ethan's, Matt drove by Rex's house. It looked quiet, deserted. The yard was in sore need of a spring cleanup. It didn't look like Rex was back yet. He'd told Matt he had no idea when he'd be back.

When Matt arrived at Ethan's, his place also looked quiet, although this yard looked ready to usher in summer. Someone had already cleaned up the mess winter left behind. No vehicles were out front or in the driveway.

He rapped on the front door and let himself in.

"Ethan, it's Matt," he announced himself. "You here?"

"Back here, Matt," Ethan yelled back.

Matt made his way through the kitchen to the family room, again admiring Ethan's handiwork. Renee was right—they needed to get Ethan out to their new house at Whispering Pines to get his input on finishes and flooring.

"Your sister may copy that floor in your new kitchen. It would look great out at the house," Matt said, finding Ethan right where he'd said he'd be—on the couch. But he didn't look like he was resting. A laptop was on the coffee table in front of him and papers were strewn everywhere. "That doesn't look like *rest*."

Ethan shrugged. "A guy can only watch so much television. I had Lizzy bring me some paperwork. Taxing my brain shouldn't pose any risk to my heart." He closed the laptop. "You've got me curious. What's up? You said you had a possible idea? Is it related to the fire?"

"Maybe. Maybe it's nothing. Don't get excited, not yet."

Ethan spread his hands out. "I get it."

Matt sat down and explained how they'd held a brainstorming session out at Whispering Pines the night before.

"No wonder my nose itched. You guys were talking about me," Ethan joked, but then his face grew serious. "I do appreciate any help I can get, you know."

"I know. And I'm not sure yet if this will help, but I figured there wasn't any harm in digging deeper. What was the name of your tenant who died?"

Ethan's face was blank. "Died? No one died in the fire."

Matt shook his head. "I mean earlier. Didn't you have one of your tenants pass away, leaving that lower unit vacant? The one you were remodeling at the time of the fire?"

Ethan looked to the ceiling. "Let's see . . . what the hell was his name? He was a quiet guy. Paid his rent on time and never reported any maintenance problems. I only met him once or twice. Last name was Smith. His first name was . . . Ben or Ted or something."

Matt waited. He didn't want to prod Ethan with what might be bad information.

"Here, wait, I'll go grab the file out of my office," Ethan said, pushing up from the sofa.

Matt stopped him. "Wait—tell me where it is and I'll get it."

Ethan shot him a hard look. "I'm more than capable. It's not like I'm stuck here using a bed pan. I'll get the damn file."

Matt shrugged and stayed put. He recognized that flash of Richter stubbornness. His wife displayed it at times, too. He'd let Ethan get the file.

"Damn," Ethan said, stopping before he even got to the kitchen. "I forgot. The file for that lower unit, and that Smith guy, was over at the fourplex. I'd been keeping measurements for the remodel in it. I bet it was lost in the fire."

"All right," Matt said as he pulled his small notepad out of his jacket pocket and reviewed the items he'd jotted down about the entry he'd found in last spring's obituaries. "That's unfortunate, but we can still figure this out."

Ethan snapped his fingers. "Theo—that was the guy's first name," he said as he walked back to the couch. "Theo Smith."

Matt nodded. "Do you know if he was in his early seventies?"

Ethan settled back down in his spot. "Yeah, that sounds about right. Poor guy. Far as I know, he wasn't even very sick."

"How did he die?"

"I think it was a stroke or something. I remember getting a call from his daughter. She was taking care of his affairs, calling to let me know her father was dead and she needed to take care of his estate, end his lease, that kind of thing."

"Did he die in your apartment?"

Ethan shook his head. "No. I think she said he'd been having trouble with his blood pressure and was doctoring. He might have even died in the hospital. Why are you curious about Theo? He's been dead nearly a year now. There's no way he had anything to do with the fire."

"Of course not," Matt agreed. "Not directly, at least."

"What do you mean?"

"Last night, when we were just kicking around ideas, Seth asked about your fourth tenant."

Ethan sat back, his face curious now. "Okay, I'll play along. Do you have some reason to believe Theo might have been *indirectly* involved in the fire? Seems like a stretch. Now that you have his name, are you thinking about doing a background check or something. You could probably give Penelope a call. She knew him."

"I already *had* the name. At least, I thought I probably had the name. I found an obituary."

"But how? You didn't have a name to start with."

"Actually, I remembered seeing 'T. Smith' on one of the four mailboxes in the entryway in your building."

"Clever."

"It's my job," Matt said. "Guess it's trained me to keep my eyes open. Anyhow, once I was relatively certain T. Smith from your building was the Theodore Smith in the obituary I found, I started poking around to see if anything jumped out at me."

Ethan rubbed his chest.

"Are you having some pain?" Matt asked.

"Sorry, no. Honestly, I think it's just become a habit at this point. Rebecca called me out on it earlier today. Nearly scared her to death. I'm fine. Keep going."

Matt wasn't entirely sure he believed him, but he continued. "Turns out your Theo had his fifteen minutes of fame when he was the foreman on a jury trial fourteen years ago."

The front door slammed and voices found their way back to the men. "Dylan and Rebecca are back, sounds like," Ethan said. "Keep going."

"I might be way off base here, Ethan, so I'm not sure I want them to hear what I'm looking in to quite yet."

Ethan nodded in understanding. "I'm fine with Rebecca hearing anything you have to say. But if Dylan comes in here, just hold off a bit."

Someone pounded up the stairs in the front of the house, and something like keys were dropped onto the granite counter in the kitchen.

"Should I be concerned about a patrol car parked in front of the house?" Rebecca joked as she came into the family room. "Hello, Matt! Good to see you again. I hope you're just here to check on our patient?"

"Hey there, Rebecca. Good to see you, too. Ethan seems to be doing well. No worries."

"How are you feeling?" she asked Ethan.

Matt watched their exchange. He could see the concern on Rebecca's face. His wife hadn't misread the signs. There was something going on between these two.

Good for you, Ethan.

"I'm feeling fine. Did Dylan go up to take a shower?"

"Yes, thank goodness. That boy stunk."

Ethan laughed. "Pretty common for that kid. Say, Rebecca, Matt stopped over because he's doing some digging into something. He was just explaining it to me."

"I can leave if you guys need to talk," she said, turning to go.

"No. Stay. I just didn't want Dylan to hear it."

Rebecca looked to Matt, who also nodded for her to stay. She sunk into one of the other comfortable recliners.

Matt gave her a quick summary of what he'd already told Ethan.

"Was there something unique about the trial?"

Matt nodded. "According to newspaper articles, it was a rape case with plenty of controversy. The defendant came from a well-connected, wealthy family. The reporter speculated in the article that the guy was convinced he'd get off, and when the jury found him guilty, well, let's just say he didn't take it well. They had to slap cuffs on him and practically drag him out of the courtroom. He screamed threats at the jury members on the way out, and some were visibly shaken by the ordeal."

He paused, giving Ethan and Rebecca a chance to process things.

"That would be a little creepy," Rebecca said with a shiver, "but I'm not sure why that might be important now, after so much time has passed."

"I agree," Matt said. "But there were a couple of pictures with the article I found. One of them caught my eye."

He stood and motioned to Ethan's computer. Ethan handed the laptop to Matt. Matt sat back down and searched again for the article. Rebecca and Ethan waited, curious as to where he was going with this. He found it and enlarged the picture that had initially caught his eye. Then he spun it around so Ethan could see the screen.

"Anything jump out at you?"

Ethan squinted. "Bring it closer."

Matt took a few steps toward Ethan and waited.

"That's . . . weird."

"*What's* weird?" Matt asked.

"Back when we first started gutting the unit over at the fourplex, Penelope saw Rex coming into the building. She asked him if he was Theo's son, but then got flustered when she remembered Theo only had a daughter. She said Rex looked an awful lot like Theo. I checked the rental file, since it was right there, and she was right. Based on a picture I found clipped inside, there was a resemblance. Of course, I had to give Rex a hard time about it, which he didn't appreciate. Rex's actual dad was a nasty drunk and Rex hated him. He died way back when."

Matt nodded but allowed Ethan to study the picture from the article.

"The picture in the rental file was more recent. This is older. Theo would have been about Rex's age in these. The similarities are even more apparent here," Ethan said, pointing toward the computer screen.

Matt sat down again. "I thought he kind of looked like Rex, too."

Rebecca said nothing, having never met Rex.

"So, Rex bears a slight resemblance to a guy who used to live in my building. A guy who got yelled at when he was on a jury twenty years ago. Why do you think that might matter?"

"*Fourteen* years ago."

Ethan sighed. "Whatever. It was a long time ago. Where are you going with this, Matt?"

Matt set the laptop on an end table at his elbow. He leaned back in his chair and crossed his arms. "I decided to check to see if the guy Theo's jury convicted was still in jail."

Rebecca straightened in her chair, placing both her feet back down on the hardwood floor.

"When did he get out, Matt?"

"The week before Thanksgiving."

Chapter Thirty-Four
Gift of a Hunch

MATT LEARNED LONG AGO that coincidences were rare. When Ethan had the same reaction to the picture of a younger Theo Smith that he'd had regarding the similarities to Rex, he knew he had to take it to the officers in charge of the fire investigation. Ethan agreed.

He called the precinct the next morning.

"Nash here," a gruff voice came over the line.

"Karl Nash? This is Sheriff Matt Blatso. I'm calling to discuss your case involving a fire last November in a fourplex owned by Ethan Richter."

There was a pause on the line.

"What did you say your name was?" the police officer on the other end of the phone asked.

Matt went on to explain who he was and how he knew Ethan.

"I've come across something I think you might be interested in, but I'd rather come in to discuss it versus going into detail over the phone. Do you have time this morning.?"

Matt drove over to the police station, his window cracked to let the fresh air in. The fickle May weather was finally showing signs of warming. He hoped the decent temperatures would hold for their camping trip in two weeks; he was ready to get away for a few days. People tended to let loose when spring finally arrived, and this year was no exception. On top of that, he'd been spending his off-duty hours on their new house. The more they could get done on it, before the early summer renters started arriving at the resort, the better.

He stifled a yawn as he got out of his patrol car. Inside, an officer at the front desk pointed him up the stairs. He found Nash's office. The man behind the desk stood and waved him in.

"Blatso, I'm guessing?"

Matt introduced himself and took the open chair next to a younger man in uniform.

"I'm Karl Nash and this is Bob Tolley. I have to admit, I was relieved to get your call this morning. We've been getting some pressure to close out this case and move on, but I'm having trouble doing that. My gut tells me there's more to this story. I just can't figure out what the hell it is."

Matt had found himself in that exact same position a time or two through the years. For some reason, a case popped into his mind at Nash's words: the teenage girl who had gone missing on Fiji when Renee and her kids were visiting that first holiday. He'd spent months chasing every lead he could uncover, but as far as he knew, there'd never been any answers. Those were the types of things that kept people in law enforcement up at night.

He pulled his attention back to Nash and Tolley.

"I might have uncovered something that could help you out on the case," he said.

The younger cop next to him sat up straighter. Matt had their attention.

"I presume you looked into the tenants at the apartment building," Matt said. It was more a statement than a question. That would have been one of the first places any good cop would look.

"Of course," Nash replied. "Didn't find anything, though. That old woman, Penelope Jarvis, she has quite the colorful background. Been married four or five times. The two men, on the other hand, had relatively bland histories. Nothing jumped out at us there. And that fourth tenant, the one who died months before the fire . . . remind me again what you found on him, Bob."

The other officer shifted in his chair. "Not much, Karl. He was a widower, retired from the post office. Clean record. I didn't see any red flags there."

Karl turned back to Matt. "Why do you ask? Do you think we might have missed something?"

"You might have." Matt nodded to Karl, then turned back to Bob. "Were you aware that Mr. Smith was the foreman on a jury, years ago? The case got some press."

Bob's blank stare was his answer.

"What kind of press?" the older officer asked. Matt caught the exasperated look Nash sent in Bob's direction.

"It was a rape case. The guy came from a rich family and, according to the articles I found, most everybody expected him to be acquitted," Matt said as he pulled his notebook out of his pocket so he'd be sure to get the details right. He read back the names and dates of those involved.

Karl pushed his desk chair back a few inches. "I remember that case. I wasn't on it, but it created quite the firestorm in the department. Oliver Gage was a spoiled rich kid, and his daddy was friends with the mayor. The kid had been in and out of trouble . . . into the drug scene . . . minor offenses. My partner before Bob here was on the case, back in the day. Said the kid gave him the creeps. Joked he was the kind who would have killed kittens for fun when he was a kid. My buddy was relieved when they got Gage off the streets."

"Any chance we could talk to your old partner?"

"Nah, he's dead. Poor guy died of a heart attack six months after he retired. A real shame. This job can do that to you," Karl replied. "Like I said, I remember the case, and it's interesting that this Smith guy who used to rent from Richter was on the jury . . . but I don't see how that could possibly have anything to do with the fire."

"Your first suspect in the fire was Rex Forde, Ethan's foreman and close friend, right?"

Karl nodded.

"I've met Rex. There was a picture of Theodore Smith, Ethan's deceased tenant, alongside one of the articles I found on the trial. The two men share some common physical characteristics. At least, they *did*, when Theodore was fifteen years younger. I had to do a double-take."

"Okay . . . ?" Karl said, obviously trying to follow Matt.

"I know. Not real unusual. Lots of white guys in their late fifties look similar. But the reason the jury on that trial was included in some of the press was because Gage shouted nasty threats at all of them when they dragged him out of the courtroom. And Smith was the foreman."

Karl rubbed at his ear, a look of deep concentration on his face. "I think I see where you're going with this, Blatso, but that's quite the leap."

"Maybe not quite as big of a leap as you might think. Pull up Gage," he said, nodding at the computer parked on the corner of Nash's desk.

It didn't take Karl long.

"Son of a bitch . . ."

Matt let it sink in.

"What?" Bob asked.

Matt could already tell the younger officer wasn't as quick on his feet as Nash.

"How the hell could you miss this, Bob? There are goddamn red flags all over this. You told me you looked into the dead guy."

"I did—"

"Gage got out of jail in November, *days before the fire.*"

"So you agree there could be something to this?" Matt asked.

"Damn right, I do," he replied to Matt before turning back to Bob. "Look up the names of the other jury members and get out there and find out if anyone else has had any trouble recently. I'll try to find out where Gage is now."

"Anything more I can do to help?"

"You've helped plenty, Matt," Karl said, standing and extending his hand. "Thank you."

Matt returned the hand shake and nodded at the younger man, sensing he was about to be on the receiving end of a tongue lashing as soon as Matt left the room. He didn't feel sorry for Bob; the man's ineptitude had resulted in both Rex and Ethan being put through the wringer. The emotional toll from the fire and subsequent investigation likely played a part in Ethan's heart attack. Stress kills. Matt had no time for sloppy police work.

"Keep me posted, will you?"

"I'll call you personally," Karl assured him.

Molly, Renee's cocker spaniel, scrambled to her feet, barking madly at the knock on the door.

"Just let me know what you decide to do, then," Matt said into his phone, getting up from the kitchen table to answer the door. "Yeah, he's here now. I'll tell him." Matt hung up and set his phone down on the coffee table on the way to the door. "Molly, be quiet. It's just Ethan," Matt scolded the rambunctious dog.

"Just Ethan, huh?" Ethan kidded as Matt opened the door. "Two weeks ago, you were all sharing plenty of love when you thought I was in danger of checking out. But I can see things are back to normal already. About time."

"Cute. Thanks for coming out," Matt said, pulling Molly out of the way and stepping back to let Ethan in.

Ethan bent and stroked the dog's head. "Thanks for the invite. I've been spending too much time at home lately. It was getting damn boring."

"I can imagine," Matt agreed. "Did you eat?"

Ethan glanced at the table and Matt's lunch. "I did, thanks. Where's Renee? It looked pretty quiet over at Jess's, too.

Matt cleaned up his lunch mess. "They were picking up flowers and heading out to the cemetery with your folks to clean up some graves."

"Ah, yes. Celia used to do that every spring, but now Mom's taken over. Don't they usually do that on Memorial Day?"

Matt wiped off the table and tossed the rag back into the kitchen sink. "Renee said they decided to go today since it's nice out and the forecast for next weekend has a chance of rain."

"Rain would suck for our camping trip."

Matt gave him a mischievous look. "But we won't let that stop us, right?"

Ethan grinned back. "I threw my old tent in the back of my truck. Thought maybe we could set it up today, make sure mice haven't chewed big holes in it or anything. I bet I haven't used it for ten years. Not since the kids were little. Damn . . . I should have taken them camping more often."

Molly rubbed up against Ethan, looking for a scratch. He squatted down to her eye level to comply. "You said you wanted to show me some things over at the new house?"

"Yep. And I thought we better plan next weekend, too, among other things. Why don't we check the tent first and decide who's bringing the beer?"

***

"This'll work," Ethan said, stepping back to inspect the old orange-and-blue tent as Matt hammered in the last stake.

Matt stood. "I've got a roll of duck tape over at the new house. A good vacuum job and some tape over that little hole in the back and she'll be good as new."

"I'm just glad Luke is lining up campers for us Old Farts to sleep in," Ethan said, referencing back to the name his dad had assigned to their ice fishing team. "Rain, possible critters, or even bears don't scare me, but sleeping on the hard ground might put me in traction."

Matt laughed. "Aw, come on, old man. Don't start complaining already."

"The boys will fill this thing up. Luke's bringing a second tent, too. No way will they want to be inside with us."

"You're probably right," Matt agreed. "Why don't I show you the progress over at the house? You wanted to leave this up for a while, didn't you?"

Ethan nodded toward the tent. "If it isn't in the way. It needs to air out."

"Good idea. Renee's been busting her tail getting Whispering Pines ready for the season, but she's not opening until next weekend. Robbie can help me pack the tent up in a day or two and we'll add it to the growing pile of camping supplies. Come on, let's head over there," Matt said, tossing his hammer into the toolbox he'd brought along.

Ethan followed him toward the other side of the resort. The path wound near the smallest cabin at Whispering Pines—what Renee had dubbed the Gray Cabin.

Ethan stopped. "Is Renee ever going to let me help her fix this old thing up? Doesn't she want to rent it out this summer?"

Matt set his heavy toolbox back down and stood with his hands on his hips, eyeing the decrepit old cabin. "Funny you should mention that. She's finally started talking about cleaning it up. We just haven't had a spare minute to get to it, what with the new house and all."

Ethan eyed the little structure with a critical eye. His sister had grown to despise the cabin, given its history, but Ethan could see potential. He'd been playing around with a way to get it fixed up. "Since I haven't been *any* help on your house, maybe I can help with this," he suggested, angling his head toward the cabin.

"You were booked up and your sister didn't want to wait a whole year on the house."

Ethan understood all that. He'd even been relieved when Matt and Renee hired someone he'd suggested. Working that closely with family on something as important as a new home could cause problems.

"I get it. Besides, you'd have nothing more than a basement at this point if I'd been trying to do it for you, given the crazy year I've had. But what if we turned this into more of a family project?" Ethan asked, motioning to the Gray Cabin. Ethan knew the faded, rundown exterior matched the interior.

"Family project?"

"Yeah, I'd love to put Drew, Dylan, and Robbie to work on it. You know, teach 'em some handyman skills."

"That's actually a great idea. But do you have time?"

Ethan crossed his arms and continued to size up the cabin, his mind already compiling all that needed to be done. He glanced back at Matt. "Funny how a heart attack can put things back in perspective. I want to spend more time with the kids. No more working every weekend. Our camping trip and a project like this would be a great start."

Matt nodded. "Just as long as this doesn't turn out to be more work for you. I like the idea of getting the boys to help. I bet my wife will *love* the idea. And she'd certainly appreciate it."

"Cool. I'll talk to her about it today if she gets back before I leave. Now let's see this new house of yours. Last time you took me back there it wasn't much more than a shell. But Renee's been sending me pictures."

Matt picked up his tools and together they walked back toward the build site.

"Say, Ethan, I've got some news about the fire."

Ethan let out a sigh. "I actually thought that might have been why you invited me out today, but when you didn't mention it, I figured you were still waiting to hear back. Did your idea have any merit?"

"It did. The two cops working the case—"

"My old *pals*, Bob and Karl?" Ethan interjected. He'd grown to despise the two men, given how they'd treated first Rex and then himself.

Matt laughed. "I can see where their lack of finesse might have set your teeth on edge. Karl does seem like a decent-enough cop. Now the other guy . . . *Bob* . . . I don't hold out much hope for him."

"Where are things at with the investigation?"

They were nearing the firepit in front of three other cabins. Matt stopped to pick up a fallen branch and tossed it into the pit.

"They've interviewed all the other jury members from the case who are still around. Turns out two of them have received threatening phone calls, but they were too nervous to report them."

Ethan stopped walking. "Really? That can't be a coincidence."

"No, turns out it wasn't."

"So . . . ?" Ethan prodded, desperate for answers that would put all of the lingering questions and doubts behind them.

"They took Gage into custody last night."

"No shit? Thank God," Ethan said as he let his head fall back. He gazed at the new leaves on the trees above. He'd waited a long time for news like this. "He had something to do with the fire, then? He admitted it?"

Matt set his tools down again. "Not right away. Karl called me this morning. Brought me up to date. It took some . . . *coercing*, shall we say, to get Gage to say much at all."

"Were you right about Gage mistaking Rex for Theo?"

Matt nodded. "They were finally able to get Gage riled up enough that he spilled the story of what happened. He'd never stopped blaming the jury for taking away his freedom, for sending him away for all those years to rot in prison. Guys like that, they seldom take responsibility for the things they've done. Always looking to blame someone else for their misery. Since Theo Smith was the jury foreman, he was at the top of Gage's hit list. It wasn't hard for him to find Theo's old address. He saw Rex going in, checked names on the mailboxes, and mistook him for Theo. Rex was working down in the lower unit, and Gage even admitted to slipping something into Rex's water bottle when he left the kitchen for a minute. The bastard snuck back outside and waited. When he went back in a bit later, Rex was passed out. Whatever that asshole put in Rex's water did the trick."

"That guy sounds certifiably insane."

"He probably is," Matt agreed. "I hope he doesn't get off on that."

"Why the fire, though?" Ethan asked. "Why not just kill the guy he thinks put him in prison?" Although he feared he already knew the answer.

"That's why I've been hesitant to bring it up today," Matt said. "I know you and Rex have been friends for a long time and this might be hard to hear. Gage is a sick, twisted man. He fully intended to kill Rex that day, but not quickly. Well, he thought he was killing *Theo*, but you know what I mean. He set the fire, hoping to make Theo suffer first, in the flames, before dying. Gage wanted to cause Theo agony before killing him, like he'd personally suffered during all those years in prison. But he didn't stop there. He set it up so it'd look like *Theo* started the fire. He left a booze bottle by Rex, used Rex's work rags to fuel the fire, and even made sure to throw some beer cans in the back of Rex's truck. Again, thinking the whole time that Rex was Theodore Smith."

"That son of a bitch," Ethan said as he began walking again. "Talk about being in the wrong place at the wrong time. Rex could have died."

Matt again caught up with Ethan on the path. "He could have, but he didn't. Keep that in mind."

Ethan smiled grimly. "And now we know with one hundred percent certainty that Rex had nothing to do with the fire."

"You never doubted his innocence, did you?" Matt asked. "I hope he knows how lucky he is to have you in his corner."

Ethan considered Matt's question before responding.

Did I? Or did I let too much doubt slip in?

He'd always known Rex battled inner demons. The man grew up in an abusive home, lost the love of his life in a horrendous accident, and had no support network at home.

As he caught a glimpse of the lake through the trees, Ethan again paused on the path back to Matt and Renee's new home, inhaling the pine-scented air. Taking his time before replying, he let the peace he often felt while visiting Whispering Pines sink in.

"Rex earned my trust. He's helped me through plenty of rough patches. I guess it was my turn to stand by him. I'll admit . . . there were days when I wondered if my judgment was clouded. But I did my best."

"I'd say you did great," Matt said, clapping him on the shoulder. "Now, come on—I want to show you what we've done in the new house."

EPILOGUE

"I hope the rest of the weekend goes better than *this*," Ethan said as he eased onto the shoulder of the highway, careful not to let the wheels of the camper he pulled sink into the soft ground.

"Daaamn, I bet Luke's *pissed*," Dylan added from the seat behind Ethan.

"Hey, cool the language, dude," Ethan warned his youngest. "We aren't even to the campground yet."

"Did you see that tire blow?" Drew asked. "I'm impressed he kept it on the road."

Ethan cracked open his door and checked for traffic. Seth had pulled in behind them.

Ethan yelled back, "Stay in the truck!" and walked around the front of his pickup. Luke was already wrestling with the tailgate of his old Ford. George climbed out of Luke's truck, yelling for his grandsons to stay put.

"You got a spare?" Ethan asked his brother-in-law.

"Yeah, buried in here somewhere. But I can't get the back open," Luke grunted as he yanked on the handle. He put his foot on the bumper for leverage. That did the trick.

George came up beside Ethan and they both peered into the back end of Luke's truck box, their view blocked by a blue-and-white cooler, an old cookstove, and bicycle tires.

"You sure you don't have a spare tire for the camper *inside* the camper? It'd be easier to get to," George pointed out.

Luke shot a look at his father-in-law; clearly he didn't appreciate the ill-timed advice.

"Come on—unhook the tarp and we can roll it back," Ethan suggested.

Seth and Matt joined them on the side of the road but wisely refrained from commenting. Ethan stood on the driver's side of the pickup box, opposite Luke, and together they rolled the tarp back out of the way.

A semi blew by with a honk of its horn.

"Prick," Ethan said as he hurried back around to the shoulder of the road, disconcerted by the hard rush of air that hit him when the truck passed. The highway was narrow here, and sitting on the side of the road wasn't safe.

The tire was buried under a tub of cookware and rolled-up sleeping bags.

George walked back up to the cab of the pickup and asked Dave to come back, reminding the two younger boys to stay put. "Your dad needs some help."

Dave hustled back to stand by Luke.

"If I lift you up, can you crawl in there and get at the tire?"

Dave assured him he could, and everyone helped lift things out or shift gear around to give the twelve-year-old access. It wasn't long before they had the blown tire on the back of the camper replaced and they were rolling again.

It was twilight by the time they reached the campground. Luke and Ethan maneuvered the two campers into their assigned spots, each parking as far over as they could to leave room to set up two tents between them. They were on the edge of the campground so only had neighbors on one side. Nathan handed out cold beers to the men and then set up two coolers beside the picnic table. He filled one with cans of soda and bottles of water, the other with more beer.

"Can we have a fire tonight?" Dylan asked as he lugged the heavy tent bag over to where Ethan planned to set it up. Seth and Nathan were in the process of putting up the other tent.

"Here," Ethan said, "help me get it out of the bag and then go grab the smaller sack in the back of my truck. It has the stakes in it. If we can get camp set up before dark, we can probably do a fire tonight."

The door on Luke's camper opened and George descended the creaking metal steps. "Say, Ethan, Matt, did you guys happen to remember firewood?"

Ethan straightened and looked around for Matt. He could hear him talking to Luke behind the campers. It sounded like they were trying to hook up the water line. He hadn't given a thought to bringing their own firewood. Matt probably hadn't either.

Damn.

"Not sure, Dad. Let me go ask Matt," Ethan said, dropping the hammer he'd been about to use to sink a stake into the ground.

As he'd suspected, Matt hadn't remembered firewood either.

"Sorry, guys, looks like we're gonna have to wait and have a fire tomorrow," Ethan said with a shrug.

A few groans met his announcement, but they had plenty of time for a campfire. No one was bored yet. They finished getting the tents up and the kids were ordered to get the rest of the gear out of the pickups. It was nearly dark and the mosquitos were out in full force. Without a fire, they'd want to get inside the tents or campers soon.

The boys squabbled amongst themselves, trying to decide how the six of them would split up between the two tents. Nathan had already passed on tenting it, since there was room in a camper for him. Once sleeping arrangements were set and gear stowed, the boys all piled into one tent. Ethan suspected their plan was to watch videos on their phones, but he doubted reception would allow it.

Good, maybe they'll actually have to talk to one another.

"Anybody up for poker?" Luke asked.

"Did we bring cards?" Seth asked.

Luke grabbed another can of beer out of a cooler. "What decent camper wouldn't come fully stocked with cards and poker chips?"

"I think I'll pass, guys," George chimed in. "It's nearly my bedtime."

Ethan laughed. "Dad, you're usually the *last* one to bed."

He was about to ask his father if he was feeling all right, when the crunch of gravel cut him off. There were plenty of other campers around, and he expected the approaching vehicle to turn in to one of the other sites, but it kept creeping their way.

Matt, who'd just tossed a pillow in to Robbie, zipped the tent closed and came to stand next to Ethan, swatting at a mosquito.

"I'll be damned," he said under his breath.

"What?" Ethan asked, glancing between Matt and the vehicle that had just pulled in behind Seth's truck and killed its lights. The moon ducked behind clouds. It was dark. "Do you know who that is?"

Matt shrugged. "I might."

A door slammed and footsteps approached. Only Ethan and Matt were paying attention to their visitor; everyone else had disappeared into the campers and tents.

Ethan could see the silhouette of a man approaching.

"I didn't know if you'd show," Matt said.

Ethan watched, curious now.

"I didn't know if I would, either."

"What the hell?" Ethan said, taking two steps forward. The clouds parted and moonlight illuminated the man. But Ethan didn't need light now. He'd know that voice anywhere.

"By the way, Matt, your directions sucked, man."

Matt stepped around Ethan and extended his hand in the moonlight to shake with the new arrival.

"Glad you could make it, Rex," he said.

"I hope you aren't the only one happy to see me," Rex replied, jamming his hands back in his pockets after shaking Matt's.

"I'll let you two catch up, then," Matt said, "Rumor has it there's going to be a hot poker game, if either of you are interested. Or there's a bar in that small building where we checked in if you'd rather talk."

Ethan's newest brother-in-law turned and headed toward the spare camper Luke had managed to arrange for their weekend, leaving Ethan alone with his old friend.

Neither said anything immediately.

Ethan's mind raced. He'd missed Rex. Once they knew for sure that Rex was the victim and not the perpetrator behind the fire, he'd been swamped with guilt. But he was still furious at him for taking off like that. He hadn't even bothered to call when Ethan had his heart attack.

If he even knows about that.

And now, apparently, Rex was going to leave it up to him to make the first move.

"This is a surprise," Ethan said, unsure where to start.

"I hope you don't mind. Matt called last weekend and invited me."

Ethan looked over his shoulder toward the camper. He'd be talking with Matt about this later. But now, he could hardly believe this was Rex standing right in front of him after all these months. Just as Matt had done, Ethan offered his hand.

Rex wasn't as quick to take it this time. Ethan left it extended.

Finally, Rex let out a sigh and took Ethan's hand. Their handshake turned into a hug. They'd both suffered over the past six months, some of which they'd imposed on each other. Ethan knew in that moment that he wanted to put it all behind them, including the bitterness and hard feelings. He hoped Rex felt the same.

"So . . . you want to go try your luck at some cards, or should we walk up and get something to drink?"

Rex looked over at their campsite, now bathed in moonlight. The boys must not have heard Rex's voice, or they would have come running.

"If you can make it a Diet Coke, I'd vote for that drink."

***

Ethan bought two cans of Diet Coke from the old man behind the counter. Matt was a bit off in his description of the place—it actually looked more like a bait shop with three tables shoved in a corner, surrounded by chairs upholstered in dusty black vinyl. Hardly a bar.

"We close at eleven," the man said as he shoved the dollar bills Ethan handed him into the till. "I gotta get me a few hours' shut-eye before I open up again to sell bait in the morning."

"Thanks. We'll keep that in mind," Ethan assured him as he turned away. Poor guy already looked exhausted, and the season was just beginning.

He set the can in front of Rex and sat down.

Rex met his eye. "I'm not even sure where to start."

Ethan shrugged. "I'm not either. I suppose we could rehash everything, but what would be the point? I'm just glad to see you and to know that you're doing all right. You *are* doing all right, aren't you?"

Rex nodded as he cracked open his soda. "Why don't I go first? I apologize for taking off on you like that, Ethan. I really, truly do. I shouldn't have left without telling you why or where I was going."

"I won't argue with you on that," Ethan said, softening his words with a grin. "But I suspected you were struggling. You seemed to be drinking more than usual, and I can't imagine how you felt when those cops accused you of setting the fire."

Rex said nothing, only shrugged.

Ethan took a drink out of his own can. "Actually, I *can* imagine. After you left, they turned their sights on me for a bit. Nothing ever came of it, but it was a shitty feeling, being on the receiving end of their suspicions."

"Speaking of feeling shitty, how are you feeling these days? Matt called to let me know about your scare, but not until you were already home."

"I'm doing fine now. Scary as hell at the time, though, let me tell you. My brush with the Grim Reaper has me reevaluating some things."

"I'm sorry I wasn't there for you," Rex said. Ethan could see that he meant it.

"And I'm sorry I ever doubted you."

Rex accepted Ethan's apology with a nod.

Their conversation moved on to lighter topics. Rex wanted to know all about the kids. He felt awful that he'd missed Lizzy's college graduation.

"Don't feel too bad," Ethan assured him. "The ceremony itself was painfully long, there were so many kids. We did go out for a nice dinner afterward. That was fun. She'll be delighted you're back. She's been worried sick."

"What did she decide to do for work, now that she's graduated?"

Ethan chose his words carefully. He wanted Rex to know there was still plenty of room for him to come back if he chose to, even though Lizzy was working for him now, too.

"Funny story, actually . . . remember that Saturday when we did some work at the house and then grabbed a burger and beer for lunch? You told me then that you thought Lizzy might want to join me in this business."

Rex nodded. "Sure. I've always thought she should do that."

"You were right. She's working for me now. But if you want to come back to work, I'd love to have you. With her on-board, we wouldn't have to put in such crazy hours anymore. I've vowed to be better about that, since my heart attack—and *you're* even older than I am."

Ethan braced himself, unsure of Rex's reaction or what his old friend was envisioning for his future these days. Neither said anything more for a minute or two. Someone was banging around in another part of the building, and a fresh wave of fishy-smelling air wafted over them.

"I think they're filling up the bait tanks," Rex said with a soft laugh. "Yeah, I'd like to come back, but I don't want to step on Lizzy's toes. She's the future for this company."

Ethan held his pop can up, as if to toast Rex's words. "You have a lot to teach her."

Rex toasted back. "It would be an honor."

Much of Saturday was spent out on the lake. They rented three aluminum fishing boats from the old guy in the bait shop, who looked as if he hadn't gotten a wink of sleep after all.

Ethan had chuckled when he heard Luke arguing with his kids earlier that morning. "Get your butts out here! You can't go on a guys' camping weekend and not fish, for crying out loud!"

More grumblings ensued, but the kids emerged from their tents, hoods pulled up over their heads, sweatshirts bearing their school logos, and followed the rest of them down to the shore.

Everyone seemed to have fun, even those who didn't catch as much as the others. Dylan and Drew fought for the chance to fish with Rex. Someone suggested a contest, but George killed the idea. He reminded them that sometimes this group's competitive nature got a bit out of hand.

Everybody caught at least one fish. Robbie caught the most. Even though he'd squashed the idea of a contest, George made sure everyone knew Robbie would have won *if* it would have been a competition. There was plenty for a fish fry. Everybody pitched in.

"I sure wish Mom was here," Noah said later as he filled his plate with fish and potatoes.

His brother Logan looked at him like he was nuts. "Seriously? This is *great*. All guys. No girls. Why would you want Mom here? Are you *lonely*, you little mama's boy?"

Noah, only one year younger than nine-year-old Logan, shoved Logan away as they both attempted to sit down at the picnic table. "'Cause I don't like potatoes, you jerk. She'd have other stuff for me to eat," he whined. "Plus, she might not make us clean up."

George and Ethan overheard their exchange. George winked at his son before interrupting their conversation.

"Val is a pretty good cook, isn't she, boys?" he asked his two grandsons. "She'd probably have half a dozen other dishes for you to pick from, but you're stuck with just us guys this weekend. And you have to admit, this might just be the best fish you've ever tasted." George held a forkful of walleye up in front of them and then popped it in his mouth. "Fresh fish, straight out of a Minnesota lake, in early springtime. I could live off this fish for weeks."

Noah and Luke shot doubtful looks at their grandfather, but they knew better than to talk back to him.

Rex joined them at the picnic table. "Have your old tenants been able to move back in yet?" he asked Ethan as he set his paper plate, bowing under the weight of an impressive heap of fish and fried potatoes, on the table. They'd rehashed everything about the guy now in custody for starting the blaze, but hadn't yet talked about the current state of the building.

"Norman is moving back in next week, but I had to find two new renters for upstairs. The unit we were remodeling should be ready in a month or so."

"What happened to your old upstairs renters?"

George laughed. "They shacked up together. No more stairs."

Rex choked on the bite of fish he'd just taken. "What? Are you serious? They seemed pretty old for that. That woman was always yelling at us to be quiet when we were working downstairs, and once she even mistook me for a ghost. The one time the guy caught me in the entryway, he talked my ear off."

"We are never too old for romance." George turned to his son. "Isn't that right, Ethan?"

Before Ethan could reply, his boys also joined them at the table, squeezing in on each side of Rex. They'd stuck close to his side most of the day.

Ethan shot a look at both his father and old friend. Any more talk of romance should wait.

"Fill me in later," Rex said.

The conversation moved on to other topics like summer baseball and who would catch the most fish on Sunday. Matt was starting to update everyone on their plans for moving into their new house when Luke approached, red-faced and carrying a smashed beer can in one hand. He'd come from the direction of the tents.

"Would someone please explain to me why I found an *empty beer can* in that tent?"

All other conversation ceased, cut short by both the tone of Luke's voice and his words.

Matt, who'd just thrown his empty paper plate away, groaned out loud. "Which tent?"

"The one Seth brought."

Ethan turned to his youngest. "Dylan, you slept in that tent, right? Do you know how that can got in there?"

Dylan was momentarily speechless, and Ethan's temper rose. If his fourteen-year-old was sneaking beer, there'd be hell to pay.

"Dylan, I asked you a question, and I expect the truth."

The boy just sat there, picking at the peeling white paint on the picnic table. He wouldn't meet anyone's eyes.

"Dylan, answer your father," Rex ordered. Disappointment was etched on his old friend's face, too.

George cleared his throat. "Dylan wasn't the only boy staying in that tent."

Dylan shot his grandfather a thankful look.

"Who else slept in that tent last night?" Matt asked, his tone even and authoritative.

"Dave, I told you that was a stupid idea last night!" Logan said. "I told you Dad would find out somehow, but you did it anyway! And then you're stupid enough to leave the empty can *in the tent*?!"

"Dave, did Dylan have anything to do with this?" Luke asked his eldest son as he waved the crushed can in the air.

Dave shook his head, his face burning red. "No. He didn't. It was just me and Logan."

Luke was about to say more, but Matt laid a hand on his shoulder. "Why don't we talk to the boys in the camper?"

Luke took a steadying breath and nodded. He tossed the offending can in the trash, motioned to his two oldest boys to get up, and went into his camper without another word. Matt followed the three of them.

Silence reigned for a minute after they left.

"I'm sorry, Dylan," Ethan said. "I shouldn't have assumed, just because you were the oldest in your tent, that you were the culprit."

Dylan's eyes shone with hurt when he looked up at his father; but, in typical Dylan style, he immediately tried to laugh it off. This time, however, it rang hollow.

The festive mood lost, everyone helped clear away the dinner mess. The other four boys took a football off to play some catch. The men got a fire going. After a while, Matt and Luke joined them, bringing lawn chairs and adding to the ring around the campfire. Dave and Logan made a beeline for their tent, their faces red. They didn't utter a word.

The other four boys returned from playing catch and joined the men around the fire.

Eventually, conversation levels returned to where they'd been before Luke's discovery.

Matt reported that he hoped they'd be settled in their new house before the fourth of July. Robbie was excited to have a room in the basement. Based on his comments, he planned to take over the whole lower level. His older sister, Julie, wasn't around as much anymore, so he fully intended to make the most of his last full year at home before he also headed off to college.

"Dad, I suppose maybe we could do something with Celia's stuff up in the attic this summer, too," Ethan suggested. "Maybe there are some things up there the kids could make use of. So many of them are getting to that age now where they're getting their own apartments, it might be a good time to let people look through it all."

"You're probably right," George agreed. "We can let the kids—or any of you, for that matter—take what they want and then decide how to get rid of the rest. It isn't really bothering anyone up there, and you have plenty of room, but I agree some of the kids might be able to use some of it. How about you, Nathan? Do you need anything?"

Nathan, the oldest of his grandchildren, was living in a furnished apartment above a bookstore now, but George wasn't sure if that was temporary or not. Nathan shrugged at his grandfather's question. "Eventually, maybe. Things are going great at the bookstore for now. Frank, the owner, isn't threatening to shut us down as often as he used to. That's a good sign, isn't it?"

Seth, sitting next to Nathan, chimed in. "Don't worry. I think Frank's all talk. He loves that place. His wife loves it even more. I'm sure having you around to help has made all the difference."

"I hope so. My favorite part is helping independent authors get more visibility in the store. The big chain stores won't, or can't, do as much of that."

"I hear from your grandma about how that whole indie business is thriving," George commented. "Can we expect to someday read a novel written by our own Nathan Rand? Do you have any interest in doing something like that?"

"Hopefully sooner than later, Gramps. Sooner than later."

A crack of thunder sounded off in the distance.

"Either that's the heavens encouraging you, Nathan, or we're about to get wet," Luke laughed as he wiped a raindrop off his face. "Anyone want to take this party inside?"

"What do you want to bet those kids are in here within the hour?" George joked.

The boys had opted to stay in the tents. Sleeping outside in the rain would be "cool," they'd said. It might get *cool*, all right.

"They'll come in when they get cold," Luke said. "We could get crowded in here tonight. But it was a fun day."

Seth pulled off his damp sweatshirt and hung it on a hook next to the camper door. "It was great. Everyone's beat. I'm glad you guys included me this weekend. Is this going to be a 'first annual'?"

"*I* think it should be," Luke said. "That is, of course, unless Val kills me when she finds out her boys drank beer."

George squeezed into the small bench seat at the kitchen table. "Boys will be boys. I think Matt put the fear of God in them, and I don't think that'll happen again.

Ethan overheard his dad's comment as he came out of the minuscule bathroom in the back of the camper. "But, knowing my sister, you'd best keep the whole incident with the beer from her if at all possible."

"No shit," Luke said. "I threatened all three of them with their lives if they don't keep their mouths shut. Besides, Val's got enough to worry about these days."

George didn't like the sound of that. "Anything you want to talk about, Luke?"

Luke took the bench across from George, sighing heavily. "Things are just a little tight these days. Four growing boys tend to eat . . . *a lot*. She's talking about maybe going back to work. And I appreciate that, but the logistics would be a nightmare, with none of the boys old enough to drive yet. I could maybe pick up a second shift at work, but they've already done some cutbacks, so I need to be careful."

Luke's comments didn't come as a surprise to George. He'd sensed as much lately. "You know, Val hasn't done anything with her inheritance yet from Celia. Could you use that to get by?"

Luke shook his head. "Absolutely not. Celia wanted Val to use that money to start something of her very own, not to pay our ever-rising monthly grocery bill."

"Is she considering anything specific yet?" Seth asked. "If it wouldn't have been for Jess's inheritance from Celia, we never would have met. Ethan's family just moved into her house. And look at how Renee has brought Whispering Pines back to life. Feel free to tell me to shut up and mind my own business, but maybe now it's Val's turn."

Luke laughed. "I wouldn't have brought it up if I didn't want to talk about it. I appreciate that, man. I want her to do something amazing with it, just like Ethan and her sisters have done. But she can't do that if she has to go back to work for someone else. She barely has any time to herself as it is. I think I just need to pick up a second gig doing something to bring in extra cash for a while. You know, a weekend here or there. Even that would help."

"I don't know, Luke, you're both awfully busy, running those boys," George said, doubtful. "Ethan, do you need any more help? Maybe not . . . with Rex back now and Lizzy working with you, you're probably full."

"Not at the moment . . . but we could have a space open up on the crew or get a big job we need some extra hands on. I'll sure keep you in mind, Luke," Ethan promised.

"You know, Luke, I've been thinking about bringing someone on part-time," Seth said, leaning against the counter. "My name is getting out there, and I've had to pass on a few buildings because I can't get to them all. It'd be flexible. Maybe we could work something out."

"I appreciate that, Seth—as long as you're not just saying that. We're not a charity case."

Seth scoffed. "Believe me, you'd earn every penny if you teamed up with me. Tell you what—stop out to the shop sometime in the next couple weeks and we can talk more about it."

George looked between the two men. His daughters did all right when they picked these two. He appreciated Seth throwing Luke a lifeline, and he appreciated Luke having the nerve to bring it up tonight.

A gust of wind howled outside and the light above the kitchen table flickered. Rain pounded against the camper.

"It won't be long now," George said, eyeing the door.

ell

Their last full day of camping was sunny but cool with lots of mud. After the heavy rains the night before, fishing was bound to be off, so they opted not to even try.

"Remember when we went out to Whispering Pines as kids, Dad? Rain like we had last night always ruined the fishing," Ethan reminisced as they lounged around outside.

"You would get *so* mad," George said, laughing at the memory. "You'd talk me into taking you out in Celia's old fishing boat and giving it a try anyway, and I could never talk you out of it. You never liked to have your plans changed. You'd get bored, though, and we'd head back in after a couple hours. You were usually cranky the rest of the day."

"I *still* don't like to have my plans changed . . . but now I can appreciate the wisdom of just chilling for a while."

A fire crackled in the firepit, taking the chill out of the air for those sitting close enough.

"Good thing you bought plenty of firewood that first morning, Ethan. We may want to keep this burning all day," George said, warming his hands over the flames.

Screams of camaraderie erupted in the open field behind their campers where the boys were tossing the ball around.

"They are going to be *so* muddy," Matt observed. "Good thing the campers have showers."

"We probably won't be popular, bringing home bags of filthy clothes . . . but they're having a blast."

Conversations continued around the fire as the men relaxed. They'd have to go home tomorrow, but right now, to relax was perfect.

Rex shifted in his camp chair, staring into the flames. "Thanks for letting me hang with you guys this weekend. I think it's about time I got back to the real world after this weekend."

"Happy to have you, bud," Ethan said, slapping Rex on the shoulder. "If we make this an annual event, we'll count you in."

"Good to know. So . . . since I haven't heard any mention of Brooke's name this weekend, I take it you two aren't an item these days?"

Ethan laughed. He'd managed to put off any discussion of his love life up to this point. Might as well get it over with, now that the kids were out of earshot and he couldn't use them as an excuse.

"No. We aren't an item. It didn't take me long to figure out that wasn't going to go anywhere."

"I could have told you that," Rex said. "She's way too hot for you!"

Laughs erupted around the fire. Everyone there had met Brooke. No one thought to argue with Rex's point. Not even Ethan.

"Since you brought her up, though," Ethan said, turning to his sister's boyfriend, "have you heard much from her, Seth? I know you two are good friends. I haven't talked to her since she told me she was leaving town for a while. You mentioned a while ago you'd heard she was coming back." He knew Jess didn't like Seth talking to Brooke, but Ethan was pretty sure her jealousy was misplaced.

Seth nodded, concern showing on his face. "We went out for lunch again last week. She got back to town in early May. As predicted, things crashed and burned with her old boyfriend. I warned her, but there's something about that guy that keeps drawing her back. He's trouble. Maybe she's finally learned her lesson this time."

George sighed. "I'm sorry to hear that. She seems like a nice young woman. What is it about old flames? Seems like those keep pulling people back in."

Ethan inwardly cringed, bracing himself for what he knew was coming.

"Yeah, Ethan, just what *is* it about old flames?" Matt tossed out with a wink.

"You just couldn't let that go, could you?"

Matt shrugged, and Rex looked between the two men.

"Do *not* tell me you're back together with Stacey," Rex demanded, looking at Ethan in disbelief.

"What? *God*, no! That ship has sailed. She did move back to town, though, so I'm having to deal with her more lately. I thought it was a pain when she was living in Minneapolis and we were having to shuffle the kids back and forth. You know what they say about being careful what you wish for. At least things are easier for the kids now."

Rex wasn't going to let it go. "Who is Matt talking about then, if not Stacey? You'd have to go back a couple decades to find a flame older than her."

This drew laughter from around the firepit.

"An old college flame," someone tossed out.

"Oh, *really?* Tell me more," Rex insisted.

"What the hell has gotten into you?" Ethan asked, uncomfortable to be the center of attention for this particular discussion. "All that talk about your feelings in rehab must have softened you up."

"I've always been a softie when it comes to the ladies," Rex countered. "Come on—spill."

Ethan knew Rex wouldn't let it drop. Once he latched on to something, he'd see it through. He explained how he'd run into Rebecca at the hospital after the fire, how they'd known each other in college, and all the while he tried to keep the current status of their relationship a bit vague.

"She's back in town then? It took a heart attack to win her back? I bet Stacey is pissed her old friend is back, stealing her man."

As tempted as he was to rise to the bait, Ethan decided to say little else. Things were still new with Rebecca. He didn't want to scare her away this time. She meant too much to him.

"We're working our way through things, and trying to keep things from getting too weird for the sake of the kids."

Rex seemed to bite back whatever he was about to say. He met Ethan's eye and gave him a brief nod.

"How about we focus on someone *else's* love life for a while," Ethan said, scanning the circle for a new target.

Matt raised his hands as if in surrender. "I'm just an old, boring married man at this point. Sorry."

Ethan's eyes traveled to Seth. "How about you, Seth? That sister of mine keeping you on your toes?"

"Wait, wait, wait," Nathan chimed in. "That sister of yours happens to be my mother, Uncle Ethan, so I'd appreciate it if we passed on discussing her love life."

"Nathan, why aren't you playing football with the kids?"

Nathan flipped his uncle off.

"Since you brought it up, Ethan, I actually have a question for you," Seth said.

"What's up?"

"You know that old trunk we found up in Celia's attic last summer? The blue one? Have you done anything with that stuff inside it yet?"

"You mean the old dresses and baby booties? No, why? Don't tell me you two need little blue booties for another baby. Isn't Harper keeping you busy enough?"

Seth burst into laughter at that one. "I *dare* you to ask Jess that question."

"Nah, I'm not that stupid," Ethan countered. "If it isn't the booties you're wondering about, and that christening gown would be too small for Harper now, I'm going to have to assume it's the wedding dress you're curious about?"

At least Ethan *hoped* that was what Seth was getting at. Seth was a good guy, good for Jess, and he'd been wondering lately what Seth's intentions were in regards to his sister.

Seth gave Ethan a brief nod and then looked over to George. "I already talked to Nathan about this yesterday. But I wanted to get your blessings, too."

"Hey, go for it, man," Ethan said. "She can't do any worse than the last one."

Ethan's reference to Jess's first husband, now doing time in federal prison for embezzlement and insurance fraud, gained him groans from around the firepit—especially from Nathan.

George seemed to be considering how best to respond. He set his water bottle down on the grass and leaned forward in his chair. "Seth . . . I sense you're a good man, and you two seem to make a good pair. But if you *ever* hurt her the way Will did, you will have me to answer to. Understand?"

Ethan chewed his lip to keep from laughing at his dad's attempt at intimidation. No one would doubt his sincerity. It was just comical to watch him try to act the tough-guy role.

But Seth seemed to take George seriously. He stood and walked over to the older man, hand extended. "You have my word."

"Thanks for cooking all this up, Dad. The smell of bacon on the griddle might have been the only way to get the kids up this morning."

Ethan set the heavy pan of scrambled eggs on the table next to Luke's camper as George pulled the last of the bacon off the sizzling griddle. He dropped the last piece on the ground when a spatter of grease burned his hand. Ethan scooped it up, blew it off, and popped it in his mouth.

"Five-second rule. Can't waste good bacon."

"Hasn't this been a great weekend?" George said, shaking his injured hand. "Bed's a little tough to sleep on, but other than that, I'd say it's been a success. *Boys, come and get it!*"

"What time is it, Grandpa?" someone yelled from inside a tent.

"*Bacon* time! Come on, before it gets cold."

It didn't take long before everyone was filling a plate.

Ethan sat next to his old friend. "Are you heading home, Rex, or do you need to go back to the facility at all?"

Rex swallowed a mouthful of eggs before replying. "Going straight home. And *damn*, does that sound good. Better than this bacon tastes. I'm ready to get back to it. Work, too, if you can keep me busy."

"That won't be a problem. I gave Lizzy a call yesterday, too. She's *thrilled* you're back."

Matt joined them at the picnic table.

"Say, Matt, did you get a chance to talk to Renee about the Gray Cabin? She wasn't home yet when I left last weekend."

"Sure did. She jumped at the chance. Loved the idea of putting the boys to work on it, too."

Robbie overheard enough of their conversation, including the mention of his mother and work for the boys, to catch his attention. "What are you two cooking up over there?" he asked as he snatched up the last piece of bacon from the tray.

"Your Uncle Ethan here wants to put you to work," Matt said, tipping his steaming coffee mug toward his wife's brother. "Dylan and Drew, too."

"Say what?" Dylan chimed in. "Summer vacation starts in a *week* and you're already signing me up to work, Dad?"

"Sure am," Ethan shot back. "I've got a project in mind. It's about time you learn a few skills with a hammer and power tools."

Drew squeezed into the last open spot at the table, next to his brother. He snuck a piece of bacon off Dylan's plate. The boy was too busy complaining to notice. "Oh, man, that *sucks*. But, wait . . . if it involves power tools, I guess I could be convinced. What's the project?"

"Renee's notorious Gray Cabin."

" 'Gray Cabin'?" Rex asked. He'd been out to Whispering Pines, but Ethan doubted he knew any of the history around the dilapidated little structure.

"I'll fill you in on it, Rex, but suffice it to say we'll spend a few weekends out there, whipping it into shape so Renee can start renting it out."

"Should I tell Renee you'll do it?" Matt asked.

Ethan glanced between Robbie, Drew, and Dylan. "Boys? We going to do this?"

He got affirmatives from Robbie and Drew, along with a reluctant nod and eye roll from Dylan.

Ethan turned to Matt. "Tell her she can start booking it out for the fourth of July.

Thank you for reading **Rebuilding Home**. I hope you enjoyed it!

The story of this close-knit family continues in **Capturing Wishes**, the fourth book in the Gift of Whispering Pines series. A very special bookstore is at risk of closing, but Celia's family is determined to help. Join in the fun that kicks off with Halloween, spans the holidays, and culminates with both new and old loves on Valentine's Day.

Be sure to visit www.kimberlydiedeauthor.com to sign up for my newsletter to get the latest on new releases and more. You will also receive a free novella First Summers at Whispering Pines – 1980 just for signing up.

ACKNOWLEDGEMENTS

The two simple words, ***Thank You***, don't seem big enough to capture the level of gratitude I feel toward all of the wonderful readers who have so graciously given their time to read one or more of my books in this series.

It all began with *Whispering Pines*. I suspect most of us hit different points in our lives when we stop and ask: Is this it? Luckily the answer to this question should always be "no"— as long as we are brave enough to try new things. Honestly, that first book was my way to start living out some of my own dreams. But life can be complicated, and we often have to reshape our perspective and expectations as life unfolds, much as we saw in *Tangled Beginnings*. And now, with this third book in the series, *Rebuilding Home*, I'm able to explore the big question of what home really means.

The themes of my stories are held together by the love and support of family. Some families we are born into, others we create through special friendships. Life is sweeter when we experience it together.

The support I've received from family, friends, and strangers as I continue on my author journey has been amazing! I was blessed throughout this past year to be invited to visit with numerous book clubs. It is an honor to sit down with readers and chat about these characters and their stories which at one time were nothing more than ideas in the recesses of my mind. One fabulous meet-up even included props based on snippets out of *Whispering Pines* (you ladies down in Wahpeton have set the bar high). I was blown away!

450

Your encouragement is the fuel behind my continued pursuit of this goal to entertain and inspire others through the written word. I cannot thank you enough.

Writing *Rebuilding Home* represented a new challenge for me because much of it is written from a man's point of view. I needed extra help from my editor in this regard. He made numerous, helpful observations throughout the process ('Kim, men don't ask a series of questions like that all at once' for example). I had many laugh-out-loud moments as I worked to keep Ethan, Rex, and a bunch of teenage boys as true to life as possible. Thank you, Spencer Hamilton, for going the extra mile with me on this one!

What does home mean to you? For me, home and family are central to my existence. It took a while for the title "Rebuilding Home" to come to me, but once it did, I knew it was a perfect fit. Aren't we constantly rebuilding and redefining what home means to us? For our family, as our kids grow up and no longer sleep under our roof every night, having them all at home becomes even more special because it's no longer an everyday event. Families change and evolve. Many of us are developing new definitions of what home really means.

I appreciate all the support my husband and our kids continue to show for my writing. This summer, we will be celebrating our thirtieth wedding anniversary. Then we will begin to "rebuild" our day-to-day lives as our youngest heads off to college. Good thing I have more books to write!

A huge thank-you to all of the amazing, selfless people on my *Rebuilding Home* book launch team. Thank you for your careful review and helpful suggestions. I have learned that writing a book begins as a solo project but getting it out to the world takes the work of many.

About the Author

Kimberly Diede writes contemporary novels that weave together family, friends, hope, and romance. She writes family sagas, suspense, and women's fiction that you'll find hard to put down. She truly believes we are never too old for second chances in life.

Kimberly enjoys spending the short months of her Midwest summers on the lakeshores of Minnesota and North Dakota. Nothing beats writing and hanging out with family and friends at their cabin. Her love of tradition and all things vintage comes through in her decorating and her stories.

Be sure to follow Kimberly on social media to catch glimpses of the junk she drags home to repurpose and to get updates on her latest books.

Website: https://www.kimberlydiedeauthor.com/
Facebook: https://www.facebook.com/KimberlyDiedeAuthor/
Instagram: https://www.instagram.com/kimberlydiedeauthor/
BookBub: https://www.bookbub.com/authors/kimberly-diede